OUT OF THIS WORLD

ALSO BY CHARLES DE LINT

Over My Head (Book 2 of the Wildlings series)
Seven Wild Sisters (illustrated by Charles Vess)
The Cats of Tanglewood Forest (illustrated by Charles Vess)
Under My Skin (Book 1 of the Wildlings series)
The Painted Boy
Muse and Reverie (collection)
Eyes Like Leaves
The Mystery of Grace
Dingo
What the Mouse Found (collection)
Woods and Waters Wild (collection)
Little (Grrl) Lost
Promises to Keep
Widdershins
Triskell Tales 2 (collection)
The Hour Before Dawn (collection)
Quicksilver and Shadow (collection)
The Blue Girl
Medicine Road (illustrated by Charles Vess)
Spirits in the Wires
A Circle of Cats (illustrated by Charles Vess)
Tapping the Dream Tree (collection)
Waifs and Strays (collection)
A Handful of Coppers (collection)
The Onion Girl
The Road to Lisdoonvarna
Triskell Tales: 22 Years of Chapbooks (collection)

Charles de Lint

OUT OF THIS WORLD

WILDLINGS BOOK THREE

razOr
bill

RAZORBILL
an imprint of Penguin Canada Books Inc., a Penguin Random House Company

Published by the Penguin Group
Penguin Canada Books Inc., 90 Eglinton Avenue East, Suite 700, Toronto, Ontario, Canada M4P 2Y3

Penguin Group (USA) LLC, 375 Hudson Street, New York, New York 10014, U.S.A.
Penguin Books Ltd, 80 Strand, London WC2R 0RL, England
Penguin Ireland, 25 St Stephen's Green, Dublin 2, Ireland (a division of Penguin Books Ltd)
Penguin Group (Australia), 707 Collins Street, Melbourne, Victoria 3008, Australia
(a division of Pearson Australia Group Pty Ltd)
Penguin Books India Pvt Ltd, 11 Community Centre, Panchsheel Park, New Delhi – 110 017, India
Penguin Group (NZ), 67 Apollo Drive, Rosedale, Auckland 0632, New Zealand
(a division of Pearson New Zealand Ltd)
Penguin Books (South Africa) (Pty) Ltd, 24 Sturdee Avenue, Rosebank,
Johannesburg 2196, South Africa

Penguin Books Ltd, Registered Offices: 80 Strand, London WC2R 0RL, England

First published 2014

1 2 3 4 5 6 7 8 9 10 (RRD)

*Publisher's note: This book is a work of fiction. Names, characters, places and incidents either are
the product of the author's imagination or are used fictitiously, and any resemblance to actual persons
living or dead, events, or locales is entirely coincidental.*

Manufactured in the U.S.A.

LIBRARY AND ARCHIVES CANADA CATALOGUING IN PUBLICATION

De Lint, Charles, author
Out of this world / Charles de Lint.

(Wildlings ; book 3)
ISBN 978-0-670-06535-6 (bound)

I. Title. II. Series: De Lint, Charles Wildlings ; book 3.

PS8557.E44O87 2014   jC813'.54   C2014-904057-1

eBook ISBN 978-0-14-319317-3

Visit the Penguin Canada website at **www.penguin.ca**

Special and corporate bulk purchase rates available; please see
www.penguin.ca/corporatesales or call 1-800-810-3104.

FOR JOHNNY'S FAIRY DOGMOTHERS,
LINDA GARRETT & KATHY HUGHES

What is life? It is the flash of a firefly in the night.
It is the breath of a buffalo in the wintertime. It is the
little shadow which runs across the grass and loses
itself in the sunset.
—Crowfoot saying

DES

A soft wind's coming in from the ocean as I pick my way from shadow to shadow through the neighbourhood.

Honestly? I'm not expecting to be right. I mean, come on. It's three in the morning. Nobody's going to be out here at this time of night. But I'm still careful. The guys from Black Key Securities gunning for Josh aren't a bunch of kids waiting to beat us up after school. They're military trained and they already took a shot at us yesterday.

Josh is in the otherworld, and if they saw what was left of Vincenzo, they might not even mess with him. But they don't have a clue about that, so I'm doing what any good bro would: making sure things are cool over at his mom's house.

I keep to the shadows, slipping through backyards as I make my way from my house to Josh's. It'd be just my luck to have Santa Feliz's finest happen to swing by on a patrol, but I do my best ninja impression and make it all the way to the Evoras' backyard without raising an alarm. Sidling along the side of their garage, I peer down the street to Josh's house.

I watch the street and yards, listening to the surf where it breaks against the beach at the far end of the street. There's no movement, not even a pack rat rustling around in the hedges or up in the dead fronds of the palm trees, no one out except for me. Then I remember where the sniper was hiding when he shot at us in the barrio yesterday. I look up, checking the rooflines.

Still clear. Except if he's on a roof, he's not going to pick a house on the same side of the street as Josh's. He's going to be on the opposite side.

So I work my way back around the block, still cutting through yards until I'm in a position to see the rooftops across from Josh's place.

And there the prick is, lying on the flat, tiled roof of the house opposite Josh's.

Sometimes I hate it when I'm right.

All I can see is his head, but I know from experience that he's going to be well armed. The big question is, is he here just for Josh, or is Josh's mom in danger, too?

And what do I do about it?

Okay. It's not like he's a Wildling or some kind of superhero. He's human like me, but no way am I stupid enough to go up against some ex-military guy with a gun.

And then it hits me. If I can break into Josh's house without his mom catching me or the sniper spotting me, I can steal Josh's phone, which the FBI are tracking, then go someplace odd enough that the Feds'll come looking to see what Josh is up to. At that point I fill them in and they can deal with it.

But how to get into the house? If I were the hero from some action flick, I'd blow up a car as a diversion, then slip in and be gone with the phone before anyone was the wiser. Hell, I'd just sneak up on the sniper, beat the crap out of him, then make him lead me to where the rest of the rogue security detail are hiding and take them all out—problem solved.

As if.

I'd even settle for having Agent Solana's number so I could just call him up right now and hand the mess over to him.

"Whatcha doing?" a girl's voice asks from directly behind me.

I'm so inside my own head that I almost scream, which, dude, would be uncool on so many levels. I never heard a thing until she spoke. As it is, I bang up against the side of the house where I'm hiding, my heart pounding in my chest.

Some ninja I turn out to be.

I look over my shoulder to find a cute, skinny, sun-browned girl around my own age studying me with an amused look. The worst of my panic starts to die down. She's sitting on her haunches and dressed for the beach in raggedy cotton pants cut off at mid-calf and a baggy T that says "Life's a beach." Her eyes are big in a narrow face surrounded by long dreads that are almost as thick as her slender arms.

I don't know what she's doing out here at this time of night, but I suppose she could ask the same of me.

"Dude," I whisper. "Give me a heart attack, why don't you?"

"Sorry," she says. But her eyes and her smile say she isn't.

"Who are you?" I ask, motioning to keep her voice low.

"I'm Donalita, not *dude*." she says. "Theo said I should keep an eye on you."

It takes me a moment to realize who she's talking about.

"You mean Chaingang?" I ask her.

She nods. "But his real friends call him Theo."

"Yeah, well, that's never going to be me. I think I irritate the hell out of him."

She grins. "Me too, but I call him Theo anyway. Why are you sneaking around in the dark?"

"How long have you been watching me?"

She shrugs. "Only a couple of minutes. You're very good at sneaking. If I wasn't me, I'd probably never have noticed you."

I put that together with her telling me that Chaingang sent her.

"You're a Wildling, aren't you?" I say.

"Don't be silly. I'm much older than that."

"So you're one of them—what do you call them—cousins?"

She laughs and says, "I'm me. Why do I have to be something else as well?"

"You need to be quiet," I remind her.

"I'm very good at that. I'm very good at everything I do."

"Yeah, that must come in handy."

"Oh, it does," she says, either ignoring or oblivious to my sarcasm. "So, what are you doing?"

I ease my head around the corner of the house. The sniper's still there.

"I'm trying to figure out what to do about him," I tell her, pointing upward and across the street.

She pushes right up beside me to have a look. Up close she smells really good—fruity with a faint undercurrent of musk. It's like having a smoothie at the zoo. She grins, her face inches from my own, before she peers around the corner.

"So is he a bad man?" she asks.

"He wants to kill Josh—you know Josh?"

"I don't *know* know him, but I know who he is."

"Yeah, well, that guy's with those men that kidnapped Josh a few weeks back. They definitely want to hurt him."

"But Josh went into the otherworld," she says, "so he's safe. From them."

I nod. "Except maybe they're after his mother, too. Maybe even me and Marina."

"Do you want to kill him?" she asks.

She has an interesting voice—girlish and throaty all at the same time—so it seems a little weird to hear her ask that so matter-of-factly. And then I start thinking about the torn-up remains of Vincenzo that we found earlier tonight. Josh literally ripped the body to shreds while in his Wildling shape.

"Dude," I say. "Are you all so bloodthirsty?"

She blinks and gives me a blank look.

"Come on," I say. "You've got to admit it's a little freaky. You look like a cute little rasta girl"—that gets me another grin—"but you sound like Clint Eastwood doing Dirty Harry."

"Is that a good or a bad thing?" she asks.

"Depends, I guess. For pretend, it's kind of hot. For real, it's kind of scary."

"But you have to deal with your enemies," she says.

"Right," I tell her. "But just killing them is a little too Wild West, dude."

"Well, what *do* you want to do with that man?"

I feel a little bad ragging on her, considering how I was just running through different violent scenarios myself. But I don't roll like that for real.

So I tell her my idea of getting Josh's phone and letting the Feds handle it.

"I can do that," she says. "Get the phone, I mean. Where does he keep it?"

"It'll be in his bedroom," I tell her. "The room that backs

on to the yard on the ocean side. The one on the right if you're facing the house. But dude, you can't just—"

I don't get to finish. One moment the cute rasta girl is there, the next I'm looking at a coatimundi. I swear she gives me a wink from her masked features before she slips by me to scurry across the street.

I suppose I should be worried. The Black Key guys know all about Wildlings. If the sniper spots a coatimundi trying to get into Josh's house, he's likely to take a shot at her just out of principle. But as she takes her animal shape all I can think is, that is so cool.

JOSH

I'm feeling a little shaky as I follow Tío Goyo into the otherworld. I can't get it out of my head. What I did to Vincenzo. The mess I left behind on the headland.

All those bits and pieces that I tore up used to be an actual living being. It's worse than when I killed the researcher at ValentiCorp. That was over so quick that I didn't have time to even think about it. I could put it down to instinct. Defending myself and Rico. A gut-reaction payback for what she'd been doing to those kids. But this …

What kind of a monster am I becoming?

It's not like Vincenzo left me any choice—not after threatening Mom and Marina and everybody. It's what I did to his corpse afterward. I can't reconcile that with who I always thought I was. What kind of a maniac does something like that?

I can't even imagine Chaingang doing it, and he's about as hardcore as they come. Yeah, he was a gangbanger, and pretty much the toughest guy I ever hung out with, but there was something noble about him, too. And now Chaingang's probably dead as well.

I think about Marina, and how she could have ended up

with a guy like him. I just can't imagine them as a couple. Marina has such a sweet, gracious nature. She's always looking out for other people's feelings. Chaingang might've had his friends' backs, but his social conscience ended there. Marina hates drugs and violence, so how did they end up together? And where could it possibly have gone? Like her parents were going to let her run around with a biker gang? Like she'd even *want* to be cruising around town on the back of Chaingang's Harley while he goes about his business, dealing dope, fighting with the Riverside Kings?

Nothing makes sense anymore.

I should be back home with my friends. Trying to fix my friendship with Marina and consoling her, and just getting past all this crap. Doing whatever it is that Auntie Min thinks I should to make sure nothing bad happens to the other kids who became Wildlings.

And Mom's going to be worried sick.

Instead, I'm literally in the middle of nowhere with some old guy I don't know and I'm not entirely sure I can trust, looking for my ex-girlfriend who dumped me. Okay, technically, I dumped her, except Elzie was the one who gave me that either-or choice.

I'm not sure if I'm doing the right thing, but with Vincenzo dead, surely Auntie Min can look out for Marina and Des.

Elzie doesn't have anybody but me, and Vincenzo's crew are sure to kill her when they find out what I did to him.

MARINA

Theo pulls over beside the corner groceteria near Papá's house and kills the engine. I hold on to him for a long moment, arms wrapped around his comforting presence. One of his big hands covers mine and gives them a squeeze. I could stay like this all night, but there's still so much to do. I give Theo a last reluctant hug, then get off the bike. Theo takes my hands before I can step away, concern plain in his eyes.

"Are you going to be okay?" he asks.

"It's just Ampora."

He smiles. "Who you were ready to beat the crap out of yesterday. She pushes all your buttons, sweetcheeks."

I know what he's doing. He's trying to get a rise out of me. Trying to get me out of myself so that I'll forget the fact that Josh literally tore a man to pieces before disappearing on us without a word.

"I could call Donalita back," he says. "I really don't think those Black Key guys are gunning for Des anyway. I'll get her to return to my grandma's and then I can stay and have your back."

I smile. "Oh, and you showing up is going to put Ampora in such a receptive mood."

"Yeah, maybe not."

"Besides, I'm not worried about dealing with Ampora. I'm worried about Josh."

Theo gives me a slow nod. "I get that. I'm worried, too. But I'm also trying to figure out what changed him. The Josh I first met wasn't all jacked up with the big *cojones* like the one I was with yesterday. And then there's that whole business with Vincenzo. I'd never have thought Josh had that in him."

I shiver, remembering the awful sight of Vincenzo after he'd been shredded by Josh in his mountain lion shape.

"Anyway," Theo goes on, "if he can take out Vincenzo that easily, I figure he can take on anybody. So that's not the problem. I'm more worried about how he's handling all of this." Theo taps his temple. "In here."

"Me too," I say. "He's on his own over there, without anyone that he can trust. Plus you know what the elders say about going too deep into the otherworld."

"He's not all alone. You saw those other footprints. Somebody took him deeper into the otherworld."

"Except, is it a good guy or one of Vincenzo's friends?"

"I hear you. Here's my take: we can beat ourselves up worrying about it, or we can deal with the problems we've got in front of us and trust Josh to handle himself over there."

"It's just …"

He pulls me close. "I know," he says into my hair. "You're in mama-bear mode. But there's nothing we can do."

I nod when he lets me go. He's right. I don't know if I'll be able to keep it all together the way he can, but I can at least try.

I take out my phone and text Ampora to meet me in the playground. Theo waits until I get an answer.

"Are you going to need a ride home?" he asks.

I shake my head. "I'll either stay over at Papá's, or I'll need the walk to blow off steam before I have to face the music with Mamá."

He nods. "I'm just a phone call away."

We share a last lingering kiss, then he gets on his bike and pulls away while I walk to the playground to meet my sister. I sit on a swing, tapping my foot on the sand. She makes me wait. It's a full ten minutes before she comes sauntering down the street from her house and drops onto the swing next to mine. I get a twinge in my gut remembering how we played endlessly together when we were kids, just like our little sisters do now.

"So, how'd your meeting go?" she asks, her voice even, which is so much better than the usual vitriol that she reserves for me.

For a moment I don't know what she's talking about. Then I remember that I told her about the meeting with some of the Wildling elders, but I didn't give any details except to tell her that if she came along, it would make things harder on Josh. Now I don't know what to say.

Do I tell her how this guy Vincenzo crashed the meeting? How he killed Tomás and almost killed Theo? That Theo—who she knows better as Chaingang—is my boyfriend and we're both Wildlings? That Cory went into Theo's head and literally pulled him back out of a part of the otherworld called the dreamlands? How Josh tore Vincenzo into pieces in his Wildling shape, then disappeared into those same dreamlands?

She wouldn't understand any of that. I can barely believe Josh ever told her he's a Wildling, or that she's suddenly crushing on him.

"Good," is all I say. "Thanks for covering for me."

"I wasn't just doing it for you," she says. "How's Josh? Is he okay?"

"Josh ... went away."

"What's that supposed to mean?"

My heart begins to sink as I hear the faint edge of her usual belligerence.

"Honestly," I say, "I don't really know. It's some kind of Wildling thing, I guess. He just took off. He didn't say where he was going. He didn't"—my voice catches for a moment—"say when he'd be back."

"This is bullshit."

"No," I shoot back at her. "This is the truth. You don't get to call it bullshit just because you don't want to hear it."

She glares at me, but I remember the advice Theo gave me earlier in the night, before I came by to get Ampora to cover me while I went out to Tiki Bay for the meeting.

Just give her the hard stare, no budging.

So instead of looking away like I usually do, I hold her gaze until she's the one to break eye contact.

"But he's okay, right?" she asks, all the aggression gone from her voice.

I want to tell her that what she's feeling for Josh isn't real. It's only because of the pheromones that Wildlings give off. But that seems mean-spirited. And really, what do I know? Maybe she really does like him. He's a good guy. I crushed on him for years—long before he became a Wildling and there was any chance that pheromones were involved. So why can't it be the same for her?

Except I can't tell her any of that, either. And for sure I don't tell her that we assume he's gone looking for Elzie. If Josh and my sister have something to work out, I'm not going to be standing in the middle. Des would say she's a bitch and deserves to feel bad, but I can take the high road.

"It's Josh," I say, answering her question. "Lately he's been surprising everybody with how he can deal with anything that gets thrown at him. I'm sure he'll be fine."

She nods. "Mamá called around eleven."

Oh, crap.

"What did you say to her?"

"Don't worry," Ampora says. "I was polite."

"But—"

"It's cool. We had a deal. You don't tell Papá and Elena about the trouble I got into, and I cover for you. She thinks you're sleeping over."

Wow. Ampora should get in trouble with the Riverside Kings and then crush on Josh more often. This is the most she's said to me in years without biting off my head. And she actually covered for me? I guess she took me seriously when I told her that if she wants to hang with Josh, she'd better get used to me being around, too.

"Speaking of which," Ampora goes on, "we should get back inside."

I nod. "What'll Papá and Elena say when they see me in the morning?"

"They'll be so happy we're getting along that they won't even stop to ask how you got there."

"I owe you," I tell her, giving the chain of her swing a little pull.

"I know," she says. "Big time. And I won't forget."

JOSH

"Don't live inside your head so much," Tío Goyo says, and I start.

But he's right. That's exactly what I've been doing. I've been walking beside him, staring at the ground and not paying attention to anything but the soap opera in my brain.

We're still trudging along a shoreline that's a counterpoint to the one south of Santa Feliz. At one point Tío Goyo began explaining how we're a few layers deeper than the part of the otherworld that I first visited. Something about them all being layered, or is it that they exist in the same space, only sideways from each other? I realize I tuned him out.

But now I look around and realize the landscape has been changing. The dirt underfoot seems pretty much the same, but the shoreline is much farther away and we're coming up on some foothills. Behind them I see mountains rising impossibly high. We sure don't have anything like that in So-Cal.

"It's kind of hard not to think about what's happened," I say.

"I told you. Vincenzo deserved to die."

"Yeah, but did Chaingang? Did Cory or Tomás?"

"I wouldn't worry about the coyote boy," he says. "They're next to impossible to kill permanently."

"What's that supposed to mean?"

He shrugs. "They keep coming back."

Which doesn't explain anything, so I just say, "Right."

Cory and maybe even Tomás might be able to come back, but it's hard to think about that big solid presence of Chaingang being gone. Marina must be sad, too.

I don't want to think about that. Not Chaingang dead, or the two of them as a couple. I just can't figure out how they ever hooked up in the first place. I can ask myself the question a thousand times and it still makes no sense.

Chaingang's the guy you'd want to have at your side when it comes to a fight, but hang with him on a regular basis? We don't have anything in common. I can't see Chaingang surfing or skateboarding. I'm pretty sure he's not much of a fan of rockabilly or surf music, so I can't see him hanging out in Des's garage during band practice. Or even sprawled on the couch with us watching movies.

Those were good times. Marina can read for hours, but she always falls asleep during a movie, usually with her head on my shoulder. And she always smells nice, her hair a mix of some fruity shampoo and salt ...

Until I messed things up, it was always good. When we walked, she'd often loop her hand into the crook of my arm, and both hello and goodbye usually required a hug.

I think about how betrayed I felt when I found out that she had been a Wildling for months and not told me. And yet I did the same thing to my mom, for the same reason: to keep the people I care for safe.

But after I blew up about it, I couldn't take it back. I could say I was sorry, but it still lay there between us—how I'd been such a jerk—and nothing's been the same since.

Maybe I drove her to Chaingang. It's a stupid idea. But then I think of Des telling me earnestly on more than one occasion how she was into me. He's such a wild exaggerator that I just laughed it off.

Except … except …

I think of other little signs.

I shake my head. Maybe I'm an idiot. All of it—the hugs, the hand on my arm when she's talking to me, even the punches. *Could* she have wanted to be more than just friends?

I just took her for granted. I knew that she'd always be there. But I never had a clue how she really felt until I pushed her away, and then it was obvious that she was hurting bad.

I drove her away. And I *really* didn't have a clue how I felt about her. Until now. When it's too late.

"You're doing it again," Tío Goyo says.

My head snaps up. "Doing what?"

"Living in your head."

"Yeah, well, I've got a lot to think about. What are we even doing here? We're supposed to be looking for Elzie. Like, now."

He nods. "And we will. But to find her we need to recalibrate your awareness of the world around you."

"How long's that going to take?"

He shrugs. "It depends on how quickly you're able to assimilate what I have to teach you. I'm hoping it won't take more than a few weeks."

"Weeks? Are you kidding me? This is nuts. She could be dead *today*."

"This is true. She could already be dead. But I prefer to assume that she's not." He holds up a hand before I can break in. "Time moves at a different pace in different parts of the otherworld. Where we are, what will seem like weeks to us will be but the blink of an eye to those we left behind."

"How's that even possible?"

"In the long ago, when the first people lived in the world—"

"You mean the Native Americans?"

"No, I mean your people—the animal people. They were here when the world was born, and in those days there was no reckoning of time. No concepts such as past, present or future. Everything happened at the same time."

I shake my head. "Time's not something that was made up. Day turns into night. The seasons change. How can that all happen at the same time?"

He shrugs. "I don't know how. I just know that here, it is as it was in the long ago. All times and places take up the same space."

"I was here before," I tell him. "A few weeks ago. Time passed the same for us here as it did in our own world."

He shakes his head. "You were not *here*, where the hours move at a slower, different pace. If you can clear your mind and focus, you will have time to learn."

"Okay," I say. "What are you going to teach me?"

The dry wash that we've been following the past while has brought us into the foothills and the mouth of a gulch. The dirt underfoot has changed to rock—big slabs that rise like a giant's staircase, the embankments growing steeper on either side the higher they rise.

"To begin with," he says, "I want you to jog up to the top of the gulch and back down. Then repeat it—say, ten times."

"You've got to be kidding."

"You can take my help or not. But if you take it, you have to do what I say."

"But what does this accomplish?"

"You'll be concentrating so hard on keeping your footing and actually fulfilling the task that you won't be able to remain distracted. You need to empty your mind before you can actually learn anything."

I want to ask more questions, tell him he's wrong. I'm ready to learn, but we need to get *going* on it. People need me *now*.

Except I realize he's right. All this ruminating is getting me nowhere.

"All right," I say. "We'll do it your way."

I take off up the gulch, jumping from one big stone to the next.

DES

I'm on pins and needles waiting for Donalita to come back. I keep expecting something to go wrong. To hear her getting caught by Josh's mom. Or worse, to hear the sound of the sniper's rifle as he shoots her down. But the night stays quiet except for the surf at the far end of the street and the occasional car that goes by on the main arteries outside our neighbourhood.

When she finally does show up, it's sudden, like the first time. She giggles when I jump, then tosses Josh's phone to me.

"Did you have any trouble?" I whisper.

"Don't be silly." She cocks her head. "Why can't I just kill the man with the rifle? Then we wouldn't have to do all this sneaking around."

I don't know how serious this bloodthirsty streak of hers actually is. I *think* it's just for show, but in case it's not …

"Well, first off," I tell her, "we don't just go around killing people. And secondly, that'll put the rest of them on guard. Right now we know where the threat is. If they take a different approach, we might not see it coming."

"Well, that's not much fun."

"It's called being sensible, dude. And I can't believe I just said that."

She nods. "Me neither. It's so strange that you think I look like a boy."

"No, I meant—never mind. Look, thanks for your help, but I need to get going."

"Where to?"

I hold up Josh's phone. "I've got to get this to a safe place where I can meet Agent Solana."

"Can I come, too?" she asks.

She seems pretty flaky—and this is me saying that—but she's an old-school Wildling, which means she's stronger and tougher than she appears. I'm not so stupid as to turn down help when I have no idea what I'm getting into.

"Sure, dude," I tell her. "I'd be happy to have you tag along."

"You did it again," she says. "You called me—"

"Dude. I know. It's just a thing. Think of it as a term of affection."

Her face brightens even more. "Really? So you want to be my boyfriend—*dude*?"

Oh boy, not again.

"What is it with you Wildling girls anyway?" I ask.

She gives me a confused look.

"Look," I tell her. "I met Joanie Jones—you know, seriously hot lead singer with The Wild Surf?—and she was all over me. I do okay with the ladies, but this was ridiculous. Pheromones, right?"

"Most of us don't have that ability—and you sure don't."

"Then what gives?"

"Did you ever think that maybe it's because you're pretty cute?"

"Yeah, right," is all I say.

"Well, *I* think you are." She grins. "You know, for a human."

"Let's take it a step at a time," I tell her.

"I can do that. I take all my steps one at a time. I'm very good at it."

"I'm sure you are."

I've decided that the old amusement park north of the pier would be an excellent place to wait for Solana. As I head off in that direction, Donalita walks beside me, exaggerating every step until she's sure I notice. Then she skips around me singing some nonsense song in which every second word is *dude*.

"Not so loud," I warn her.

She nods and puts a finger to her lips, but she keeps on singing in a whisper, still dancing circles around me the whole way to the Santa Feliz beach boardwalk. I sit down on a bench where I can look out at the old park, the abandoned rides lost in the darkness. Donalita finishes her song with a flourishing *"Doo-deet-dee-dude!"* and jumps up onto the backrest of the bench where she sits on her heels, perching like a bird. Her gaze goes to the park.

"Can we go on one of the rides?" she asks.

"They're all broken."

"But we could still climb up the Ferris wheel and sit at the very top and try to catch the moon."

"We could, but let's not."

"Poo. You're no fun."

That's a new one for me. Usually "You're no fun" is my line.

Before I can brood over that, Donalita pokes me in the shoulder with a stiff finger.

"Can we at least run up and down the beach?" she asks. "And then spin around in circles until we fall down?"

"Go ahead," I tell her. "I'm just going to wait here to see if Solana shows up."

"That's so boring."

"One of us has to be the responsible one," I say.

Then I have to laugh. If Marina were here, she'd be killing herself because that's *her* line.

"What's so funny?" Donalita asks.

"I think I'm turning into my father. Just call me Ted from now on."

"I don't understand."

"Because you're me and I've turned into an old man."

She cocks her head and studies me carefully.

"Not literally, dude," I say.

She grins. "Waiting is boring, but you're funny. You're much more fun than Theo."

"I'll be sure to tell him that."

"You could give him lessons on how to be more fun—except he *does* have a motorcycle. Do you have a motorcycle?"

"Not even close."

It goes on like that for a while until she suddenly sits up straight and looks across the beach to the parking lot.

"That's interesting," she says.

I follow her gaze, but it's too dark out here and I can't tell what she's looking at. I don't have a Wildling's enhanced vision.

"What is it?" I ask.

Instead of answering, she shifts to her coatimundi shape—

and jumps down to the ground. A moment later she's pressed up against the backs of my legs.

The fact that she's hiding from whatever she sensed out there makes my pulse jump. I try to take comfort from the fact that she said "interesting." She didn't say "terrifying," or even "dangerous." Except why is she hiding?

A car door opens in the parking lot, and by the interior light, I can see someone getting out, but it's too far away for me to recognize them. The door car slams and whoever it is comes walking along the concrete path where I'm sitting.

Okay, dude, I tell myself. Just be cool.

I drape an arm along the back of the bench and wait. It's not until he's almost upon me that I realize it's Agent Solana. He doesn't beat around the bush. Hands on his hips, he looks down at me and demands, "Where's Josh?"

"Dude, you'd never believe me."

"Try me."

What the hell.

"He went into this kind of other dimension," I say.

"By himself?"

"*Really?* I say he's gone into some parallel universe and all you ask is whether he went on his own? Dude, who *are* you?"

He studies me for a moment before he says, "That depends on what Josh has told you."

This is starting to tick me off.

"He said you were the bitch boy for a bunch of hawk uncles," I tell him.

He laughs. "Close enough."

He takes my snarkiness so well that I feel a little bad.

"Except he didn't put it quite like that," I add.

"Well, he wouldn't, would he?"

"So what's the real story here, dude?" I ask. "Are you like some kind of mole inside the FBI?"

Solana smiles, teeth flashing white in the dark.

"I don't mean that literally," I say. "Well, maybe I do."

"No, the job's real. My work with *los tíos* is more like … a hobby."

"What about Agent Matteson? Is he in on this with you?"

Solana shakes his head. "Paul just likes Josh and his mother. We have some history with them, remember? You know, contrary to what some people think, looking out for Wildlings is as much a part of our job as looking out for regular people. There could be trouble at this Householder rally on Saturday, so we want to keep tabs on anyone who might be at risk."

Sure, I think, but they still get their paycheques from the government. The *human* government. When push comes to shove, I know where their loyalties are going to lie. For all I know, they might even be secretly tight with Congressman Householder, the asshole who just wants to lock up Wildlings and throw away the key, problem solved. But I keep those thoughts to myself.

"You know I've been tracking Josh's phone," he goes on, "so I assume you were trying to meet with me by bringing it here."

I nod. "Josh is gone—like I said—but I'm worried about his mother, too, and maybe even Marina and me."

"How so?"

"Remember the guy taking potshots at Josh and me this afternoon? Well, right now he—or one of his friends—is on the roof of the house across from Josh's place with a rifle. You can't tell me that's a good thing, dude."

He shakes his head.

"So are you going to send in a SWAT team or something?"

"That'll just scare him off and he'll alert the others. We need to round them all up so we don't have to think about them anymore."

"Didn't some of those Black Key guys turn themselves in for protective custody?" I ask. "Why don't you just lean on one of them?"

"We don't 'lean' on people."

I don't really believe that, but I let it pass.

"So, what?" I ask. "You wait until he shoots Josh's mom, or one of us, and *then* you bust him?"

"I won't let it go anywhere near that far. But let me think about it."

Donalita nudges the back of my leg with her snout and I remember what she's actually capable of.

"How about if I deliver him to you, dude? All gift-wrapped with a pretty bow and everything?"

"Don't you even *think* about trying to take him on. All the Black Key personnel are military trained and highly dangerous."

"Dude. I didn't say *I* was going to do it."

"And I don't want any of your Wildling amigos involved, either. They may be fast and strong, but they're no match for professionals."

"So, no citizen's arrests."

He sighs. "That's right. No citizen's arrests. Let me handle it. The next time you need to get in touch with me, just call."

"I don't have your number."

"Didn't Josh use your phone to call me yesterday?"

I feel like slapping my head. Of course he did. The number's sitting there in my Recents. We didn't have to go through all this spy crap.

"And I'm serious," Solana says. "Don't go trying to play hero."

"Dude, I heard you the first time. What are you? My mother?"

He studies me for a long moment, then nods and starts back across the sand to his car. I wait until the interior light goes on and the door closes.

"What do you think, Donalita?" I say. "Can we take this sniper guy without killing him or getting ourselves killed in the process?"

The coatimundi scurries out from behind my legs and jumps up on the bench where she changes into her human form.

"Piece of cake," she says.

JOSH

It's farther to the top of the gulch than I thought. Despite my Wildling strength, I'm breathing hard when I finally approach the top. But I'm looking forward to the view and to seeing Tío Goyo way down below.

Except when I get to the top, he's up there sitting cross-legged on a rock and humming something tuneless. The thin spiky branches of an ocotillo fan out behind him.

I stand half bent over, hands on my knees, trying to catch my breath enough to ask, "*Huh—huh*—how did—*huh*—you—*huh*—do that?"

He just shakes his head, like he's embarrassed for me.

"Maybe I'll tell you down below," he says. "And be careful. Descending this terrain can be harder than going up."

I stand there staring at him, still trying to catch my breath.

"What are you waiting for?" he asks.

My head is spinning with questions. But then I remember what he said below and it's still true. I'm too much in my own head.

I turn and start back down. He's right about this, too. It is harder. I can't go as quickly as I did coming up without losing my balance. But I push myself to go as fast as I safely can because I need to get my brain to just shut up.

He's waiting down below, but this time I don't talk to him. I just give him a nod and start back up the gulch.

MARINA

It's weird, tiptoeing through Papá's house in the middle of the night. I feel like I'm in somebody else's house even though I'm usually here a couple of times a week.

But everything familiar looks different in the dark. It *feels* different without the girls underfoot, Elena's cheerful presence, Papá watching the news channel. Everybody's in bed and I can't shake the sensation that Ampora and I are a pair of burglars creeping through a house that belongs to strangers.

What's even weirder is Ampora being nice to me. Okay, maybe saying *nice* is a stretch, but she is making an effort to do more than just tolerate my presence. She's even starting conversations.

"Josh was asking me about these guys called *los tíos*," she says when we're lying beside each other in her bed.

Her voice is a quiet whisper, right beside my ear. I'm very aware of the closeness of her body to mine and savour the sisterhood that I can't help but feel.

"You mean the hawk uncles," I say.

"So you know about them?"

"Just what I heard from Josh. I'd actually never heard of them before."

"Me either. I said I'd see if Papá knew anything about them."

"Does he?"

"I think so. But he wouldn't talk about them."

I turn my head to look at her. "That's weird. Usually he can't *stop* talking about the old folk tales and stories, once you get him going."

"I know. I'm going to ask Elena about them tomorrow."

She doesn't say anything else, so I figure she's gone to sleep. I listen to her breathing even out and lie awake awhile, staring up at the dark ceiling, worrying about Josh. I know Theo says I shouldn't. And it makes sense. Josh handled Vincenzo like it was nothing. He took that psycho elder out when Theo couldn't even lay a hand on him. But still. It's Josh. My Josh doesn't have a mean bone in his body. Or at least he never did before.

I flash on Vincenzo's shredded body and suddenly the warm bed feels cold.

"So who is your new boyfriend?" Ampora asks just as I'm finally starting to shake that memory and drift off.

I was afraid this would come up at some point. I just didn't expect it so soon.

"I know he doesn't go to Sunny Hill," she goes on when I don't answer right away, "because I only ever see you with your usual crew."

"It's complicated," I finally say.

"Complicated how?"

"If people knew we were together, they might misunderstand."

She turns to me, head supported by her forearm. "Now I'm really intrigued."

I don't know why I tell her. Maybe it's because this is how I always wanted it to be, the two of us hanging out like real sisters, talking late into the night, sharing our secrets.

"His name's Theo," I say. At her blank look I add, "Theo Washington."

It's like somebody just threw a switch. She sits up, revulsion twisting her features.

"Are you for real?" she says.

I sit up and hold her forearm. "Before you start—"

But she yanks her arm away and cuts me off. "God, you're such a hypocrite. You're all in my face because you think I'm running with the Kings, but meanwhile you're banging Chaingang Washington."

"I am *not*—"

She doesn't let me finish. She leaps out of bed and points toward her window.

"Just get out of here. Go back to Mamá—the two of you deserve each other," she says. "I mean it," she adds when I don't move.

I take a breath to steady myself because all I really want to do is smack her.

Be calm, I tell myself. Take the high road.

"This is exactly why I didn't want—" I start, but she cuts me off again.

"I'm serious," she says. "Get out or I'll wake Papá and we'll see how happy he is when he finds out you're in a gang."

"I'm *not* in a—"

"Get. Out."

There's no give in her face. Everything's shut down. I don't think she even sees me. From the set of her features, I know that all she sees is some awful *thing*—like I'm a piece of crud on the bottom of her shoe.

"Okay," I tell her. "I'm going."

I'm mad at her, but I'm more mad at myself for getting sucked into thinking it could ever be any different. Tears well up in my eyes but I refuse to cry in front of her.

I get up from the bed and dress as quickly as I can. She doesn't look at me. Not while I'm dressing. Not when I pause by the window. She's probably still staring at the wall after I've gone through the window and I'm walking down the street away from the house.

I make it as far as the park before the full enormity of it all hits me.

Ampora knows about Theo and me. By tomorrow morning everybody's going to know about us. Papá will be so pissed off. Mamá will have a heart attack.

This is almost as bad as being outed as a Wildling. Maybe worse. Becoming a Wildling isn't something I ever chose.

Why did I confide in her? What was I thinking? I can't even threaten her that I'll tell Papá about her getting mixed up with the Kings yesterday because me being a Wildling trumps that by about a million.

I sit on a swing and let my feet drag back and forth in the sand as I try to figure out what to do.

It's while I'm sitting there that I realize I'm not alone.

JOSH

I think I'm going to die by the fourth time up.

"Remember," Tío Goyo says. "The mountain lion is yours to control."

I hit a wall halfway up. I'm all set to just say screw it and sit down right where I am, but I don't want to give Tío Goyo the satisfaction of being right. So I push on, cursing him with each painful step.

The mountain lion is pissed. It wants to break free and lope up the gulch, then maybe swat Tío Goyo around a few times to let the old uncle know what it thinks about this pointless exercise.

But as I go back down, I think about it—the faster and stronger element of being a Wildling, but also the increased stamina. So why am I having so much trouble?

The mountain lion is yours to control.

Yeah, so? I've been controlling it. I haven't been cheating and shifting to its shape. I haven't knocked Tío Goyo's head off. Yet.

But then I realize I'm not using its full capabilities, either. I can take more from its strength and speed and stamina without having to shift into the full mountain lion shape.

So, coming up the fifth time, I push through the wall of

exhaustion and actually feel lighter on my feet by the time I get to the top than back when I started. This is cool.

When I reach the top on my seventh trip, Tío Goyo grabs my arm before I can start back down.

"How's that conversation inside your head?" he asks.

It takes me a moment to get out of the zone and register what he's asking, then a moment longer to answer.

"What conversation?" I ask, grinning.

He nods. "Good. I think you can stop."

DES

"So," I say when we're back in the shadows of the house across from Josh's place. "How do we do this?"

I can't see the sniper from where I'm standing, but Donalita pokes her head around the corner of the house and assures me he's still there on the roof.

"I've got a great idea," she says.

I turn to look at her. She's got a gleam in her eyes that makes me nervous.

"Okay," I say. "But it doesn't involve death or dismemberment, right?"

"Well," she says, drawing out the word. "Not on purpose."

"Dude!" I start, except then she gets that big grin of hers.

She holds up a hand. "I know. It's just a word. Like *yo*, or *wassup*."

"Exactly. One I obviously use too much. And you're changing the subject. What's your plan?"

I almost wish I wasn't asking.

She leans close, filling my nose with her fruity musk smell.

"You," she says, laying her palm on my chest, "walk up to the front door of Josh's house, all casual, la-la-la, and while Big

Stupid on the roof is watching you, I'll bang him on the head and knock him out."

"You want me to be bait."

"More like a distraction."

"Dude, he'll probably just shoot me!"

"I won't let that happen."

My eyebrows go up.

"Because," she says, "you're going to give me a head start. Count to three hundred and twelve and then step out onto the street. I'll be ready to do the rest."

"Why three hundred and twelve?"

"It's kind of a fun number."

"In what universe?" I ask.

She shrugs, then slips away.

"Hey!" I call after her in a loud whisper. "I never said I'd do this."

But she's long gone. I sneak a peek around the corner of the house, but I still can't see the sniper.

Sighing, I start to count. When I get to Donalita's "fun" number, I take a deep breath and walk along the side of the house.

I realize I'm an idiot. Why did I let her talk me into this? If I'm also a target and she doesn't get to the sniper fast enough, this could be the last chapter in the very short book of my life.

I force myself to not look where the sniper is hidden as I step out onto the street. I imagine Marina hearing about this plan of Donalita's. *Are you a complete idiot?* she'd say. Even Josh would try to talk me out of it.

But they aren't around and the only person in my corner is a bloodthirsty Wildling who's more focused on the fun of taking out the sniper than what might happen to me.

Let's face it. I *am* an idiot.

The hairs on the nape of my neck are standing straight up and I've got a crazy itch crawling up and down the length of my spine. I try to keep my pace casual, but it's all I can do not to break into a run and take off as fast as I can go.

Eventually—like about a century later—I turn up the walk to Josh's house. I get all the way up to the front door when I hear a short sharp whistle.

I freeze until it's repeated, then I slowly turn to scan the flat roof on the other side of the street. I expect to see a rifle pointed at me, a muzzle flash. Instead it's just Donalita, silhouetted against the sky, waving at me.

I let out a breath I didn't realize I was holding and wave back. Looking up and down the street, I trot across, stopping under where she's standing.

"Is everything okay?" I whisper up to her.

She gives me a mad grin and a thumbs-up.

"And he's not dead?"

"He's just tied up."

"Okay. Good. You should come—"

Before I get to finish, she's already jumped, landing lightly on her feet beside me. Man, would I like a little dab of Wildling in me to be able to do that kind of thing. The tricks I could pull off on my skateboard.

"That was so fun. Now what do we do?" she asks.

"Now I call Solana."

I pull out my phone, punch in the FBI agent's number and start walking. Donalita falls in step beside me. When Solana answers, I rattle off the address where we left the Black Key Securities guy and tell him to look on the roof.

"What the hell did you do?" Solana asks. "I told you not to—"

"Relax. I never even went up. I just saw somebody take him out and tie him up."

"Yeah? And what were you—"

I thumb the End button and stow the phone back into my pocket. When it rings, I see it's Solana calling back, so I turn off the power and put the phone away again.

All this time, Donalita's walking along beside me, a bounce in her steps.

"Where are we going now?" she asks.

I almost wince at the perkiness in her voice. I was already exhausted before we got into all of this. Now that the adrenalin rush has worn off, I just want to crash.

"I don't know about you," I tell her, "but I'm beat. I'm going home to bed."

"Can I come?"

"Dude, I live with my parents."

"I'll be good. I'll be as quiet as a mouse—quieter really, because they're always making these scritchy-scratchy sounds and I won't make a single one."

"Do you have any idea how long I'd be grounded if my parents caught me with a girl sleeping over?"

"I'll be a coati girl and sleep in a corner and no one will ever know I was there."

"I don't know …"

"Please please please please. I've nowhere else to go. And Theo said I'm supposed to watch out for you."

I'm too tired to argue, so against my better judgment, I let her tag along.

JOSH

Tío Goyo tosses me a canteen. The water is warm and has a metallic tang, but I don't think I've ever tasted anything as good. I have another long pull. That's when I see the two big backpacks sitting on the ground by his feet.

"Where did those come from?" I ask.

He shrugs.

"And how did you get up and down so fast? Did you change into a hawk and fly?"

"Where do these stories come from?" he says.

"Well, you know—"

He holds up a hand. "Is the conversation in your head starting up again?"

I got through the last ordeal faster than he expected, but I don't feel like starting all over again.

"I'm fine," I tell him. "Head empty, ready to rock and roll."

He nods. "All right, then. I'm going to walk out of your sight. I want you to call up a map of the area in your head and figure out where I am."

I watch him leave, tiny plumes of dust rising from his footsteps. Then he's gone. I take another pull from the canteen.

Sitting on his rock, I close my eyes and try to tune in to the GPS thing in my head. It was so strong back home I had to damp it down or I thought I'd go crazy. But here? Nothing. It's like I never had it.

I find my thoughts starting to drift, and force myself to concentrate on locating Tío Goyo. But no matter how hard I focus, I get nothing.

I stand up and turn in a slow circle. I can't even catch his scent. When the wind shifts and I finally do, I follow it to where he's sitting on the edge of a flat rock. The ground drops away from the edge in a sheer cliff. The bottom has to be a couple hundred feet below.

He looks at me over his shoulder and smiles. "You found me."

"With this," I say and touch the side of my nose.

"Ah." He shrugs. "That's okay. We'll figure it out."

He hops to his feet with more agility than I'd expect for an old guy, and with way more *cojones* than I'd have on that precipice. But I guess if he can turn into a hawk, what does he have to worry about?

"What makes you think I can fly?" he asks.

I'm sure my mouth hangs open.

He laughs. "No, I can't read your mind. But I can read your face and your body language."

I close my mouth, then clear my throat. "Well," I say, "I've heard that you—*los tíos*—the uncles from Halcón Pueblo, you're not cousins, but they say you can still take the shape of hawks."

"Huh. Wouldn't that be something? Imagine what the world looks like from up there."

I can't tell if he's being disingenuous or if it's really not true.

I can't think of any reason for him to lie to me, but if he can't turn into a bird, how does he get around as quickly as he does? It's not like—

"You're making friends with that conversation in your head again," he says.

I smile. "And I suppose you've got nothing in yours."

He cocks his head like a bird and considers it.

"Only what I need," he tells me. "Come on," he adds, heading back to the top of the gulch. "Let's get our gear and make camp."

I open my mouth to ask him where these backpacks came from—because he never did answer me—then shut it again and just fall in behind him. He shoots a grin over his shoulder.

"Now you're learning," he says.

MARINA

I really wish I had Josh's weird GPS ability—this topographical map inside his head that tells him where every nearby living thing is in relation to him. My Wildling sense of smell and hearing are acute, but they can only do so much. Right now I can't hear anything out of the ordinary approaching the playground, and if someone *is* creeping up on me, they're doing so with the breeze taking their scent away from me. All I have to go on is a warning prickle at the nape of my neck.

If I were Josh, I could pinpoint right away if someone's not where they're supposed to be. I might even know whether they present a danger. But I'm not Josh, and anybody wandering around at this time of the night is probably up to no good, no matter how often I tell my stepdad that it's perfectly safe.

I try to figure out who might be after me. Josh stopped the Riverside Kings from beating me up, but what if they've found out that he's not around anymore? And what about the original animal people—the ones who were here before any of us kids in Santa Feliz started changing? Vincenzo and his pals were pissed that the Wildlings showed up on their turf and wanted to get rid of all of us. Josh killed Vincenzo, but what if one of his buddies is sneaking up on me right now, ready to get their genocide started?

My nose and ears are on full alert. I glance around as casually as I can. If someone *is* stalking me, I don't want to let on that I know. I want to establish who or what it is, so that I know how to confront them.

Out of the corner of my eye I catch a glimpse of movement just past the far side of the park. I turn for a better look, caution forgotten, my pulse quickening, and then I have to laugh. It's only a stray barrio dog, long-legged and skinny, soft-stepping like a coyote as it walks along the pavement.

Talk about letting your imagination run away on you.

Except then I see another. And a third.

I get the little warning *ping* in my head that tells me they're Wildlings—no, not Wildlings. This *ping* is stronger. These dogs are cousins, part of the original animal people. Now that I know what I'm looking for, I spot maybe a half-dozen of them coming from all directions. I get the sense that there are even more out of sight in the shadows.

My laugh from a moment ago dies in my throat. It has to be Vincenzo's crew. So this is how they're going to take us Wildlings down. I almost have to admire the simplicity of their plan: the guise of a rogue pack of dogs suddenly attacking people, one by one. And once again, the elders will fly under the radar, with the general public none the wiser.

I stand up and turn in a slow circle, trying to keep them all in sight—an impossible task. Again I think of Vincenzo and how incredibly strong he was. I am so screwed.

I have nothing to defend myself with.

I might have a chance of outrunning ordinary dogs, but these will have the same extra speed and stamina that I do.

My head fills with should-haves as I mark their steady approach. I should have just gone home instead of mooning here in the playground. I should have called Theo to come pick me up. Really, I should have toughed it out and stayed in Ampora's bedroom, no matter how unwelcome she made me.

I make myself stop. None of that's going to help me now.

I continue to turn, trying to keep them all in sight, the seat of the swing banging against the back of my legs. I'm surprised they haven't rushed me yet. I count at least eight or nine of them. They have the numbers. Why aren't they attacking? They're fast and strong. They're—

They don't know what I can do, I realize. They're holding back, taking my measure. They know Josh tore Vincenzo to ribbons. What if Vincenzo was way stronger than them? Theo said that Vincenzo handled him like he was a little kid.

So, if Vincenzo was so powerful, but Josh—who's just a Wildling kid—could take him out as easily as he did ...

Maybe they're wondering what the other Wildling kids can do.

Maybe they're wondering what *I* can do.

That's a good question. Even I don't know what I'm capable of. I'm faster and stronger than a normal human, but by how much? I've never truly tested myself. Whenever I'm in human shape, I just keep my head down and try to fit in like I'm an ordinary girl. I've never let loose. Not ever. Not even once.

I bump into the seat of the swing again as I make another turn to keep an eye on the dogs. The chains going up from either side of the seat rattle from the movement. The sound makes me look up. One of those chains could make a decent weapon, and they're only attached to the bar by a link at the top of each side.

I'm strong enough to break those, aren't I? And then at least I wouldn't be empty-handed when the dogs finally get up their nerve to attack.

I'm full of confidence. I get a fistful of chain in either hand and pull down hard.

And nothing happens.

The pack is still moving in closer to me. The closest of the dogs is twenty feet away.

I give the chains another yank. Harder.

Still nothing.

The lead dog shifts into his human shape. He's tall, with black hair and skin much darker than the tan brown of his fur when he was a dog. He stands barefoot in black jeans and a leather vest. There seems to be a mark on his shoulder—no, it's a tattoo of a circle with a lightning bolt stamped across it like a no-smoking sign. His eyes flash with cruel humour, but I keep my gaze steady, trying not to show my fear.

"Hell," he says, shaking his head. "Why would Sandino tell us to be careful? You're nothing like the mountain lion. You're just a girl."

Then he laughs and starts to walk forward. The other dogs close in.

I glare at him, anger washing away my fear.

"Just a girl?" I mutter.

I don't know if it's something to do with being a Wildling that enrages me so quickly, or if this is just the final straw in a long, crap-filled day. Nothing's gone right, from my sister and the Kings, to Josh abandoning us on his dumb quest for Elzie, to all these stupid haters like Congressman Householder who just want to lock up every Wildling because we're different. And now these so-called cousins who'd rather kill us than protect us.

Something in me just snaps.

I channel all my anger into a last attempt to yank down the chains and this time they break from the bar at the top of the swings. I almost bean myself with them as they come flying down, but I jump back and they crash to the sand beside me. I grab one of the chains where it's attached to the swing seat and break it free.

When he sees what I'm doing, the guy with the big mouth charges. The dogs move in from all sides, growling and snarling. But I'm good and royally pissed off now.

I swing an end of the chain at the lead guy and he catches it easily. He grins at me, so full of himself that he doesn't twig to what I'm doing until it's too late. With all my might and speed, I whip the other end against the side of his head. There's a loud crack and it drops him like a dead weight, blood gushing from his temple.

I don't waste a second celebrating his fall. I move away from the swing set, whirling the chain above my head like it weighs nothing more than a skipping rope. The charging dogs break off their attack and beat a hasty retreat, but they don't go far.

"Come on!" I yell. "What are you afraid of? I'm just a girl."

I'm pumped with adrenalin, but not so stupid as to forget that I've only bought myself a moment's respite. I might be able to get one or two more of them, but there are too many for me to ever get out of here in one piece.

My options are so limited. I could run for Papá's house, and

I might even make it, but I don't think anything will stop the dogs from busting in and going after my family. Except there's nowhere closer, nowhere to hide. Unless ...

It's a crazy idea, but what if I escape into the otherworld?

I've never even tried it before, but I've watched Cory do it, and it's not like he uses some kind of magic incantation. It seems to work the same way as shifting into my otter shape. You just have to will it to happen, though I doubt it's all that easy on the first attempt. You probably have to concentrate pretty hard, the way you do when coming out of your animal shape and you want to be wearing clothes.

The pack can follow me, of course—that snarling gang of dogs observing a safe distance from the end of my chain while keeping me penned here. But I remember Cory and Auntie Min talking about how the otherworld holds endless layers. If I can get over there in the first place, and then keep shifting from that first world deeper into the others, I'll bet I could lose them.

The chain's getting heavy. I stop swinging and hold it loosely at my side. When one of the dogs gets bold and starts moving toward me, I flick the end of the chain in his direction. The dog yelps even though I missed by at least a couple of feet. As he retreats I see that he has the same tattoo on the upper part of his front leg. No, not a tattoo. It's a brand, like in a cowboy movie where they burn the mark on the cattle.

So whose brand is it? The first guy mentioned somebody named Sandino.

I hear a scuff in the sand behind me and whirl the chain again in a big circle. This time the end connects with one of them and the high-pitched yelp is for real.

Part of me is aware of the danger I'm in, and part of me is

trying to figure out what these marks on the dogs mean. I tell myself to stop getting distracted. Right now, the only thing I need to concentrate on is getting over to the otherworld.

I lower the chain and put all of my focus on what it was like to be there. What it felt like and smelled like. How clean the air was.

But when I reach for it—nothing.

I push and push. Still nothing.

I hear one of the dogs sneaking up behind me again. Up goes the chain and I whirl it around, except this time it stops dead, then yanks me forward. I wasn't expecting that. The chain flies from my hands and I stumble, turning as I go down. I land on my hands, gaze fixed on the dog who's shifted into a man holding the chain.

Like the first guy, he's got this big grin on his lips. Mean eyes mocking me. I hear an echo of that dismissive comment his friend made.

Just a girl.

So I do the last thing he's probably expecting. I come up off the ground and charge him.

He doesn't have time to use the chain. He doesn't have time to do a damn thing before I barrel into him. He goes down with me on top and the impact knocks all the breath out of him. I hit him hard and fast, my fists drumming against his face.

Now the rest of the pack surges forward.

For most of us, moments of stress trigger our change into Wildlings.

I guess it doesn't get much more stressful than being attacked by a pack of rabid, snarling dogs. As I'm about to go down under them, I reach out for the otherworld one more time.

One of the dogs hits me in the back and we both pitch forward, except instead of landing on the loose sand of the playground, we're on dry rough grass and dirt. I can still hear the other dogs howling and snarling. The one on my back snaps at my neck and yanks a mouthful of hair upward, pulling my head with it.

I don't even bother to try to fight it off. I suck in the pure air of the otherworld and then push deeper again, away from the pack. For the moment, I've lost the dogs and I'm in a glade in some forest. Big trees rise up all around me and the night is gone. The sun is high in the sky and sends down shafts of light. I seem to be alone, but I can still hear that last dog growling so I push farther still.

This time I'm standing in—snow? It's up to my knees and a cold wind gusts, spraying snow into my face. As far as I can see, there's an endless expanse of white.

There's a So-Cal world that gets this much snow?

No, this isn't some parallel unspoiled version of Santa Feliz anymore.

I remember somebody—Cory, maybe, or Auntie Min— saying that the deeper worlds get stranger and stranger, the farther you go. I've hardly gone anywhere and it's already too bizarre for me. And cold. And I can still hear that howling dog.

I push again, and again. Landscapes flicker around me. Jungle, desert, arctic tundra, a mountaintop. Once I appear in the middle of a town square straight out of some medieval movie, startling the people around me. I push on quickly before somebody grabs me.

I know I'm panicking, but I can't seem to stop the unreasonable fear from pushing me on and on. I haven't heard the dogs for a while. The worlds continue to flicker by. I've got a sharp pain in my temples now and I'm getting more and more nauseous.

Finally I manage to stop pushing. I collapse on what feels like broken asphalt. I curl up, holding my head, and try not to throw up. I know if I start, I'll never stop.

I don't know how long I lie there before I finally feel like I can move without being sick. The pain in my temples has receded to a dull ache. I listen hard, but I don't hear the dogs. I lost them a long time ago.

I sit up and look around. I'm in the middle of what was a street, in what once was a city. But something flattened most of it and the forest has grown back over the rubble. Parts of buildings covered with vines and moss are still standing. There are remnants of streets like the one I'm on, but trees and other vegetation have pushed up through the pavement, and you can only see the shape of the road by the rubble of the buildings on either side. Judging by the size of some trees, whatever happened here happened a long time ago.

It's when I stand up to get a better look at my surroundings that the quiet hits me. It's not just the lack of traffic. I can't hear the ocean anymore, either, and that's just creepy. I've never been away from the coast before. Distant or close, the sound of the waves is always somewhere nearby.

But not here. Wherever *here* is.

My stomach's settled down, but the headache hasn't gone yet and I'm weak as a kitten. I massage my temples. I need to rest up a bit before I can start to make my way back. Until then, I'm not moving from this spot. I can't see the door, or portal, or whatever it is that will take me home, but I do know that there's a way back close at hand. If I start wandering and try to shift back, who knows where I'll end up?

I'm pretty sure that's not exactly the way it works—I've seen Cory cross over at whatever random spot he happens to be—but I'm not taking any chances.

Except then I hear voices.

My pulse quickens. I lift my head to read the wind, but it betrays me, sending my scent in the direction of the sound and giving me nothing in return.

Friends or foes?

More of the dog men or possible allies?

Weak as I am, I can't face the dog men right now.

So … risk outweighs hope.

I take a loose rock and scratch a mark on the pavement, then head to the closest side of the road, where I take shelter in the rubble of a building.

JOSH

We leave the desert world behind. From one step to the next, the red dirt underfoot turns dark and we follow a trail through a thick forest, its canopy so dense that it feels like twilight down here.

As we walk I catch a glimpse of something moving off to our left. My nose tells me it's a deer a moment before I catch a glimpse of its disappearing flanks, white tail bobbing. The mountain lion's hunting instinct wants me to chase after it and grumbles when I stay on the trail with Tío Goyo.

He shoots me a questioning glance, which I ignore.

I haven't particularly noticed the land rising underfoot, but a moment later the trail takes us out of the forest to the top of a broad plateau. There's still vegetation here—tall fir trees, some kind of browning grass, along with lots of big rocks, some flat and the size of a city lot, others rounded.

"This is as good a place as any to camp for the night," Tío Goyo says.

When he drops his backpack under one of the towering fir trees, I do the same.

"You're sure about this time thing, right?" I say. "I don't want Elzie to get hurt while I'm off camping in the woods with you."

"I'm sure. But consider this: until we fix the map in your head, you won't be able to find her anyway."

I don't want to think about that.

I watch as he starts to scoop together pine needles. When I realize he's making himself a mattress, I copy what he's doing, rolling out a blanket on top of the makeshift bed just the way he does. Then we gather wood and he makes a small fire on a flat slab of stone that abuts the nearest of the big rounded rocks. He pulls a frying pan out of his pack and I expect him to make some kind of meal, except he just takes out a couple of foil-wrapped burritos and heats them up. I want to ask where they came from, but decide to live in the moment, letting the delicious flavours explode in my mouth.

It's been a long day with way too much to process, but for once my mind's not running at a mile a minute. I don't know if I'm just tired from racing up and down the gulch earlier, or if it's something about this place, but after we've eaten I'm content to bunch up my blanket and lean back to watch the sky.

The sunset is amazing—the sky fills with colour from one end of the western horizon to the other. When the sun finally slips away, it gets dark even for my Wildling eyes, but not for long. The sky is impossibly big, the stars spilling across it in a dazzling array. When the moon rises it's just this side of full and so bright that everything is as clear as day around me. The air's so clean and sharp it tastes the way I imagine winter would.

"It's beautiful here," I say.

Tío Goyo nods. "A night like this is a gift from the Thunders."

DES

I'm in that in-between moment when you're not quite awake, but not fully asleep—where if you're left alone, it could go either way—except then I hear my little sister open my bedroom door.

"Mom!" Molly yells. "Des has a girl in his room!"

I come all the way awake to see Donalita curled up beside me on the bed. She's outside the covers and I'm under them, but still.

I am so dead.

Donalita's eyes open. She smiles at me. I can hear my mother coming down the hall. She won't be smiling at all.

"Get out of here," I tell Donalita even though there's no time.

Mom's pushing the door open.

Donalita winks and rolls off the bed. She lands with a soft thump on the carpet, then disappears under the bed.

"Desmond Wilson!" Mom starts as she bursts in.

Then she stops because what is she going to do? Yell at me because I'm still in bed at seven on a Friday morning? I never get up until the last minute. And it's obvious there's no one in the room with me.

But she's not completely trusting.

"Jeez," I say. "A little privacy maybe?"

We've had discussions before about knocking before coming in, but Mom's on a mission this morning.

"Do you have a girl in here?" she asks.

"I can honestly say I don't."

And I can because Donalita's one of the animal people. Sometimes she can look like a girl, but she's not one. For starters, she's older than everybody in this room combined.

"And I'm not going to find her if I look under the bed?" Mom asks.

Busted.

I sigh as she goes down on one knee to peer underneath. When she lifts her head again she has a funny look on her face.

"You're hiding a kitten?" she says.

Molly does that thing where every bit of her starts to tremble with excitement.

"A kitten?" she cries. "Can we keep it, Mom? Can we?"

My heart sinks. Sure, Donalita might look like that in the darkness under the bed. In the poor light it might be easy to mistake a coatimundi for a cat. And yeah, a coati's not as bad as having a girl, but how am I supposed to explain what I'm doing with one?

Molly's on her knees beside Mom, reaching under the bed.

Don't, I want to say.

But when Molly sits up she's got a kitten in her arms. Sort of. Because I see two things: my sister holding a cute little kitten, but superimposed over the kitten is a kitten-sized Wildling girl that Molly obviously doesn't see. It's like the two of them—kitten and coati girl—occupy the same space. I shoot Mom a look, but it's clear that she only sees a kitten, too.

Mom sits on her heels.

"Why is there a kitten under your bed?" she asks me.

"I, um, found her on my way home?"

Mom's eyes narrow. "And why are you home? I thought you were staying at Josh's house last night."

I can't stop staring at my sister cuddling a kitten that's also a tiny Donalita.

"Des?" Mom says.

I drag my gaze back to her. "I was. I mean, that was the plan. But Josh is still pining over Elzie."

"I liked that girl," Mom says.

"Right. Who wouldn't? She's great. But sometimes it gets a little old, him mooning over her all the time—especially when he's the one who broke them up. Last night I just got tired of hearing about it, so I came home."

"And found the cat along the way."

"More she found me—but yeah."

"We're keeping it, aren't we, Mom?" Molly asks. "Forever and ever. I'm going to call her Kitty-poo."

The Donalita part of what she's holding rolls her eyes and I smile.

"That's a good name," I tell Molly, "but we can't keep her. I need to take her back to the street where I found her and find out who she belongs to."

Mom gets up off the floor and sits on the edge of the bed. She reaches out and ruffles the fur between Donalita's ears.

"That's not true, is it?" Molly asks her.

"I'm afraid so. How would you feel if you lost your kitty and nobody brought her back to you?"

"But I don't even have a kitty."

Mom pulls the kitten from Molly's reluctant arms and plonks her on the bed.

"And you still don't," Mom says, shooting me a dirty look as Molly's eyes well with tears. "Come on, missy," she tells Molly. "You have to get ready for school. And you," she adds, looking at me, "better get up right now because you need to find out where that cat lives before you go to school. I'm not having it running around the house scratching the furniture and doing its business everywhere."

"What kind of business?" Molly wants to know.

"Number one and number two," I tell her.

She pulls a face and lets Mom lead her out of my bedroom. Mom pauses in the doorway to look back at me.

"I mean it," she says. "Get that cat back to its proper home today."

"I will."

She closes the door and I fall back against the headboard. I can't believe I got away with that. Donalita returns to her normal size, minus the kitten ghost she seemed to be wearing, and sits cross-legged on the bed beside me.

"How come they couldn't see you?" I ask.

"Of course they could see me. Did you take a stupid pill when I wasn't looking?"

"I mean, all that they saw was the kitten. They didn't see a kitten-sized you laid over the kitten."

"And you did."

"Well, yeah."

"Huh."

"Dude, what is that supposed to mean?"

She shrugs. "Some people can see through illusions and I guess you're one of them."

"Cory said something about that yesterday, except all I saw was him, not some other thing superimposed over him at the same time."

"Oh yeah? Well, I'm good at lots of things he isn't."

I hold up my hands. "Hey, I wasn't dissing you."

"Okay." Then she grins and adds, *"Dude."*

I leave the house carrying Donalita/the kitten, which Donalita thinks is hilarious, but I find kind of creepy and awkward. I'm not sure how to hold her because she's both a cat and a girl at the same time. I try to adjust for one, and then the other, and I just end up feeling like a klutz.

Before we left I sent Marina a couple of texts, which she never answered, so instead of swinging by her house like I'd usually do, I head for school. I guess she stayed with Chaingang last night, and I'm sorry, but them being together still weirds me out. I don't care how okay Josh is with it, it's just wrong on so many levels.

Donalita, or maybe just the kitten part of her, is purring in my arms. She thinks she's coming to school with me—like that's going to happen. Can you imagine her running around the halls of Sunny Hill following after me? Detention would be the least of my worries. But I've given up arguing with her. As soon as I'm far enough away from home, I plan to drop this kitten off. The last thing I need is for one of the neighbours to rat me out on animal abandonment to Molly or my mother.

That's the plan, anyway, but before I get the chance to put it into action, a dark sedan pulls up beside me. The window whispers down and there's Agent Solana giving me the evil eye.

"Remember last night?" I ask. "You know, when I told you Josh took off—as in, he's no longer around?"

"I'm here to see you."

"Seriously, dude?" I say. "Shouldn't you be out fighting crime somewhere instead of following a nobody like me around?" I bend to look in the window and see that the shotgun seat is empty. "See, even your partner doesn't approve of you making me your new project now that Josh is gone."

"Get in the car, Wilson."

I shake my head. "Not going to happen. I don't know what your deal is, but I'm not going anywhere with you."

"My deal," he says, "is that you called me last night and when I brought the team in to pick up that shooter on your say-so, we found him in pieces."

"What?"

"He was dead. Torn apart, just like the others."

I flash on stepping into the otherworld last night and us finding the remains of the elder that Josh ripped to shreds.

A bit of my breakfast comes up my throat.

"Now get in the car," Solana says.

I shake my head. "Dude, I never touched the guy."

But Donalita did. Bloodthirsty Donalita, who thinks the best way to get rid of problem people is to kill them.

I unconsciously tighten my grip on her and her purring changes to a low growl.

But she wouldn't have done that.

"Car," Solana says. "Now."

Crap.

"I never called you last night," I try. "I told you where the guy was when I met you on the beach, but then I just went home."

"Bullshit."

"Come on, dude. You really think I killed this guy? You think I'm a Wildling now?"

"I know you're not."

Yeah, and how does he know that? But that's a question for another time.

"So why are you hassling me?" I ask instead.

"Because you know who *did* kill this guy."

"I don't know anything."

Solana sighs. "Look," he says. "I could have picked you up at home in front of your mother and family …"

He lets his voice trail off. I wait a beat, then fill the space: "But you didn't."

He nods. "As a favour—which I'm quickly regretting."

"Unless you don't want your people to know that you met with me last night."

Something flickers in his eyes and I know I'm on to something.

"Okay," I say. "I'll come with you. I won't be saying anything about the dead guy because I don't know anything. But dude? I'll be able to talk all day about how you've been following Josh around and now you've switched your little obsession to me. I'll tell them about hawk uncles and secret societies and any other damn thing that comes to mind. That what you want?"

He gives me another sigh. "I want this butchery to stop."

"Yeah, because these same guys running around with snipers' rifles—that's not a problem."

"Of course it is."

"Then why don't you go do some actual investigating, and I'll go to school, and we'll pretend none of this ever happened."

His dark gaze settles on me, half warning, half threat. He is *so* pissed off.

"I know you were involved," he says.

"Dude, that's no secret. I called you about the guy. But that's where my part in the story ends."

I can tell he doesn't want to let it go like this, but he *is* going to back off and we both know it.

"Don't leave town," he says.

A dozen responses to that cliché come to mind, but for once I'm smart and I keep my mouth shut.

"Later, dude," is all I say.

I start to walk away, the back of my neck prickling until he pulls away from the curb and drives off down the street.

I keep on walking. I look down Josh's street when I'm passing by. The cop cars are still there, yellow tape marking off the yard of the house across the street from his. Half a block later, I duck behind a hedge and put Donalita on the ground. She immediately turns back into a girl.

"I didn't kill him," she says. "I promised you I wouldn't, so I didn't."

"I never said you did."

"But you were thinking it."

"It's not an issue, dude. We're all good."

She grins. "So what are we going to do now?"

"I don't know what *you're* going to do, but I'm going to school and you can't come."

"But I want to. And Theo said I'm supposed to guard you."

"Except I'm not going to need guarding. Nothing's going to happen to me at school."

"But—"

"And if Chaingang's that concerned, he can do it himself."

She gives me a pout that would do my little sister Molly proud. "You *do* think I killed that man with the rifle. That's why you don't want me to come."

I shake my head. "No, I don't want you to come because you don't go to Sunny Hill and I can't have you hanging around when you're not even supposed to be there in the first place. It'll just get us both into trouble."

"But what am I supposed to do?"

"I don't know. What do you usually do?"

"I could change into something very small," she says, "and then I could just ride around in your pocket. No one would ever know I was there."

"Dude, I'm not walking around school with a mouse or a lizard in my pocket."

"Please please please please."

I shake my head again. "It's just not going to happen."

She looks so dejected I almost change my mind. Then she brightens up.

"I know," she says. "I'll change into a pebble. You don't mind carrying a pebble around in your pocket, do you?"

"You can do that?"

"Of course I can, *dude*. But you'll have to wake me up when it's okay for me to be a girl again."

"A pebble."

The physics of a human being turning into a rat or a bird is confusing enough for me to get my head around, but this seems off-the-charts impossible.

"Why is that so strange?" she asks.

"Well, it's just—I mean, come on. A pebble." That makes me think of something else. "Are you telling me everything's sentient?"

"Everything has a spirit, silly. How else could it know what it is?"

"I have to tell you, I'm having trouble wrapping my head around this."

She shrugs. "It's just the way things are. Everybody knows that."

"So you're going to turn into a pebble."

"Yes. But you have to remember to wake me up later because when we take shapes like that, we can lose ourselves in them unless there's someone around to call us back."

"And all of you can do this?"

"Oh no," she says. "Only the very smartest and tricksiest of us."

"Okay." It's not really okay, but every time she explains it to me it gets a little weirder. So I settle for agreeing and ask instead, "So how do you wake up a pebble?"

"Oh, that's easy. Just tap me against a wall or something."

"Tap you …"

"Now, hold out your hand, palm up."

"Wait a minute," I start, but I do as she says.

Before I can go on she leaps into the air, changing as she does. There's a confusing flicker of strobing images as the normal-sized girl shifts and becomes something else. A moment later a pebble lands in the palm of my hand. Except with my double vision, I see both a pebble and Donalita curled up like a baby. I reach out with a finger. All I can feel is the hard surface of the pebble.

So maybe it's a pebble, but it's also Donalita, and the whole thing creeps me out. I slide it carefully into my pocket, but keep reaching in to make sure the pebble's still there. I want to give it a rub with my thumb the way you do with that kind of thing, until I remember that it's also a tiny Donalita, and somehow, that would just be wrong.

I'm still quietly freaking out about it when I get to school. For a change, I'm happy to be here because at least I'll be able to talk to Marina about the latest weirdness going on.

Before I can go inside, Bobby White, one of the Ocean Avers, steps in front of me, blocking my way.

"Theo wants a word with you," he says.

He nods to where Chaingang's sitting on his usual picnic table under the eucalyptus trees, shades on, shaved head gleaming. Great. Now everybody's going to think I'm a drug dealer, too.

Two weeks ago I'd have thought it was cool having Chaingang want to talk to me. Now it's just a pain in the butt. What does Marina even see in him?

But you don't turn your back on a summons from the big guy.

Chaingang lifts his shades as I walk up and gives me a nod.

"What's up, bro?" he asks, then he studies me, an odd look in his eyes. "There's something different about you—like you're a Wildling and you're not, all at the same time."

"That's because I've got Donalita in my pocket."

"You've got—"

"Don't even ask, dude."

He lets the shades drop. "Right."

I stand there for a moment waiting for him to tell me what he wants.

"Some of us have classes to go to," I say.

I figure that might get me a laugh, but he just nods like I said something profound.

"You heard from Marina?" he asks.

I shake my head. "We usually walk to school together, but when she didn't answer my texts, I thought she was catching a few waves or … you know …"

He cocks his head, waiting.

"Or that she was with you."

"No, I dropped her off near her old man's house in East Riversea last night when we got back. She's not answering my texts, either."

Maybe that's because she finally wised up, I think, except then I remember the way she was looking at him last night and how freaked she was when we all thought he was going to die. Time to take the high road.

"Did you try calling her dad's house?" I ask.

He chuckles without any humour. "Yeah, like that would go over well."

I dig in my pocket for my phone. "Do you want me to try?"

"Nah, it's all good. I haven't seen Ampora this morning, either. They'll be along."

"Not together they won't."

He shrugs. "If she gets in touch, ask her to shoot me a text."

"Sure."

"Later, bro."

I stand there for a moment longer than I need to before I realize I've been dismissed.

"Right," I say. "Later."

I add "asshole," but only in my head because I don't have a death wish.

"Des," he says as I start to walk away.

I look back at him.

"How the hell do you have Donalita in your pocket?" he asks.

I smile. "Sorry, dude. That's strictly need-to-know."

He lowers his shades and studies me for another long moment before he smiles as well. Then he pushes the glasses back up again and he looks away.

JOSH

I turn to look at Tío Goyo sitting on a rock in the moonlight. "What exactly are the Thunders? I thought it was a cousin thing, except it kind of sounds Native American, too. But you're Mexican, right?"

"No, I am Toltec."

"Right. Solana told me about that. So, the Thunders is a hawk uncle thing?"

"It's just a word," he says. "You can call the creator God, or gods, or Thunders. It can be an old man with a beard, a woman with the moon in her eyes, maybe a whole pantheon, each responsible for this or that bit. Or you can say that Raven stirred his pot back before the long ago, and this world is what came out. Whatever expression you use, it's just a way to describe what's impossible to comprehend."

He waves a hand to encompass the whole of the starry night sky. "How can we even begin to imagine the being that brought all of this into existence?"

"We could call it evolution."

He shrugs. "The first people believe that Raven woke the Thunders before he made the world."

"Well, I don't."

"What *do* you believe?"

"I don't know what to believe anymore. But even with everything that's happened to me, it all sounds like a fairy tale."

He nods sagely, as if I've just said something profound. Then he takes out a pack of cigarettes and offers me one.

"No, thanks," I tell him.

He shakes one out for himself and lights up. Standing, he turns in a slow circle and lifts the cigarette so that its smoke rises up to the stars. He does that four times before he sits down again. He leans back against a rock and takes a drag.

In the distance I hear a vague rumble of thunder.

"Think we'll get a storm?" I say.

He only smiles and exhales a stream of smoke.

"So what do you think?" he asks. "Is what happened to you purely random, or did somebody plan it?"

"I have no idea."

He nods. "I would guess random. If it were planned, somebody would have approached you by now."

"Cory did, pretty soon after I changed," I say. "He was there when I woke up as a human again. And Auntie Min keeps trying to convince me that I'm some big chosen one."

"So you think they're responsible for what's happened to you and the other young people in Santa Feliz?"

"Cory? No. I'm not too sure about Auntie Min."

Tío Goyo shakes his head. "She is too connected to her land to have grander designs. You know nothing of your heritage, do you? What it means to be a cousin—one of the animal people?"

I shake my head. "But I don't buy into this crap of me being some kind of hero saviour. I mean, come on."

"How can you be so sure?"

"I grew up my whole life being *me*. I love my mom, but our family doesn't have any special heritage, in the way you're saying."

"What about your father?"

I shrug. "He's just a loser that I don't think about." That's a lie. Not the loser part, but I've been thinking about him my whole life. I try to figure out why he left Mom. She's beautiful and smart. She's a good woman. It never made any sense that he'd just walk away from her. Why he'd walk away from *us*.

But that's nothing I want to share with anyone, and I'm not going to start with Tío Goyo. He's looking at me—studying me—but I can't get a read on him.

"With all you've experienced so far," he finally says, "how can you be so sure that you don't have a destiny?"

I have to smile. "Like I'm going to believe that, coming from yet another person who wants something from me?"

"I told you before. There are no strings attached to whatever help I can give you."

I nod. "Except you're just being more subtle than the others. You've all got an agenda. You figure if you help me, I'll feel obliged to help you when all of this is done."

He studies me for another long moment, then shrugs.

"We should get some sleep," he says.

He butts out his cigarette on the stone and puts what's left in his pocket. Then he gets up and goes to his makeshift bed.

I stay where I am, looking up at that big moon in a bigger sky. My thoughts start to drift. When I realize that I'm not thinking of Elzie, but of Marina and what the hell is she doing with someone like Chaingang, I give my head a shake and go to my own bed.

MARINA

I crouch behind what's left of a wall in the ruins of the building where I've taken shelter, holding a length of rusted pipe that I guess was once part of the plumbing system. There are no ceilings or a roof. The walls that still exist are a mix of brickwork and cement, and rise up at least two storeys with the hint of a third. There's rubble all around me. It was like that as far as I could see before the voices I heard sent me scurrying here for shelter—just abandoned and ruined buildings, and broken-up city streets choked with junked vehicles and brush—everything falling down and reclaimed by nature.

It's all so different from back home—or even from those other times I first crossed over to the otherworld. There's not even a single salty hint of the ocean in the air. It's humid rather than dry. The overcast sky just makes everything seem even more gloomy, especially to someone like me who's used to her So-Cal sunshine.

I'd like to explore a little instead of hiding—try to figure out what happened to this place—except now I can hear the approach of whoever owns those voices. Unlike me, they're not trying to hide. Their footsteps crunch in the dirt and they're talking away to each other. I hear three, maybe four different voices. I still can't make out what they're saying—I don't even know what language they're speaking.

I haven't dared peek out yet to get a better look, so I don't know if they're human or cousins. I'm hoping for human. I've got a little advantage in terms of strength and speed against a human. But a cousin who can sniff me out? Not so much, though I did pretty good holding my own against that pack of dogs back in the barrio.

Oh, who am I kidding? The only way I escaped in one piece was pure blind luck, and since luck isn't something you can count on, I'll have to play it smart.

Like hiding from strangers until I can figure out if they're friendly or a threat.

The voices are abreast of my hiding place and my heart sinks a little when I get that *ping* of recognition that tells me they're cousins. And if I can sense them, then they must be able to sense me. I swallow hard and tighten my grip on the pipe, ready to come out fighting.

And then … nothing happens.

As the voices start to move away, I finally peek over the wall. The receding figures are a quartet of tall, human-shaped figures. But I know they're not human.

They wear dusters over jeans and boots, and walk with an easy swing to their steps, black braids bouncing on their backs. I don't see any weapons except for the staff that one of them is using as a walking stick. Something flutters from the top—a tangle of ribbons and bird feathers.

If I were Cory or Auntie Min, I'd be able to tell exactly what their animal shapes are. But I'm not and right now I don't care. Just so long as they keep moving.

Except then one of them stops. He lifts his head and sniffs the air, and I hold my breath until he finally turns away again and catches up with his companions. He says something to them and they all laugh.

I watch until they're out of sight and I can't hear their voices anymore. Then I drop behind the wall again and sit on a stone. I turn to put the wall at my back and come face to face with a man squatting on his haunches not three feet from me.

A wordless *gah* jumps out of my mouth and he puts a finger to his lips. Somehow I manage to remember the cousins that passed by a moment ago, and don't vocalize my surprise any more than that one sound.

I scuttle sideways along the wall, putting more distance between us while I get a good look at him. I lift the pipe, ready to whack him.

The way he snuck up on me is creepy enough, but he's also so *strange* looking: short and bulky, with a wide, dark brown face, a thick matt of long hair and a full beard, both braided with buttons and shells, ribbons and thin tendrils of vines. He's probably not much more than four feet tall, standing up. His raggedy clothes are a collection of muted browns and greens, and look like they came from the discard bin in an alley behind a thrift shop. His feet are dirty and bare.

He regards me with curious eyes, the piercing blue of a husky's. They're cool in a dog. Way too intense in a man. If he even is a man.

"We have to go," he says.

"What?"

"The hounds. They know you're here. They were just playing with you when they went by—pretending they didn't notice, but how could they not? You reek of an otherworld."

"Whoa, whoa," I manage to get out. "Say what?"

Hounds. That sounds way too much like the guys who jumped me in the park and then chased me here.

He stands up and beckons me to come. "Quick now."

"I'm not going anywhere with you."

I hear the sound of a hunting horn. It's not close, but it's not far, either.

"Suit yourself," the raggedy man says. "But whatever you decide, make sure it includes running away from here as fast as you can."

Without another word, he jumps over the wall at the back of the building. The horn sounds again. This time it's answered by another, coming from the opposite direction. Then a third, and a fourth. They're on all sides.

That can't be good.

I'm on my feet and over the wall just in time to see the raggedy man disappear around the corner of a building, the walls still standing covered in vines.

"Hey, wait up!" I call after him.

I put on a burst of Wildling speed, winding my way through the rubble and brush, but he's motoring along at a good clip for all his bulk and it takes me a couple more blocks to catch up to him. When I do, it's only because he's crouched down beside a rusted old car. I'm about to ask what he's doing when I see the dog. I get a momentary glimpse of it, maybe three blocks away, then it's behind some brush and lost from sight again.

"They're closing in on us," the raggedy man says.

The horns sound again, one answering the other, all around us. They're much closer now. I don't think I was entirely convinced before, but I am now: the men with the long hair and black dusters are definitely hunting us. Maybe with a pack of dogs. Maybe they can turn into dogs.

"How do we get away from them?" I ask my companion.

"We need to be invisible," he says. "Sight, sound and smell." He taps his brow. "In here, too."

I look at him like he just grew a second head. "How are we supposed to do that?"

"The same way you do anything—you will it to happen."

I shake my head. "I don't have that party trick. How's it even possible?"

"Look away," he says.

I hesitate.

"Go ahead," he says. "Trust me in this one little thing."

He's odd-looking, but since he hasn't seemed threatening so far, I decide to give him the benefit of the doubt and do as he asks. But I'm ready to swing the pipe if he tries anything.

"Now look back," he says.

His voice comes from the same place, except when I turn back around he's not there anymore. I mean he's *really* not there. I reach out with my free hand, then jump back when I touch his invisible chest.

He reappears like the Cheshire Cat: first a grin, then the rest of him.

"You see?" he says. "It's easy."

I shake my head. "Falling off a board is easy. That is just impossible."

"Think of Prince Jayden with his magic cloak," he says.

I give him a blank look.

"Like in the old story," he explains. "Remember? He got it from the thrushes to help rescue his sister, Princess Maika, when she was trapped in the Iron Tower."

"We don't have that story where I come from."

"Really? That's sad."

"We have other stories," I assure him.

The horns sound again.

"What about this cloak?" I add.

"Pretend you're wearing it—or it can be a blanket. It doesn't matter. Just make it whatever's easiest for you to imagine. Wrap it all around you so that no one can see you, or smell you, or even sense you. Use it to block anyone from being aware of you."

"But I don't *have* a cloak or blanket."

He sighs and glances down the street before turning back to me.

"*Imagine* you have one," he says.

I guess the panic I feel is written on my face because he sighs again.

"I can show you how to do it," he says, "the way we teach our infants survival skills when they're still too young to understand language."

That doesn't sound too dangerous. But I still have to ask, "Is it going to hurt?"

Maybe wherever he comes from infants are way tougher than So-Cal teenagers.

"It's more startling than anything else," he says. He shoots another worried look down the street. "We don't have much time."

"Okay," I tell him. "Go for it."

Please don't let me regret this. And can I just say how much I wish I had a do-over before I escaped the dogs by coming here in the first place? Make that before I let Ampora chase me out of Papá's house.

The raggedy man reaches out toward my brow with a finger and I flash on Cory doing the same thing with Theo, back on the headland near Tiki Bay.

Oh, God. Is he going to step inside my head, or my dreams, or whatever it was Cory did to Theo?

But then my head fills with a flash of—not exactly light. It's more a momentary rush of information that flares inside me like stepping out of a dark house into the noontime sun. I see how to pull off the trick. I also see a cascade of confusing images that I realize are pieces of my companion's life. It's like watching somebody flip pages in a book, but they flit by so quickly, it's almost like they were never there in the first place.

"Now quickly," he says in a soft voice. "Disappear."

I use the new information he stuck in my head and discover that he was right. It *is* like enfolding yourself in an imaginary blanket or a cloak. I imagine a blanket that I pull over me and I guess I go invisible. I know I did everything just like the info-dump showed me. Except …

"I can still see my hands," I say.

"But I can't."

"Seriously?"

"Yes. Now, on our lives, be still."

I'm about to ask why, when I hear the soft pad of paws on the other side of the wrecked car. I grip my length of pipe and hold my breath.

The dog is there, standing as high at the shoulder as a wolf. It's the same breed as the pack that came at me in the park.

That reminds me of the one I hit with the chain last night. I hope I didn't kill him.

I get a flash in my head of the surveillance video footage where Josh is killing that ValentiCorp researcher while he's in his Wildling shape, quickly followed by the memory of the torn-up remains of Vincenzo that Josh left in the otherworld.

I don't want to go there. I don't want to be like that.

But today I don't have to fight. The dog looks right at us— no, right through us because his gaze slides away as though we're not even there. He shifts in a blur of movement and the dog becomes one of those tall men in a duster. He pulls a horn from an inside pocket and blows a quick call to his companions.

The sharpness of the sound, coming from so close, startles me. I can feel my imaginary blanket slide a little from my imaginary shoulder and reach up to adjust it. It's only when the man turns in my direction that I realize I forgot I was supposed to imagine the adjustment. Instead I reached with my hand and the movement broke the spell.

His eyes widen in surprise at my sudden appearance and then he grins before lifting the horn again.

JOSH

My butt is starting to hurt. We're sitting crossed-legged on one of the big flat stones, facing each other under the morning sun. I'm supposed to close my eyes and use all my other senses to "see" Tío Goyo, then when I'm locked into him, I'm supposed to use my tracking sense to place him in the landscape.

"How long before we finally give up?" I ask after we've been doing this for a half hour. "Something about this place is blocking my ability to find that GPS I had in my head."

"We're not going to give up," he says.

"Yeah, but—"

"It will return," he tells me before I can finish. "Trust me. We can try other exercises, but let's not abandon this one too soon."

I think of montages in movies where they fast-forward through the hero's training to the beat of some rocking tune. Why can't that work in real life?

"Let's give it another few minutes," Tío Goyo says, "then we'll take a break and try something else."

I nod and close my eyes. His breathing is quiet, but I can easily find it. Ditto his scent. But when I reach for more, I can't—

A faint movement breaks my concentration. It's followed by a whooshing sound, and then all sense of him is gone. I open my eyes to find he's vanished.

Great.

CHAINGANG

Ampora doesn't show up until the last bell's just about to ring. As soon as I spot her, I get up from the picnic table and move to cut her off from the door. She sees me coming and picks up her pace, but I add a little Wildling juice to my step so I still get to the door before she does, blocking her entrance.

She glares at me. "Get out of my way."

"Soon as you answer my question."

"I don't have to answer anything," she says. "And I sure don't have to take any of your gangsta crap. So move, or you'll be sorry."

I ignore the empty threat. What's she going to do? Take a swing at me?

"Where's Marina?" I ask.

"Stay away from me, you freak."

She starts to walk away, but I grab her arm and I'm not particularly gentle about it. She tries to pull free—good luck with that. When she looks around she realizes that it's only the two of us out here.

"I asked you a question," I tell her.

"Yeah, and I could give a flying—"

I pull her in and hoist her up until her face is inches from my own.

"Listen, little girl," I tell her. "You might think you're badass, but I could break you in two without even trying. Now. Answer. The. Question."

I set her back down hard, directly in front of me, keeping a light hold on her shoulders. She shakes her entire body as though trying to rid herself of fleas. Nothing kills the belligerence in this one.

"Why? Or you're going to go after my family?"

"That's not the way I roll. I'm not like the little dipshit cartel wannabes you run with."

"I don't run with the Kings."

"Right. You only dress the part."

"I dress like this so that the jerks in school just leave me the hell alone—not that my fashion choices are any of your business."

I nod. "You're right. It's not my business and I don't care. Where's Marina?"

"Let me go."

"We'll be doing this all day until you answer my question."

"I don't know where she is—okay? She left around four or five in the morning and I haven't seen her since."

"She just left."

Ampora grits her teeth and stares right into my eyes. "So maybe I told her to go when I found out she's banging you. I don't want any gang crap around my little sisters, doesn't matter if your skin is black or brown."

I let go of her shoulders. "You've got your facts wrong. We're not banging."

"She said you were."

"In those words."

A shrug. "She said you were her boyfriend."

"So you just kicked her out in the middle of the night."

"I already told you. I've got little sisters—"

"Who don't deserve an asshole like you for an older sister."

"Hey, I look out for—"

I grab her arm and she winces. "Marina's your sister, too, and you put her out into the barrio in the middle of the night. She never made it home. She's not at school. She's not answering her phone."

"Not my problem."

"That's where you're wrong, bitch," I tell her. "If anything's happened to her, I'm coming after you. Not your sisters. Not your family. You. And if you think you're going to breeze your way out of the hurt I'll put on you, you haven't begun to understand what you're dealing with. Doesn't matter where you go, or who you get to protect you. I'll find you."

I let her go and give her a push away.

I'll give her this. She's got *cojones*. Because she comes right back at me.

"Don't think you can threaten me," she starts.

"I'm not threatening you," I tell her. "A threat means it might not happen, but that's not the deal here. I'm telling you how it will be."

Then I turn away and head for my bike.

Ten minutes later I'm cruising by Ampora's house. I make a circuit of the block and this time I pull up at the little park just down the street. There are toddlers in the playground area. Babies in carriages. Mothers and grandmothers and aunts sitting on the benches or standing around in small groups, watching over them.

I ignore the suspicious looks they give me and put the Harley on its stand. Then I walk into the park and start casting for scent.

Marina likes it here. This is where she was meeting up with Ampora after I dropped her off last night. I doubt she'd have stayed here very long after Ampora kicked her out, but I'm willing to bet that she at least passed through on her way to wherever she went. Bottom line, it's as good a place to start as any.

It's been hours, with who knows how many people walking through, but I've always felt connected to Marina. I could single out her scent in the middle of a crowded beach a week after she's been there, no problem. Today's no different. I pick up her scent right away and it leads me straight to the swing set. At first I don't notice either the broken swing or the way the ladies are shooing their charges away from me. I'm just focused on what my nose can tell me.

Marina was here recently, and more than once. Ditto Ampora. There's a mess of other smells. Kids, grown-ups—all the people you'd expect in a place like this. But then I catch a scent that stops me cold.

Cousins.

Lots of them, and none that are familiar. I see dog tracks in the sand. Scuff marks that look like a fight.

And then I realize that I'm totally freaking out the women in the park. They're gathering up their kids and bunching up on the other side of the teeter-totter. As I look up, one of them's taking out her phone. I figure she's planning to call either the cops or the Kings. Neither's a good option.

I put up my hands in the universal sign language that says I'm not going to hurt anybody.

"I'm not here to cause trouble," I say. "I'm just looking for a friend. I think she's in trouble and I want to help her." I describe Marina and add, "Have any of you seen her?"

Nobody responds for a long moment, but at least the woman with the phone hasn't punched in a number yet.

"How do we know you're not the trouble?" a grandmother in her black shawl finally asks.

She looks to be a thousand years old, her brown skin a road map of a lifetime of experience. Her eyes are so dark they seem to swallow light.

"I guess you don't," I tell her. "I don't know how to prove I'm on the level."

The women exchange looks, then turn to the old woman who first spoke to me. She studies me for a long moment.

"I think I know you," she finally says. "The young man with the large motorcycle. You are the companion of the boy who drove the bandas away from our park, aren't you?"

"Yes, ma'am. His name is Josh and he's my brother."

Her eyebrows go up.

"My spiritual brother."

That makes her smile.

"Can I ask ..." I say. "Are you also from the Halcón Pueblo?"

A few of the women make the sign of the cross, but the grandmother's smile gets bigger. The humour reaches all the way up into her eyes.

"Do I look so much like an old man?" she asks.

"No, ma'am. You surely don't."

"What do you know of *los tíos*?" she asks.

"Not a hell—I mean, heck of a lot. I don't even know where their pueblo is."

"I've been told," she says, "that the Halcón Pueblo is not a place, but a state of being, much like your relationship with Josh. The old hawk uncles are spiritual brothers—to each other and to their namesakes. But what that means exactly is unclear to me as well." She turns to the other women. "Can anyone help this polite young man?"

"The person you described," one of the younger women says to me, "sounds like Ampora Lopez."

"Close. It's her sister Marina I'm looking for."

"She doesn't live here anymore."

"I know that. But she was staying at her father's house last night and left in the early morning, when it was still dark. Do any of you live close to the park? Maybe you were up and saw something? Or heard something?"

Another of the women gives a slow nod. "My husband, Ricky, said he was woken up early this morning by the sound of dogs fighting. By the time he looked out to see what was going on, it was already over. But he did say he saw a man carrying the body of a dog."

I get a sinking feeling. I know there were dog-shaped cousins here.

"Are you sure it was a dog?" I ask.

Because in the dark, a sea otter could easily be mistaken for one.

She shrugs. "That's what Ricky said."

"Did he know the man?"

She shakes her head. "It was still dark and they left too quickly for him to see much." She pauses, then adds, "When we arrived this morning there was that."

She points to a broken swing that I barely registered earlier. I see now that it was pulled from the bar at the top of the swings. One of the support chains was ripped from the seat and lies a few yards away from the broken swing seat.

When I walk over to the chain I smell Marina's scent all over it. There's blood on one end, and a small pool of congealed blood in the sand.

Crap.

I didn't want to think it, but it can't be avoided now. Last night some pack of dog cousins came at Marina while she was here. Alone. Because her bitchy sister tossed her out on her ass.

I'm going to kill Ampora.

But first I have to find Marina.

I feel like breaking something, but I manage to school my face so that nothing shows.

"Thanks," I tell the women. "You've been a big help. I'm just going to look around a little more, then I'll be out of your hair."

"Take your time," the grandmother says. "If not for you and your friend, we would have had to find another park for the children to keep them away from the bandas."

"It was our pleasure," I tell her, even though it was Josh who did all the heavy lifting.

I leave them and walk around the park some more, sifting through the scents. The story becomes pretty clear. Marina was by the swing set. The dogs came at her from all sides. What I can't figure out is where they all went. The scents all lead into the park. Most of them don't lead out—including Marina's.

That confuses me until I realize it's because they *didn't* go out. They went sideways. Into the otherworld.

To follow them I'm going to need help.

I go back to my bike. Before I can start it up, I see the old grandmother coming across the park to have a last word with me. I don't have time for this, but my own grandma raised me to be polite to her generation. So I wait for her beside the Harley. She takes her sweet time, but I don't let my impatience show. When she gets close enough she lays her hand on my arm.

"The girl you're looking for," she says. "Marina. Is she like you?"

I shake my head. "She's not in any gang."

The old lady frowns. "I don't take you for a fool. You could at least do the courtesy of treating me the same. I may not be a *brujá*, but even a *curandera* can see the animal spirit living under your skin."

I know that *brujás* are witches, but I've no idea what a *curandera* is. I know she's not a cousin because I'm not getting a Wildling *ping* from her. But I don't like that she can just spend a few minutes in my company and know that I'm one.

"And that would make you—what?" I ask.

"A healer," she says. "A medicine woman."

"Okay."

"So your friend—Marina?" she asks.

"Yeah, we're both Wildlings—but you can't spread that around. Seriously."

She gives me a withering *as if* look that would do my

grandma proud and changes the subject. "You were asking about *los tíos*," she says, "and I thought I should warn you about them."

My eyebrows go up.

"Please remember that this is only based on hearsay," she goes on. "But you are a young animal spirit and will be unaware of the stories that are told about them. You know they fight an ongoing war with evil spirits?"

I nod. "Along with some really big and bad thing that's at the center of the world or something."

Which is why they want Josh on their side, but I don't add that.

She nods. "They welcome allies—especially animal people— but they are more concerned with winning their battles than keeping their allies alive. Be careful in your dealings with them."

"Thanks," I tell her, "but I don't need the warning. I don't trust anybody."

She pats my arm. "How sad for you," she says.

Then she leaves me beside my bike and returns to where the other women are standing.

I don't waste time wondering why she's sorry for me. Instead, I start the Harley. I need to find Cory or Auntie Min to help me get to the otherworld. I'd prefer Cory, but he can be hard to track down. I know where Auntie Min should be, so I head for the underpass where she has her camp.

I get maybe a block from the park when I feel the first *ping*. I start looking around, but it takes a few more *pings* for me to spot them: a handful of rangy barrio dogs the colour of dirty sand, tracking my progress by running full tilt through the dirt yards on either side of the street. At least that's what they'd look like to someone who doesn't have Wildling radar in his head.

I make a few turns just to be sure they're really on my ass, then I pull over to the side of the street.

I take out my phone and punch in J-Dog's number.

He answers on the first ring. "Yo, little bro. Where you at?"

"You in the mood to shoot something?" I ask.

"Always. Is this a *me* thing or a *you* thing?"

He means, does it involve the gang, or Wildlings.

"Bit of both," I tell him. "I've got a pack of dogs on my ass and I thought I'd lead them back to the junkyard behind my crib. I think they've got a connection to the guy who killed Lenny."

J-Dog was seriously pissed off when he found out that Josh had killed Vincenzo. He'd wanted that pleasure.

"Oh yeah?" he says. "Then they've got to die a little slow."

"One of them needs to not die at all."

"You telling me my business?" he says.

"I need to be able to question one of them."

"Well," he drawls. "Maybe we can make that happen."

JOSH

"Come on, Tío Goyo," I say into the thin air.

There's no response. I'm all alone here, wherever here is. Except then I hear the sound of voices. I stand up and turn to see a couple of figures approaching from under the big fir trees.

Obviously Tío Goyo didn't want to be seen by them, which is why he did the quick fade. But what about me? Am I supposed to hide, too?

Too late. The figures are closer and now they've seen me.

They don't look particularly threatening, so when they stop, I walk toward them. Of course, when it comes to animal people, well, cousins don't have to look tough to be tough, and vice versa. I mean, Chaingang has a mouse under his skin and I have a mountain lion. How weird is that?

These two are slight, about my height with darker skin and straighter hair. A man and a woman, dressed in unbleached cotton trousers and tunics. The man has a sack hanging from one shoulder. He and the woman are holding hands.

I stare at them intently, trying to figure out what made Tío Goyo take off. The only thing I know is that they give me an old-cousin *ping*, and then I realize that I can actually see their animal shapes just outside of their skin, hovering around them like an aura. What I'm seeing is a pair of rabbits.

The mountain lion inside me rumbles with interest. The woman moves closer to her companion.

DES

"Hey, skater boy," somebody says from behind me.

I'm in the hall, heading to my next class. Turning, I find Ampora.

"I need to know where my stupid sister is," she says.

"Really, dude? That's how you ask for a favour—by dissing my friends?"

"Look, I kicked her out of the house last night and now Chaingang's all on my ass about it. I need to know where she is."

"You kicked her out?"

"Are you deaf? I just said that."

"Dude, Chaingang's going to be the least of your worries if anything happened to her."

"What? Now you're threatening me, too?"

"I don't need to. Josh is going to tear a strip from you."

She rolls her eyes and waves a hand like that's nothing.

"Seriously?" I say. "You're not afraid of the guy who shut down the Riverside Kings?"

Not to mention ripping apart a badass cousin that even Chaingang couldn't take on. But I don't say that aloud. I don't have to.

Her expression gets uncertain and her face goes pale.

"I need to find her," she says. "Help me out."

I'd have more sympathy for her, except I figure she's only interested in saving her own ass. Knowing her, she'd probably be glad if something bad happened to Marina. That's not cool.

"Okay," I say. "I'll look for her."

But only because I'm worried myself.

"Where do you think we should start?" Ampora asks.

I shake my head. "There's no 'we' here, dude. You've already done enough damage."

"You can't just cut me out—"

I hold up a hand. "The places I'm going, nobody's going to want to see you. Nobody's going to talk to you."

"What is *with* you people? Ever since Josh became a Wildling, you're being high and mighty, acting all mysterious. You, Marina …" Her voice trails off and she studies me for a moment before she adds, "You're one, too, aren't you?"

I have to laugh. "I wish, dude. But yeah, we've got secrets and they're none of your business."

The warning bell rings. The halls are empty except for a few stragglers. We're all supposed to be in class now.

"Go," I tell her. Then I throw her a bone. "I'll let you know if I find out anything."

"But—"

"Seriously."

Before she can argue anymore, I duck into the boys' washroom. I half expect her to follow me in, but maybe she thinks I actually have to use it. I wait a few moments, the weight of Donalita's pebble heavy in my pocket. When I think the halls must be empty, I slip out and head for a side door.

For once, my luck actually holds. Nobody stops me to ask to see the hall pass I don't have. There's no one around at all. I smile when I heave the door open and step out into the hot sun. Free. I mean, it's not great why I'm skipping classes, but I can't help but feel a lift in my heart all the same. My only worry is Marina. I hope she's just out catching waves.

I check around to make sure no one's watching before I take the pebble out of my pocket. It would be hard to believe that Donalita's inside this thing, except my double vision still sees her curled up in a ball at the same time as I see the pebble.

"Okay," I say. "So, um, here goes ..."

I tap the pebble against the side of the school. For a long moment nothing happens. I'm about to tap it again when the pebble goes weirdly soft in my fingers. I wasn't expecting that and it drops out of my hand. I start to grab for it at the same time as Donalita shifts into her normal shape and suddenly I've got an armful of girl. I stagger back against the wall under the unexpected weight. She drapes her arms around my neck, bringing her face inches from mine.

"Hi, dude," she says and kisses the tip of my nose. "But shouldn't we be doing this somewhere else?"

I have to laugh as I set her on her feet.

"This is serious," I say. "I need your help."

But before I get the chance to explain, the door beside us opens and there's Mr. Goss glaring at us. He's so hard line when it comes to rules that everybody calls him Mr. Boss. This is, like, the last thing I need right now.

"To the office, Wilson," he says in a sharp voice. "Right now. And you, young lady—"

I don't get to hear what he was going to add. Donalita scoops me up in her arms and takes off at Wildling speed. We're a block away between one breath and the next.

"Dude," I say as she puts me down.

"That was okay, right?" she asks. "We didn't want to be there, did we?"

I can't believe this little girl just carried me like a baby—talk about crushing my studly rep—but I can't stop grinning, either. What a rush. My blood is pumping. I felt like we were the Road Runner just going at batshit crazy speed and leaving Coyote in our dust.

"That was *awesome*," I tell her. "I would've killed to have seen Goss's face when you took off like that, even though I'm going to pay for it later." I laugh. "Let's just pray that no one else in school was looking out a classroom window. I'll never live it down, dude."

Donalita's laughing too, but this time she's the one to bring us down to earth.

"Why do you need my help?" she asks.

"It's Marina," I say. "If even her bitch sister from hell is starting to worry about her, then it's serious. We need to find her."

"Where would she go?"

"I don't know, dude. Can't you use some witchy Wildling power to track her down?"

"No," she says. "But Auntie Min probably could. She could get every lizard and bird in town out looking for her."

"Then we need to go see Auntie Min. Donalita?" I add when she doesn't respond.

She nods, but she's looking down the street, her body

language stiff. When I follow her gaze, all I see is a rangy barrio mutt sniffing at the base of a palm.

"What is it?" I ask.

"That dog's a cousin," she says.

"Yeah, so?"

"There's something off about her."

I take another look, but I can't see whatever it is that Donalita does, except the dog's maybe taller than most that roam loose in the barrio.

"Off how?" I ask.

She shrugs, then swivels to look the other way down the street. There's another dog sitting at the far end of the block. This one's not pretending to do anything but look at us.

"Okay," I say. "This isn't good, is it?"

Her only response is to hook her fingers together and offer them to me as a step, though a step up to what, I don't know. We're standing on the sidewalk under a tall palm. There's nothing else around.

I look up—way up—to where the broad fronds stick out like the tree's got bad bed hair.

"Dude," I say. "What are you thinking?"

She gives her hands an impatient shake. "Step in—and be ready to grab yourself a perch."

"Dude, you can't be serious."

"Now!"

The word jumps out with such an authoritarian crack that I'm putting my foot in her hands before I even realize what I'm doing.

"Keep your body straight," she says.

"Seriously, I don't think this is such a good—"

I don't get to finish. She snaps me up like a kid playing with an action figure. And I mean *up*. Like fifteen, twenty feet. I think I'm going to shoot right over the top of the palm, but I manage to grab hold of a spray of fronds and haul myself to relative safety in the branches, with only a few cuts on my hands from the sharp edges of the leaves. I hardly get there before a coatimundi pushes through the crest of big fronds to join me.

"Are you out of your freaking mind?" I yell at her. "You almost sent me to the moon!"

The coati shifts into Donalita's familiar features.

"Don't be such a baby," she says.

"It's not being a baby when—"

"Look," she breaks in. "We might have stood a chance against one of them. But two? Not as much. And three …"

"What three?"

"There's another one across the street."

I hold on tight and lean over to have a look, trying to ignore the vertigo fluttering in my stomach. Sure enough, there's a third dog crossing the street. By the time I get settled again, all three are at the base of the palm.

"If they're cousins," I say, "can't they just shift into human shape and climb up?"

She nods. "But here, we have the advantage. We can knock them down before they ever get close."

"What do they want with us?"

"I don't know. And as long as we're stuck up here, we're not going to find out, either."

I sigh. "So now what do we do?"

Donalita pulls a phone out of her pocket.

"Now, dude," she says with a smile. "We call for help."

JOSH

"My pardon, sir," the rabbit man says, standing stock-still with his partner. "We meant no offence."

I smell their fright. They're about to take off. It's like coming suddenly upon an animal. First they freeze, then they bolt.

"What are you talking about?" I say. "You didn't offend me."

"If you say so, sir. We just came for a picnic. We didn't know you'd already claimed this place for your own. If we had, we would never have intruded on your privacy."

"You can stop calling me 'sir.' I'm probably half your age."

"Yes, sir. But you're Mountain Lion Clan, though, pardon me, I don't know which one."

"So?"

He looks at the ground, to the side, anywhere but at me. Then the woman nudges him. "It's *him*," she whispers. Her voice is soft as a breath, but I hear her clearly with the mountain lion's ears.

The man raises his gaze to my face. He doesn't seem as scared or even nervous anymore. He looks at me with awe.

"It is," he murmurs as though I'm not standing right there in front of him.

Then he catches himself.

He lets go of his companion's hand and sets his bag on the ground before giving me a formal bow. The woman bows as well. Then he stands ramrod straight and meets my gaze with steady eyes.

"Young lord," he says, "I am Manuel de Padilla of the Long Mountain Hare Clan and this is my mate, Lara."

I'm not sure what to do, so I say, "And I'm, um, Josh Saunders from Southern California."

"You do us a great honour in allowing us to speak with you."

I shake my head. "Guys, you've got me confused with someone else."

Manuel smiles. "I don't think so. Might I ask with which Mountain Lion Clan you are affiliated?"

"I'm not part of any clan."

He gives me a puzzled look.

"I'm not like you," I explain. "I wasn't born into a, you know, clan or anything. One day I just got a mountain lion living under my skin."

Lara lays a hand upon her breast. "A miracle."

"I guess that's one way to look at it."

"It isn't my intention to instruct you," Manuel says, "but you do know that you and the mountain lion are one and the same? There is no end to one and beginning to the other."

I nod. "Yeah, I know that. Intellectually. I just find it helps me cope to think of him as a spirit living under my skin."

They look at me without comprehension.

"Forget it," I say. "So how do you know about me?"

"Every cousin has heard the story by now," Manuel says. "How the Thunders sent the seed of the animal clans into a group of five-fingered kits and one of them grew into the spirit of one of the old clans."

"And do the stories say why this happened?" I ask.

Manuel smiles. "We are only small cousins. Why would the Thunders explain themselves to such as us?"

"But it means something," Lara says. "It whispers in our hearts."

This kind of throws me. "What does your heart say?" I ask.

She exchanges a glance with Manuel and something passes between them. It's like when Marina and Des and I are in the zone, and we can communicate without speaking: an abrupt shift into another song during practice, all of us hitting the mark on the same beat. A look across the hall at school that tells a story nobody else can read. Riding our boards, the three of us turning sharp the way a flock of starlings do, all at the exact same time.

"That something's going to change," Lara answers, "and when it does, it'll be better for everyone."

I'm not sure what that means.

"And you think I'm a part of this?" I ask.

Another glance at her mate.

"We *know* you are," she says.

I don't believe her any more than I do anybody else who's tried to tell me what my destiny is, but I don't tell her that. There's something so earnest about her, as though she thinks some big prophecy is coming true.

I guess they read the disbelief in my face.

"If we've offended you ..." Manuel begins.

I wave that off. "It's not that," I tell him. "I just wish *I* knew what's going on with as much conviction."

He nods. "Destiny is a knife with two blades and no handle. There's no easy way to hold it. Some might say it's better not to try to pick it up at all. But destiny doesn't care what you think or believe. It will carve out your life for you regardless."

There's a pleasant thought. But I don't let it change the good feeling I get from these two.

"Why don't you stay and talk for a bit?" I ask. "You could go ahead with your picnic."

"We would be honoured to visit with you, sir, but we will wait until later to eat—unless you care to share our food?"

I sigh. "No thanks. Any chance you could dial the 'sirs' down a little? I mean, I'm grateful for your respect and everything, but it's nothing I earned. I'm just a kid with a big lion under his skin who's trying to figure out what it all means."

Lara puts a hand to her lips. I can't tell if she's shocked or hiding a smile.

"We can try," Manuel tells me, but he can't hide the reverence in his eyes.

I lead them over to our camp area. They stare at the two beds, two backpacks. Their noses are working, reading the scent trails in the air.

"We *have* intruded," Manuel says.

"No, it's cool. Really. My friend and I are trying to wake up this map thing in my head, but he's off taking a break."

I give a vague wave around the campsite. "Grab yourselves a seat," I say.

MARINA

As the dog man lifts his horn again, I know I can't let him send a warning to his friends. I don't even think before I act. I just sweep my length of pipe in an arc and whack him across the back of the leg. I don't have the room to put any real power behind the blow, but it's enough to make his knee buckle. The horn drops as he goes down. Still on automatic, I give him a hard tap on the top of his head and he collapses.

Time seems to stop as I look at him lying there. Blood trickles from the gash on his head and he's not moving at all.

I think I might have killed him.

I feel sick.

The raggedy man doesn't share my concern. I turn to find him holding a big chunk of rock. When I realize that he plans to bash it on the dog man's head, I get between them.

"What are you *doing*?" I ask.

"He's still breathing."

"Well, thank God for that."

He gives me a puzzled look, but at least he lowers the rock.

"You know he wouldn't give you the same mercy," he says.

"I don't know any such thing. I just know that if we start

bashing in their heads when they're already unconscious and can't hurt us … well, we'll be no better than them."

"But we'll be alive."

"We're alive right now," I tell him.

"For the moment."

I refuse to move. His strange eyes study me for a long beat.

"Fine," he says finally and puts the rock aside. Then he nods. "You're probably right. If we've only hurt him, they'll be angry and looking for settlement of the wrong, but they won't make it their life's work. If we finish him off, they'll never stop until they've hunted us down and killed us."

"Thanks," I say.

I dust myself off and pick up the pipe again. I might not want to kill anybody, but I'm not stupid.

"I need to go back," I start to say, but the hunting horns sound again.

"It's too dangerous at the moment," he says. "Right now we need to find a better place to hide."

I think about the mark I scratched on the road where I arrived. I think I can still find it, but if I follow him now, will I get too turned around?

The horns sound once more. Closer.

The raggedy man sets off at a quick jog. I have no choice but to fall into step behind him.

It's another hour of winding through the streets of this ruined city before the raggedy man deems it's safe enough for us to rest. He leads me up to the third floor of some kind of old warehouse building, most of which is still standing, although the whole north wall is missing. It's a huge cavernous place. We sit near the missing wall, which gives us a good view of the city. There's dirt here—three floors up—with weeds growing out of it. Vines trail down the sides of the building where the missing wall would have connected to it.

A cool breeze blows in, fresh and clean compared to the closer air in the streets below. This So-Cal girl isn't used to the humidity.

When I look out over the view, I can't believe how huge this place is—as big as New York City, I'm sure. The ruins seem to go on forever. The buildings are taller here than they were where I first arrived, but nature's also reclaimed them. We haven't seen anybody. Just birds and animals. We haven't heard the horns for the past half hour. The last time we did, they were faint and distant.

The raggedy man pulls something wrapped in cloth from his pocket. It proves to be flatbread and cheese. He breaks each in two and offers me half.

"Are you sure?" I ask.

He smiles. "Go ahead."

I was just being polite. Truth is, I'm starving. I can't remember the last time I ate. The raggedy man also shares water from a metal flask. I can see it's supposed to have a screw-on top, but I guess he lost it because he's using a chunk of wood as a cork instead.

"Now, aren't you interesting," he says when we've finished.

Me? Has he never looked in a mirror?

"Why do you say that?" I ask.

He shrugs. "You feel like a cousin in here." He touches a fingertip to his temple, by which I suppose he's referring to his own version of the *ping* that I get in my head whenever I'm near a Wildling or cousin.

"But you seem to be newly born," he goes on. "As though you're only months old, rather than years. So, who are you?"

"Just a displaced girl who wants to go home. Who are you?"

He brushes the question off with a wave of his hand, but I can't help but be curious. What he really reminds me of is one of the dwarves from those Lord of the Rings movies that Des and Josh have made me watch way too many times.

"Okay," I say. "Can you at least tell me where we are?"

He gets a puzzled look. "You should know. I saw you arrive. No one brought you."

"I didn't come here on purpose."

"There's that," he agrees. "No one comes here on purpose." He scratches his beard, then adds, "It's called Dainnan—the city, I mean."

He says it grudgingly, as though he detests the word. I decide to push my luck.

"I'm Marina," I tell him. "What's your name?"

Those bright blues of his fill with sadness before he looks away.

"People call me Thorn," he says, "and I've been in this miserable place for far too long."

"If you don't like it here, why do you stay?"

His laughter has no humour in it.

"Good one," he says.

"It wasn't a joke."

He studies me for a long moment. "You have no idea, do you?" he finally says.

I shake my head.

"Dainnan's a midden. A refuse heap. It's the place they send the undesirables and leave us to rot. There are a thousand ways in and only one way out, and that way is guarded by the chief of the hounds."

"Whoa, whoa. Back up a bit. What do you mean, 'there's only one way out'?"

"Exactly what it sounds like."

The bread and cheese feels heavy in my stomach.

"So, how do I get to this place that the chief guards?" I ask.

"It's not a place. I've been told that it's a token—something the chief carries on his person. I've never actually seen it. I've only spied him once, and that was from a distance, mind you. It's not something I'd care to repeat."

"Why not?"

"He's rather formidable."

Is there anything *not* crappy about this place?

"You've never tried to get out?" I ask.

"I did at first, before I knew about the token. It was a pointless endeavour. I soon realized that ours is not the power in this ruin of a city. The hounds rule it. They chase us to this world—to this city—and we can't get out. And then, if the fancy strikes, they hunt us, and when they catch us, they string us up."

"But you've managed to stay free."

He shakes his head. "They've caught me twice. The first time, one of the other prisoners climbed up and sawed through the ropes with a sharpened stone. The second, I had to free myself. It took a week."

He pushes up his sleeves and shows me the white scar tissue encircling each of his wrists.

"It was not an easy escape," he says.

What is he saying? He was strung up with no food or water for a week and he still managed to free himself? How's that even possible?

All I can do is stare at the scars until he finally pushes his sleeves back down.

"Nobody sent me here," I say after a long moment. "I mean, there was this pack of dog cousins on my heels at the start, and they were like the hounds, but I'm the one who picked this place to hide out."

"Unless they only want you to think that. Perhaps chasing you here was their plan all along."

"But I didn't *do* anything."

"That you know of."

"What got you sent here?" I ask.

He doesn't move, but it still feels as though he withdraws from me.

"That's not a question we ask each other in Dainnan," he says, his voice stiff.

"Sorry, sorry," I say quickly. "New girl, remember? I don't know the ropes. And I don't want to be here long enough to have to know them."

"I'm afraid that's not up to you," he says.

I nod. That's beginning to sink in now.

"The hounds that I fought back in my world," I say. "They had a mark on them. It was a brand when they were in their dog shapes and a tattoo when they looked human."

I draw it out in the dirt: the circle with a lightning bolt stamped across it. Thorn frowns.

"That's how I've heard it described," he says. "The symbol of the chief's token."

JOSH

"What did you mean about waking a map in your head?" Manuel asks. He and Lara sit side by side on a wide flat rock facing a smaller one where I'm seated.

I tell them about that moment in the skatepark when I suddenly got this 3-D image of the landscape in my head with every living thing placed on it, exactly to scale.

"I had to learn how to tone it down really fast," I say, "but once I had it under control, it was really cool. And useful. But it disappeared when I came here, and I'm trying to get it back."

"Lara has something like that," Manuel says, "though not nearly so complex."

She nods. "Once I've been somewhere, I can return any time. It's how I navigate my way through the worlds. Otherwise, the choices would be too bewildering and I'd be lost in moments. But I can't see everything around me, only the route I need to take."

"How does it work?" I ask. "Did you just always have it, or did someone teach it to you?"

"I was born with the raw ability, but my grandparents taught me how to use it." She smiles and looks up at the sky and the trees. "The first time, they brought me here because it was one of their favourite places."

"It is beautiful," I say, following her gaze while discreetly scanning our surroundings. There are no hawks in view. I wonder where and why Tío Goyo's hiding.

"I could try to teach you what my grandparents taught me," Lara offers, "but it sounds very different from what you described."

"Maybe you can help. I'm looking for a friend of mine who's in danger. I need some directions."

"Do you think we might know him?" Manuel says.

"She's a her, and it seems doubtful. She hasn't been in the otherworld very long. Her name's Elzie—she's a jaguarundi."

Lara shakes her head, a rueful look on her face. "We don't know her, or even what that is," she says.

"It's a kind of a big cat, but that doesn't matter. She was captured by a member of the Condor Clan named Vincenzo. Do you know anything about him? Where he might have been camped or where they'd hold a captive?"

Manuel sighs. When he replies his voice resumes a more formal tone. "You must understand, young lord, that Lara and I, we are simple people. We don't involve ourselves in the affairs of the greater clans."

"No, sure. I get that. I'm not asking you to be involved. Like I said, I was just hoping you could point me in the right direction."

"Had I the knowledge you require," he says, "I would happily give it to you. But alas, I do not. The Condor Clan have nests in the great mountains of La Vendyr. Perhaps Lara could tell you how to get there, but you won't find Vincenzo or his brothers there now. We've heard that they left to carry out other … plans, but we don't know where they are now."

He glances at her and she nods.

I shrug. "Well, it was worth a shot. Thanks, anyway."

Manuel puts a hand on my arm. "You are, of course, a member of the great clans yourself, young lord, and it is not my place to advise you, yet my conscience would not let me rest if I didn't warn you against involving yourself with such as the Medinas. They are dangerous and make formidable enemies. Especially Vincenzo and Stephano."

"Vincenzo's dead."

They look at me as though I've just told them that Elvis is not only alive, but has recorded a rap album.

"How is this possible?" Manuel says.

"He finally ran into someone who could stand up to him," I say.

"You *saw* it?"

"I saw what was left of him."

Lara gives me a considering look. If she's guessing what I'm not saying, she keeps it to herself.

Manuel shakes his head in wonder. "That is really something," he says. "I can tell you this. No one among the cousins but his brothers will mourn his death."

Whoops. I should have kept my mouth shut. If this place is like any other, gossip is the main entertainment.

"I'd prefer you kept this to yourself for now," I say. "I still need to rescue my friend."

"Of course, of course," Manuel assures me. "We will tell no one."

"And we should let you resume your search," Lara adds, standing up. Manuel rises, too, and I follow suit.

"Thank you for your kind hospitality," Manuel says.

He embraces me and gives me a kiss on either cheek. I don't quite know what to do—I mean, I hardly know them—but I return the hug and give him a couple of awkward pats on the back. Then Lara takes his place.

"Be careful," she whispers as she kisses my cheeks as well.

I nod and watch them go, walking hand in hand again between the big trees. They're no sooner out of sight than Tío Goyo comes sauntering back into our camp. I can't believe this guy.

CHAINGANG

By the time I pull off the Pacific Coast Highway into our compound, eight or nine of the dogs are following me. I rev my bike through the yard beside the gang's clubhouse, peel past my crib into the junkyard behind it, then spin to a stop so that I'm facing the way I came. I don't see J-Dog and the boys. I can't smell them, either, through the dust the Harley kicked up.

That's okay. I trust they're here.

It doesn't take long for the dogs to come loping in after me. I know what they're thinking: I've done their work for them. Got myself someplace where there's no one around and nowhere to run.

Suckers.

The dust that keeps me from smelling J-Dog and the others is hiding them, too. I kill the engine and put my bike on its kickstand. Pulling my crowbar from its holster, I step away from the bike.

The dogs fan out, snarling and snapping, eager to take me down. I don't know why they've got a hard-on for me. Truth is, I don't care. I've been so worried about Marina that I need to hit something.

"Okay, girls," I say. "Bring it on."

The dogs think I'm talking to them, but that's my signal to J-Dog. The pack charges me. Two in the lead, the rest moving to flank me on either side. That's when J-Dog stands up from where he's been hiding behind a rusted beater of a '67 Chevy with that big Glock of his in his hand.

His first bullet hits the front dog and pretty much shears off its head. The other one's startled, but stays committed to its attack. I figure he plans to bowl me over with the force of his charge. I brace myself and yell to J-Dog, "This one's mine!"

Killing it would be easier, but I need one of the pack alive to answer some questions.

But only one.

I hear J-Dog's Glock fire again, then a flurry of other shots as the rest of the gang takes out the pack. I'm half aware—as you are in a fight like this—of everything going on around me. My Ocean Aver brothers standing on either side of the junkyard, weapons still ready. The dogs all shot to pieces. But my main focus is on the one coming straight for me, still intent on taking me out. There's no give in his flashing eyes.

I move forward to meet his attack, then step to one side, bringing the tire iron down on his shoulder.

I hear bones snap.

I hear J-Dog yell: "Put down your goddamn guns."

I'm guessing one or more of the boys was ready to help me out.

But I don't need help.

The dog's game—I'll give him that. His right leg gives way under him and he sprawls in the dirt. But he's up on three legs, snapping at me as soon as I close in on him.

Man, you have to admire his determination. He's hurting bad, yet still not backing down.

But this is a done deal now.

I kick him in the head and the blow sends him sprawling. Before he can get up I've got my boot on his neck and he can't move. He can barely breathe. But I hold the position, our gazes locked until he finally gives up and looks away. Under my boot I feel all the tightness in his muscles go limp.

I ease up on the pressure. Just enough to let him breathe.

"Grab yourself a shape with a face that can talk to me," I tell him, "or this is going to get a lot messier."

He doesn't respond, so I let the end of the tire iron brush against his bloody shoulder. It catches on a piece of bone that's sticking out of the matted fur. I know that had to hurt like a sonofabitch, but all he does is hate me with his gaze.

"Yeah," I tell him. "Everybody knows you're tough. And you want to rip out my throat. I get it." I push down with my foot. "But your friends are history and nobody's coming to save your ass."

The other Avers are gathering in the dirt, checking out the dead dogs. I've gotta tell you, I'm a little surprised that the pack members are still in the shape of dogs. I thought we returned to our true shapes when we died—like both Lenny and the rat girl, Laura, did. But maybe that's only Wildlings. Maybe cousins don't. Or maybe these are their true shapes and they only borrow human forms.

I turn back to my prisoner. "Either you talk to me, or you bleed out here in the dirt. Live, and maybe you'll get another shot at me. Dead, and that's all she wrote. Your choice. So what's it going to be?"

"Yo, J.," I hear one of the Avers say. "Your bro losing it?"

Yeah, I know what it looks like. I'm talking to animals like they're people. But I don't care what anybody thinks. I'm getting the cousin *ping* in my head. I know what this dog is.

"Shut your mouth," J-Dog says in a conversational voice that means he's getting pissed. "Or you want me to shut it for you?"

The boys are smart. Nobody responds.

Again I let the tire iron brush the piece of bone that's pushing out of the dog's shoulder.

"Last chance, Rin Tin Tin," I tell him.

J-Dog comes to stand beside me, the Glock dangling from his hand.

Just when I figure the dog's ready to die before talking, he does his shift and I've got my boot on the neck of a dark-skinned, black-haired man in jeans, barefoot and bare-chested except for a leather vest. The shoulder wound is gone and I can feel him tensing, getting ready to make a move.

I hear gasps of surprise from the other Avers, but J-Dog just nods like he's seen this a thousand times before. He squats and presses the muzzle of the Glock against our prisoner's head.

"You're not feeling frisky, now, are you?" he asks.

The man swallows. The hate's still there in his eyes, but all he says is, "No."

"Good. Now answer my brother's questions."

"Who told you to take me out?" I ask.

"Who do you think?" the man says.

J-Dog gives him a casual whack with his free hand. There doesn't seem to be much power in the blow, but I can almost see the stars in our prisoner's eyes.

"Answer the question," J-Dog says. Then he looks at me. "I think I'll call this one Little Bitch, yo."

"Who told you to take me out?" I repeat.

"Vincenzo."

"Bullshit. Vincenzo's dead."

"Yeah, but it's on Vincenzo's orders. His brother Stephano gave the go-ahead."

"Steph-*aan*-o?" J-Dog drawls, looking at me. "Seriously? And he thinks that's some kind of kick-ass scary name?"

I shrug. "Nobody probably thought much of the name Adolf until he invaded the rest of Europe."

"Bro," J-Dog says. "Why do you even know that?" He turns back to Little Bitch. I've got to say, I'm liking the name.

"What else were you supposed to do besides a drive-by on my bro?" he asks. "What was your *mission?*"

"We're going after all of the mountain lion's friends."

I put a little pressure on his throat. "Yeah? And what did you do with the otter?"

He finds a little cockiness. "Hopefully she's dead—like you're supposed to be."

I push down on his throat until the smirk leaves his eyes and he starts to gag.

J-Dog taps my leg. "Easy there, bro. Dude can't talk if you bust his windpipe."

I let up the pressure. Reluctantly.

"She's not dead," I say when I trust my voice. "You chased her somewhere out of this world."

"Not—not me," Little Bitch rasps.

"But one of your crew did," J-Dog says. His voice is silky smooth, which I know means he's right on the edge of going hardcore with the butt of his gun on Little Bitch's face. "So the question is, where would they chase her?"

"If she went into the otherworld, it was under her own steam. We wouldn't chase her there. It's too easy to lose her in that place."

J-Dog looks at me. "That make sense to you?"

I shrug. As much as anything does.

"So this guy Stephano," I say. "He's in charge now?"

"I don't know who's in charge. We took our orders from Vincenzo and Stephano and their other brother Lucio, but somebody higher up was pulling the strings."

"And are Lucio and Stephano as hardcore as their brother?"

"I don't know that, either. But that whole clan's been around since the first days, so probably."

Perfect. And with Josh off looking for Elzie, we've got nothing to stop them with if they decide to come after us, which they obviously have.

J-Dog turns to me. "Anything else you want to ask Little Bitch?"

I shake my head. What I need to do now is track down Cory or Auntie Min—find a way to get myself over into the otherworld and find Marina.

"Will you let me go now?" Little Bitch asks. "I've told you everything I know."

J-Dog nods. He pats Little Bitch on the head. "You did good."

Then he pulls the trigger on the Glock and blows Little Bitch's head away.

For a long moment I'm too surprised to do anything.

"What the *hell* did you do that for?" I demand.

"He was part of the crew that did Lenny. You think I was just going to let him walk away?"

Of course he wouldn't. What was I thinking?

J-Dog stands up and rolls his shoulders. He looks around at the other Avers and everybody starts talking at once. I'm going to have one hell of a lot of explaining to do.

I look around at them. Shorty, Bull, Dekker, Edwin, Tall Boy, Nas-T. I've known these guys for most of my life. I've had their backs and they've had mine. Like the way they stood up today. I owe them an explanation.

Before I can start, my phone rings its 50 Cent theme. I'd ignore it, but it could be Marina. When I look at the display, I see it's Donalita. I almost let it go to voice mail, but maybe she's got news. I push Talk.

"Yeah?" I say.

"Have you seen any dogs around today?" she asks.

"We just put down a pack of them."

And then I remember what Little Bitch said.

We're going after all of the mountain lion's friends.

"Is Des with you?" I ask. "Are you guys okay?"

"They've got us treed in a palm."

"Tell me where."

"We'll be fine. Cory's on his way. But I wanted you to think about your grandma and Josh's mother."

"Fuck me. I never thought of that. Call me back if you still need help."

I don't scare easily—not for myself. But for Grandma?

I cut the connection.

"Everybody shut up!" I call above the hubbub of voices in the junkyard, putting some of J-Dog's command into my voice.

The boys' heads come up and they all look my way. J-Dog raises an eyebrow as if to say, *WTF, bro. Keep it cool.* Which would make me laugh any other time because I'm not the hothead in our family.

"This pack wasn't working on its own," I say. "They might be after Grandma, too."

J-Dog's face changes and I would not want to be the cousin— dog or man—to get in his way today. He shoves the Glock behind his belt at the small of his back and starts for the bikes. The rest of us hurry after.

JOSH

"So what's with the disappearing act?" I ask Tío Goyo.

"What do you mean?"

"You—taking off the way you did."

He shrugs. "I had no way of knowing what sort of cousins they would be."

"So you just left me to them."

"You seemed to do well enough. And besides, you killed Vincenzo—what do you have to be afraid of?"

"Something happening to Elzie."

He nods. "Then we should get back to work."

"Not so fast," I tell him. "What difference does it make what sort of cousins the de Padillas were? You disappeared like a scared mouse as soon as you knew someone was coming. So who are you hiding from?"

"It wasn't fear, so much as caution."

I sigh. "I don't care what you call it. I want to know what's going on, or this ends now."

"Then how will you find your friend?"

"I'll figure something out. Now dish." He gives me a confused look. "Spill. Talk already."

For a moment I don't think he's going to say anything. Then he nods.

"We don't always get along with all the cousins," he says.

"When you say 'we,' do you mean you and the other uncles?"

He nods.

"Because?" I prompt when he doesn't go on.

"Because sometimes evil spirits take up residence in them—especially here. We've been calling this the otherworld, but there's more than one."

"I get that already."

"And the deeper you go, the more tenuous its hold on reality."

"And in plain English?"

"This place has many names," he says. "One of them is the dreamlands, and as you go deeper into them, you start to enter more individual dreams."

I put that together with what Agent Solana told me.

"And these evil spirits come from dreams," I say.

"Exactly."

"That still doesn't explain what the beef is between you and the cousins. Or why you'd have to hide from them."

"I wasn't hiding. I was merely avoiding needless confrontations."

"Can't you just talk plainly?" I ask.

"I am. The problem is, you're not listening."

"So enlighten me."

"We're warriors, my brothers and I from the Halcón Pueblo. When we find evil spirits, we destroy them."

"You kill the spirits, or the people they're living in?"

"If the evil has taken root in someone, what they once

were has already died. Their friends and kin aren't always so understanding about why we do what we do."

"Jesus. Can you blame them?"

"That's not a question we dwell upon."

"And it's just cousins you're killing?" I ask.

He shakes his head. "But here in the dreamlands, cousins are usually the target of these spirits because they seek to inhabit powerful beings."

I've had nightmares from time to time. I think about some creepy spirit taking over my body, and how unfair it would be to have these hawk uncles just kill me outright instead of helping me. It could happen to me, or any of my friends. Elzie, for example. She's had enough crap in her life to give her bad dreams. I feel sick just thinking about it.

"Isn't there some other way to get rid of the evil spirits without killing their hosts—like an exorcism or whatever?"

There's genuine surprise in his eyes.

"Of course not. It is usually too late, and this is what we've always done," he says.

He starts to go on, but I hold up a hand.

"Not now," I tell him. "I need to process this."

"But your friend—"

"Time moves differently here, right? However long we're here, we can still get back into the regular time stream when we need to. Isn't that what you said?"

"Yes, but—"

"So I need some time."

I walk away before he can argue further. When he starts to follow, I shift to the mountain lion. I turn and snarl at him before loping off into the trees. He doesn't try to come after me.

DES

Donalita thinks it's a riot to be stuck up here at the top of a palm.

"Look at the view!" she says. "This is the way birds see the world."

She called Cory, then Chaingang. Now she's sitting on her precarious perch, dangling her legs like she's on a park bench. She divides her time between teasing me and yelling insults down at the dogs.

The three of them are at the base of the tree, looking up. People walk by. Traffic passes on the street. Nobody takes any notice of the two of us up here with the dogs below.

"How come nobody even looks up?" I say. "I mean, are we invisible?"

Donalita shrugs. "People only see what they want to see. They're not like you, with your third eye."

She raps a knuckle against my forehead.

"Ow." I rub my forehead. Then I think of what she said. "What's 'third eye' supposed to mean?"

"You see what's really in front of you."

I rub my forehead again. "Dude, do you really think I've got a third eye?"

She laughs. "Not literally. But you can see through a glamour, which most people can't. And you see the dogs, while other people's eyes just slide on by."

"So that's my superpower." I shake my head. "Wow, talk about getting the short end of the stick. Why couldn't it be super strength or speed? Or teleportation? I'd love to be able to teleport."

"Me too. I'd appear right beside one of those dogs and whack it smack on the head and then—*poof!* I'd be back up here again."

"Dude. Why not use your imagination and teleport someplace cool, where nobody could bother you? If it were me, I'd go check out all the cute surfer girls in Hawaii."

She frowns. "Why would you want to do that when you've got me?"

"Because ..."

Then I remember that she's got this thing for me.

"No harm in looking," I say. "And there'd be all kinds of surfer dudes, too."

"Why would I want to look at them?"

Really? We haven't even made out. Okay, technically, we slept in the same bed last night, and she has this hot, out-of-control vibe—like Elzie ratcheted up a couple of notches. But it's not like we're an *item* or anything.

Yeah? the part of my brain that tries to keep me out of trouble offers. Maybe I should tell *her* that.

I might be better off taking my chances with the dogs.

Luckily, I spot a familiar figure coming around the corner and I don't have to put my other foot in my mouth. I point and say, "Here comes Cory."

Though what he's going to do against the three dogs, I don't know. He's not a whole lot bigger than Josh, and even if he shifts into his coyote shape, these dogs are still going to tower over him, even the female. And outnumber him. But he doesn't seem perturbed. He's just ambling along, hands in the pockets of his hoodie. The dogs haven't noticed him yet.

"What can Cory do that you can't?" I ask Donalita.

That puts her right back in a good mood.

"Oh, I'm much fiercer than he is," she agrees, "but he's brought backup."

"I don't see any backup."

"What do you think those crows are?"

There *are* a lot of crows around all of a sudden, maybe ten or twelve on this block, all on this side of the street. One of them lands in the palm fronds just a few feet from where we're perched. He dips his head and croaks at us with what I assume is a greeting.

"Dude," I say and nod back.

I want to ask what a bunch of crows can do, but I keep the question to myself. I probably don't want to insult them if they're here to help. But really. They're crows. Big birds, sure—but up against dogs?

Donalita's not paying attention. She's hanging precariously from a long frond to see what's going on below.

"Though this could still get messy," she says. "It all depends on how stupid the dogs are."

The crow croaks again—this time I think he's laughing.

Below, the three dogs stand shoulder to shoulder, waiting as Cory approaches. I don't get how nobody seems super concerned about anything.

"We should go down to get a closer look," Donalita says.

"Maybe we should stay out of the way," I tell her.

"Oh, pooh. Don't be a baby."

"I'm not. But if it's so safe, why did we have to hide in a tree?"

"That was before Cory and the crow boys showed up."

The big black bird chitters and preens his wing feathers. I could swear he's grinning.

"That was then," she says. "It's safe to go down now."

"Okay, seriously? I don't know how I'm going to get off this tree without a fireman's ladder."

"Is that all?"

Before I know it, she's swung me onto her back. I start to complain, but she's already scampering down the trunk and all I can do is hang on for dear life. When we get to the ground, my legs feel too wobbly to stand up. I hold on to the palm, happy that I didn't wet my pants.

The dogs turn, snarling and growling, teeth bared. Donalita steps between them and me.

"Don't even think about it," Cory says.

The air is suddenly thick with the beating of crow wings. As the birds land on the sidewalk around us, they turn into dark-skinned men with long black hair. One of the dogs, also a male, takes human shape.

I look around. Cars are driving by. A couple of kids are sitting on a stoop on the opposite side of the street, one of them texting, the other listening to something through his earphones. There's a woman at the end of the block having an intense conversation with some guy who's probably her boyfriend. Scratch that. Her *ex*-boyfriend, from the way she's yelling at him.

Okay, so all these people have their own lives happening, but how can *nobody* be paying attention to any of this?

"We don't answer to you," the dog man tells Cory.

"Nobody says you do," Cory says. "But I'm here as an emissary of Señora Mariposa, and so long as she watches over this land, you'll do as she says."

"Or what? You'll sic your little flock of pet crows on us?"

I remember how powerful Vincenzo was—he took out three elders without even breaking a sweat—so I'm wondering about these dogs. What if they're just as strong? If that's true, then it won't matter that Cory and the crows outnumber them three to one.

But Cory seems unconcerned.

"That's an interesting symbol you're wearing," he says, his voice mild, like they're just having a conversation.

I've noticed it too. A thunderbolt in a circle. The one in man-shape has it tattooed on his bicep. The other two dogs wear it like a brand on the shoulders of their forelegs.

The dog man shrugs, "It's just a tat."

"I can see that," Cory says. "I'm just wondering what it means, seeing how all three of you have the same one. Is it a pack emblem?"

"Sure," the dog man says. "Let's go with that."

Cory nods. "But it's interesting. Whenever I get a tat, it disappears when I shift to my other form. I just can't get them to stick."

"Guess you need a better tattoo artist."

"I guess I do," Cory agrees. "But it makes me wonder. What if it's not a gang emblem, or even a tattoo? What if it's a binding mark that someone's put on you, and now they're just putting you through your moves like a puppet?"

"You need to do a little less thinking," the dog man says,

"and a whole lot more of getting the fuck out of here. We've got business with the human and it's not your concern."

Cory shakes his head. "I guess that binding mark's doing something to your memory. Didn't you hear me say that I'm Señora Mariposa's emissary and she doesn't want you conducting your business here?"

The dog man laughs. "Everybody knows your Señora's a tired old hag that nobody pays attention to anymore. She can't even remember the stories she's supposed to hold in care for the spirits of this land."

"I wouldn't be so quick to—"

"Face it, pup," the dog man says. "She's a has-been. Stick with her, and you'll go down when she does. And if she gets in our way, trust me, she's going down."

It's been one of those cloudless days—blue sky above with the sun just beating down on us, its brilliant glare washing everything out. Let me tell you, I felt it, sitting up in that palm with Donalita, and it's not even noon yet. So when a dark shadow washes over us, it feels all the more dramatic.

"Tell her yourself," Cory says.

He nods with his chin to something behind us. I look back there—like everyone does—and all I can do is stand with my jaw hanging slack. That was no thundercloud passing in front of the sun. Instead, there's a monstrous dark-winged moth floating above us, so vast it seems to fill the sky.

I flash back to that moment on the clifftop last night, when a huge moth came rising up from the beach, and realize that this is Auntie Min in her animal shape—amped up to an impossible size.

She floats there for a long, suspended moment in time. It feels like all the air has been sucked out of the sky, but finally the enormous moth shrinks down to her more familiar form of an old Native or Mexican woman with a ghostly impression of moth wings rising behind her like a grim echo. She fixes the dog man with her gaze, eyes dark and seriously pissed.

"Here I am," she says to him. "Standing in your way. Now, just how do you plan to—how did you phrase it? Oh, yes. Put me down."

The dog man looks like he's about to drop a load in his pants.

He starts to say something, but only a garbled noise comes out. He clears his throat and tries again.

"Señora," he says. "We meant no disrespect."

"Oh?"

The dog man stares at the pavement. His companions stand with their heads drooping, tails between their legs.

"Pay attention to me, now," Auntie Min says. "Every person in Santa Feliz—cousin and five-fingered being—is under my protection from the likes of you. Do you understand?"

"Yes, Señora."

"And if I should need to send another emissary to speak on my behalf, next time you will heed what they have to tell you—correct?"

"Yes, Señora. Of course."

"Good. Now go."

The dog man shifts back to his dog shape, and just like that, the three of them trot off. Donalita claps her hands.

"Nicely done," Cory says with a grin. "The threat's gone and no one was hurt."

"It's too early to congratulate ourselves," Auntie Min tells him. "There's been more serious trouble down by the highway. I'll meet with you there."

"Meet with you where?" Cory asks.

"At Theodore's home."

Then she just takes a step and vanishes. I know she's only moved into the otherworld, but I still can't help but be impressed.

"Dude," I say to Cory. "That's so cool. Can we go there the same way?"

He smiles, but shakes his head.

"I've never been there in this world," he says, "so I'd have trouble finding a place to cross back over if we were on the other side."

"Huh. But Auntie Min knows where Chaingang's crib is?"

"In Santa Feliz," Cory says, "Auntie Min knows where everything is."

The dark-haired crow men shift back into their bird shapes and fly off. They move fast, like they're fuel-injected. Sighing, I fall into step with Cory and Donalita as we trudge off.

"So, I'm curious about something," I say to Cory.

He lifts a brow.

"If Auntie Min's so powerful, why didn't she take out Vincenzo back on the cliff? Why doesn't she just wave her hand right now and deal with all the crap that's going on?"

"That's not her way," Cory says. "She's a caretaker. A healer. She couldn't take a life—it's not in her DNA." He grins. "Of course, those dog cousins don't know that."

"Yeah, but Tomás *died*."

His humour leaves him. "I'm pretty sure she didn't think Vincenzo would take that road."

JOSH

It's good to feel the play of the mountain lion's muscles as I run.
I go about a half mile, then circle back to the mesa top. When I
get near the edge of the cliff, I leap up into the thick branches of
one of the tall pines. I look out across the valley from my vantage
point, my tail flicking with irritation as I think about what I've
learned.

I knew *los tíos* weren't necessarily nice guys. I remember the
way the bandas deferred to them. Hell, those tough Mexican
gangbangers were *scared* of them—there's no other way to put it.
It wasn't respect. It was fear.

And now there's this whole business of the uncles executing
cousins who play host to evil spirits. Evil spirits that choose the
most powerful cousins to inhabit.

If *los tíos* are capable of that, then they really have something
big going on.

Question is, do I want to be a part of it? I don't mean, do I
want to help them, but do I even want to associate with them?

The mountain lion's getting restless hanging around here in
this tree while my brain goes around in circles. Tío Goyo's right
about that. I spend way too much time in my own head.

But then I think of something else. Something Lara said: how her grandparents showed her how to move between the worlds.

Lara moves through the worlds.

Why not track her, and when the trail takes me into a different world, I'll just put all my attention on what's going on around me as I step from one world into another? Maybe I'll be able to figure out what she sees and then reboot the map in my head.

The mountain lion likes this tracking idea and I find myself making a lazy leap to the ground, then heading in among the trees where I saw the de Padillas disappear from sight.

Their scent is easy to pick up and I follow it with a new confidence. I'm not going to need the uncles if I can figure this out for myself.

The trail takes me about a half mile deeper into the forest, where it suddenly disappears. No matter how much I cast around, I can't find it. I can tell where they appeared, and where they disappeared, but I just can't follow.

I bat at a pine cone with a big paw and send it skittering along the ground.

"Ready to get back to work?" Tío Goyo asks.

MARINA

"Where are you from?" I ask Thorn as we make our way back down to street level.

I step over a missing stair, my hand on the stone wall of the stairwell for balance. I'm already missing the fresh air from where we had our lunch above. It smells like an animal's den in here.

"I mean, if that's okay to ask," I add.

"My home was in Tal Avelle," he says, "in the part we call the Sea Dales. And I tell you, without fear of sounding like a braggart, that the Dales are the finest jewels in Tal Avelle's crown, I don't care what the steppe dwellers say. Our coves and beaches and cliffs are rich and diverse—nothing like this pissant little pocket world."

"'Pocket world'?" I repeat. "What do you mean by that?"

He spreads his arms in a wide gesture. "Dainnan—this city—*is* the world. Or at least it is the world we're in now. It was pulled out of a dream, or created whole cloth by some mage—truth is, I've no idea how it came to be. But it's no bigger than the city as we saw it from above, and then about the same acreage of bushland surrounding it."

I'm trying to understand this, but it's not making sense.

"What's past the forest?"

"Nothing," he says.

"There can't be *nothing*."

"Go see for yourself. You have the time."

I shake my head. "No, I need to get home."

He starts to say something, then seems to think better of it. It's not until we get out on the street again that he finally responds.

"Let me take you to see Canejo," he says. "Maybe he can explain it better."

"Who is he? Your leader?"

And what's his real name? I wonder. Because *canejo* just means rabbit in Spanish.

The raggedy man shakes his head. "We have no leaders. Canejo is simply a wise man who finds himself in the same situation as ours. He has been here a long—"

Suddenly, he breaks off and shoves me back into the building.

"Hey!" I start.

He cuts me off. "On your life, be silent. Go invisible."

I have a thousand questions, but he looks so serious I keep my mouth shut and do as he says, letting the imaginary cloak of invisibility fall over me again. It's easier this time. It feels just like shifting to my otter shape—all I have to do is think about it and it happens.

Thorn has pulled his own vanishing act. I look out through the open door and can't spy anything, dangerous or otherwise. I can't hear anything, either. Then finally, after long minutes of nothing, I see the shadow of a large bird drift across the broken pavement in front of the building. A moment later a second shadow trails in its wake. I hold my length of pipe tighter.

The shadows wheel in slow circles—once, twice—before drifting away again.

I want to ask Thorn what they were, but I figure I'll just stay still and keep my mouth shut until he judges we're safe. When he slowly comes back into view, I let my own invisibility fall from me.

"What was the danger?" I ask.

He spits on the floor. "Condors."

My heart seems to stop in my chest. That's what Vincenzo was, and he was almost invincible until Josh finally dealt with him. But before that happened, Vincenzo killed Tomás, tossed Cory off a cliff and broke Chaingang's back.

"What—" I have to clear my throat. "What were they doing here?"

"What do they ever do except bring misery into the world?" He cocks his head to study me for a moment before he adds, "You've seen them before."

I shake my head. "Not them. I mean there was only *one* of them. This guy named Vincenzo."

Thorn spits again. "They should have called him Verminzo."

"Well, he's dead now," I say.

"Dead?" Thorn gives me a look that tells me I must be mistaken. "How can he be dead?"

"My friend kind of killed him."

Thorn's eyes widen slightly. "Kind of," he repeats.

Actually, Josh tore him into little pieces that he scattered all over a clifftop, but all I say is, "I can guarantee he's dead. I don't think even an old cousin like that can come back to life when he's in as many pieces as Vincenzo was that last time I saw him."

I remember his head lying there in amongst all the gore, and a sour taste comes up my throat.

"You have powerful friends," Thorn says.

I shrug. I don't really want to get into that.

"The problem is," I say, "I think that maybe those condor guys are looking for me."

Thorn stares at me as though he's seeing me for the first time. The moment hangs so long that it starts to creep me out.

"Or maybe not," I tell him just to say something. "I could just be paranoid."

He blinks as though he's coming out of a trance.

"We really have to talk to Canejo," he says.

JOSH

I heard Tío Goyo approach, but saw no point in acknowledging his presence. But now I shift back into human shape and rise to my feet. My stomach growls. As usual, I'm starving after the change, but I make myself ignore it.

"I won't kill cousins for you," I say.

"I didn't ask you to."

"But that's what *you* do."

"You're still not listening," he says. "We rid the world of evil spirits in whatever host we find them, but that's not our principal task. Our main effort is to rouse people from their sleeping lives because if they're awake, the spirits can't take root."

"But if you're too late, you kill them."

"Why are you so focused on this?"

I shove him so hard in the chest that he stumbles backwards.

"Because I'm tired of people dying!" I yell at him. "Killing each other. You, Vincenzo. Me. *I've* killed people. I'm just a kid and I've already killed people!"

I step forward and shove him again. He lands on his butt in the dirt, but calmly stands back up and brushes the dust off himself. I wish he'd come at me so that I could really let him have it.

"Chaingang's dead. Elzie could be. And you go around killing innocent people that you've decided have evil spirits in them."

He doesn't flinch as I go to push him again. I stop myself and turn away.

I feel sick. I just wish there was somebody I trusted here. Marina. Des. My mom.

"We don't take our duties lightly," Tío Goyo says in a quiet voice. "And we find no pleasure in taking a life. Each adds to the burden we carry."

"Then why do it?"

"To keep the world safe."

"*Your* vision of safe. As both judge and executioner." I spit on the ground beside me.

He shakes his head. "We don't kill indiscriminately, and it's a far rarer occurrence than you imagine. We don't kill evil people, of which there are many. We only rid the world of evil spirits."

"Meaning what?"

"Vincenzo was evil, but he chose to do the things that he did. There was no spirit riding in his body, so we left him alone. Just as we ignore the gangs, the thieves and the murderers that infest the world."

"But what if by stopping *them*, you could help people?" I ask.

"Are we also supposed to be *luchadores* now, off fighting crime when we're not in the wrestling ring?"

"No. It's just—"

"Make up your mind," he says. "Just now you were criticizing me for taking justice into my own hands, and now you expect me to be a vigilante. There are laws and police for common criminals. The responsibility of the Halcón Pueblo is to banish parasites that infest the sleeping mind—to stop evil spirits that manage to escape dreams and possess a soul."

I sigh and shake my head. A minute ago I wanted to punch him in the face. Now my anger has drained away and I only feel tired and confused. If I'm claiming that it's wrong to persecute these so-called possessed cousins, it's just as wrong to do it to gangbangers and criminals.

"Nothing is simple," Tío Goyo says. "For now, let's concentrate on finding your friend. I think it's time I taught you how to fly."

"Say what?"

CHAINGANG

We're seven strong, riding our bikes down Grandma's street. Though we're not all wearing our colours, no one's going to mistake us for anything but what we are: trouble on wheels. The roar of that many bikes is enough to make windows rattle as we go by.

In any other neighbourhood someone would have been on the phone to the cops as soon as we turned onto the first street. But this is the Orchards. Our turf. Having J-Dog pass through is like getting a glimpse of some famous warlord, or the Godfather—if there ever really was such a thing. Let's face it: Italian gangsters are like any kind of gangster. They're ruled by profit, not honour. Even the Ocean Avers—tight as we can be—we're out to make a buck. The difference between us and the big banks is that we're up front about it.

The first thing I see when we pull up to Grandma's place is the dead dog at the foot of the stairs leading up to the porch. It lies in a sprawl of limbs and blood, flies already buzzing around it. My gaze tracks up to find a big hole in the screen door—where other dogs entered, I think, my heart in my throat. But then I see Grandma. She's sitting on a chair on the porch, a shotgun on her lap.

Damn. She blew that dog away right through the door.

I kill the engine and put my bike on its stand as quick as I can, but J-Dog is up on the porch before I can get there. I'm right behind him.

"Well, look at you boys," Grandma says, "riding in like the cavalry."

J-Dog looks from the dog to her. "Are you okay?"

She pats the shotgun I didn't even know she owned, never mind knows how to use.

"I'm fine," she tells us. "The situation's under control. But how'd you even know there was trouble? I only just got off the phone with animal control."

"We had a hunch," I say before J-Dog can answer. "What happened?"

She shrugs. "Damn dog went crazy. I was starting down the hall to collect the mail when I saw him charging down the street. I didn't know that he was coming for me, but I grabbed my shotgun, just to be safe. When he came up onto the porch and charged right through the screen door, I had to shoot him."

"Where did you even get a shotgun?" I ask.

"From the hall closet. I'm living in the Orchards, boy," she adds at my surprised look. "People have to know that you're serious about protecting your own."

I can see J-Dog bristling.

"Anybody ever even looks at you sideways," he says, "you give me a call and it won't happen again."

"Oh, like starting a war solves anything. I swear, Jason, you are your own worst enemy."

The other boys are still straddling their bikes behind us, engines off. I hear one of them chuckle. I have to smile myself, watching the little old lady that's our grandma lay down the law on J-Dog.

She looks from him to me. "Now enough of the bullshit," she tells us. "Both you and I know you never had any hunch. How'd you know to come riding in like a pair of half-assed John Waynes with an entourage?"

"We already had a run-in with some other mutts," J-Dog says, "and we got word they might be coming for you."

"But *why?*"

J-Dog just looks at me.

I sigh. "It's a long story and I'll tell you whatever you need to know, but first I have to make a call."

Grandma's eyebrows go up but she waves her hand, telling me to go ahead.

I dial Des's number.

"Do you know where Josh's mother works?" I ask when he picks up.

"Sure," he says. "She runs Dr. Esposito's office."

"Would she be working there today?"

"What happened?"

I can hear the worry in his voice.

"I don't know, bro," I tell him. "They took a run at my grandma, but she stood them off with a shotgun. And Marina, too. I think she took off to, you know, over *there*."

"Not again, dude," Des moans.

"Don't worry, bro. I'm going to find her as soon as I can

get my ass over there. But it makes me think they're probably gunning for Josh's mom, too."

I hear him say a muffled, "I have to go," to someone.

"Who are you with?" I ask.

"Cory and Donalita. We're on our way to your compound to meet up with Auntie Min. She says something big went down there."

Oh, crap.

"Do you have the number of Josh's pet Feds?" I ask.

"Yeah, but—"

"Send them to check on her. I'll see you at the clubhouse."

"You'll see who at our crib?" J-Dog wants to know when I hang up.

"Wildlings," I tell him. "Really old Wildlings who've been around forever, and might be a little pissed off with how we handled things back there."

J-Dog frowns. "Yeah, well, maybe they'd like a taste of the same medicine."

"Is *anybody* going to say *anything* that makes sense?" Grandma asks.

I can't believe how messed up this is. What I really want to do is find Marina, but the crap just won't stop piling up.

I point a finger at J-Dog. "You go ahead and tell them that," I say, then turn to Grandma and gently put my palm on top of her head. "I'm sorry," I tell her, "but the explanations are going to have to wait. I promise I'll tell you everything first chance I get."

Grandma swats my hand away and gives us a stern look. When I was a kid, that would have had me scrambling for a place to hide.

"What have you boys got yourselves into now?" she asks.

"You remember Donalita?" I say.

"That nice girl you were helping?"

"This is part of the same problem. But we're handling it."

"So she's still in trouble?"

I nod.

"Well, what are you waiting for, boy? Go help her. Don't you worry about me. I've got everything under control here."

I give another nod. But all the same, when we're back on our bikes, heading for the clubhouse, we leave Tall Boy behind to handle the dead dog and keep an eye on things.

JOSH

Tío Goyo turns and walks back to the camp. I watch his back for a moment, then trot until I catch up with him. When we get to where our blankets are still spread out, he fills the kettle from the canteen.

I grab some cheese and bread and eat it standing at the edge of the mesa where I can look out across the valley, trying not to think about the argument we just had. My brain obliges, but with perverse humour, has me going back to the usual ruminations about my messed up life.

"Josh!"

I turn to Tío Goyo. "I know," I say. "Too much in my own head again."

He shrugs then lifts the kettle. "I just wanted to tell you that the tea's ready."

"The tea," I say. "Right."

I accept the mug he pours for me. He clinks his own against mine, the sound of the metal muted. It's cool enough to take a sip. Another. I wonder how long Tío Goyo was trying to get my attention that the tea cooled this much.

He drinks his all in one go.

"It's better to have it all at once," he says.

So I follow suit.

"It seems a little bitter," I say.

He nods. "That's the mescal. But don't worry. I used only a pinch—just enough to wake up your spirit, not enough to poison you."

"You gave me ... a drug?"

"No. Or at least not recreational."

"I don't do drugs."

He gives another nod. "Which is highly commendable. But this isn't doing drugs. This is a learning experience."

"Why would you *drug* me?"

I feel like hitting him again, but my arms and legs are tingling and they don't seem to have any strength.

"Trust is a two-way street," he says. "I realize now that I've given you no good reason to trust me, so I'm going to show you one of the secrets of the Halcón Pueblo as a measure of good faith."

"By drugging me ... against ... my will ..."

I'm slurring my words. I want to call up the mountain lion. Maybe if I do the switch, I can clean out my system the way shifting shapes has healed me previously. But my brain feels as thick as my tongue and I can't seem to focus.

"I'm ... going ... to kill ... you ..." I tell Tío Goyo.

"You have my permission to try," he says. "But first absorb this wonderful experience."

I don't feel wonderful. I feel kind of sick.

I'm overcome with the sensation that I'm sinking and floating at the same time, and I get the distinct impression that my body is no longer mine to control. Never mind getting to my feet. I can't even keep upright.

Then I make the mistake of looking down, only to realize I'm looking at myself, swaying back and forth. I'm floating in the air, but my body is still sitting on the ground below me. As it starts to tumble over, Tío Goyo catches me and lays me carefully on the ground.

Except that's not me. I'm up here, floating.

And as I watch from this disconcerting perspective, my body starts to dissolve. It just melts away until it's absorbed into the ground.

What the hell did you do *to me?* I yell.

Except I don't have a physical body, so I don't have a physical voice. It's just my thought that rages out into the afternoon air.

In. Which. I'm. Floating.

Without a body.

Relax, a familiar voice says.

I don't have a head or eyes, so it's my awareness that turns to find a hawk riding an updraft beside me.

Relax? How am I supposed to relax when you just made me melt away?

You didn't melt away, the voice answers. *Your spirit is who you are. Your body is just matter, and you borrow it as needed from the earth, to which it will return. It will be waiting for you when you need it back.*

What are you saying? I ask.

Did you never wonder how a boy such as yourself can take on the bulk of a mountain lion with a mere thought?

Not really.

It's because you take as much matter as you need to shape yourself.

But it's only borrowed. What never changes is your spirit. That always belongs to you. But since your spirit has no matter, you have no true shape.

Except you're a hawk.

No. You only perceive me as a hawk. The same way anybody looking up at the moment would perceive you as one, too.

It all makes a crazy kind of sense. And for some weird reason, it calms me.

You couldn't just tell me what you were going to do? I ask.

I've learned that people don't truly understand an experience such as this until they've lived it. Trying to explain it in advance is futile. Are you really so upset?

Honestly, I tell him, *it's kind of cool.*

I feel him smile in my head.

So how long does the effect last? I ask.

It's not an effect. It's reality. It's what you see when you stop dreaming and wake up to how the world really is. And it lasts as long as you wish. When you're ready to reclaim your place in the physical world, return to the earth and will your body back to you.

How do I do that?

The same way you change from human to mountain lion.

Which means that I'd better remember that I want to be wearing clothes when I come back.

Does this work anywhere, I ask, *or only in the otherworld?*

The first time is always easier in the otherworld, but you can do it anywhere.

So how do we move around?

Again the smile in my head. *All you are is spirit, so all you have is your will.*

I consider that for a moment, then imagine myself being

closer to the ground. As fast as I can think, it happens. I'm so close that every piece of dirt and pebble is enormous in my perception. I let myself rise back up through the air until again I'm beside the hawk that is Tío Goyo.

So this is the secret of the Halcón Pueblo, I say. *You don't turn into hawks. You turn into spirits that look like hawks. It must be good for spying.*

I'm thinking of all the times I've seen hawks watching me.

It is a secret, he says.

And now this is something that I can do?

Normally, I would say no. But to the best of my knowledge, no one has ever shown this to a cousin before. Since the knowledge to make it work is the same as what you apply to change shapes ...

I get the equivalent of a mental shrug.

After that we spend a while getting me used to moving around. We fly fast in between the big trees and drop straight off the mesa's edge, pulling up from the ground at the last moment to soar high in the air again. So high that we can take in the whole slightly oval shape of the mesa.

It's exhilarating. Like skateboarding on steroids. I wish Des and Marina were here and able to experience this with me.

Finally, just as the sun is setting in a sky of reds and oranges, we return to camp. I watch the hawk that is Tío Goyo descend. When his talons touch the ground, his human shape rises up out of the dirt and stone, and wraps itself around the hawk. The last I see of it is the beak disappearing as it's swallowed into his chest.

Then it's my turn.

You're wearing clothes, I tell myself. Just like you were before the tea melted you away.

My own talons touch the ground and my body rises up to

embrace my spirit. I know I'm doing it right because climbing back into my body is the most familiar sensation I've ever felt. I cheat just before the transformation is complete, so that when I'm standing in front of Tío Goyo, my little dreadlocks that got shaved off from my time in the ValentiCorp lab are back. And longer.

I push them back over my shoulder.

Now that's cool.

Tío Goyo regards me with surprise, but all he says is, "Interesting."

DES

I walk with Cory and Donalita as they trek along the Pacific Coast Highway, both of them showing a confidence I don't feel. Think about it. I don't want to come off as a pussy, but dude, we're going to the Ocean Avers' compound—a place that's off limits to everyone but the gang. Sure, we know Chaingang and he's all cool with us and everything, but the other guys? Not so much. Let's face it: they have a rep to maintain and there isn't going to be any welcome committee when we go waltzing into their backyard.

It's not like Auntie Min's going to ask permission, considering how she feels she owns all of Santa Feliz, and don't even get me started on what Donalita's reaction would be if someone tells her she can't do something. So yeah, I'm worried about what kind of first impression we'll make.

Out of nowhere I hear the theme to the last James Bond movie. Then I realize it's my phone.

"Dude, your pants are singing," Donalita says.

"Better than having them on fire," I tell her.

But then I answer my phone, and as I talk to Chaingang, all

my humour drains away. So much for hoping that Marina's out catching waves, and looks like Josh's mom is still in danger.

"Dogs attacked Theo's grandma?" Donalita asks when I've hung up.

Sometimes you forget how good a Wildling's hearing is.

I hold up a finger. "Just a sec."

I call Agent Solana and tell him that Josh's mom might be attacked by dogs. He starts to ask more questions, but I just say I've got to go and hang up.

"But she's okay," I tell Donalita. "His grandma, that is."

"Good. I like her."

"What did he mean about her standing them off with a shotgun?" Cory asks.

"No clue, dude, but sounds like she's cool. It's Marina and Josh's mom that I'm worried about."

We get to the lane leading into the compound way sooner than I'd like. Eucalyptus and oaks line the narrow roadway, and you know what? It's actually kind of pretty till we get to the homemade wooden sign that reads: "Private—Keep the Hell Out!" in drippy red paint. Nice. Beyond the sign is a dusty lawn with a couple of chopped motorcycles parked in front of a long rambling ranch house.

At first there doesn't seem to be anybody there, but then we hear angry shouting around back. Cory picks up his pace, where I might have beat a quick retreat. I follow, craning my neck to see if there's some dude hiding with a shotgun, ready to take our heads off.

There are more bikes in back, not all of them in working order. Bike and car parts are strewn all around. A rusted panel truck and a couple of cars are also parked in that dusty yard.

There are a few more oaks back here, but beyond the open space, it's mostly just scrub and dead grass. We pass a small building on our right, which I think Josh described to me as Chaingang's personal crib, before the scrub opens up into a junkyard. Who knew they had all this crap back here?

But the shouting gets even louder and my attention locks on this big black dude who's towering over Auntie Min and yelling at her to get her ass out of here. Like that's going to happen. But on the plus side? He seems to be the only one of the Avers here at the moment.

I'm sort of looking forward to hearing Auntie Min tear a strip off him, except knowing her, she'll probably sweet-talk him into calming down. But now I start to notice the dead dogs scattered around in the dirt. Five or six of them, or what's left of them. Worse, there's a dead dude lying on the ground right beside Auntie Min and the Ocean Aver. The dogs and the dead guy are a mess, covered in blood. Pools of it are seeping into the dirt all around them. A heavy-duty battle went down over here. Flies are buzzing and crawling all over the open wounds.

Cory drops to his knees beside the nearest of the dogs. His shoulders sag as he lays a hand on the bloody fur. The dog was shot a couple of times and half its head is gone. There's not much brain matter left in there, and the wound in its abdomen has spilled bloody intestines onto the dirt.

I don't know why Cory's so upset. I mean, it's horrific all right, but dude. These are more of the dogs who wanted to kill us, aren't they?

But the longer I stand here, the more gross it all looks. It's nothing like it is in a movie. The colour of the blood isn't even the same and the flies are starting to drive me a little crazy. In the end, I have to turn away. Out of the corner of my eye, I see the Ocean Aver make a threatening move toward Auntie Min and suddenly she seems twice her size, now looming over the biker. The dude takes a quick step back.

"You should go," she says in that calm voice of hers that also holds a touch of menace. Sure, Cory says she wouldn't actually hurt anybody, but I'm not sure I believe it. The biker doesn't seem to think she's kidding, either, but he's got his rep to think of and he doesn't back down.

"Like hell I will," he tells her.

He reaches behind his back and starts to pull out a handgun from under his T-shirt. Before he can do anything with it, Donalita is over there and on him, gripping his wrist. She yanks it up behind his back with all her Wildling strength, forcing the big dude to yelp and drop to his knees. She snatches the gun away as he goes down, and throws it aside, out of reach. It lands with a thump in the dirt.

The guy struggles to get free, so she applies more pressure until he's lying flat on the ground.

Cory's hand is still on the dead dog. "I knew him," he says, a dazed look on his face. "His name was Hector. This wasn't something he'd do. Hector would never try to hurt anyone."

"Look at his shoulder," Auntie Min says softly.

I look down and see a mark there—the same one that was on the dogs that treed Donalita and me. It looks like a brand, the kind you'd see on horses or cattle in a cowboy movie.

Cory nods. "I saw the same brand on the others. When one of them shifted into his human shape, it became a tattoo on his shoulder."

"It's not a brand or a tattoo," Auntie Min tells him. "It's a binding."

Cory gives a slow nod. "I figured as much. Clever to target *los perros.*"

"Anybody want to tell me what you're talking about?" I ask.

Cory touches the brand on the dead dog's shoulder. "These symbols on their skin bind their will to someone. Whatever he or she tells them to do, they must obey. And our foe is clever to use the barrio and rez dogs because there are so many of them. Tío Coyote never could keep it in his pants."

"Who's he?"

"My uncle. Old Man Mischief. Over the years he's fathered hundreds of these dogs."

I have to ask. "Dude. Are you talking about the Coyote from all the stories?"

Cory just shrugs. I look from him to Auntie Min. She doesn't answer, either.

"Okay," I say, "so if this binding makes them do stuff that's totally out of character, why would they let anybody burn a brand onto them? I mean, that's got to hurt like hell, right?"

"That's an excellent question," Cory says.

The Ocean Aver that Donalita's got in lockdown picks that moment to try to break free again. Donalita puts more pressure on him without any real effort on her part. The guy strains, veins popping in his neck and arms, but he might as well be trying to lift a truck off himself. He gives up with a grunt of pain.

"Señora," Donalita says to Auntie Min. "When do I get to break his arm?"

Auntie Min smiles at her without any humour. "Patience, little coati. Maybe, later."

"You hear that?" Donalita tells the Ocean Aver pinned under her.

As she gives his arm a little jerk, Auntie Min turns her attention back to me.

"I don't know what *los perros* hoped to gain from this alliance, but I think they trusted and respected whoever did this to them. I think they were chosen because of their loyalty."

"And then," Cory says with a bitter tone in his voice, "Chaingang had them butchered."

"Dude, if they were attacking him ..."

Cory stands up, but his shoulders are hunched as though he's in pain. He wipes the blood from his hands onto his jeans.

"It doesn't matter," he says. "Chaingang still needs to answer for this."

I don't think I want to see a knock-down between those two, but it looks like I'll have no choice. Above the sound of the surf comes the roar of motorcycles pulling off the highway and racing up the narrow lane to the Avers' clubhouse. A moment later the gang pulls into the junkyard, tires spitting dirt as they bring their bikes to a sudden stop. I recognize Chaingang and a couple of others from seeing them around town, where I always make sure to give them a wide berth. But the guy straddled on the chopper beside Chaingang I know from pictures in the paper. That's J-Dog, Chaingang's brother and the leader of the gang. He's also supposed to be completely batshit crazy.

He puts his bike on its kickstand and jumps off it to glare at us. It's weird. The dude's not as big as Chaingang—not by a long shot—but he seems taller, like he takes up more space. He's like one of those tough guys in a rap video—all tats and muscles and a thousand-yard stare that tells you he'd just as soon shoot you as to have to look at your face. And here we are, on his personal territory.

"You people know who I am?" he yells. "You know where you are?"

Chaingang puts a hand on his arm. "Jason," he says. "This is not a fight you can win."

J-Dog shrugs him off. "Have a little faith, bro. This is our turf. These dipshits need to find out why I'm the one says what's what here."

Those crazy eyes fix on us again, tracking us one by one until they settle on where Donalita still has the other guy pressed face down in the dirt.

"—The fuck?" J-Dog says. "What the hell's the matter with you, Coltrane? You have any idea how little the girl holding you down is?"

Then J-Dog pulls the biggest, shiniest gun I've ever seen from behind his back and points it in Donalita's direction. She smiles back at J-Dog and grinds this Coltrane dude more into the dirt.

"Don't worry," Cory says softly to me. "We can take them. Except for Chaingang, they're only human."

"Dude," I tell him. "So am I."

"This ends—now," Auntie Min says.

She's doing that whole I'm-bigger-than-you-think deal, but all it does is focus J-Dog's attention her way and now the gun's pointing at her.

"Shouldn't have done that," Cory mutters.

He moves so fast it's like he's invisible. One moment he's standing beside me, the next he's plucked J-Dog's gun out of his hand and kicked the gang leader's legs out from under him. By the time Cory stops moving, J-Dog's lying on the ground and the gun's now in Cory's hand, the muzzle on J-Dog's temple.

It takes a moment before what happened even registers on the other bikers. When it does, their hands fill with guns. But we all know J-Dog will be dead before they can pull a trigger.

"Don't do anything stupid," Chaingang tells Cory. "These people are my brothers."

"What about *my* brothers?" Cory says, yanking J-Dog to his feet while keeping the gun on his temple. "It's okay to kill them?"

Chaingang's eyes go dark and his whole body tenses. I realize that I've never seen him seriously pissed off before.

"*You* sent those dogs?" he growls.

Cory meets that dark gaze with his own anger. "Don't be any more stupid than you've already been. These boys you killed were being forced to do what they did, but I wasn't the one who put the order on them."

Chaingang shakes his head. "Doesn't change anything. They were coming after us. They went for my grandma. And Marina."

"You're wrong. It changes *everything*," Cory tells him. "Do you blame the weapon, or the hand holding it?"

"You better shoot me right now, boy," J-Dog says before Chaingang can respond, "or first chance I get I'm going to cut a new asshole for you in the middle of your face."

Cory looks at his captive like he's only just remembering J-Dog is there with the muzzle of a gun pressed up against his head.

"Here's what we do with tough guys in my world," he says.

And then they both disappear.

Chaingang's eyes narrow. Behind him, the rest of the gang

starts shouting. Chaingang raises a hand and they shut up—just like that. He points a finger at Auntie Min.

"Bring. Him. Back," he says.

She shakes her head. "This is between you and Cory."

"Then take me to him so I can finish this, and then you're going to help me find Marina."

She shakes her head again. "I will not interfere."

"Bullshit. You've done nothing but interfere since the first day I became a Wildling."

She regards him steadily for a long moment before she says, "Tell your men to put away their weapons."

"Yeah, not going to happen."

Did you ever hear the sound of a hundred or so pairs of wings? Let me tell you, dude. Shades of Hitchcock and seriously creepy. I don't know where they came from, but suddenly the sky is full of crows, not making a sound other than the beating of their wings. They settle in the raggedy trees. More still perch on the junked cars.

Chaingang's gaze leaves Auntie Min's to take in the birds. He shakes his head and looks back at her. "Maybe from where you're standing, we don't seem so important," he says, "but you don't want us to be your enemy."

"You're right," she tells him. "I've always considered us allies."

"Then what's with the army?" he asks, waving his arm to take in all the crows.

She shrugs. "They are here of their own accord. Most likely, they think you are threatening me."

"Chaingang," one of the bikers calls out. "Just say the word. We'll take out the birds just like we did the dogs."

"They aren't birds," Chaingang replies without turning. "And I need her," he says, still looking at Auntie Min.

Man, I so hope this is like a team-up in the comics and we get done with the fighting and yelling at each other. Maybe Chaingang is thinking the same thing.

"Everybody," he says. "Put down your guns."

Another of the bikers shakes his head. "No way—" he starts.

"Don't make me have to come and do it for you," Chaingang says, still not turning around. Then he focuses his attention back to Auntie Min. "What do you want from us?" he asks her.

"Nothing more than I ever have. For you to stand by us, as we stand by you."

"You've got my man Coltrane on the ground and you've taken my brother. In my book, that's not standing by me."

"Let the young man go," Auntie Min tells Donalita.

Donalita frowns, but she releases his arm and steps aside. Coltrane comes up, grabbing her ankle and swinging at her, so she punches him in the side of the head. He goes down and lies very still in the dirt.

"Sorry," Donalita says. She's trying to look contrite, but the laughter in her eyes gives her away. I hold my breath until Chaingang sighs.

"Not your fault," he tells her, then he's back glaring at Auntie Min. "Now, my brother."

"Do you vouch for him?" Auntie Min asks.

"Vouch for him? What kind of bullshit is this? You come onto our turf, and walk all over us and him, and you expect him to say, 'Yes, ma'am, thank you, ma'am'?"

"*Your* turf?" Donalita says. "You're going to tell Auntie Min that this land is *your* responsibility?"

"Okay, point taken. But you've got to see it from his point of view. Bunch of dogs attack us, then you show up disrespecting him. The guy's got a rep to maintain."

"Do you vouch for him?" Auntie Min repeats.

"He's my brother. I've got his back, he's got mine. Of course I freaking vouch for him."

"Donalita?" Auntie Min says.

I'm expecting what happens next, so I look at the Ocean Avers when she disappears. I'm not kidding myself—I wouldn't want to go one-on-one with any of them. But dude, even tough guys look dumb with their mouths hanging open like that.

She and Cory are back a moment later. Cory's still holding on to J-Dog, who's now covered in red dust, like he's been up in the hills somewhere, fighting. His body language says he's defeated, but his eyes are full of rage. Cory's jeans and hoodie don't have a speck of dust on them. Donalita's holding J-Dog's big gun. She snaps the barrel off and drops both pieces in the dirt.

"Oops," she says, and winks at me.

J-Dog shakes off Cory's grip and walks over to Chaingang, wiping the dirt from his face with his trashed T-shirt.

"What the fuck did you get us into?" he growls at Chaingang.

Chaingang nods. "My bad. You and the boys should walk away."

"Yeah, like that's gonna happen any time soon."

He turns so that he and Chaingang are facing the Wildlings. Auntie Min looks solemn; Donalita's still amused. Cory's eyes flash with an anger as dark as J-Dog's.

"So, are we going to keep up this pissing contest," Cory says, "or are we going to work together?"

"What about the dead dogs?" Chaingang asks.

"Oh, you'll still be answering for that," Cory answers.

Chaingang stands a little taller. "To you?"

"Enough," Auntie Min says. "Both of you." Her gaze lifts to take in the other bikers. "All of you. There is work to be done. Those of you who won't help must leave now."

"Or what?" J-Dog says.

"You will be removed."

"Yeah? By you and what army?"

Crows start drifting to the ground from the trees and their perches on the junked cars. As they reach the dirt, they turn into tall, lean, dark-haired men. In moments there are dozens standing around us and the trees are still full of birds.

J-Dog nods like he sees this all the time.

"You got all your homeboys," he says, "so what do you need us for?"

"I never said I did," Auntie Min tells him. "But Theo appears to want you with us, and I don't care enough one way or the other to argue with him about it."

Donalita starts to giggle, but she stops as soon as Auntie Min gives her a stern look.

J-Dog's eyes narrow like he's trying to figure out if Auntie Min's dissing him. I'm trying to figure it out myself.

"So what's the gig?" he asks finally.

Auntie Min counts it off on her fingers. "The rally on Saturday. Keep the congressman from being killed and becoming a martyr." She raises a second finger and waves her hand toward the nearest dog corpse. "And find out who's behind all of this," she says, "and stop them."

"And find Josh and Marina," I say when she pauses.

J-Dog gives me a glare. "Who the fuck are you?"

I want to take a step back, but I force myself to hold my ground.

"That's Des," Chaingang says before I can answer, "and he's my man, straight up. Nobody messes with him unless they come through me first."

Wow, really?

I suppose Chaingang sees something in my face because he gives me a look that says, "Zip it." I keep my mouth shut.

"Considering how ... efficiently Josh dealt with Vincenzo," Auntie Min says, "I don't think we have to worry about his safety. As for the otter—"

"We need to get Marina back—*now*," Chaingang says. "And if Vincenzo's brothers are as strong as he was, we're going to need Josh's fire power."

"I'm hoping we can resolve this without more butchery."

Ouch. She's looking around at the carnage. The dead dogs. The dead guy. I feel like she expects Chaingang to apologize, but I don't see that happening. It's just not the way he rolls.

While nothing shows on Chaingang's face, I don't have to guess about what J-Dog's thinking.

"Are you fucking kidding me?" he says to Chaingang. "Why are you even listening to these fools? What kind of a Wildling are you, anyway? A pussy?"

"Shut up," Donalita tells him.

"Listen, little girl—"

She waves a hand at him. "Yeah, yeah. We get it. Everybody's an alpha—especially you. Now shut your stupid mouth and let Auntie Min speak."

J-Dog's voice goes quiet. "Oh, you're going to pay for that slow, bitch. And Auntie *Min*? What kind of a douche name is—"

"Seriously, Jason," Chaingang tells him. "Either walk away, or shut up."

"What the—" J-Dog starts, but Chaingang holds his hand up, glares at him and mimes zipping his lip. Then he turns his attention back to Auntie Min.

"The dogs didn't give us a choice. Come after me or mine and you go down, end of story."

"Your grandmother—is she protected now?"

"We left Tall Boy to keep an eye on things. He's one of ours."

"I will send extra guards," Auntie Min says.

"Josh's mom, too," I put in. If my phone call worked, Solana and Matteson might already be over there, but it can't hurt to send reinforcements, especially ones that can fight fire with fire. I don't know what to do about Marina.

Auntie Min nods. I don't see her say anything, but a half-dozen of the dark-haired crow men shift into birds and fly off, three heading in the direction of the Orchards, the others toward town.

"Now—" Auntie Min begins, but Chaingang cuts her off.

"I know you've got your own agenda," he says, "but here's my priority number one: we find Marina and bring her back. And then we lay a little righteous head-busting on whoever was stupid enough to grab her."

"We are all concerned about the young otter," Auntie Min says, "but our first priority is to keep the congressman alive."

"I don't care about no asshole congressman," Chaingang tells her.

"You don't understand," Auntie Min says. "If they kill him and make it look like the work of a Wildling, the authorities will not rest until they have every one of you locked away."

Chaingang shakes his head. "Doesn't matter. I don't turn my back on my friends."

"Or girlfriends," Cory mutters.

Chaingang fixes Cory with that hard stare of his. "Say what?"

"You heard me."

"It doesn't matter what Marina and I are," Chaingang tells him, "I'm not about to let her hang out to dry without doing whatever it takes to get her back."

"That's commendable," Auntie Min begins, "however—"

"You're not *listening*," Chaingang cuts her off.

"I'll go find her," Cory says. "I'm the best of any of us at tracking somebody through the otherworld. And I'll do it better if I bring someone with me who knows her well."

"That would be me," Chaingang says.

Cory shakes his head and points at me. "No, that would be Des."

"That's bullshit."

"Oh, and have *you* known her for the better part of your life?" Cory asks. "Because that's the kind of knowing I'm talking about."

"Maybe I haven't. But you're going to need somebody who can fight and that's me—no offence, Des."

Cory nods. "Which is why Donalita's coming, too."

Auntie Min extends her hands toward Chaingang and interlaces her fingers. "We can achieve all of our goals by working together," she says. "Some have unique skills that will provide a surer success. If Des goes, it doesn't mean he's better than you."

"You think I give a rat's ass about that?"

No one says anything. I know what he's thinking. He wants to be the one to ride in and save Marina. I don't mind that it's me who gets the role, but not for the same reason. Dude, I just want to do something useful around all the people with their superpowers. But I totally understand.

We stand there in the hot sun for a few long moments until Chaingang finally nods.

"Okay," he says. "We'll do it your way. But"—he points at Cory, and then me—"don't you screw it up."

The look on his face is so dark I almost want to throw up my arms and tell him, "No, dude. You do it."

But I've got this. I think. Whatever the *this* is that Cory figures I can do.

I clear my throat. "We won't," I tell him.

Then Donalita's on one side of me, Cory on the other. They each take one of my arms.

"Just take a step," Donalita says.

I do, in unison with them, but we don't move a pace forward in the dusty junkyard. Instead the step takes us someplace else entirely.

Seriously, this is so cool.

JOSH

We have a dinner of rice and beans washed down with tea that isn't laced with any drugs, recreational or otherwise. I don't ask, but I take a long, considering sniff before I drink any. Tío Goyo makes no comment. The night's clear and the stars feel very close. I lie back looking up at them, and absorb the pleasing mix of scents from around me. Pine and wood smoke, and a hundred messages that the wind carries up from the rocky landscape below the lip of the cliff.

"So, are you guys like priests," I ask, "or did you ever have a girlfriend?"

"What kind of a question is that?"

I shrug. "You seem to know everything about *me*."

He studies me for a moment, then slowly adds another piece of wood to the fire, poking the burning pile with a stick and staring into the coals.

"No girlfriend," he says.

"Never? Really?" Sounds like the priesthood to me, but I don't say that.

He waits another moment before he answers. "When I was

your age, yes. But then I became involved with my brothers of the Halcón Pueblo and there was no longer time."

"Hobbies?" I ask. "You know, other than spying, and killing evil spirits, and drugging people?"

"You're still angry."

"I just wonder, when you go around interfering with people living ordinary lives, having normal bad dreams, if you ever consider how you're intruding on their right to privacy."

"It's only because of what my brothers do that they are able to live ordinary lives."

"Unless you kill them."

He sighs and shakes his head. "You know it's not like that. I'm turning in. We'll try again tomorrow morning to see if we can wake the map in your head."

"You shouldn't be surprised that I'd want to know what I'm getting into with you."

He doesn't answer. Instead he sets his mug by the fire and lies down on the bed. I hear his breathing even out. I look back up into the night sky.

When I'm sure he's asleep, I shift to my mountain lion shape and pad off silently into the darkness. Though it's not dark to my eyes. There's enough light from the moon and stars that I could read a book. But the mountain lion is only interested in reading the night.

I run for a while, following the rim of the mesa until I come to a dry waterfall. In the monsoon season it's probably a roaring torrent. Right now there's not even a trickle of water. I follow the tumble of boulders down until I reach the lower ground. I move without making a sound, but wherever I go, the night falls still. The nocturnal animals think I'm hunting. I can smell them:

jackrabbits, javelinas, mice, rats. Once, a pair of mule deer. But although the mountain lion wants to hunt, that's not why I left the camp.

I leap high into the lower branches of one of the big ponderosa pines and stretch out along a limb. As the minutes go by, the night life returns to its business once more.

I need to get the map in my head working again.

If I got anything from what Tío Goyo's been talking about today, it's that everything is all about … oh, let's just call it magic. And everything to do with magic works because of our will.

I can change shape because I will it.

I dial down intense smells and sounds by deliberately willing that to happen.

I've shut down the flow of pheromones I was putting out because I willed it to stop.

I know I can rise into the air in spirit form and safely return because I can will it.

So that's what I do now.

I don't try to relax, or empty my head, or anything else we've tried before. Instead, I imagine a wall in my mind and behind it is the map I'm trying to access. I study the big stones of the wall for a long moment, then I will it to come down.

In my imagination the wall explodes as though a giant boot kicked it aside. I have a moment to smile, thinking about Des and those old Monty Python shows he likes, and then there's my map—that weird GPS thing that first appeared in my head, back when I was in the skatepark. Like it never went away.

It's so stupidly easy.

I can see it all in my head, the landscape and everything around me for a radius of a hundred yards or so. I push it out farther, taking in the route I took to get here. The dry waterfall, the rim of the mesa, the camp. I note Tío Goyo, still sleeping.

Why does it work now, when it wouldn't before?

Because this time, I *believed* it would. I was relaxed about it. It's that simple. Just like you don't think about reaching out and picking something up. You don't forget how to move your arm, your fingers. You just do it.

I shut the map down and call it back up a few times, just to practice and explore it. I keep it close, let it spread out for miles, then reel it in again. Not until I'm sure I can call it up whenever I want, do I practice the other thing I came here to try.

I let my mind fill with everything I felt when my spirit rose out of my body—every part of that disconcerting sensation of slipping out of my flesh that I experienced after drinking Tío Goyo's special tea. When I'm sure I've got it all figured out, I let it happen again.

It's like throwing a switch. One moment I'm in my body, the next I'm looking down at myself in my mountain lion shape. Then that tawny shape dissolves into the long branch of the pine it's lying on and I shoot back to the camp, quick as a thought. I mean *literally*.

I hover there, high in the night sky, and look down at Tío Goyo's sleeping form.

I don't entirely trust him. I suppose I should take him at face value, seeing how he hasn't steered me wrong so far. Or at least not that I know. He could honestly be helping me find Elzie. But he could also be pulling some kind of mental sleight of hand, making me think he's my friend, and instead leading me into a confrontation with one of those evil spirit monsters he and his brothers are chasing. Maybe he needs my help to defeat one of them. Well, I'm not about to join their little priesthood.

I watch for a few moments longer before I zip through the sky and I'm above the spot where I lost the de Padillas' trail earlier. I drop down to earth and pull my physical shape out of the ground.

I have a bad moment, wondering, what if I get it wrong? What if when I re-form, my legs are sticking out of my shoulders or my head's in the middle of my chest?

But nothing goes wrong. I even remember to be wearing clothes, and my new longer dreads are still with me. I don't even have the hunger that I get when I shift from the mountain lion shape to this one.

In spirit form I detected a faint trace of the de Padillas' passage—a slight, lingering echo of where they'd walked. Now I can only smell the fading remnants of their trail. I wake up the map in my head and try to push it—not away from me to take in the surrounding terrain, as usual, but right at the place where the de Padillas crossed between the worlds.

Nada.

I've positioned myself at the exact spot where they disappeared, but the map in my head tells me nothing. It just shows the ground at my feet. My nose tells me more, but nothing I don't already know.

Damn. I was so sure I could make this work.

Okay. Time to try something else. I keep the map in my head and let my body fall away so that I'm just a spirit floating a few inches above the ground.

I have a little trouble keeping the map in place, but once I'm sure I can hold it, I superimpose the map in my head with the spirit's ability to see the residue of the de Padillas' passage. I don't know what the residue is, but it doesn't matter. All that matters is that I can see it.

I lay them on top of each other, like putting a transparency of one map on top of another, and focus on the point where the residue disappears.

This time I get a sense of something—a faint thrumming sensation in the air—sort of like a heat mirage. As though the border between the worlds is just a little weaker there. I push at it, not hard, but firmly, and suddenly I'm through. When the map in my head explodes with a whole new topography, I'm still able to hold on to the map of the world I left behind.

Now I've got two maps, with the trail of the de Padillas laid upon them. This world's not a whole lot different from the one I left. The forest is denser—smaller pines, with cedar and birch instead of the towering ponderosas. I expand the map for a couple of miles, but there's no sign of people or habitation. Still, the path is there, following a game trail as it switchbacks down a steep incline, the forest thick all around it.

I follow along above the trail until it disappears again.

Now I know what to look for. As soon as I find that weakness that marks the border, I push through again.

It's easier this time, and now I've got three maps superimposed over each other with the de Padillas' trail marked on each. The mesa world. The deep forest world. This new, third one is flatter. The de Padillas' trail follows a narrow road now, and I can sense a village nearby.

I congratulate myself as I follow this new trail through the third world, happy to have finally figured out how it's done.

But my self-congratulation comes too soon. Just as I'm nearing the end of this third segment of the de Padillas' passage through the worlds, I lose hold of all maps and I'm whipped back to my starting point. It happens with the abruptness of the rubber-band wars I have with Des, when I'm about to take a shot and the elastic snaps in two in my hand.

MARINA

Thorn does a thorough scan of the sky to make sure the condors aren't making a return sweep, then leads me deeper into the city. Debris still litters the streets—the wild reclaiming the once-tame blocks. We step around fallen rubble from the buildings, skirting our way past rusted cars, trucks and buses. At one point we pass by a tree whose limbs embrace a bicycle that's now embedded in its trunk, which pretty much says it all. But as we get closer to the city center, the buildings are much taller and many are in better shape, though their windows are mostly busted out.

Twice we have to do the invisible-cloak thing. The second time we're out in the open and one of the condors comes swooping down, snatching something out of the weeds down the street from where we're standing, the two of us frozen and invisible. When the bird rises, that something is wriggling in its talons, but even with my Wildling sight I can't make out what it is. A young tabby cat maybe. Or a baby raccoon.

The bird rises until it's near the top of the buildings, then it lets go and the little animal comes plummeting down, a terrified mewling echoing on the buildings as it falls. The *splat* when it hits the pavement seems magnified—a horrible wet sound that's way louder than you'd think it would be. It's all I can do to just keep hanging on to my invisibility and not throw up. My hands are clenching my length of pipe so hard they're starting to cramp.

The birds continue to circle above until I just want to scream. But finally they drift away and we can let the invisibility drop. Thorn's face is pale.

"This … this is new," he finally says.

"What do you mean?"

"The condors don't hunt here—they leave that to the hounds, and the hounds only play games with us. Fierce and unpleasant games, I'll grant you, but games nonetheless. Games we can survive. Not … not like that."

He nods in the direction of where the little creature died.

Neither of us says anything for a long moment. Then Thorn sighs and heads that way.

"Do we have to see it?" I ask.

"This is the way we're going," Thorn says. "You can always avert your gaze."

Which I totally plan to, but it's like rubbernecking at an accident. You tell yourself you're not going to do what everybody else does, but as soon as you're close enough, the morbid scene draws your gaze like a magnet.

We get to the other side of the rusted car, pushing through weed and brush until we find the body sprawled like a broken doll, abandoned, like everything else in this awful place.

It's worse than I expected. The condor didn't kill a cat. It killed a Wildling who changed back into a boy at his death. It's so sad and horrible. The face is turned away. The body lies with its limbs at awkward angles. The back of the head is cracked, and blood and brain matter are seeping out.

When I see that, I turn away.

I'm aware of Thorn going around to the other side of the body and crouching down on his haunches.

"I don't recognize him," he says.

"Shouldn't we do something?" I ask, still not looking. "Like bury him?"

"No time. We don't know when the condors will be back."

I wait until I hear Thorn stand again and start to move, then I walk around to join him. I'm doing fine until I get to the other side of the body and my morbid curiosity makes me look at the dead boy's face before we go on.

I stop in my tracks, staring.

"Marina?" Thorn asks.

For a long moment I can't speak. I clear my throat.

"I ... I know him," I finally get out. "That's Jeff Phelps. He goes ... went ... to my school."

My gaze lifts to search for something that makes sense in Thorn's eyes, but he just looks sad and bewildered.

"How could he have gotten here?" I ask.

"He must have been chased here, the same way you were."

I'm about to say that I never knew he was a Wildling, but that's not true. I made a point of knowing who all the Wildlings were in school—mostly so that I could avoid them and not have them figure out that I was one, too. It's easier than you think to pull it off, or at least they never let on that they knew I was a Wildling. I suppose we were all in denial, praying that no one would find out. But even if I did manage to stay under the radar of the other kids, you could never hide it from one of the elders like Auntie Min or ...

I glance up at the sky.

Those awful condors.

I shiver, remembering the horrible sound of impact when Jeff hit the ground.

"If that's true," I say, "and they killed him because he came from Santa Feliz, then they'll be looking to do the same to me."

Thorn gives me a sympathetic nod. "But you already guessed that."

"I suppose. It just didn't seem entirely real before."

Thorn glances at the body. "It's real now," he says. His nostrils flare and he kicks at some debris before he turns away and starts off down the street once more. His pace is fast enough that I have to hurry to keep up with him.

Ten minutes later, he stops at the edge of a sunken roadway filled with water. It goes off in either direction like a canal cutting through the city, reeds and brush choking the sides. Right in front of us is a makeshift bridge of boards crossing the water, and we use it to get to the other side, walking in a single file. The wood creaks and sags under our weight, but otherwise holds up just fine.

On the far side, Thorn points to a tall building where the street ends a few blocks away. It towers over its broken-down neighbours and seems relatively unscathed until I realize that it's missing all of its top floors. I can't imagine how tall it must have originally been.

I've been walking with a prickle of anxiety gnawing at me deep between my shoulder blades. I keep anticipating that the condors will show up so suddenly that we won't have time to hide from them. I can almost feel their talons digging into me, ripping me from my footing as we go up and up.

And then the long fall.

I shake my head, trying to push the fear away.

"Is that where we're going?" I ask.

Thorn nods. "Canejo's warren."

"Warren? What's *that* supposed to mean?"

"You'll see."

And that's when we both freeze.

From somewhere behind us we hear the hunting horns. With all the echoes bouncing around, it's impossible to tell how close or far away they are.

Thorn gives me a push forward. "Run!"

He doesn't have to tell me twice. I take off at full Wildling speed, and whatever kind of being Thorn is, he has no trouble keeping up with me. The tall building gets closer and closer.

Now I can see our reflection in the windows of its foyer— two figures running hell-bent, dodging back and forth through the rubble and brush. There's a wide, clear space in front of the building's double glass doors. We're almost there. The doors are so close.

Then the shadow of wings flashes over us. I hear the whistle of wind in feathers. I don't even think of what I'm doing. I turn and slash up with my metal pipe and connect with one of the condor's wings. The blow throws him off balance and he careens into the brush just beyond the cleared area.

When he rolls to his feet, he's a man who could be Vincenzo's twin.

Another shadow cuts across the asphalt.

I brace myself, pipe held ready, but then Thorn grabs me by the back of my shirt and pulls me inside the building.

Like the windows, the glass door is still intact and it works, hydraulics pushing it closed behind us. I shrug free of Thorn's grip and stand there breathing hard, flushed with adrenalin, pipe still in hand.

I watch the second condor drop, raising its wings to ease its fall. When its talons are about to touch the ground he changes into another Vincenzo twin. His companion crosses the cleared area and the two of them stand on the other side of the glass doors. Any damage I managed to do to the first one doesn't show.

I'd like to believe we're safe, but I know a few sheets of plate glass aren't going to stop this pair.

"They can't enter," Thorn says from behind me.

"Are you kidding me? I know how strong these guys are, and that's just plate glass."

"Doesn't matter how strong they are. They won't set foot in the building."

I turn for a moment to look at him.

"They can't come in," Thorn says. "They may have trapped Canejo in this pissant little world, but they're afraid to face him."

When I look outside again, I see loping figures approaching from the far end of the street. The wild dogs. It's hard to count them, they're moving so fast. Less than a dozen, more than half.

"And the dogs?" I ask.

"Same thing."

"Get her out of here!" a new voice yells from behind me.

I turn around to see a guy coming at us from the shadows that pool deeper in the building's foyer. The light's not great in here, especially after staring through the windows to the outside. As he comes closer, I see that he's a lean, compact man, just a little taller than me, dressed in loose pants and a shapeless shirt, black hair sticking up from the top of his head like a rooster's crest.

More to the point, he's totally pissed off.

"Now!" he says.

I see his teeth for a moment when he spits out the word. There seem to be far too many of them, sharp and pointed, like the inside of his mouth belongs to a barracuda. My fingers tighten around my pipe. I don't want to have to start swinging it, but I will if he comes at me.

Thorn moves so that he's between me and the stranger, who I figure must be this Canejo guy. But I don't know if Thorn's protection's going to be enough because Canejo's not alone. Moving toward us out of the shadows from behind him comes a whole crowd of beings—between twenty or thirty of them. They're mostly human in shape, but all sizes. Tall, short, fat and thin. Dressed in raggedy clothes like Thorn and Canejo. But there are others that aren't human-looking.

A tall figure who seems to have bark for skin, and hair that looks like thin vines with tiny leaves. A pair holding hands, with long, scaly faces and crests like fish fins. A girl with a wing for an arm, which hangs limply at her side.

And then I see three more kids I know from school: Matty Clark and Fernando Hill—neither of whom share any classes with me—and Stacy Li. She and I have biology in the same period. We aren't lab partners or anything, but we know each other well enough to exchange small talk before and after class. She disappeared a month or so ago. I thought she'd gone into the FBI program, or that her parents had taken her away from town. Now I know she's been here all this time, and I feel like I somehow abandoned her.

She starts to raise a hand, then drops it and looks away.

I'd feel hurt, but I'm not so uncaring that I don't understand.

She's been with these people for a month now. I'm somebody from an old life that must feel a million miles away. She's bonded with them. And I've just brought the monsters right to their front door.

I wonder what kind of a Wildling she is. I know she's not alone. I'm getting *pings* like crazy from the crowd, but I can't tell if they're all cousins. With this many, it's hard to focus in on just one.

Thorn raises himself up a little taller and wider as he faces Canejo. "You'd throw her to the hounds and their masters?" he asks.

"What were you *thinking?*" Canejo shoots back. "If they've sent the condors after her, what meagre protection we have against them won't hold. You've put us all in danger."

Some of the heads in the crowd behind him nod in frightened agreement. Others look away or at the ground. But no one else speaks up.

Canejo starts to move forward.

Thorn positions his arms like those of a wrestler. "Take another step and I'll throw *you* out to them," he says.

"Now, now," a new voice says.

The crowd parts and an old, long-haired man approaches us. I blink when I realize that he doesn't have long hair—those are drooping rabbit ears hanging down on either side of his face. And he's got small horns sprouting from his brow, tined like an antelope's. But even though he's doing the half-Wildling/half-human thing, it doesn't look creepy. I sense a calm strength coming from him, along with the strongest Wildling *ping* I've ever felt. Like Auntie Min times a hundred. If you think of all the other cousins here as decent-sized curls, he's the Big Wave you're always waiting on when you're floating out in the water on your board.

"Lionel," he says, placing one hand on the shoulder of the guy with the barracuda teeth and then his other on Thorn. "Thorn. I need both of you to calm down."

Lionel? I think. And then I realize that *this* is Canejo.

Thorn and Lionel move farther apart and Canejo drops his arms and interlaces his fingers. Lionel glares at Thorn, but Thorn doesn't seem to care anymore. Canejo steps up to me.

I'm hyperaware of everything. Lionel's animosity, the crowd's. The condors and dog cousins outside. But when I meet Canejo's gaze, it all seems to melt away.

"Look at you," he says, opening his hands. "You're just a slip of a girl with an otter living under your skin. What could you have done to make everyone so angry?"

"Nothing."

"Her friend killed Vincenzo," Thorn says.

Canejo's brows go up in surprise, but all he says is, "Ah."

"I didn't have anything to do with it," I say.

"There are those who would laud you as a hero if you did have a hand in it."

"I don't want to be a hero," I tell him. "I just want to go home."

Lionel gives a derisive laugh. "You think you're the only one? Now you've screwed us all."

Canejo nods toward the front of the building. "We have nothing to fear from them."

"Then why are they hanging around out there?"

"They're waiting for Nanuq," Canejo says.

His voice is mild, but a collective shudder goes through the crowd. Canejo gives me an apologetic look.

"I'll admit he's a formidable figure," he says. "But somewhere inside us, we each have the potential to be just as strong and fierce."

"I don't," Thorn says.

Canejo gives him a smile. "And because of your humility, you could be the strongest of us all."

"Good," Lionel says. "Let *him* confront Nanuq since he brought them here."

"You speak out of turn," Canejo says without turning to look at him. When he does turn, it's to speak to everybody. "We gain nothing by milling about down here, feeding each other's fears. I would ask you to disperse, so that I might speak to our guest without a crowd of onlookers hanging on to our every word."

He says "ask," but it's taken more like a command because the crowd immediately breaks up and fades back into the shadows. The last to go are Stacy and Lionel. For a moment she looks as if she's about to talk to me, but then she drops her gaze again and follows the others.

Lionel remains rooted to the spot, his face clouded with anger. "We have to make a plan," he says.

Canejo shakes his head. "We already have a plan. You will go away because you're making our guest uncomfortable. She and I will remain here with Thorn to get to know one another."

"But—"

"If you feel the need to be doing something, you might brew us a pot of tea to drink while we await Nanuq's arrival."

Lionel draws back his lips and gives me such a glare that I

feel the only thing he really wants to do is bury that mouthful of sharp teeth in my neck. But then he gives Canejo a brief nod and stalks away.

"You must forgive them," Canejo says as he ushers me to some couches on the far side of the foyer.

I'm surprised everything's so well taken care of in here. Outside, it looks like World War III hit a decade or so ago and it's all gone downhill since. Inside, we could be in the foyer of some corporate building in my own world—without power, of course, but the polished marble floors are spotless, the couches are firm and clean, and the air smells fresh instead of like old pee, the way it did in the stairwell of the building where Thorn and I ate lunch.

Thorn drops onto one end of the couch and the whole thing shivers a little from his weight. I take the other corner, leaving room for Canejo, but he opts to sit on the low, wooden coffee table facing both of us. I look past him to the other side of the glass doors and walls, my length of pipe laid across my knees.

Outside, the condors are as motionless as statues, but the fury in their eyes speaks volumes, while around them more and more dogs arrive. Some take human form, both male and female. They stack brush, then start fires in the piles they've made.

The whole scene is eerie as hell, but if everyone's sure they'll stay outside, I suppose I should relax. I lean my pipe against the side of the sofa and ignore the twitch in my hands that wants me to keep holding it.

"How did you come to find yourself in Dainnan?" Canejo asks.

I nod toward the dog men. "They chased me here. I thought

I was escaping them, but I guess they were just herding me to this place."

"They had no choice, you know," Canejo says.

I glance over at Thorn and back at Canejo before speaking. "Thorn says that they're controlled by somebody—one of the condors, I guess. Or this Nanuq guy, if he's the one that's carrying around the controller."

I pause for a moment, then add, "But you're not scared of any of them, are you? Not the dogs outside, not Nanuq. Even though everybody else is."

Canejo shrugs. "They can't hurt me. I wasn't supposed to be in this little prison of theirs. I stumbled upon it when they took some students of mine. But once I was here, they couldn't let me leave for fear of what I might reveal to other cousins. I'd been looking for a good place to conduct my teachings, so it hasn't been all bad."

"So you can't get out, either?"

"There is only one passage out of Dainnan and that's controlled by whoever holds the token."

"You've tried to get hold of it?"

That gets me another shrug, then he says, "I can do my work anywhere, but here, my students need me more than ever."

"What work is that?" I ask.

"I teach my students how to fulfill their potential—to become the best that they can be."

I look past him at the condors and the dog cousins. "That doesn't explain why *they're* all scared of you."

"They aren't scared, so much as cautious. I am an old cousin. I wasn't here when Raven first pulled the world out of that big black pot of his, but it wasn't much longer after that before Coyote was chasing me through the new world. Young pups like those outside are no match for me—not even with their greater numbers—and I have dealt with the Condor Clan a time or two. They know better than to test me."

I imagine Theo here, rolling his eyes, but I believe him. He sounds a lot like Auntie Min.

"And Nanuq?" I have to ask. "What about him?"

"He's Polar Bear Clan. We have never had occasion to physically assess each other."

I look again at Thorn sitting quietly on the other end of the couch, then back at Canejo.

"And you don't think trapping you in this world is reason enough to take him down? Or at least to try?"

"I told you. I have—"

"Your work. Right."

It seems the older a cousin is, the harder they are to understand. How can he not be mad at being stuck here? And how can his students reach their potential in such a confined setting? But I decide to let those questions lie. Straight answers from elder cousins are few and far between.

"So now, little otter"—Canejo leans forward, cupping his chin, elbow on his knee—"tell me how Vincenzo died."

JOSH

Snapped back to the world Tío Goyo brought me to, I sense that the fragile reality of my spirit form is about to dissipate into the air all around me. I forget how magic's all about belief, focus and will. Instead, I panic and rush toward the ground where I'm somehow able to call up my body from the earth, no worse for wear except for a splitting headache. I lie face down on the ground, grateful to still have fingers to dig into the earth and anchor me. Content to press my cheek against the dirt and weeds.

It takes me a few moments to regain my composure enough so that I can sit up. The pain between my temples feels like a snare drum that Marina's using to bang out an energetic drum solo. I shift to my mountain lion shape, then back, and the pain's gone, the same way that bruises and other hurts are healed by the shift, though now I'm hungry. I try to ignore the hollow feeling in my stomach.

With my head clear again, I try to figure out what went wrong. Because I was doing so well ...

I take a steadying breath and call up the map in my head. It appears as soon as I think of it, and with it are the maps of

the other two worlds I visited, which surprises me. I thought I'd
have to work at reclaiming them. I study them from all sides.
They're laid on top of each other, but I can see them together,
or separately. It's like looking at a three-dimensional tic-tac-toe
board, only from different perspectives.

It's weird and takes a bit of adjustment.

Once I figure it out, it's easy to trace the trail of the de
Padillas as they moved from world to world.

So what kicked me out when I got to the third one?

The only way to find out is to go back and do it all again—
only this time, pay close attention to everything around me. I
also decide to return to human form once I've arrived at each
world, which is how I eventually end up standing on the narrow
road where I got snapped back to my starting point.

I don't move, anticipating a repeat of what happened before.
But this time I remain in place. I hear the night sounds of a forest
all around me. My map lets me pinpoint where each comes from.
A pair of deer. A hunting fox. Innumerable mice, voles and other
rodents going about their business. Expanding the map, I locate
the village again. Almost everybody is asleep.

I roll my shoulders to ease my tension.

Okay. Time to move on.

I repeat the whole procedure and end up on a slightly larger
road. There's still forest all around me, but the air's cooler and it's
closer to dawn than it was in the world I just left. The first hint
of the rising sun pinks the eastern horizon.

I follow the de Padillas' scent trail, staying in human form,
until it vanishes between one step and the next. I cast around to
be sure—on the road, in the overgrown hedges on either side.

But just before I let my body fall from me again, I sense someone approaching.

I hesitate, caught between wanting to move on and curiosity. My head tells me nothing of who this stranger might be—only of his approach and that he's a cousin. His animal shape is a—hummingbird? I can deal with a hummingbird cousin. I've got a mountain lion under my skin. I can take a step and be back in the last world I was in. I can drop my body completely and be just a spirit. There's no need for me to feel anxious at all.

So I wait for his approach.

CHAINGANG

I won't lie. I'm pissed that I'm not the one going over to find Marina, but I can't pretend to know her as well as Des. And if that's what it's going to take for him and Cory to find her, I'll step aside. But not for long. And there'll be hell to pay if they blow it.

Auntie Min tells me what she wants me to do, then she and her crow boys step away into the otherworld, taking the bodies of the dead with them. A few of the crows are still hanging around in the trees.

J-Dog makes a finger gun and pretends to shoot at them.

"Just say the word, bro," he tells me.

I don't bother to answer. I head back to the clubhouse. I can feel the guys checking with J-Dog before they fall in behind me. When we get inside I pop a beer and sit down on a sofa, prop my legs up on a plastic milk crate and wait until everybody's settled with their beers in hand. Then I tell them what they need to know, about Lenny, and me, and the whole Wildling thing.

"What kind of Wildling are you?" Shorty wants to know.

He's skinny and tall, hair in cornrows, a dagger tat under his left eye. It's ballpoint blue—a jail tat made with a pin and ink from the cartridge of a pen. He's got his feet up on the same crate I'm using to rest my own.

I boot his feet so they fall off the crate. "Doesn't matter and don't ask," I tell him.

J-Dog chuckles. "Which means he's some little lame-ass sparrow or lizard or something."

Close, but I just shrug. Like I'm going to give them the ammo to rag on me for the next ten years. Soon as they know, I'll go from Chaingang to Mouseboy. Yeah, not going to happen. But the guys laugh and a tension I hadn't really registered leaves the room.

Dekker lifts his beer bottle to get my attention.

"Yo, bro," he says. "Why you let that old lady talk trash to you?"

"Same reason I let my grandma. She deserves the respect."

"You don't always do what your grandma says. If you'd listened to her, you'd never be riding with us."

"Some things, nobody else gets to decide for you," I say.

"Yeah? So's your grandma as much of a—"

J-Dog points a finger at him. "Careful where you're going with that, homey. She's my grandma, too." Then he turns to me. "You serious about this, bro? You jump at that old lady's word? You going to get into bed with the goddamn po-leece?"

"It's not like that. It's just using the right tools to do the right thing."

"Since when do we care about that shit?" Bull asks. He gets his name honestly. He's not tall, but he's built like an ox.

"I'm not asking anybody to step up," I tell him.

J-Dog shakes his head. "You don't get to make that decision."

"Yeah, then who—"

He cuts me off. Turns to the guys.

"Anybody got more questions?" he asks.

He looks around at them all, and one by one, each shakes his head.

"Chaingang's one of these animal freaks now," he says, "but he still rides with us—am I right? Once an Ocean Avenue Crip, always."

"We're family," Shorty says. "A brotherhood."

Bull nods. "Nobody walks away and we don't turn our back on any of us."

Shorty smiles. "Even if he is a sparrow."

I point a finger at him. "I told you. Don't even start—"

"Shut up," J-Dog says. "It's settled. Go talk to the Feds. Figure out what you need. Then you come back and tell us, and we'll take it from there."

"Sure, but—"

"End of discussion, bro. You need backup on this?"

I shake my head.

"Then get your butt outta here and do what needs to be done."

I step outside and call the number that Auntie Min gave me—I guess she got it from Josh or Des, though knowing her, she could have just pulled it out of her ass. It rings once, then I hear Agent Solana's voice.

I name a place, then add, "Be there. I'm on my way."

I hang up before he can ask his first question.

I'm waiting at the picnic table on the beach where Donalita first took me to see Cory—man, was that only yesterday? The weather's nice—warm and sunny, with a light breeze coming in from the ocean, so the usual crowd's out. Surfers waiting on the swells that they'll ride in to shore. Dog walkers. Joggers. Families. Kids playing volleyball or just chilling. I get an ache thinking about how Marina would love to be out there on her board.

I hardly get settled on the bench before a dark sedan pulls into the parking space beside my Harley. I watch the two FBI agents get out and look around themselves, assessing the situation. The lot's about two-thirds full and between the cars and the people, there's plenty to check out. They're studying every vehicle and every person with suspicion. When they see me, they approach from either side, hands under their coats, ready to draw their sidearms at the first hint of danger.

I stay where I am, palms flat on the table, and wait. The last thing anybody wants is a firestorm on a crowded beach.

"You know what we do with assholes who yank our chain?" Matteson says when he finally reaches the table.

He leans on the slats, towering over me. I want to grab his throat and show him exactly who's the asshole, but I let it ride. For now.

"No," I say, keeping my voice mild, "but I'm sure you're dying to tell me. But if I were you? I'd hear me out before running off at the mouth."

Solana is still scanning the beach, the parking lot, like he's expecting an ambush.

"Sure, tough guy," Matteson says. "So start talking before we pull you in."

Good luck with that, I want to say. Yeah, it could play out

that way. He takes me in, J-Dog's lawyer will bust me out within the hour. But that won't get us anywhere.

So I ignore him. Instead, I turn to Solana and jerk a thumb in his partner's direction.

"How much does he know?" I ask.

"Know about what?" Matteson cuts in.

"Everything," Solana says.

"Is that right?" I say.

Which begs the question, how much does Solana really know? But hey, not my problem. I'm just the messenger today. The elders want to keep secrets, they should let me know which ones.

So I lay it out for them with a few edits. I leave out that Josh killed Vincenzo; I just say that we found out the condor dude is dead. I don't bring up how I had the dog men ambushed— their bodies are gone now, anyway. And I don't talk about my relationship with Marina.

Mainly, I deliver Auntie Min's warning that Congressman Householder—and maybe a bunch of innocent bystanders—is going to end up dead unless we protect him at his damn anti-Wildlings rally this Saturday.

Matteson sits down on the bench opposite me. "You know what this sounds like, right?" he says. "I mean, how do we know you're not setting this up to get some intel on the congressman's schedule?"

"You don't. But we both know that asshole never shuts up about his freaking save-the-poor-humans rally. It's as public as you can get."

"So now what?" Matteson asks. "Are we supposed to give you a merit badge, or a get-out-of-jail-free card?"

I'd like to tell him where to shove his merit badge, but I clamp it down. "You can do whatever you want," I say. "I just passed along a message."

"We can still run you in," Matteson says.

I ignore him again and turn my attention to Solana. "Auntie Min thought you might feel that way. She told me to say, 'Alejandro Maria Solana, I bid you to help this man, by my word and the will of the Halcón Pueblo.'"

Matteson stares up at Solana. "Your middle name is *Maria*?"

Solana ignores him, his gaze steady on my own. "What does she want from me?"

"Jesus," Matteson says. "You're not actually going to listen to this—"

Solana holds his palm up and Matteson shuts his trap. There's a long pause, then Solana turns to him and says, "Maybe you should walk away. Right now, while you still can. What you don't know, they can't hold you responsible for."

Matteson sits up straighter, squaring his shoulders. "That's what you want? You'd swap your partner for this low-life?"

"Hey. Sitting right here," I say. But I might as well be on the moon, for all the attention they're paying me.

Solana is shaking his head. "If this goes bad, I don't want to drag you down with me."

"And if it was me, telling you to walk away?" Matteson asks.

"I wouldn't listen."

"Exactly. If you're in, I'm in. End of discussion."

"Anybody ever tell you two that you're like an old married couple?" I ask.

They both look at me.

"Shut up," Matteson says.

He puts his elbows on the table and studies me for a moment. "So Josh up and left," he says. "Of his own accord."

"That's how the signs read."

"His poor mother," Matteson says. "That lady's already been put through the mill. You'd think he'd at least say goodbye before screwing off."

I guess that means they went to check on her, but I'm not going to ask. Instead I just shrug. "Not my business."

"And you say Marina Lopez has gone missing?"

I nod.

"She's not the only one," Matteson says. "We've got missing persons reports on almost a dozen kids in the past few weeks— all of them with some kind of Wildling connection. And don't even start trying to tell me that you and your friends aren't Wildlings, too."

"I knew there were kids who went AWOL," I say, "but I just thought they were runaways, or that you guys grabbed them."

"We don't *grab* people," Matteson says. "Believe it or not, we've been trying to help these kids. The whole world is watching this shit go down. Half the press thinks this whole Wildlings thing is some elaborate scam created with special effects, but they're still on our chief like flies on shit. We couldn't kidnap kids even if we wanted to."

"But you keep them locked up on the old air base like research monkeys."

Matteson's finger is pointed straight at my face before I can even blink.

"Don't you *ever* equate us with those sick freaks at ValentiCorp—you got me?"

"Those kids on the base came to us," Solana says. "They had

full amenities—TV, Internet, games. They were being tutored, their parents could come see them whenever they wanted."

"Until one of you broke them out," Matteson adds. "And you know what? Most of them came back to us of their own free will. We're keeping them off the streets for their safety as much as the public's. If Josh had come to us, a lot of his problems would never have happened. And we could have contained the Black Key assholes gunning for him."

"Speaking of Black Key," I say. "Have you rounded them all up now?"

Solana shakes his head. "We've still got two more on the loose. Kelvin Barrett and Santos Morris. We've got good leads on both."

"Why do you want to know?" Matteson asks. "You sure Wildlings aren't killing those Black Key guys—maybe sending dogs after them?"

"Like the one we nabbed going after Josh's mother?" Solana adds.

So they did take care of her. I hope they blew the bastard away like we did the others.

I shake my head. "It's nobody I know. Maybe Auntie Min can tell you more."

"Auntie Min," Matteson says with a sigh. "That old lady really have that much mojo?"

Both Solana and I nod.

"What, exactly, does she want us to do?" Solana asks.

I shrug. "Like I said, stop the congressman from dying—not that I give a shit. But she thinks if someone offs him at his rally, he'll become a big martyr, and then everybody's going to be out for Wildlings."

"You said Vincenzo's dead," Matteson says. "So what are you not telling me? Who wants to off Householder?"

"Vincenzo *is* dead, but he's got pissed-off brothers. And apparently they're all working for someone bigger and badder—with a real hard-on for Wildlings."

"But *they're* Wildlings, so they hate themselves?"

I shake my head. "They hate the new ones—kids who changed here in the last six months."

"Even if he kills you all," Solana says, "the fact that you existed won't go away."

I don't reply. I just want this conversation to be over.

"So when can we meet with Auntie Min?" Matteson asks.

"Let's go. I'll take you to her right now."

Matteson nods. "All right," he says. Then his finger is back in my face. "But if you're yanking our chain—playing some kind of angle—let me tell you, Washington, you're going to be all kinds of sorry when I'm done with you."

I get up from my seat.

"Are you kidding me?" I say. "I'm already all kinds of sorry we ever even met."

I don't wait for a reply. I just head for my bike and roll out of there, making them scramble to get back to their car to follow me.

JOSH

He comes around the corner of the road and stops when he sees me. I feel a faint tickle touch me and I realize he's reading me. It's weird—and creepy. Cousins have been reading me for months, but I've never felt anything like that before.

After a moment, he continues to approach.

He's not much taller than me, but with much darker skin and a shaved head. At first I'd thought he was wearing white cottons like the de Padillas, but I see now that it's a white suit tailored to his slender frame, with a black shirt and a thin white tie. Very sharp looking, if you like the hipster look, but totally incongruous on a dirt road in the middle of a forest. And then I notice his feet are bare. What's up with that?

"Hey," I say when he's just a few paces away. "Nice to see someone out here in the middle of nowhere. My name's Josh."

His eyes narrow.

"I should punch you in the face," he says.

"What?"

I take a step back. Okay, wasn't expecting that.

"What makes you think I want the burden of your name?" he goes on.

"I have no idea what you're talking about," I tell him. "I was just being friendly."

"Giving me your name without my asking for it is *not* friendly."

"Yeah? Well, it is where I come from."

"Where you come from," he repeats in a mocking tone.

His eyes focus sharply on me and I feel that tingle again. He looks disgusted.

"I thought as much," he says. "You're one of them—the unborn."

"Excuse me?"

"You were made into your skin, not born into it."

"Yeah, so?"

"*So*," he says, leaning into the word, "you have no clan affiliation and are only bound to attract trouble."

"I'm not here to cause trouble."

He nods. "Yet you will still attract it. The cousins argue constantly about your kind: are the unborn miracles or monsters? Are you to be welcomed or shunned? Do you upset the balance of the world or are you here to set it right? Pissant little cousins can't feel the balance shift, but I do. You don't fool me."

I raise my hands, palms up. "Dude, I have no idea what you're—"

"Exactly," he cuts in. "You have no idea, yet you appear in the land under my care, without even the courtesy of paying your respects to the spirits who make this place their home."

My hands have dropped and are now clenched fists at my side. The mountain lion stirs, but I ignore the urge to bite this jerk's head off.

"Well, first of all, I didn't know that was the deal here," I tell him, "and secondly, I'm just passing through. If I hadn't stopped to talk to you, I'd already be gone."

"Then go."

"You know, we have a name for people like you where I come from."

His brow creases in even more displeasure. "I'm sure you do. And we have name for you as well—meddler. Now go."

He's got the little-guy macho of angry hummingbirds jockeying for position at a feeder. I can almost hear the buzz of his wings, except he's using words instead of dive-bombing me.

I remember his opening line.

I should punch you in the face.

I feel like doing that to him right now, but I'm not going to play into his negativity any more than I already have.

Instead I just say, "I'm gone," and let my body fall back into the earth.

The look on his face is priceless as my spirit rises up above the road. I guess he sees a hawk, which has got to be totally throwing him off because earlier he had to have read me as a mountain lion.

But that's his problem.

I call up my maps, focus on the de Padillas' trail, and head into the next world.

I find myself on a vast plain. There's no road, just grass for as far as I can see, with a vague trail running through it. The sun's a lot higher here. I let the map of this place expand and detect nothing but rodents and birds.

I follow the scent of the de Padillas until it disappears, then go through my whole process again.

When I call up my body from the earth, I'm standing on

a ridge overlooking the ocean. I could almost be back in So-Cal. Between the ridge and the shoreline is a scattering of adobe buildings.

It's midmorning here and my map's showing lots of people and animals. Not wanting a repeat of what I went through with the hummingbird cousin, I return to spirit shape and drift down the slope, still following the de Padillas' trail. It leads me to one of the houses. An adobe wall spreads from the back of the house, penning a cow and a handful of goats. A cat sleeps on the top of the wall. A dog is stretched out on the dirt by a table near the back door.

Manuel and Lara sit at the table, the remains of a recent meal between them. As I drift down toward them, the cat opens an eye to look at me. The dog stands up and whines, its gaze on me as well. Manuel looks up, shading his eyes.

"Redtail," he says. "A big one."

I'd like to talk to them, but I've got what I came for. I was able to track and find them across the worlds, and now I've got five maps in my head that I can access as I need to.

I mentally line up those maps until I can see both the beginning and the end of the trail that brought me here, then I will myself directly back to my starting point.

If I had features, I'd be grinning from ear to ear as the now-familiar ponderosa pines rear up around me.

"Cool," I say as I rise up in my physical shape once more.

Then I turn around because my maps show me I'm not alone.

DES

"Dude, this is *so* cool."

The words pop out of my mouth before I can edit them. I know I'm geeking out like—well, the geek I am. But I can't help it.

We've stepped from the dusty yard behind the Avers' clubhouse into what feels like some kind of rainforest. I can almost feel the pores of my skin open up with the humidity in the air. The trees rise up forever, long, hanging branches dripping water and vines. There are ferns everywhere, taller than us. Birds that I can't see make a racket in the boughs above. And all it took was one step to get here from So-Cal. Just like *that*.

I freaking *love* magic.

Cory and Donalita smile at each other.

"Are we going to meet elves?" I ask them. "I mean, the tall, Peter Jackson kind, not little Tinkerbells—though I guess they'd be cool, too."

"Sure," Cory says. "And unicorns and dragons."

"Really?"

He gives me the same wry look my friends did when I still believed in Santa Claus and they were all *so* over it.

"What do *you* think?" he asks.

Donalita elbows him. "This was all new to you once, too," she tells him. "You're just no fun anymore."

Cory's eyes darken. "Maybe that's because somebody put a binding on my brothers so they can't control what they're doing, but gangbangers like Chaingang are slaughtering them all the same."

"Dude," I say. "I'm sorry. I didn't mean—"

He waves off my apology before I can finish. "We're here to do a job," he says. "Let's just get it done."

I'm thinking he was pretty harsh to the dogs that treed Donalita and me, but then I realize it's true. He just talked to them. He didn't lure them into an ambush and blow all their brains out.

"What can I do to help?" I ask.

"Nothing for the moment. Let me see what I can pick up on my own first." He starts to walk off through the rainforest.

I go to follow him, but Donalita puts a hand on my arm. "Give him a little space," she says.

"What's he doing?"

"Trying to hone in on Marina. If he can't do it on his own, then he'll use you."

I'm not sure I like the sound of that.

"What's that going to involve?"

She shrugs. "He's Coyote Clan. I don't know how they think or what they do to make things happen. But dude," she adds, letting her eyes go big. "It'll probably hurt. A lot."

Her face splits into a grin at the look on my face.

"Kidding," she says with a chuckle.

She slips her hand into the crook of my arm and steers me

in the direction that Cory took, but at a much slower pace. We catch up with him at the lip of a large pool of clear, still water. Though the trees rear up impossibly tall on all sides, here on the flat stones by the water, we can see the sky. A cloud drifting by is echoed on the surface of the pool. Cory's sitting on his haunches. He dips his hand into the water and stares down as the ripples spread.

"Any luck?" Donalita asks.

He shakes his head. "I've got a knack for finding the thread of a person's passage through the otherworld and then following it to where they are. But not today."

"You can't find any sign of her?"

"That's the funny thing," he says. "I can find her thread, but it doesn't lead me anywhere. It just fades into a dead end."

"So isn't that where we should go?" I ask. "The place where it ends? Won't we find her there?"

"It doesn't work like that," he says. "None of us are dead ends. Wherever we are, we're connected to where we've been and where we can go. It's a huge web of history and possibilities. But her thread doesn't go forward."

I swallow hard, feeling like a piece of lead just dropped into my belly. "You're not ... Are you saying ..."

"I'm saying I don't know. I don't think she's dead, or at least I haven't seen or felt anything to make me think she is. But I can't find her, either.

"You see," he goes on, standing up and wiping his hand on his jeans, "the otherworld is capricious, at best. You have to either be someone like me, who can figure out the patterns, or have a sense of direction that works in at least five dimensions. Past, present and future all take place at the same time here.

Dreams—hell, anything you can imagine, and a lot you can't—exist here somewhere. But not in any way you can map.

"Everything's on top or underneath, or a step sideways, and it shifts around so that just because you found your way once, doesn't mean you'll find it again. Or that you can see how to get out. And if you're a five-fingered being, you might be a whole somebody else when you do return to your own world."

Great—thanks for the warning, I think.

"Is that what they mean about fairyland?" I ask. "You know how in the stories, if a mortal goes there, they come back either a poet or mad?"

"Maybe. But the more I live among you people, the more I believe that you're already all out of your minds. The things you do to each other." He shakes his head.

"Oh yeah?" I tell him. "Dude, what about ..."

I'm about to bring up how heavy Vincenzo was, but I let it go because he's right. We humans don't need psycho cousins to bring hurt down on us. We already do that to ourselves. And dude, that's a sobering thought.

"You were saying?" he asks when I trail off.

"Nothing. So what now?"

He shrugs. "We find her the hard way."

I swallow again and try not to let my nervousness show. Whatever happens here, I tell myself, I'm doing it for Marina. She and Josh would do the same for me. I just hope I'm the same *me* when I get back.

"So, what?" I say. "You take a walk around inside my head and somehow that leads you to her?"

"Something like that. Just fill your mind with her. Think of all the things she means to you—the good and the bad. Let the memories come and keep filling in details. I'll do the rest."

"Dude, tell me first. *What* will you do?"

"It's a coyote thing," Donalita says. "You know how you let a bloodhound smell a piece of clothing that belongs to the person you want him to track?"

"Sure, but—"

"This isn't any different, except you're giving him a taste of all the things that make Marina who she is. It's like you're laying down a scent trail, and that long nose of his will lead us to her."

Cory nods. "That's a good way to put it. And it works best with someone who knows her really well."

"So I just think about her."

"More than that," he says. "Close your eyes and try to make her real inside your head—so real that if you opened your eyes, you'd expect her to be standing right here in front of you."

"Dude," Donalita says, punching me lightly on the shoulder. "You can *so* do this."

"I know." Though honestly? I'm not so sure.

"You're not going to stab me are you?" I ask Cory, thinking of how I heard he did that to Chaingang.

Cory flashes that coyote grin of his, obviously aware of what I've been thinking.

"If I do, it'll only *feel* real," he says.

Donalita kicks him in the shin.

"Ow!" he cries and steps out of range, almost falling into the water. "It was a joke," he adds from a safer distance.

She glares at him and points a finger. "Well, don't be such a Big Stupid. How's Des supposed to know that?"

Girls. Didn't she just play the same kind of joke on me?

"Okay, okay." He rubs his shin and looks at me. "Word of warning—don't ever get on the wrong side of a coati girl."

I hold up my hands. "I'm not stupid, dude."

Donalita laughs, then turns serious. "I'm going to make things easier for you," she tells Cory. "You'll only have to worry about bringing Des along."

"Wait," I say. "You're not coming?"

"Did I say that?" she says. Then adds, "Catch!"

She jumps toward me, shifting into a pebble in mid-air. I'm so unprepared that my fingers only close around air. But hours of playing hacky sack with Josh pay off with an instinctive save. I tap the stone with my heel before it can hit the ground, and this time I catch it.

"Man," Cory says, "would I like to figure out how she does that trick."

"I thought it was something all you tricksters can do."

Cory shakes his head. "I can look like someone else, but I can't actually *become* something else."

I look down at the pebble in my hand and see Donalita curled up, superimposed on the pebble. I can only feel a pebble, but just like back at Sunny Hill, I can *see* them both.

"Don't drop her," Cory says, "or who knows where she'll end up."

I nod and stick the pebble in my pocket. "But what did she mean about making things easier for you?"

"Now I only have to concentrate on bringing you along."

I shift from foot to foot. I have no clue how he's planning to bring me anywhere. "Okay, so what happens now?"

"Just stay still and fill your head with Marina."

I feel totally out of my depth, but I nod. He steps up close and puts his palms on my temples.

"Just think of her," he says. "Not only what she looks like, but what her skin feels like, how she smells, what she cares about—everything that makes her real to you."

I close my eyes and start with how she looks—that's easy. But beyond that it gets complicated. She hid that she was a Wildling for six months, so how am I supposed to know what she thinks about or what she feels? She's been mooning after Josh for pretty much as long as I've known her, but suddenly, wham bam, she hooked up with Chaingang, who's not even remotely like any of the dudes she's ever dated.

I don't even want to get into the crush for her that I've carried for years.

"Man," Cory says. "You guys are like a bad reality show."

His voice seems to come from somewhere behind me, but I can still feel his hands on either side of my head. I open my eyes to look at him and then vertigo hits me.

We're standing on—dude, I don't know *what* we're standing on. It's like we're floating in nothingness and my stomach just won't stop doing flips.

"Wh—where are we?" I manage.

I feel like I might puke, so I start to pull away, but he holds my head more tightly.

"Don't break contact!" he says.

"Dude—what the hell is this place?"

Cory shrugs. "Hard to say. Feels like a piece of something you might have dreamed once."

Like that makes any sense. But I'm feeling too nauseous to ask him to explain.

"You're doing good," he says. "Close your eyes. Keep concentrating."

I want to argue that I'm not doing good at all, but if I open my mouth again I'm pretty sure I might barf. So instead, I close my eyes.

And just like that, the queasy feeling goes away and I'm visualizing Marina again.

"Dude," I say, keeping my eyes firmly closed. "That was weird."

"Concentrate. Don't get distracted."

"Yeah, but—"

"Focus."

Yeah? On what?

I've got a thousand pictures in my head of Marina. She's surfing—on her own or with the school club. She's banging the drums, head keeping time, her hair flying. She's on a skateboard and laughing because she can't get her balance on wheels like she can on a wave. She's sitting across from me at a table in the lunchroom, trying not to smile at some stupid thing I said.

And then I remember the Sadie Hawkins Dance last year. She was gorgeous in that pink dress, hair all done up, but wearing a radical pair of high-tops that she'd painted a million colours in art class. Being a Sadie Hawkins Dance, I'd been sure that she was going to invite Josh, but instead she showed up with some loser whose name I can't even remember. I can't remember who asked Josh, or who I went with, either. All I remember is her watching Josh, and me watching her, and Josh being oblivious to it all, as usual.

"Got it!" Cory says.

I feel like we're falling—but it's a sensation that's only in my head. I still feel Cory's grip, and the ground underfoot. Then Cory lets me go and I stagger.

I open my eyes and all around us is a dead city. Like a big city, except it's been all bombed out or something, and there's trees and vines and crap growing over everything.

"Where are we?" I ask. "The end of the frigging world?"

But all he says is, "Fuck."

I don't like the sound of that.

"What? What is it?"

"I need to talk to Donalita."

"Dude, you're freaking me out."

Instead of answering, he cocks his head.

"Fuck," he says again. Then he turns to me. "Donalita. Now."

I take the pebble out of my pocket and kneel down to tap it on the asphalt underfoot. A moment later Donalita's kneeling in front of me. We're nose to nose. She starts to grin, but then she frowns and shoots Cory a dirty look.

"Where did you bring us?" she asks, her voice sharp.

"She was here," Cory says. "Maybe a half day ago."

"But this is a *closed* world."

"You think I don't know that?" he says. "And it gets worse. Hear that?"

Donalita cocks her head like he did.

"Hunting horns," she says.

I still don't hear anything, but I already officially hate this place.

"Somebody want to tell me what's going on?" I say.

"Sometimes," Cory says, "a cousin will carve out a little

pocket world. It might be no bigger than a room, or it might be like this—going on for who knows how far. But there's only one way in and one way out."

"Yeah, so? Can't we just go back the way we came in?"

He shakes his head. "This one's set up differently. Anything can be funnelled in, but there's no way out, except through whoever set it up in the first place. They control the exit."

"And these horns you're hearing?" I ask.

"I think this world is somebody's private hunting preserve," he says. "Which means that either Marina stumbled onto it and is now stuck here—just like we are—or it could be Vincenzo's people chased her into this world."

"So the horns ..."

He nods. "Mean that the hunters have noted our arrival and are coming for us."

I feel the blood drain from my face. I get up from the ground a little too quickly, and that strange feeling that comes just before you faint hits me. I lean over and brush off my pants, trying to tamp down my panic. I stand back up, more slowly this time.

"So what you're saying is, we're screwed."

"I'd like to see someone try to hunt me," Donalita says.

She flashes a mouthful of way too many sharp, pointy teeth, then they're gone again. She looks at my white face and wide eyes and laughs.

"Oh relax, dude!" she says. "This will be *fun*. I just wish Theo was here because he knows what to do to hunters."

Cory bristles. "We're not killing anybody," he tells her.

"Oh, pooh. What are you going to do? Sweet-talk them into letting us go on our way? Tra-la-la."

"We don't know that anybody's trying to kill us."

"We don't know that anybody's *not*, either."

"Vincenzo was," I say. "We know that. And now we know he's got some brothers running around—and some dude who's the boss of them."

Cory shoots me a dirty look. "The dogs that treed you didn't try to kill you," he says.

"Only because you called in a thousand crows," Donalita says.

"There weren't a thousand—"

"Do you have some crows here to help us?"

"No, I—"

"Right," Donalita says. "So you want to greet the kind hunters and have a nice little civilized chat with them because everybody knows that dogs don't run in packs and rev each other up."

Cory closes his eyes and takes a deep breath.

The horns sound again, closer. I know because now I can hear them.

"Look," Cory says. "Somebody has put a binding on them. They don't *want* to do this."

"Unless maybe they do," Donalita says.

"Can we just—"

"You know, I smelled *you* on that roof," she says to Cory.

"What—"

"Yeah, you do know," she says wagging her chin smugly. "The one across the street from where Josh's mother lives."

"Wait a minute," I say. "How could you know that? You were in my room with me all night."

I really want to blow this popsicle stand—I don't need

another confrontation with these dogs, so the sooner we're out of here, the better—but what she's saying has me rooted to the spot. I look from her to Cory.

He's looking back and forth at us like he thinks we're an item or something.

"Dude, it's not like that." I turn back to Donalita. "Are you telling me you went back to kill that guy anyway?"

"Of course not, silly. I promised you I wouldn't. Besides, he was already dead when I got there."

I shift my attention to Cory. "*You* killed him, dude? Hypocrite much? You're pissed that Chaingang kills a pack of vicious dog cousins who go after him and a whole bunch of us, but it's totally cool for you to go kill this unconscious guy? And before you say it, I *know* he was an asshole assassin. But the cops were going to pick him up. The dude was totally out of the game."

Cory shakes his head. "I didn't kill him."

"He didn't," Donalita agrees. "The snake cousin did it. But he was there."

"Wait a sec—what snake guy?"

Cory sighs. "Rico."

It takes me a moment to place the name.

"You mean the dude who was in the lab with Josh?" I ask. "The one who got his leg cut off?"

Cory nods. "The one who saw a bunch of cousins get dissected to see how they tick. He's been after these Black Key Securities people, taking them down one by one."

"But the word is, it looks like some wild animal's tearing them apart. A snake can't do that. Wait. How big a snake can he turn into?"

"Just a regular rattler," Cory says. "He kills them while he's in human form and it's not pretty. At first I didn't know it was him. When I finally did figure it out I tracked him down, but I got there too late. He'd already killed that latest one and disappeared."

Him saying "killed" brings me crashing back to our own situation.

"Come on," I say. "Let's split so the same thing doesn't happen to us."

"Too late," Donalita says. "Here they come."

I turn to look where she's pointing and see a half-dozen lean dogs loping steadily in our direction. They're far down the street, bounding over rubble and junked cars, but it won't take them long to reach us.

JOSH

Tío Goyo sits cross-legged in the dirt a half-dozen yards away, his back against a tree. Busted. So much for working this out on my own.

"I was practicing," I tell him. "You know—that spirit thing you showed me. I think I'm getting the hang of it."

"Good."

He studies me for a long moment, then rises in a smooth motion and starts back to our camp. I follow along, trying to decide how much to tell him.

In the end, I decide to tell him everything because what's he going to do? He gets the fire going and brews us some tea while I talk. By the time he hands me a mug, I'm done.

I sniff the steam coming from the mug, but I can't tell if anything's in there that's not supposed to be. I look over the brim to catch a smirk on his face, like he knows just what I'm thinking.

What the hell. I blow on the surface of the tea and take a sip.

"Why didn't you search for the de Padillas directly?" he asks.

"What do you mean?"

"You followed their trail, which was clever, but you already know this couple. You should be able to focus on them and go directly to where they are. It's how you'll find your friend."

"Uh … I didn't realize that." Great. Something else I have to learn. I figured as soon as I got the GPS map in my head up and running again, the main stumbling block to finding Elzie would be over.

"Don't be so worried," he says. "Look what you've already accomplished in just a couple of days."

"I suppose. But what about that hummingbird guy I met? Talk about having a chip on your shoulder."

Tío Goyo shrugs. "It's most unusual. The Hummingbird Clans are among the most joyful of the animal people. Their kindness and generosity are legend. I've never heard of an aggressive one."

"I don't know about that. Mom's got a feeder on the porch and they're always dive-bombing each other and trying to drive the other off. They seem pretty aggressive to me."

"Ordinary birds, perhaps, but I'm talking about cousins."

"Yeah, well, this cousin was a racist dick looking to pick a fight. I've been called a lot of crap but being an 'unborn' is a first."

"Family and clan are important to the cousins," Tío Goyo says. "The idea of not having either makes them uncomfortable."

"I *do* have a family. My mom and my grandparents are amazing. If they're not good enough for him, that's his problem."

"It's also yours," Tío Goyo says, his voice mild. "At least it will be if you intend to lead the cousins."

I let out an exasperated sigh. "I'm *not* leading anybody anywhere."

"Look at it this way," Tío Goyo goes on as if I hadn't spoken. "For someone from an old clan like Hummingbird, your lack of an affiliation makes you appear potentially dangerous. Here, in a society without laws or courts, respect, trustworthiness and clan affiliation all serve to keep excesses in check."

"Hey, I'm not trying to disrespect anyone. All I want to do is find Elzie and get us back to the real world. I don't even want to be here."

"He couldn't know that. You arrived in his territory without adhering to normal customs, so there was already a sense that something was off. But on a broader cultural level, in circumstances where a member of one clan causes harm to someone in another, the injured party can go to your clan and demand justice. Your clan will then either take your side—if you were in the right—or punish you if you were not. Without affiliation, only the individual can be held responsible, and then problems are solved only by who is stronger. Might is right. It's how despots are born."

"Okay, but why would he be pissed when I told him my name? The de Padillas and I exchanged names, and they weren't upset. I was just trying to be friendly to him, too—and respectful."

"Often one fears what one does not understand," Tío Goyo says. "It seems that some of these older cousins are distrustful of you and your Wildling friends because you are new. They don't necessarily want to pledge friendship and mutual respect—yet, anyway. According to past convention, giving someone your name puts the receiver in the immediate position of either accepting you as a friend, or refusing, which is a major insult and can give you justification to attack them."

"That's messed up."

Tío Goyo nods. "I agree. But what do we know? I am only a man, while apparently you are"—he smiles—"an unborn."

"Well, screw him. It's not like I'll ever see him again."

"Perhaps not, but you will meet more cousins who will judge you for how you came by your mountain lion aspect. They will either embrace you or hate you. The latter could prove dangerous if you run into a large number of them."

I kick the dirt beside me. "It's not as though I chose this."

He shrugs. "Neither of us chose the colour of our skin, yet we're still judged by it."

"Well, I had the last laugh on that jerk. You should have seen his face when I dropped my body and he saw a hawk lifting up into the air. Because he *knew* I had a mountain lion under my skin."

"I'm sure," Tío Goyo says, "though you ought to have been discreet about it."

"Oh, crap. That's one of your uncle secrets, isn't it? And I totally gave it up to him."

"It's done now."

In the east the sun's rising. Fat shafts of light slice through the boughs of the ponderosa pines.

"Get a few hours' sleep," he says. "Then we can go back to finding your friend with clear heads."

"I'm not tired."

"You've been up all night."

"It's weird," I say. "Every time I call up my body from the earth, it's like I get the perfect version of it. I'm not hungry or thirsty and I'm super alert. It's not the same when I shift back from my mountain lion form. Then I'm always really hungry."

Tío Goyo nods. "But if you don't sleep, you won't dream, and dreams nourish your spirit in a manner that nothing else can."

I think about how I've already slept right near him. There's been so much crap in my life that it wouldn't surprise me if I had a nightmare. Would he go into my brain and kill whatever was in my dream? Would he kill me? I'd rather not take that chance.

I stand up and poke at the fire with a nearby stick. "But I'm not even remotely tired," I say. "I need to be doing something. Like finding Elzie. Can you teach me about how this focus thing works?"

Tío Goyo sets his empty mug down and rises as well. "All right," he says. "So the map has returned to your head."

I nod. "I've got five different ones layered on top of each other right now."

"And how much of each world do they show?"

"I'm not sure, but I feel like I could let them expand to include as much of each world as I want to see."

"I don't advise that," he says. "In fact, it would be best for you to shut all the maps down if you can."

This is nuts. As soon as I get the GPS working again, he wants me to shut it down. What's with this guy?

"I'd rather not," I say. "What if I can't get them back?"

"Then we work on that. You'll need them later, perhaps, but not to find your friend."

I drop the stick into the fire. I feel anxious about doing what he says, but then I remind myself, if I believe the ability is still inside me, it will be. I've already proved that, haven't I?

So I go ahead and close all the maps—even the one for this world we're in. I wait a couple of beats—long enough to hum a few bars of a Bo Diddley riff—then call back the map of the de Padillas' home turf. It comes up in an instant, all the topography and every living thing in it. I let it expand a little until I can "see" Manuel and Lara, then shut it down again.

"Okay, I'm good," I tell Tío Goyo. Then I have a thought and give him a curious look. "How do *you* move between the worlds?"

"If I've been in one before, I can simply step into it," he says. "The same way I assume your friends the de Padillas can."

"And if you haven't been there before?"

"I search with my hawk's eyes—as you did to locate the de Padillas."

"You mean in your spirit form?"

He nods. "I was going to have you try that today, but you've already taught yourself."

"So now what?" I ask.

"Try to recall as many memories of your friend as you can. Fill your head with the look of her, the scent, the sound of her voice, but especially whatever it is that you *feel* when you think of her."

I have to laugh. "You mean confusion?"

His brows go up.

"I'm kind of conflicted with how I feel about her," I tell him.

"But you still have feelings for her?"

"I ..."

Sure, I do. How could I not? I've never been with anybody as wild and sexy as Elzie. The confusing thing is, I have all this longing for Marina, which is so wrong. She's either mourning Chaingang—or with him, if he somehow survived. And even if she hadn't hooked up with Chaingang, I screwed things up between us so badly that she'll never completely trust me again.

"Josh?" Tío Goyo says.

I give him a rueful grin. "I know, I know. In my own head again. Okay, so I think about Elzie and then what?"

"Focus on the need to find her and drop that need into wherever it is that you store your maps."

"How am I supposed to do that? I don't know where the maps are. You made me shut them down."

Tío Goyo nods. "All right, why don't we try this: imagine a book in your mind and inside it are all your maps."

The skepticism I'm feeling must be written all over my face because he adds, "Just try it."

This is the kind of thing Des is so good at. He can close his eyes and paint a word picture of something he's imagining, which, as you're listening to him, starts to sound so real that you end up seeing it yourself.

So how would Des do this?

I smile. The first thing is, the book would be some big, fat, old leather-bound volume like the one from the credits of *Buffy the Vampire Slayer*. It'd have embossed gold lettering on the front, in some kind of spooky Gothic font. The title would be … all I can come up with is *Book of Maps*. Des'd have a far better one, only he's not here. But it doesn't matter. I can picture the book now, just kind of floating around inside my head.

All the maps are in there, I tell myself. Maps of all the worlds I've visited so far, as well as every place I haven't been to yet. That book's not just any book. It's my magical GPS atlas and it's always going to be there, as normal to access as it is to shift into my mountain lion shape.

"I think I've got it," I say.

"You *think*?" Tío Goyo asks.

"No, no. I've definitely got it. So now I just focus on my need to find Elzie and drop it into the book?"

Tío Goyo nods. "Wait!" he adds before I can let my body fall back into the earth. "If you do find her on one of those maps, don't go directly to her. Instead, arrive somewhere nearby, so that you'll be able to scout the area instead of appearing directly in the middle of a situation you might not be able to handle."

"Good point. Maybe I should go in my spirit form."

"You could," Tío Goyo says. "But remember how you snapped back when you were first trying it last night?"

"Yeah, what was up with that?"

"It's because when you let your body return to the earth here, it serves as an anchor to this world. If you haven't established a similar anchor in the new world, any momentary distraction can snap you back."

"And I create an anchor by …?"

"Calling up your body from the matter of the new world."

"Okay, that sort of makes sense. Anything else?"

"Be careful of the cousins you meet. They might be like the de Padillas, but they might also be like the one you met from the Hummingbird Clan last night, or worse."

"I could have handled him."

Tío Goyo shakes his head. "Which would only cause more problems. Right now, you only have an issue with the Condor Clan. You don't need to add the enmity of other clans. Feuds among the cousins can last for generations, and their lives are already long."

He's echoing what Cory told me back when I first changed: don't get cocky.

Yeah, I was able to deal with Vincenzo, but what are my odds going up against his two brothers at the same time? The smart way to play this is to avoid a situation where I have to find out.

"Low profile," I tell Tío Goyo. "Got it." Then something occurs to me. "You're not coming?"

"I will if you want me to," he says. "But I think things will go more smoothly if you don't arrive in my company. The hawks of the Halcón Pueblo don't have many friends among the cousins."

"Should I be worried hanging around with you?"

He gives me a humourless smile. "Only if you become infected with an evil spirit."

I hold his gaze and realize he's really not kidding. Nice.

"Right," I say. "Well, on that cheerful note ..."

"I will be nearby," Tío Goyo says, "if you should need me. But I'll wait for a signal before approaching."

I close my eyes and take a breath, let it out slowly. I've got my handy dandy *Book of Maps* floating in my head, ready and waiting. I fill my thoughts with Elzie. The sway of her walk and the lilt of her voice. The smell of her hair, the touch of her skin. Her body against mine. I can't help getting an erection from some of these memories.

I totally believe I can do this. I *will* it to happen.

But nothing does.

After what feels like forever, but has probably only been a few minutes, I open my eyes again.

"I'm not getting anything," I tell Tío Goyo, feeling a little awkward about the bulge in my pants.

He nods, kindly ignoring the obvious. "You're doing well," he says with a wry smile, "but perhaps you're a little self-conscious. Try it again, this time in your spirit form," he says. "But when you get there, make sure you shift immediately to your human form."

"Okay," I say and let my body fall away.

As soon as my spirit rises, everything feels clearer inside me. I'm unencumbered. I call up the book. I think about Elzie again, then roll everything I know and feel about her into a tiny pulse of light that I drop onto the cover of the book. As the light sinks into it, I imagine the book opening to turn page after beautiful page, revealing maps known and unknown. The little blinking light pulses until it holds steady on a particular page.

I stare at it for a long moment. I've no idea what world that is, but I'm certain it's where I'll find Elzie.

If I had a body, I'd be grinning.

MARINA

Canejo is quiet for a long time after I finish describing the events leading up to Vincenzo's death, the awful things he'd done and intended to do, and hardest of all, how he died. Looking at him and Thorn while I talked, I was almost able to forget the dogs and condors gathered outside. But now my gaze goes beyond the window and their eerie presence fills every part of me, like a cloud shadowing the sun, like a huge wave about to pull me deep into the ocean with its undertow.

Dusk has fallen and the fires the dogs lit earlier cast a flickering light through the windowpanes. The condor men stand motionless, staring back at me. The dog cousins lie by the fires, some in human shape, others in their four-legged forms.

I wait for Canejo to comment, but Thorn speaks first.

"This friend of yours," he says. "Josh. He must be a mighty warrior."

I start to shake my head, except then I think of everything I just told them. If someone told me those things about someone they knew, I'd have the same impression.

"I guess he's turning into one," I have to admit. I don't suppose it ever really sank in until this moment.

Never mind his small stature. Josh isn't a boy anymore. He's a man. A Wildling. A freaking mountain lion, capable of … I try to push those memories aside.

For the first time in a long while I get a pang in my chest, missing him so badly because, even if he were standing right here in front of me, he wouldn't be my Josh anymore. I'm never going to get that Josh back.

"He must be confused," Thorn says.

I blink and focus on what he's saying.

"Imagine," he goes on. "To be so young to his new nature and already so formidable."

Canejo nods. "I hadn't heard this story before—all you children waking to the animals that had been living hidden under your skin. And your Tía Min says the Thunders are responsible?"

"She's not my aunt. That's just what people call her. She's this big deal back where I come from—not that you'd ever know it by looking at her."

Which you could maybe say about Canejo, too. He doesn't look like much, either, but those condor men are wary of him and I know just how powerful they are from watching their brother Vincenzo in action.

"I don't think anybody knows why it started happening," I add. "The only thing we know for sure is that after Josh became a mountain lion, kids stopped changing. He was the last one."

"Interesting."

I think about what Canejo said a moment ago. "Some of the kids with you here are Wildlings, too," I say. "Did none of them tell you about this?"

He shakes his head. "We deliberately don't talk about who or what they were before because it doesn't matter. All that matters is who they are now, and what they will become."

"I think they were chased here—just like I was—and not to study with you."

"None of us came here willingly," Canejo admits. "But how we came here doesn't change what we can accomplish now. Worldly concerns lose their potency as we teach our spirits to walk large."

I'm starting to get the prickly feeling that I've walked into a cult. I glance at Thorn, but he appears unconcerned, slouched in his seat, legs crossed at the ankles. He produces a twig from his pocket and uses its sharp end to clean his fingernails.

"Are you starting a religion here?" I ask Canejo.

"Hardly. Religions bind the spirit and I don't believe we should have intermediaries between ourselves and the Grace at the heart of the world."

I like the sound of that. It seems not so much poetic, as deep with meaning. Then I start to worry that I'm falling under the spell of the cult, if that's what they are.

"And that's what you're teaching the people who study with you here?" I ask.

He smiles. "Not really. Many arrive in a weakened emotional state. I'm teaching them how to be strong and accept themselves. My hope is that once they adjust and become stronger, they will want their spirits to grow, as well."

Movement outside catches my eye. All the dogs are on their feet, looking back in the direction that Thorn and I came from earlier. The firelight's distracting, but my Wildling vision is still good enough to pierce the shadows beyond them where a tall man approaches.

I don't have a good scale of reference, but he appears to be huge, muscular and broad-shouldered. As he gets closer I see that he must be at least seven feet tall. He has a wide face with narrow, almond-shaped eyes, a substantial nose and long white hair that dangles in a dozen or so narrow braids. At first I think he's in half-animal shape, but then I realize he has a white fur cloak draped over his shoulders. His chest and feet are bare. The only other thing he's wearing is a pair of loose-fitting trousers.

A large medallion hangs from his neck. As he continues his approach I see that the medallion has the same symbol of a thunderbolt in a circle that the dogs wear as brands and tattoos.

"I guess—" I have to clear my throat. "I guess that must be Nanuq."

Thorn's sitting up straight, staring out the window. He gives a slow nod.

I hear the faint shuffle of feet on the marble floor behind us and look over my shoulder to see that Canejo's followers are moving in our direction, Lionel at the forefront, as they also peer outside. Lionel shoots me a bitter look, then returns his gaze to what's taking place outdoors.

The dog men make a path for Nanuq; their body language as they move is that of submissives giving way to an alpha. Nanuq doesn't pay them the least bit of attention. He strides all the way forward until he's standing directly in front of the glass doors separating us. Canejo sighs and stands up.

"I suppose we have to talk to him," he says.

Can we not? I want to say. *You're a rabbit cousin. Don't rabbits always have a hidden back door out of their burrow? Couldn't we just make a break for it?*

Because there's something old and horrible in Nanuq's eyes that just makes me want to flee right now.

But when Canejo approaches the door, I find myself following him. Thorn walks beside me. Canejo's students stay mostly in the shadows beyond the firelight that comes in through the window—all except for the snarky Lionel, who steps up so that he's flanking me on the other side. I kind of don't mind. At this moment, the more of us presenting a united front against Nanuq, the better.

I take a deep breath as Canejo pushes the door open. He steps outside and we follow suit. I steal a glance at the condor men, but they've got the same submissive vibe as the dogs.

Nanuq fixes his gaze on me and it's all I can do not to back up. "I want the girl," he says.

Canejo stands with his hands in his pockets. "You know that's not how it works," he says. "She's here under my protection, unless she decides otherwise."

"She's neither your kin nor clan."

I'm trying not to react but it's hard to breathe. I can't figure out why Nanuq doesn't just grab me and haul me off. It's not like the rabbit man presents a formidable figure.

Don't get me wrong—I'm happy that Canejo's standing up for me. I just don't understand how he's able to be such a deterrent.

"That's debatable," Canejo says. "By that same argument, none of my students are kin or clan, but nevertheless they are all under my protection. As is she."

God, I wish there was somebody I knew here. Theo or Josh, or even Des. Stacy Li and the other kids from Santa Feliz hiding back there in the shadows don't count. I want somebody who really cares for me. Somebody to hold my hand and tell me, yeah, this sucks, but everything's going to be okay.

"Her friend killed Vincenzo," Nanuq says. "He needs to pay for that."

Canejo shrugs. "So take it up with her friend."

"No," Nanuq says. "He loses everyone dear to him first."

"And how does that make the world a better place?" Canejo asks. "That's still your plan, isn't it? To make the world a better place?"

"A clear message needs to be sent that I will avenge any who murder my people. Who will follow me if I don't protect them from this threat?"

"Honestly, I don't know why anybody follows you as it is."

A deep growl rumbles in the bear man's chest.

"Just give me the girl," he says, "or maybe I'll rethink my promise to leave you alone in this little warren of yours."

"Why do you really want her?" Canejo asks.

"I told you. She's the friend of the kin-slayer."

"The Condor Clan were never your kin."

"Perhaps not by blood or birth. But I have chosen them as kindred because they stand by me against a common enemy."

"I don't."

Nanuq studies him for a moment. "Be careful what side you choose. If you stand against me ..." He shrugs. "I can make quick work of a jackalope."

A jackalope? I think. Canejo's a jackalope? They're not even real. I'm mean, they're *more* not real than animal people. Animal people at least make a kind of sense. The next thing they're going to say is that yetis or elves are real.

"Can you?" Canejo asks. "I was here before the volcanoes

gave birth to cadejos. Before the winds gave dragons their wings. Before the glaciers spawned your clan."

His tone of voice reminds me of Auntie Min: calm, soft-spoken, but there's an edge of steel underlying his words.

A flicker of something flashes in Nanuq's eyes—not exactly fear, more like a moment of unease. Then it's gone.

"Don't make me ask you a third time," he says.

"You don't really think you can hurt me, do you?" Canejo asks, the edge in his voice growing sharper.

Nanuq shrugs. "Sooner or later we'll find out, but not today. Today you should consider your students. Continue with this stubbornness and I'll do more than let my hounds tease them with the odd torment. Though of course, I'd rather they stay in your warren with you, never again to dare to venture out of doors. They are lucky to be contained in Dainnan, otherwise I would have already dispatched them."

Canejo stands a little taller.

"If that's your final word," he says, "there'll be no 'later.' We'll find out where we stand right now."

"This is bullshit," Lionel says. "Just give him the girl and they'll leave us alone."

Nice, I think. The fear I've been trying to hold at bay starts up a trembling in my legs and I feel like I have to pee.

"Exactly," Nanuq says. "Be smart for a change."

"And if he tells us he wants you next," Canejo asks Lionel, "we should just give you up as well?"

"I won't," Nanuq says.

Canejo ignores him, his attention still on Lionel. "Then where does it stop?" he asks. "How many is a reasonable number before we take a stand and say enough?"

"He doesn't *want* anybody else."

"For now," Canejo says, turning back to Nanuq. "I say one is too many."

"Well, I don't," Lionel says.

Before I know what he's doing, he gives me a hard shove and I go stumbling forward. I'm too off balance to dodge Nanuq's big meaty hand as it closes over my shoulder and hauls me toward him.

"Now, was that so hard?" Nanuq asks.

JOSH

Got you, I think as I let my spirit dart through the worlds, aiming for a half mile away from where the light pulse is blinking.

I'm there in an instant, high above a wooded landscape with a ribbon of road cutting through the treed hills from east to west. To the east I can see what looks like a village or an encampment before I zoom down in among the trees and reclaim my body from the earth.

I stand there, waiting to see if anything's going to happen. I half expect to snap back to where I left Tío Goyo, but I seem to have gotten the hang of this.

I call up the map in my head and look a mile or so all around me. There are hundreds of birds everywhere, big and small. An owl, crows, cardinals, jays … mammals, too. Deer, rabbits, a fox.

And cousins, in human form. A half-dozen of them are hiding in the woods, just before a bend in the road that leads to the encampment. They're canid—I'm guessing dogs—and I assume they're guards. I look at my map more closely, then follow a game trail that runs through the forest in the general direction I want to go, but avoiding the dog people.

Through a break in the tree boughs, I note a hawk drifting

high above the forest's canopy and nod to myself. Tío Goyo followed me.

It's cool here under the canopy, the air crisp. The trees are thick with ferns and underbrush, but the game trail lets me move quietly at a good pace. I'm just congratulating myself on how I'm playing this so smart when I'm suddenly pulled up into the air, entangled in I don't know what.

It takes me completely by surprise and I start to thrash until I realize I got caught by the oldest trick in the Looney Tunes cartoon playbook. I stepped into a hidden net, and now I'm dangling six feet or so above the trail. I could rip this thing apart in moments, but I decide I want to see who comes to collect me.

I don't have long to wait.

I hear excited voices and track the approach of three of those guards I noted when I first arrived. It doesn't take them long to reach me.

They're tall, with that muscular leanness you see in a barrio dog. Their skin is darker than mine, their hair thick and a glossy black, hanging down their backs like braided ropes. They kind of remind me of extras from a Spaghetti Western: barefoot, dressed in cotton shirts and pants.

Their excitement dies down once they see me.

"It's just a kid," one of them says, clearly disappointed.

"Not just any kid," another replies, his excitement growing again. "It's *him*."

"Well, fuck me. You're right. He doesn't look like much, does he?"

"Should we cut him down?" the third asks.

"No," the first one says. "Bobo's gone to get the boss. She'll know what to do."

I just hang there letting them talk.

She, I think. Call me sexist, but I didn't take Vincenzo's boss to be a woman. Maybe it's because the two biggest role models in my life are my mom and Marina, and they're so nurturing.

The one who spoke first is talking. "What's he doing here? I thought Vincenzo said this is the kid who's going to strike the first blow of the revolution."

When he says the word *revolution*, a big dose of déjà vu fills me. I almost don't need my mental GPS to know who's approaching. But then Elzie comes around a turn in the trail, her stride loose and confident.

It hits me like a punch in the gut. She's not a prisoner. She's the boss.

CHAINGANG

Of course Auntie Min's gotta have her center of operations on the bluff overlooking Tiki Bay. Where Lenny died. Where Vincenzo also killed Tómas, threw Cory off the cliff and broke my back.

Man, I'm really starting to hate this place.

But I lead the Feds up the Pacific Coast Highway and pull into the dirt parking lot. I phoned ahead to tell J-Dog what was up, and it looks like he called in all the troops. There must be thirty, forty bikes in the lot.

Up on the cliff I can see Auntie Min's crew of crow men standing guard at the edge of the bluff, with more in their bird shapes patrolling from the sky above.

The Feds have slowed right down, stopping at the entrance instead of following me in. When they step out of the car, Solana is carrying a pump shotgun. His partner's hands are empty, but I know he's got at least one revolver at his belt, probably another in an ankle holster.

I shut off my bike and give J-Dog a nod before I walk back to the Feds' car.

"You think this is funny?" Matteson says. "You think you can get away with ambushing Federal agents?"

"This look like an ambush to you? Nobody's even got a weapon in their hands—except him." I look at Solana.

"Don't get smart with me, Washington," Matteson says.

I put up a hand before he can go on. "You're the one that's being stupid. If your partner's going to keep waving that shotgun around like a big dick, there *is* going to be trouble. Get your panties out of your ass-crack and take a couple of deep breaths."

He takes a step forward and grabs the front of my T-shirt. "Listen, you piece of shit—"

He breaks off as a lot of guns come up and point in his direction. Solana brings up his shotgun, but *come on*. What's he going to do? We've got them way outnumbered and outgunned.

"Told you," I say as I swat his hand away. "We wanted you dead, it'd already be over." I point up to the bluff. "That's where you're headed if you want to hear what Auntie Min's got to say."

"And your gang just happens to be here?"

"No. This is how we survive when the shit storm hits—by sticking together. Now tell your partner to put down his gun and come talk to the old lady."

Matteson has a sour look on his face. "This is bullshit," he says, then spits on the dirt beside him.

I turn to Solana. "Is it? You think *los tíos* set you up for an ambush? You think I'm using their name just so that we can blow your asses away?"

Solana glares at me for a long moment before he finally lowers the shotgun.

"He's right," he tells his partner.

I give a small shake of my head at J-Dog. He makes a motion

with his hand and all of the gang's weapons disappear back into waistbands and the holsters on their bikes. I turn toward the bluff and give J-Dog a nod over my shoulder. He breaks away from the others and joins me, then we start to climb up the hill.

"I've got this," I say to J-Dog. "Let me do the talking."

He doesn't look happy, but he gives me a nod.

The Feds have taken a moment to have a little confer with each other, but now they tag along behind us. Like I knew they would.

Going up the incline, I remember the last time I was here, walking hand in hand with Marina. It was dark; now it's day, and she's not here. I feel a pang of loneliness. The only thing that's the same is the sound of the waves pounding on the rocks below, the salt tang in the air.

We pass through the perimeter guarded by the crow men and keep going through the tall grass until we reach the top of the bluff. There's a bunch of cousins up there and I don't know any of them except for Rico, who was locked up with Josh in the ValentiCorp labs before they escaped. He and Auntie Min are facing off, and I've never seen her so pissed. But Rico isn't backing down. He's not a big guy—paler than most of the cousins I've seen, except for Vincenzo, with short-cropped yellow hair—but he's tall on attitude.

"—doesn't matter," he's saying to Auntie Min. "It's done."

"Of course it *matters*!"

"You weren't there. You didn't see what they did to the kids in the labs and those guys knew it all along. But they still rounded us up and dumped us there to be diced up. They cut off my freaking leg!"

"I know, but—"

"They deserved a harder death than I gave them."

We're far enough away that only I can hear what he's saying, but I shout out a warning anyway: "Hey, Auntie Min! I brought those Feds you wanted to see."

Rico immediately gives me a look to let me know he registers the warning. The tension's still thick between him and Auntie Min, but at least they're not talking about whether or not the guys from Black Key deserved to die.

Do I need to tell you whose side of the argument I'm on? I don't know Rico all that well, but if he's the one who's been hunting down those sons of bitches, I'd like to pin a medal on that skinny little chest of his.

We climb the rest of the way and make the introductions. Several of these cousins are unfamiliar to me, and I can't tell what their animal skins are, either. The older cousins can just look at each other and know, but I haven't got that trick figured out yet. I do see—maybe *feel* is a better way to put it—the rattlesnake that's a part of Rico, and Auntie Min's big-ass moth, but I already knew their animal shapes.

The others? Not so much. One guy looks a lot like the crow men guarding the perimeter, so I figure he's one of them. Maybe he's the boss, if they have that kind of hierarchy. Crow boy is Lalo. Then there's a pair that look like twins—a Native American cast to their colouring and features. Male and female, but they both have long black hair hanging in braids. They're dressed in plain white tees, jeans and pointy-toed cowboy boots with a lot of fancy tooling on them. She's Ana, he's Jimmy and they're both glowering. It's hard to tell what they're so pissed off about—our arrival, the other cousins or maybe the whole world.

The last one's standing with his back to us, looking out over the ocean. When Auntie Min calls his name and he turns, I realize he's not a cousin. He's an old Mexican man, long grey hair tied back in a ponytail, his brown features heavily creased with age lines.

"Tío Benardo," Solana says, surprise in his voice.

I'm not surprised to find out he's one of the hawk uncles. It's not just that he looks like he's related to Tío Goyo—he's got that same "there's more to me than meets the eye" vibe going for him. But I was under the impression that *los tíos* and the cousins aren't exactly BFFs, which makes me wonder what he's doing here.

Tío Benardo steps up to Solana and takes his hand with both of his own.

"It's good to see you again, little brother," he says. "You're looking as well as Goyo told me you were."

Then he steps back and nods to Matteson. Matteson gives back a stone face.

"Any word from Cory?" I ask Auntie Min.

She shakes her head. "I understand your worry, but if anyone can find her, it will be Cory. You will just need to be patient."

"Not exactly my strong suit."

"Who's Cory?" Matteson asks.

"It's a whole other business," I tell him before anyone can answer. "We're here about Householder, the ass-wipe congressman."

Matteson doesn't like to be shut down. No surprise there.

"Sure, but—"

I cut him off, saying, "I just want to go on record to say that saving him seems counterproductive to—well, pretty much everything."

Matteson gives me a sharp look.

"'Course," I add, "I've been outvoted on this, so I'll have to go along with saving his sorry ass."

Auntie Min shakes her head. "You are eloquent as ever, Theo."

"Somebody *else* want to tell us why we're here?" Matteson asks.

"As Theo says, to prevent the assassination of Congressman Householder," Auntie Min says.

Matteson nods. "Right, except I thought you'd already stopped the guy behind it."

"Vincenzo *was* stopped," Auntie Min tells him, "but he wasn't working alone. We've learned that his brothers are also involved, and that there is someone else behind them—the same unknown entity who has enslaved a number of the Canid Clan."

Matteson puts up his hand. "Wait a minute," he says. *"Enslaved?"*

I ignore him and look at Auntie Min. "How do we know they didn't *choose* to join Vincenzo's gang?" I ask.

I hear a growl in somebody's chest and realize it's coming from either Ana or Jimmy—the pair that look like Native American twins. So I figure they're dog cousins and now I know why they're so pissed off. Considering what went down back at the clubhouse earlier today, I must be at the top of their shit list.

Lalo—the guy I take for one of the crow men—answers me. "The brands they wear make it clear."

"Brands?" Matteson and Solana both repeat at the same time.

"Just gang tats," I say, to shut them up.

Auntie Min nods. "Some may have chosen to follow this unknown leader, but several others were coerced. We have no idea how many we face in total. But we do know that Vincenzo and his brothers planned to force Josh to kill the congressman."

"Where *is* Josh?" Matteson asks.

No one says anything for a long moment. Then Solana clears his throat.

"I've already told him about the otherworld," he says.

Auntie Min shakes her head and sighs. The other cousins seem pissed.

Tío Benardo nods. "A man must trust his partner."

"Except he's a goddamn Federal agent," Jimmy the dog man says. "Next thing you know, they'll be trying to put us on reservations while they strip-mine the otherworld."

"Watch your mouth," Matteson snaps at him before he glances at Solana, then turns back to Auntie Min. "My partner here already explained how all of this can't go any further than us." He waits a beat, then adds, "Josh is really in this otherworld?"

She nods.

"What the hell's he doing there?"

"Looking for his ex-girlfriend," I say, "because Vincenzo was planning to kill her. Josh is hoping to rescue her before Vincenzo's friends find out that he's dead."

"The kid's got balls," Matteson says. "I'll give him that." He returns his attention to Auntie Min. "So why do you need us?"

Lalo answers for her. "Extra security. We can field enough bodies to keep an eye on the crowd," he says, "but we need you to survey everything behind the scenes."

Solana nods toward the ring of crow men guarding the bluff. "You're going to stand out like a sore thumb," he says.

"We won't all be going as five-fingered beings," Lalo replies.

"Most will watch from the skies and other vantage points. Theo's men will be in the crowd itself, where they'll—"

"You must be kidding me," Matteson breaks in. "You'd trust crowd control to a bunch of gangbangers? Are you out of your minds?"

"Hey!" J-Dog and I say at the same time.

"You want us or not?" J-Dog adds, obviously pissed. "As though we give a shit about your ass-wipe politician."

Matteson ignores us both. "And what makes you think we even believe you?" he asks Auntie Min. "For all we know, *you're* the problem and you're just trying to use us to get inside intel."

"We don't want intel," Lalo tells him. "We just want your eyes watching out in the places we can't go."

"Secret Service will take care of that," Solana says.

Lalo nods. "Yes, and if any of them are in on it? We can't get access to their inner circle to find out. You're FBI. They won't stop you."

"Why don't we just advise them about the threat?" Matteson asks. "Then they'll up their own security, or maybe even cancel the stupid rally."

"Sure," Lalo says. "We'd prefer that it be cancelled. But we've been told that Householder isn't the kind to listen to advice."

I've heard all of this before, so I tune them out. I can't stop thinking about Marina. I just want to take Auntie Min aside and have her show me how to do the world-walking trick so that I can go find her. But Auntie Min's caught up in this circling conversation and anyway, even if I could get her alone, she probably wouldn't help me.

I look around the headland. The crow men are doing a good job keeping the perimeter safe. They've all got their backs to us, checking for danger instead of listening to all this bullshit. When I turn back, both Jimmy and Ana are staring daggers at me. If they're dog cousins, I suppose the same rules apply as they do with actual dogs. If you don't want to seem aggressive, you look away.

I lock my gaze on theirs.

None of us have hackles in our human shapes, but if we did, they'd be bristling.

Everything around me fades away: the headland and the crow men guards, the Feds, my brother, the cousins. I don't hear the pound of the waves below or the—let's be polite and call it "conversation" between Matteson and Lalo and the others. Instead, I'm completely focused on the silent exchange I'm having with these dog twins.

You want a piece of me? I'm telling them. *Bring it on. If you think you've got the balls to—*

A slap on the back of my head brings me back to the present.

"Enough!" Auntie Min says. "And that goes for you, too," she tells the twins. "There's too much at stake here for you fools to indulge yourselves with your petty disputes."

J-Dog can't repress a snicker. "Shades of Grandma," he whispers to me.

"Petty?" Ana says. "You call butchering our brothers *petty?*"

Auntie Min shakes her head. "No. But they were hunting Theo. I don't excuse how he dealt with the problem, but I know he did what he felt he had to do."

"Just like we're going to, right now," Jimmy says, baring a mouthful of canine teeth and taking a step toward me.

Before he can get any closer, this huge moth starts to manifest above Auntie Min and her face darkens and shakes with anger.

Except for the dog twins and me, all the other cousins take a cautious step back, out of the line of fire. Solana looks like he's about to crap his pants. Matteson's jaw drops and his hand inches toward the holster on his belt. Tío Benardo watches with interest, but doesn't move. J-Dog—bless his twisted little heart—just stands there, arms folded across his chest like he sees this kind of thing every frigging day.

"No," Auntie Min says, her voice hard. "First, we will finish *this* business and then you can see to your own follies. Or you can leave. But you will *not* disrupt us a moment longer. Is that understood?"

Auntie Min likes to pretend the cousins don't have bosses, but who are we kidding? When she says jump, pretty much everybody asks how high.

The dog twins give quick nods, then hang their heads.

Me, I'm sorry she stopped the bastard. I would have loved to take him and his bitch sister.

Matteson lets his hand fall away from the butt of his gun as the moth vanishes back into Auntie Min.

"What the hell was *that*?" he asks.

"*La Mariposa de la Muerte,*" Solana says in a soft voice.

Tío Benardo laughs. "There's no such thing."

Solana turns to him. "But—"

"You saw her cousin aspect—formidable, to be sure, but nothing more."

Either *los tíos* have *cojones* bigger than anybody here, or Benardo knows something the rest of us don't.

Auntie Min ignores him. Her hard gaze is now on me. "And you, little mouse," she says. "You're as much to blame as these dogs. Stop this juvenile behaviour or go."

"Sure, happy to," I tell her. "Just show me how to cross over so that I can look for Marina myself."

She sighs. "I told you. Have patience. You have no idea what it's like. You'd get so lost so quickly that even Cory might not be able to find you."

"Maybe that's the chance I need to take."

"Wait one more day," she says. "Help us with this rally and I swear we'll find her. If Cory doesn't track her down, I'll take you over myself."

I don't say anything for a long moment. I glance at the dog twins, then look back at Auntie Min. What do I care about that jerk-off congressman or even the other cousins? I owe Auntie Min for helping me out when I first changed, but how much do I owe? When is the slate wiped clean?

"Are we in or out of this dog-and-pony show?" J-Dog asks me.

I raise a hand to shut him up.

"As soon as the rally's over and the congressman is safe," I say to Auntie Min, "then you'll show me how to cross over?"

"As I said, I'll take you myself," she says.

"If I don't take care of you first," Jimmy says.

J-Dog stiffens beside me, but I put my hand out to remind him to cool it. I'd love to put this dog bastard down, but it's not going to happen now.

"Maybe you've got a solid beef with me," I say to Jimmy, "and maybe you don't. But you get in my way before I can find Marina and I'll cut you down. And then I'll make it my personal business to get rid of every mongrel cousin in a fifty-mile radius, just to drive the point home."

Jimmy makes another move toward me, but stops when

J-Dog pulls that big handgun of his from out of his belt. The muzzle points right at the dog boy's head and doesn't waver.

"Theo," Auntie Min begins.

"I'm not starting anything," I tell her. "But I'm not taking crap from anybody, either." I motion for J-Dog to put away his gun.

"So we're back on board?" he says.

"I was never not on board," I tell him. "But if Auntie Min would've shown me how to get to where Marina is, I'd leave this part to the rest of you."

I turn to Matteson and Solana. "What about you guys?"

"Look, no offence," Matteson begins, but he breaks off when J-Dog laughs. "Something funny?"

J-Dog nods. "Every time somebody says that, they're just setting up to diss you."

"Yeah, well—"

Solana turns to Matteson. "We *have* to do this," he says. And just like that old married couple that I imagined them to be a while ago, they look at each other and have this silent conversation. Finally, Matteson nods and looks Auntie Min in the eye.

"Okay," he says. "We'll keep an eye out for problems on our side. But we're not passing along intel, and if it looks like it's going to impact national security, we'll have no choice but to bring the chief in on it."

Lalo the crow man nods, then pulls out a roll of paper and opens it up to show a hand-drawn map of the park and the neighbouring blocks.

"Let me show you where our people will be," he says.

JOSH

"Josh?" Elzie says when she recognizes me, a big grin spreading across her face.

"*You're* the boss?" I say, hoping against hope that I'm wrong.

Her smile gets wider as she gazes up at me. "Yeah. Cool, huh? We're working on a plan for cleaning up the earth. I'm so happy to see you."

Maybe I shouldn't be surprised. When I was going out with her, we had a lot of talks about the state of the world and the environment, and the reactions of people to Wildlings and cousins. I agreed with her on some points, but never on her extreme ideas about how to solve the world's problems.

Like killing people who happen to get in the way.

I still don't know *how* that's supposed to solve anything. Or why she'd align herself with someone like Vincenzo, who hates Wildlings probably even more than he does humans.

She's dyed her short hair blond, with about a quarter inch of dark auburn roots showing. As always, she looks effortlessly gorgeous.

Elzie laughs. "But I'm not the big boss," she says. "I'm just doing my bit to make our world a better place. The guy that runs this camp is named Sandino, but he's off with Nanuq at the moment. God, it's so good to see you." She looks at me like she wants to eat me up. If you catch my drift.

I don't say anything in reply. I still can barely believe that she actually sided with these creeps.

The pause grows longer and more awkward until I guess she sees something in my face.

Her face softens, and she motions to the lush woods all around us. "Look around you, Josh. Our world was like this before humans put their destructive stamp on it. Nanuq says it's still not too late to make things better."

"By killing people."

She clenches her fists in frustration. "Why do you always have to go there?" she asks. "Nobody's deliberately *planning* to kill anybody. Sure, some people might get hurt if they get in the way of the process, but nobody's making them put their lives at risk."

"How does murdering Congressman Householder fall under your plan of not killing anybody? Or how about a bunch of kids who, through no fault of their own, became Wildlings? Or what about Vincenzo killing Tomás? And Chaingang? And threatening to kill my mom and everyone I care for—including *you*?"

"I don't know what you're talking about."

She turns to one of the dog cousins who first showed up when I was caught. "Would somebody cut him down? I'm getting a crick in my neck talking to him like this."

"Don't bother," I say.

I stand up in the netting, rip a hole in it, then drop to the ground. I land lightly on my feet right in front of Elzie. She doesn't flinch, but the dog cousins do, then pretend nothing ever happened.

I look Elzie directly in the eye. I can't believe I was so stupid as to think she needed to be rescued.

"Why are you staring at me like that?" she says. Her expression softens and she puts an index finger under my chin. I swat her hand away.

"Like what? Like I'm looking at somebody I thought I knew, but it turns out she can cold-bloodedly murder God knows how many people?"

She grabs my shirt. "How many times do I have to tell you that nobody's planning to—"

"Shut up," I tell her, swatting her hand away again.

"Hey," one of the dog cousins says. "Don't talk to her like that."

I turn in his direction and he takes a step back. Then he realizes what he's doing.

"Don't get smart, kid," he says. "We outnumber you, in case you haven't noticed."

"Well, you'd better go get yourselves some reinforcements," I tell him before turning back to Elzie. "Where's this Nanoo guy?"

"Nanuq," she corrects me. "Why are you being like this? Why are you even here? Vincenzo said you were going to help get the first phase of the revolution into motion."

"Vincenzo figured that wrong. I wouldn't be his puppet, like you."

She bristles. "Where is he, anyway?"

"After he killed Tomás and Chaingang, he had a fatal accident."

"What?"

I'm studying her. Except for the hair, she looks the same, but I can't believe she's all caught up with these people.

"He's dead," I say. "Killed by a Wildling he was threatening. He picked the wrong side to be standing on. Just like all of you."

"No way," one of the dog cousins says. "Vincenzo could take down a hundred Wildlings."

"Who's Tomás?" Elzie asks.

"An elder from L.A. One of the elders who *doesn't* have a hate-on for Wildlings."

"Nobody has a hate-on for Wildlings except for humans."

"Keep telling yourself that while you take me to Nanuq."

"He's not here."

"Then take me to where he is."

"Listen, Josh," she says. "You can't just waltz in here and start insulting me and ordering me around."

"Try me," I tell her.

Part of me really hurts that I was so taken in by her. The other part wants to drive her in the face. I'm not proud of that. But here's the thing: it turns out that no matter how fast or strong you are, or what kind of superpowers you get, you still can't make somebody else be the person you want them to be.

She glares at me. "What the hell's the matter with you?"

I want to say, *you betrayed me*, but she didn't. She's exactly who she's always been. Same beliefs, just ramped up a notch. I'm the one who had the movie running in his head that she needed to be rescued.

And maybe she does. She might be naive enough to think of Vincenzo as some kind of golden boy, but the truth is, he was planning to get rid of all the Wildlings, so her head was on the chopping block, too. But there's nothing I can do about it. I know how stubborn she is, and nothing I say is going to change her mind.

She's picked her side. She'll just have to live or die by her choice.

I realize she's waiting for me to say something, so I just say, "Where'd you get the hair dye?"

She lifts a hand and ruffles her hair. "I had somebody pick it up back in our old world." I can see her start to relax a little. She cocks a hip, posing. "You like?"

"And you don't see a problem with introducing pollutants into this perfect world of yours?"

Her eyes flash. "Oh, for God's sake."

I sigh. "Yeah, I didn't think so. Just bring me to this Nanuq guy."

"I don't know where he is," she says. "You can wait for him at the camp."

I'm trying to make smart choices instead of letting my temper take over. What my gut wants is to wait for Nanuq and somehow demobilize him and this crazy plan. But if Nanuq is Vincenzo's boss, he's probably even meaner and tougher than the condor cousin. Plus there's Vincenzo's brothers to take into account, and who knows how many dog cousins. I can't take them all on by myself, and though I can still sense Tío Goyo floating in the sky above, he's not going to drop down to help me. Not unless Nanuq's hosting an evil spirit.

Just before coming here, I told myself to avoid these guys. The only reason I came was to save Elzie, and now it turns out she's one of them. It's all so crazy. The smart thing is to go back to Auntie Min and Cory with what I know, and then plan how to deal with this.

"Yeah, not happening," I tell her.

"I thought you wanted to meet Nanuq."

"I changed my mind."

She shakes her head. "It doesn't work that way, Josh. You're here now. You know where we are. So you're coming back to the camp with us. Nanuq will decide what happens next."

She's just as cute as ever, but any attraction I once felt is completely gone. It's ironic. Here I am thinking about how misguided and naive she is, yet the signs that she was headed in this direction were all there and I chose to ignore them.

"And if I refuse?" I ask.

"Don't be stupid. Like Lil' Toro said, we've got you outnumbered. Don't make this go hard on yourself."

"I never really knew you, did I?" I say.

She shrugs and doesn't respond.

"But you don't really know me, either."

She frowns. "What's that supposed to mean?"

"Well, you'd think you'd be a little smarter before making threats to the guy who dealt with your big scary Vincenzo. Do you really think there are enough of you to make me do *anything* I don't want to do?"

"Liar!" one of the dog cousins says. "There's no way a little twerp like you could take him on and still be standing."

The others are nodding.

But Elzie's giving me a careful study. "Is this true?" she says. "You really went up against him and came out without even a bruise?"

"Man," Lil' Toro says. "Vincenzo hears that bullshit and he's going to hunt you down and cut you up into so many little pieces, ain't nobody going to know what you once looked like."

"Funny thing," I say. "That's exactly what happened to Vincenzo."

I think it's starting to sink in that I'm telling the truth, because their body language has gone from swaggering to wary.

"But don't worry," I say, turning back to Elzie. "Unlike you and your little gang of terrorists—"

She stamps her foot. "We're *not* terrorists!"

I shake my head. "You only get to say that if you win, and are the ones in charge of lying to the history book. But right now that's exactly what you are."

"So you're going to do what?" she says. "Try to take us all down?"

"Oh, I'm taking the high road. I'm going after the one who's in charge—not you pissy little drones."

I know Tío Goyo's going to be mad, but I don't really care. I let my body fall away and rise up above them in my spirit form. They stare up at me with open mouths.

"—the fuck?" Lil' Toro says, turning to Elzie. "He's supposed to be Mountain Lion Clan."

"He is," she murmurs.

"Then why am I seeing a freaking hawk?"

"I ... I don't know ..."

I'd laugh, except nothing about any of this is funny. Not Elzie and her wannabe revolutionaries below. Not Tío Goyo above me, who's probably totally ticked off about what I've just done.

I am so fed up with this. Sick of fanatics, and racists, and all these people that I can't trust but who still try to tell me what

I'm supposed to do. Humans, cousins, hawk uncles—they're all the same.

What I need is to be with people I *can* trust.

Des. Marina.

I don't have to work to call up a little pulsing spark to represent either of them. They're always alive in my head. I take the one of Marina and drop it into the book of maps in my head. When the pages flip by until the light stops on a map, I will myself to where she is.

DES

"Tell me you've got a plan," I say to Cory as the dogs come charging down the street toward us.

"The plan is, we wait to see what they want," he says.

"And if they want to eat us?"

"Don't be stupid. They'll no more want to eat you than you would them."

"But if they do attack?" I ask.

"They won't. We'll talk this out. I won't raise my hand against my brothers."

I don't have his faith. I take a few steps to the side of the road and pick up a couple of good-sized stones. When I glance at Donalita, she flashes her teeth and nods her approval.

"Don't worry," she tells me. "They come at us and I'll hurt them."

"Nobody does *anything* until I say so," Cory warns us.

"Yeah?" I say. "Who died and made you God?"

But now the dogs are here circling around us, shoulders hunched, hackles up and tails raised. They look like the kind you see in the barrio—lean and tough, with a lot of pit bull and

Rottweiler in the mix. Six of them, each a little more hard-eyed than the next. They've all got the lightning brand.

Three of them change into humans and their brands become tattoos. Cory nods and smiles at the one that appears to be the leader.

"*Que pedo, wey?*"

"Don't try to make nice with me, pup," the dog man responds. "You're not my *buddy* and you've just walked yourself into a situation that you can't bullshit your way out of."

The other two dog men laugh. Maybe the dogs do too, but it's not something I could ever tell.

Cory stiffens and stands a little straighter. I don't know what's made him more mad: the leader's rude dismissal of his friendly overture, or the pack's mocking laughter.

"Do you know who I am?" he asks.

The leader nods. "You're one of Coyote's pissant little whelps. Oh, wait. That's what you call us. Let's call you a little Coyote wannabe."

Cory's eyes narrow. "Don't make me change my mind."

"What the hell's that supposed to mean?"

"It means," Donalita says, "that he's letting me off the leash."

The leader looks even more confused.

"Maybe you'd like to start over," Cory says. "And this time show us a little respect."

The dog man spits in response. Before the gob hits the pavement, Donalita's in motion. She moves so fast that I don't really see how she does it, but between one breath and the next she has the dog man down on the ground, his cheek on the gob and the blade of a knife pressed against his throat. She's applying enough pressure to make the skin pucker and I half expect to see a gusher of blood any second now.

Where'd she get that knife?

"Make a move," Donalita says to the rest of the pack, "and he's dead. I'll get at least one more of you, and Cory's good for two. Who dies next after this one?" She smiles. "La-la-la. The ones that are the bravest, of course."

The dogs growl. Their human counterparts glare. But not one makes a move.

Cory sits on his haunches beside Donalita.

"Last chance," he tells the leader. "Play nice—like you should have in the first place."

Donalita adds a little more pressure and I have to look away for a second.

"You're out of your territory," the dog man says, speaking carefully out of the side of his mouth with that knife still at his throat. Strings of filthy spit reach across his lips as he talks. It's gross, dude.

Cory shakes his head. "Don't play that game. We're neither five-fingered beings nor animals. Every territory belongs to every cousin."

"Not this one. He made this place."

That makes no sense to me, but Cory nods.

"Who are we talking about?" he asks.

"I can't say."

"Can't or won't?"

The dog man just looks at him. Cory reaches out and touches the tattoo on the dog man's bicep.

"Because of this?"

Still no response, but Cory nods again. "What are you supposed to do with us?" he asks.

The dog man glances from Cory to Donalita and back again. Clearly, it's almost impossible for him to talk with the knife's edge about the break the skin.

"Easy, cousin," Cory tells her and I see the dog man's neck muscles relax as she puts less pressure on the knife. Still, she holds it in place, ready to draw blood.

The dog man swallows. "Normally, nothing. It's easy to get in, but there's only one way out. We just let you go your own way unless we get the order to run a hunt."

"But today?" Cory asks.

"Today we're supposed to round up whoever we find and take them in to see the boss."

"Okay, then." Cory stands up. "Let him go, Donalita."

She says "What?" and I say "Dude!" at the same time, with the same disbelief.

"They're going to take us to see the boss," Cory says. "I want to look him in the face, this cousin who puts such a binding on members of the Canid Clan that they don't show even a modicum of respect to their kin."

Donalita holds Cory's gaze for a long moment, then shrugs. She flows to her feet. I catch a glimpse of a leather sheath at the small of her back as she slips the knife back into it. Then she's standing beside me.

The leader gets carefully to his feet and wipes the spittle from his face with his sleeve, eyeing Donalita the whole time. Then he puts his hand on his throat and looks at the palm, but there's no blood. Donalita never broke the skin. Finally he turns back to Cory.

"The boss takes a dislike to you," he says, "you don't survive."

"He's not going to do anything to me," Cory says, his voice cheerful. "Why would he? I'm just a little Coyote wannabe."

The dog man's gaze slides away from Cory's.

"But the thing about my great-grandfather's bloodline," Cory goes on, "is that it doesn't matter what you do to us. We always come back. We're the story that never ends and our memories are long."

"We're just following orders," the dog man says.

"I know," Cory says. "So follow your orders. Take us to see the boss." He starts walking in the direction that the pack came from.

The leader looks at us. Donalita bares a mouthful of sharp teeth at him, then takes my hand and we follow Cory, trailing a dozen or so feet behind him. A pair in dog shape lope ahead to flank Cory on either side. The rest of the pack falls in behind us.

"What did he mean by that?" I ask Donalita. "That thing about always coming back?"

"The story goes," she says, "that you can't kill his ancestor—the original Coyote. Or rather, you can, but he just shows up again, good as new. The whole Coyote Clan are supposed to carry that ability in their blood."

"Good for him. But if they kill us, we're not coming back."

She smiles. "Thoughtless little shit, isn't he?"

"Enough talking!" the leader of the dog men says from behind us.

Donalita lets go of my hand. She turns so that she's walking backwards, facing the dog men.

"What about singing and dancing?" she asks. "Are they taboo, too?"

"Just shut up and keep walking."

Donalita's smile gets bigger, but it doesn't reach her eyes. Those have gone dark and cold.

"I can still kill you," she says, her voice sweet and friendly. "Without even breaking a sweat. Or maybe I'll just cut out your tongue so that *you'll* shut up. What do you think about that?"

We're outnumbered two to one. When those other dog men had us treed in the palm, she was worried about the odds of taking them on. Now she just doesn't seem to care. Maybe that's why she's able to face them down. Or maybe it's because they saw how fast she took down their leader, but not one of them meets her gaze.

"Yeah, I didn't think so," she says. "Anybody have some gum?"

Remind me to never get on her bad side.

She turns around again so that we're walking side by side and gives me a nudge with her elbow.

"So, dude," she says. "What do you think of the otherworld so far?"

I try to match her upbeat mood.

"Pavement quality sucks," I tell her.

CHAINGANG

"These people are a bunch of douchebags," J-Dog says.

I nod. "Can't argue with that."

We drove over to city hall in a beat-up Toyota that we borrowed from Tall Boy's sister. Now standing in civvies, we watch workers putting the finishing touches on the stage that's been set up in front of city hall. A big "Humans for Humanity" banner hangs above the back of the structure. I wonder if the mayor sees the irony of hosting a rally that wants to see so many of his constituents put in camps. I guess since we're too young to vote, he doesn't care.

"So why are you giving them backup?" J-Dog asks.

"Remember when I did your time in county?" I say.

"Well, sure. Like I'm ever going to forget how you—"

I wave off whatever he's going to say. "Stuff happened in there. Everybody knew why I was inside—whose time I was doing."

"Yeah, so?"

"I got props for being a stand-up guy. Not just from our crew, but from the Kings that were in there, too. Hell, even the skinheads let me be, which is almost the same thing as respect for them."

"Because they knew I'd put a bullet in their head if they messed with you."

"No—because they understood about having somebody's back. I got respect for doing your time. I didn't make friends, but nobody took a run at me."

"Your point being?"

"Some of these douchebags aren't actually douchebags. They've got my back and I have to do the same."

"Okay," J-Dog says. "I get that."

"The real question is, why the hell are *you* helping out?" I say.

I let the pissed-off look start to build before I laugh, letting him know I understand.

"Asshole," he says.

We go back to scoping out the area.

"Well, the old lady's already got her troops on site," J-Dog says.

I nod. I've seen the crows watching from trees, telephone poles and the roof of city hall. And there are more dogs around than you'd expect. Yeah, call me paranoid. I checked them for brands and they came up clean. But that doesn't mean I trust them.

We spend another half hour on site, walking the perimeter of the grounds in front of the stage. We note the cheap fencing that's been erected behind the stage, creating a corridor to a door on the ocean side of city hall.

"What's that supposed to keep out?" J-Dog asks.

I shrug. "Considering it'll be crawling with Secret Service, it should do the job of keeping the crowd away."

"I could be through that flimsy piece of shit before they'd even think about drawing their guns."

"Yeah, but we're not here to take on the Secret Service. We're working with them, even if they don't know it."

"Huh. We should tell Grandma—give her something to be proud about for a change."

"You want to start that conversation?" I ask.

He chuckles. "You mean, start with you being able to change into a mouse? Hell, yeah."

I roll my eyes.

"Which reminds me," he goes on. "When do I get to see this happen? I've got some cheese back at the crib if you're looking for incentive."

I take the high road and ignore him.

We plan out where we'll put the boys to get the widest coverage of the crowd, then finally head back to the car. Halfway there, we're met by Matteson and Lalo.

"Well, no one's going to let you into their country club," Matteson says, "but the pair of you clean up pretty good."

I can feel J-Dog getting annoyed beside me, but I take Matteson's comment for what it is: a little friendly ribbing. This is Matteson doing his best to work with us.

"How're things going on your end?" I ask.

Matteson frowns. "Tomorrow's shaping up to be a real clusterfuck," he says. "I just found out that Householder's team is busing in hundreds of people. We're probably looking at double the crowd we planned on."

That's not good.

"Did you check out the security behind the scenes?" I ask.

"You mean, are any of them Wildlings? How the hell would

I know? Is there even a way to tell?" He gives me a hopeful look, but even if there were a way for regular people to spot us, I wouldn't tell. That'd be all the ammunition they'd need to round us up.

"Only if you're a cousin yourself," I say. "Can you slip me or Lalo back there?"

He shakes his head. "But we've run down everybody on the security detail and nothing's jumping out. Al and I and that dickwad Danny Reed have been assigned to liaise between the Secret Service, the sheriff's department and our own people, so that's good. So long as Reed doesn't screw things up."

"Who's Reed?" I ask.

"One of you. I think he's some kind of antelope."

"And he's a freakin' FBI agent?" J-Dog asks.

Matteson ignores the implied insult. "Nah. More like a consultant. But maybe he can check for other Wildlings back there."

"Probably," I say, "but what do you know about him?"

Matteson shrugs. "Not much. I don't like him, but he's been working with us for a while now, and the chief wants to keep him."

"What if he's the assassin?" Lalo says.

"Then we take him down," Matteson says, "but I don't see it. He's not smart enough—has one of those faces that can't hide what he's thinking. And anyway, he doesn't have the balls. The important thing is, some of us are behind the scenes. Al's talking to the sheriff right now."

I look back at the stage.

"So now we wait for tomorrow," I say, "and hope the whole thing doesn't blow up in our faces."

MARINA

As soon as Nanuq's hand closes on my shoulder, I know I'm finished. It doesn't matter what anybody does in retaliation, Nanuq's going to kill me first. He can snap my neck without even trying. It's like that moment just as you're wiping out on some huge wave—you know you're coming down hard and there's not a thing you can do about it. You just go limp and hope nothing gets broken.

But there's no way I'm going to survive this.

I hear Canejo yell something, but my blood's rushing in my ears and I can't focus on what he's saying.

My whole awareness is narrowed down to those rock-hard fingers on my shoulder.

God, I wish Chaingang was here with a big gun in his hand.

Or that Josh would show up and tear Nanuq into little pieces the way he did Vincenzo.

But there's only me. Chaingang and Josh don't even know where I am. Canejo—even if he has all kinds of powers—won't be able to move quickly enough to save me. I'm sure Thorn's heart is in the right place, but I can't see him even being in the running. As for Lionel ... well, he's the reason Nanuq's got me.

The little freaking *puto* pushed me right into the giant's grasp. I wish I could wipe that ugly smirk off his face.

It's thinking of Lionel that does it. The idea of him getting away with this.

I know that whatever I do is only going to postpone the inevitable, but I've never just given up without a fight, and I'm not going to start now.

I hang limp in Nanuq's grip as he's arguing with Canejo. He's not paying any attention to me—why would he? What could I possibly do?

Well, I can do this.

With all my Wildling strength and speed, I knee the big jerk right in his *cojones*. I don't care how big and tough a guy is. Hit him where it hurts and you do some pain.

The roar that pulls out of him makes my heart sing.

His grip loosens enough for me to pull free and I roll away— but not before I rip that medallion from his chest.

And then I go invisible, just like Thorn showed me. I pull that mental cloak of invisibility over me and disappear.

If Nanuq was pissed off at getting kneed in the groin, my stealing his medallion makes him crazy.

I'm right in between the two condors and Nanuq, so not in any kind of a safety zone. All someone has to do is bump into me and they'll know where I am. But I don't dare move. I don't think I can keep my invisibility except by staying utterly still.

"Find that little bitch!" Nanuq orders.

The condors start to look around, then stop when they see that none of the dogs are moving—neither the ones in human shape, nor the ones that are still canines.

Nanuq focuses a glare on the nearest group.

"Are you deaf?" he says. "Find her. Bring her to me."

One of the dog men shakes his head. "No. You don't command us anymore."

"I could break you like a twig," Nanuq tells him.

"Probably. But could you break us all?"

The other dogs are drifting over from the various fires.

It's the medallion, I realize. It doesn't only open a way out of this world. It also controls the dogs, and if Nanuq doesn't have it, they don't have to listen to him anymore.

Then another thought comes to me.

I'm holding the medallion now. Does that mean they have to listen to me?

Could I command the whole pack to take on Nanuq and bring him and the condors down?

DES

The dog men flanking Cory on either side stop so suddenly that I almost run into the one on his left. I back off quickly when he growls at me. The ones guarding Donalita and me stop just as abruptly.

"Huh," the one to Cory's right says. He looks around at his companions. "You feel that?"

They nod.

Some unspoken communication goes between them, then the ones that are in human shape shift into dogs. The whole group takes off, loping down the street ahead and leaving us behind.

"Wait!" Cory yells.

They just ignore him and keep going.

"What the hell just happened?" I ask after we all stand there for a moment, nobody saying anything.

"I have no idea," Cory says.

"So, just to be clear here," I say, "are we actually in a situation where Cory doesn't know everything about everything?"

When I'm nervous, I joke. Oh, who am I kidding? I'm always a wise-ass. It's in my DNA.

"Des!" Donalita says, but she can't help smiling.

"Is that the way it seems?" Cory asks me.

"Kind of," I tell him.

"Because I could fill a library with what I don't know," he says.

"Did anybody notice if the dogs still had their brands and tattoos?" Donalita asks.

Cory and I shake our heads.

"I didn't, either," she goes on. "But the way they stopped dead and then just took off—I'd guess that whoever had a hold on them just lost it, and they're heading for some payback. I wouldn't want to be in the shoes of whoever was yanking their chains because …"

Her eyebrows rise and she draws a finger across her throat.

"You're probably right," Cory says. "So we'd better make tracks if we want to see who it is."

He sets off at a quick run. Donalita and I follow, but he soon leaves us behind. The only reason she doesn't keep up with him is because she's holding pace with me.

She holds out her arms. "Want a ride?" she asks.

"No thanks. I'd rather not get into the habit."

Yeah, I know. She's a cousin—stronger, faster, blah blah blah. But she's still a girl.

I'd rather show up late to wherever we're going.

She laughs, picking up the pace just enough to make me have to work for it.

"I. Know. People," I get out as we jog along. "I. Could. Have. You. Killed."

That just makes her laugh harder.

Sympathy? There's none.

JOSH

I appear in the sky above what looks like a fairly serious confrontation between a whole bunch of people I don't know. If they looked up, they'd just see a hawk. But no one does. They're all cousins—some of them really old—and all their attention is on each other. I see bunches of dogs grouped around fires. A pair of condors—which I take to be Vincenzo's brothers. A—really? A polar bear? Well, why not?

He and a jackrabbit are doing most of the talking, except the jackrabbit appears to have little antelope horns, so what does that make him? The rabbit only has two people standing with him. One's some kind of fish like a barracuda, the other—I don't know what he is. He could be a cousin, but he doesn't have an animal shape that I can read. I just see a big stone that stands somewhere overlooking an ocean.

The real problem is, there's no Marina down there. Sure, the little GPS pulse in my head indicates her presence on a spot on my map, but she's not where it says she is.

I pull up higher to get a better look at my surroundings.

I can't figure out what this place is. It looks like it was once a modern city, but for as far as I can see, there's just block after block of broken-down buildings and rubble—the way New York City might look after some devastating earthquake.

I'm about to drop lower to make a more concerted effort to find Marina when I see a half-dozen more dog cousins heading this way. I can't tell if they're running toward the group below, or away from something that I can't see. I let my awareness expand farther in the direction they came from and get a serious surprise: someone familiar is approaching along one of the rubble-strewn streets.

Cory.

What's *he* doing here?

And then my heart skips a beat because trailing a couple of blocks behind Cory is Des in the company of a coatimundi girl.

Marina, Des, Cory. Did they all come looking for me?

If that's the case, then the fact that Chaingang's not here means that Vincenzo really did kill him back on the clifftop. Crap. I know I've been fighting this jealousy about him being with Marina, but I'd never have wished for him to die.

Now I do drop back down and hover above a cornice of the building. With everything going on, nobody would give any notice to a hawk perched up here, or the other one circling high above. The map in my head shows that Tío Goyo's followed me here.

I ignore everything else and concentrate on Marina. My map says she should be right there on the cracked pavement, pretty much equidistant between the polar bear and the condors, but there's no sign of her.

So I shift my focus to what this confrontation is all about.

"—would have given her a quick death," the polar bear man is saying, "but because of what she's stolen from me, I'll see that she suffers and dies slowly now. And that same slow death will be yours if you don't speak up now. So tell me. Where. Is. She?"

The jackrabbit man doesn't seem particularly phased by the threat.

"Why not have your hounds find her for you?" he says. "Oh, wait. You no longer control them, do you?"

"I know you, Canejo," the polar bear says. "I know how old you are, the gifts that the Thunders have given you. But they won't support you in this. The girl is mine by kin-blood law. They won't lend you strength if you stand against me."

Canejo shakes his head. "I'll say it again. Your bully boy wasn't blood kin to anyone but his miserable brothers, so you have no justified cause to go after his killer, and especially not his killer's friends. If you have the need to avenge a dead condor, then go and deal with this as you should, cousin to cousin."

"He's unborn, not a cousin!"

"And the girl is innocent."

"She *stole* from me!"

"Only after you threatened her life," Canejo says. "Carry your fight to the mountain lion cub if you must, but she is under my protection and you will not harm her."

"You don't get to tell me what—"

"And Nanuq," the rabbit man continues. "I don't need any gifts from the Thunders to deal with the likes of you."

I never get to hear what the polar bear man responds because it's all been coming together for me as they speak. I know who they're talking about. Me. Vincenzo. Marina. I don't have a clue who this Canejo is, but I do know that Nanuq is the one who sent Vincenzo after me and my friends and family. He's the mastermind behind it all, and now that I've got him in front of me, and know that he's threatening Marina, I just see red.

I drop from my perch and go for him, my hawk spirit screaming, talons outstretched.

I'm fast, but he's faster. Even though he's surprised, he dodges easily, but I couldn't have touched him even if I had been faster. How could I? I'm a spirit. He sees a crazed red-tailed hawk, but I'm no more substantial than a blistering lick on my guitar. You can't ignore it, but you can't touch it, either.

He raises his arm and peers upward, so I decide to give him another shock. I drop to the ground and call up my body from the earth, then stand there, right in front of him.

He lowers his arm and stares back at me. I can see that my appearance throws him off. First he saw a hawk, but now I'm the boy with a mountain lion under my skin. He can see the lion as easily as I can the polar bear under his. They all can. The condors, the dogs, the rabbit man. They can't figure it out and it makes them cautious. The only one who doesn't bat an eye is Canejo, who just nods to himself, all Zen-like.

Nanuq recovers first.

"You," he says.

"Me," I agree. "What do you think? Is this a good day to die?" I wish Des were closer. He'd love to hear me quote Bruce Willis.

Rage flares in the polar bear man's eyes.

I know this is stupid. I was barely able to handle Vincenzo on my own, and now I'm up against Nanuq, a pair of condors and a few dozen dogs all at once. I'm so pissed off I don't care. I just want this to end, and I think I know how to do it. I'll do what Tío Goyo must do: take my spirit shape again and then re-form *inside* him. I'll take him down and it'll be over. The others can come at me. I have no experience at this, so no doubt they'll kill me, but the important thing is that Nanuq won't be able to hurt anyone else. And especially not Marina. Wherever the hell she is.

I don't get the chance to see how it will play out. Nanuq roars and takes a step in my direction. I'm about to implement my plan and let my body return to the earth when the nearest dog men move in between us. I growl, low in my chest, but they're not facing me. Others join them, making a wall of dogs and cousins between Nanuq and his condors, and me.

"You're done here," I hear Canejo say to Nanuq.

I see the same anger in Nanuq's eyes as in mine. The same indifference as to what will happen to him, just so long as he gets to take me out.

But his face changes and he lets it go. He straightens his back and nods. "You're right," he says.

The condors have moved in to flank him. He puts one big hand on each of their shoulders and takes a step forward.

And they're gone.

I'm ready to follow, wherever it takes me. I raise the maps in my head, trying to track him, except as suddenly as he disappears, Marina appears, a little bit behind where he and the condors were. Through a gap between a couple of the dog cousins, I see her crouched on the ground, eyes big as she stares at me.

My anger disappears as quickly as Nanuq's did and I push through the dogs until I can pull her to her feet. She throws her arms around me and holds me tight.

As I hug her back, I know she's just relieved to see me. This doesn't mean anything more than that. But holding her in my arms like this, I've never felt as whole and complete as I do right now.

Yeah, I know. How messed up is that?

I start to pull away, but she holds on a moment longer before she lets me go. Tears glisten in her eyes, and mine are pretty much the same. Her right hand is closed in a fist with the broken ends of a fine chain hanging loose from it. Her left grabs mine and holds it tight.

"How were you invisible?" I say at the same time as she asks, "How can you turn into a hawk?"

"It wasn't what it looked like," we both answer at the same time.

Even through our tears I see a flash of laughter in her eyes that I know is echoed in my own. How many times have we said the same thing at once? I see a lot more in her eyes. They seem older, more serious, more determined—if that's even possible because once she sets her mind to something, she's more tenacious than anyone I know.

"You first," I say. I need to swallow this lump in my throat before I can continue talking.

But then Cory's here. He starts yelling at Canejo—thinking he's Nanuq, I guess, because he's putting the blame for a lot of things on the jackrabbit man's shoulders. One of the female dog cousins puts a hand on Cory's arm and starts to fill him in on what really happened.

The next thing I know, Des shows up with his new friend. He's too out of breath to talk, but he's grinning from ear to ear. Even though he's winded, he pulls me out of Marina's grip, picks me up and swings me around before setting me back down. God, I hate it when he does that, but this time it feels good.

"Dude!" he says. "Check it out. We're over here in this crazy place together! I thought we'd never find either Marina or you."

He reaches over and rubs Marina's shoulders as if to make sure she's real. She grins back at him.

Meanwhile his coati friend keeps staring at me with big round eyes, like I'm some kind of rare animal she's come across in a zoo. Marina grabs my hand again and tells me her name is Donalita. The coati girl smiles widely.

"How do you do, *dude*," she says, bouncing on her toes and looking smugly at me, then Des. Obviously he's been rubbing off on her.

It takes a few moments for everybody to calm down enough so that we can sort things out.

"Nice trick you pulled there," Canejo tells Marina before making formal introductions.

He gives one of the guys beside him a knowing smile, then introduces him to us as Thorn. Damned if he doesn't look like a dwarf right out of one of the Tolkien movies.

The other guy—the barracuda—is named Lionel. I don't know how he fits into the hierarchy of whatever's going on around here, but from the vibes, it's clear that nobody seems to like him.

Marina lets go of my hand. She steps up to Lionel, and with no warning, punches him right in the face. He goes down holding his nose, blood streaming out between his fingers. Nobody seems surprised except for Des and me.

"Dude," Des says in a mild voice. "What was that for?"

When she tells us, a rumble starts up in my chest and I start for him. Marina grabs my hand and pulls me back.

"It's okay," she says. "He's not worth it."

There's dead silence and I realize everybody's waiting to see what I'll do. I force myself to calm down.

"Whatever you say," I tell her.

"Hit the road, Lionel," Canejo says.

The idiot totally wants to argue the point. He looks from the rabbit man to Marina. Then he meets my flat gaze and scrambles to his feet. Still holding his nose, he heads off down the street. The dog cousins make way for him. The ones in dog shape are stiff-legged and growling, but no one prevents him from leaving.

"So," Canejo says to Marina, like nothing ever happened, "did you order the canids to step up like that?"

Before she can reply, one of the dog men answers. "No," he says. "That was our own decision."

"Why would you think Marina could make them do anything?" I ask Canejo.

Marina opens her closed hand to show me a medallion. It seems to be made of fired clay, and has a symbol on it that seems familiar. Then I realize it's because all the dog cousins have that same symbol—a circle with a lightning bolt inside—as tattoos on their arms if they're in human shape, or as brands on the dogs.

"This is what Nanuq was using to control them," she says. "It's also the only way out of this pocket world."

I call up my maps and see that she's right. The only thing that comes up is this broken-down city around us.

"So why did you help?" I ask the dog man.

He shrugs. "We have the same enemy."

"Just like that?" Donalita asks, another irrepressible grin on her face. "Suddenly we're all friends, tra-la-la?"

"No," he says. "But it makes us allies."

There's obviously something going on between them that

I don't understand, but right now I'm more concerned with Nanuq.

"If the medallion is the only way out of this world," I say, "how come Nanuq was able to leave without using it?"

"He made this world," Canejo tells me, "so he can come and go as he pleases without the medallion. But the world exists on its own now, so he can't unmake it."

"How do we make this world open to anyone who wants to come in or get out?" Marina asks.

Canejo points to the medallion. "You break that."

"Except that would also free the dogs, wouldn't it?" Donalita says. "Which maybe isn't such a good idea, seeing how they outnumber us."

I sense the hackles rising on the dogs closest to me and hear a few low growls.

"But you don't have anything against us, do you?" Marina asks the dog man who spoke earlier. She must also have noticed the slight edge in his exchange with Donalita.

He shakes his head, but there's a banked fire in his eyes that I don't trust. "You rule us now," he says. "It doesn't matter what we think."

"How could this happen?" Cory wants to know.

The dog man shrugs. "A few worried individuals made the mistake of joining Nanuq's cause, then they convinced others. Because of the pack bond, the medallion soon controlled the majority of us, whether we agreed to the binding or not."

"What do you mean, I rule you?" Marina asks him.

"Whatever you ask of us, we will do—or we will die trying."

Handy, I think, except it doesn't sit right with me.

Marina holds up the medallion. "Because of this?"

The dog man nods.

Marina's brow creases in displeasure. "No way," she says.

She drops the medallion onto the ground and smashes her foot down on it, grinding the clay into dust. As soon as she does, maps spread out in my head, world after world. I look up and see Tío Goyo is still high in the dark sky, turning in lazy circles. I wonder if the fact that there is or isn't a gate makes any difference to him. I also wonder how pissed he is that I showed off my own little hawk trick again.

All around us everyone is still, their gazes locked on the crushed medallion. Then the dog man goes down on one knee and raises his hands to Marina.

"My name," he says with a formal tone, "is Hernán de la Costa, of the Hierro Madera Yellow Dog Clan. We are forever in your debt. If we can ever be of aid to you or your kin, you have but to ask, and we will come."

Marina shoots me a confused glance before she looks back at him.

"What are you talking about?" she says. "I thought I just freed you from all of that."

He rolls up his sleeve to show that the tattoo has disappeared.

"You did," he says. "You had everything to gain and nothing to lose, yet you still broke the binding on us. For this, you have our gratitude and friendship."

"Sure, but—"

"Don't friends look out for each other?" he asks.

Marina looks at me, then Des, and nods. "Of course."

"So that is what we will do for you."

"Okay," Marina says, "but it's not a one-way deal. The same goes for me and your clan—you know, if you need anything."

Hernán grins with a joy that seems to radiate from every part of him. If he had a tail in human shape, I'm sure it'd be wagging.

The dog man gets up, but before we can move on to something else, the woman who was speaking with Cory takes Hernán's place and assumes the same position. She's lean and dark-haired like the men.

"My name," she says in the same formal tone, "is Lupe Gonzalez of the East Riversea Blue Dog Clan. We are forever in your debt. If we can ever be of aid to you or your kin, you have but to ask, and we will come."

Marina is gracious with her, as she is with the next three canids, accepting their thanks and friendship and promising her own to each of them in return. I guess these five are clan leaders because when the last of them stands up, all the canids raise their faces to the sky and let rip with a joyous howl that echoes and bounces back from the buildings around us.

Marina glows. She looks like one of the saints in her mother's shrines. Everybody's smiling, even the coati girl Donalita, who was full of dire warnings a few moments ago.

All the canids who aren't already in dog shape begin to shift. The huge pack lopes off and starts to disappear in twos and threes. I watch their progress on the maps in my head as they move from world to world, going back home.

I turn my attention back to the business still at hand.

A whole group of people have filed out of the building behind Canejo and Thorn. The weird thing is, I recognize a few of them as kids from school.

"Marina was just telling us about you," Canejo says, drawing my attention back to him. "She told us about the mountain lion under your skin, and I can see that aspect of yours as plainly as you see mine. But what puzzles me is how you appeared here, and the fact that you can also wear a hawk's shape."

I think of Nanuq's plan to kill all the Wildlings. Of the hummingbird man's reaction to me.

"I'm unborn," I say. "Isn't that what you call us? You think that makes us less than you, but maybe it makes us more."

Marina nudges me and rests her head against my arm. "Don't be pissy," she says. "He's my friend. If it hadn't been for him, Nanuq would have had me and taken me away before you ever got here."

I don't correct her. It doesn't matter where Nanuq would have dragged her—the maps in my head would have led me right to them. But I take her point.

"I'm sorry," I tell Canejo, "but not every cousin I've met has been pleasant."

"That's unfortunate."

I shrug. "And I can't tell you about the hawk because it's not my story to tell."

His gaze flickers skyward to where I know Tío Goyo is still circling above us.

"Of course," he says.

I figure he knows something, or at least guesses, but we leave it at that.

"Speaking of carrying more than one aspect," I say, "you seem to be both jackrabbit and antelope."

"Jackalope," Marina, says, grinning.

"That's too cool," Des says, pushing forward. Then he turns to Thorn. "And are you a real dwarf?"

"Des!" Marina says, eyes wide.

He gives her an innocent look. "What?"

But Thorn smiles, obviously not taking offence. "No, I'm a stone warden."

"Cool. And what's that?"

"The cliffs of the western Sea Dales in Tal Avelle are under my care."

Des nods like he has a clue. "This is my first time ... um ... off-world," he says and I know he feels like he's waited his whole life to be able to say that. Now just give him a cape and a superpower, and he can die a happy man.

"I can't believe you guys came looking for me," Marina says, "but I'm so relieved that you did." She grins at me. "And your timing was impeccable. I don't think I could have stayed hidden much longer."

"No problem, dude," Des says.

"I'll be honest," I tell her. "I didn't even know you were missing."

"Then why—"

"I really needed to see a friendly face," I tell her, "and you were the first person that came to mind."

Maybe it's just the light cast from the fires, but it looks like she's blushing. Her smile fades and she squares her shoulders as though she needs to be brave again.

"Did you find Elzie?" she asks.

I nod, then look down, remembering what a lost cause that was.

She puts a hand on my arm. "Oh, God. You were too late. I'm so sorry."

"What makes you say that?"

"You have this really sad look," she begins, but I cut her off.

"That's because it's maybe worse than me being too late.

She wasn't their captive. She was with them—one of their bosses."

I remember the first time I told Marina about meeting Elzie. Marina called her a skank. She ended up warming to Elzie, but it turns out Marina wasn't far off the mark.

"That's awful," she says.

"Dude!" Des says.

"Yeah, she's messed up all right. Claims not to believe that they're killing people," I say, "but she's totally on board with Nanuq's idea of remaking the world." I look around. "Which is a little confusing," I add, "considering he made *this* place, and it looks like a scene out of one of the *Resident Evil* games instead of some pastoral paradise."

"Totally," Des agrees. "Except," he adds, with an apologetic look aimed at Marina and Donalita, "without the babes carrying the big guns—no offence."

"Or the zombies," I say, then turn to Canejo. "You don't have zombies, do you?"

He smiles and shakes his head.

"So you found Nanuq's camp," he says.

"I was in the woods outside of it just a couple of hours ago."

"Did you note what clans are siding with him?"

"All I saw were canids, so maybe they're not even there anymore," I say. "And there was Elzie, who's a Wildling jaguarundi. I still can't believe she bought into his bullshit."

"Nanuq can be persuasive," Canejo says. "And he's not entirely wrong about what's happening in your world. Some of those first canid followers may still be with him."

I know what he means about our world. I'm all too aware of how corruption and greed have screwed it up. But you don't fix it by murdering everybody and starting all over. I say as much to Canejo.

"Of course not," he says. "But you have to understand it from our perspective. We were first on every continent. Usually we were allied with the initial wave of five-fingered beings— what you call indigenous, or native, peoples. Things only changed with the coming of the Europeans with their church teachings and their sciences. First they denied that we—the wilderness, the cousins, even the early peoples—had souls. Then they denied that we had consciousness. And finally, even today, they deny that there's any kind of sentience to the natural world.

"Most of them pay at least lip service to the idea that anyone with darker skin is as human as they are," he continues. "But they look at us and see only animals. They regard animals as their chattel. They look at a river, a forest, a"—he glances at Thorn— "cliff or mountain, and see only resources to be harvested—no reverence for the land or the spirits that lie at the heart of it. It's little wonder that so many cousins grow frustrated."

"But over here, there are so many worlds that are still unspoiled," I say.

Canejo nods. "True. But they each have their own spirits, and inhabitants, and guardians. If we were to take up residence in them, we'd be no better than the five-fingered beings, displacing the indigenous inhabitants for our own gain."

"Okay, I get that."

"But more importantly," he goes on, "the world of your birth—which is also the world of our birth—is the first world. It needs its wild places and guiding spirits, or it will shrivel and die.

And when it does, so do all the other worlds because they are all echoes and dreams of the first world."

"So you think he's right," I say. "Nanuq."

"Not his methods, but I understand his frustration. He comes from a part of the world that is slowly being destroyed by the encroachments of the five-fingered beings with their smoke and gases.

"His people refuse to suffer the same fate as the clans of the passenger pigeons, the pronghorn and the bison. They fight the threat of the tundra and ice floes disappearing like the grasslands, the old-growth eastern hardwoods and the western conifer forests.

"Something needs to change or there will be nothing left for anyone," he concludes.

"Okay," I say. "I get that, too. But if he's so noble, why is he also targeting Wildlings—what he calls the unborn?"

Cory and Donalita have been pretty quiet up to now. While I don't know Donalita, it's uncharacteristic for Cory, and I keep expecting him to jump in with a comment. But it's Donalita who speaks up.

"It's because Nanuq believes you were made by the five-fingered beings," she says. "He can't believe what many of us do—that you are a gift of the Thunders, to be cherished and honoured, not a threat."

And here we go, back to my so-called destiny. But at least she's including all Wildlings in it.

"None of this matters," I say. "I'm still going to protect my family and friends, and if that means I have to destroy Nanuq and Vincenzo's brothers, then that's what I'll do."

No one makes a comment.

"The thing I don't get is," I go on, "if Nanuq wants to get rid of Wildlings, why was he dumping them here? Vincenzo said they were going to kill us all."

"I think it's pretty obvious," Cory says. "It looks better if he exiles them to a prison world rather than killing them. A lot of the cousins have yet to make up their minds about where they stand in all of this. Slaughtering Wildlings wouldn't sit well with them."

"But what about beings like Thorn?" I ask.

Canejo nods. "Some stumble into this place and get trapped, others are here for some perceived wrongdoing."

"I was organizing my fellow wardens against Nanuq," Thorn says.

"And you?" I ask Canejo.

He smiles. "I am ever the anomaly. When I ended up in this place, I thought it would be as good a place as any to open my school. You have to admit that there aren't many distractions."

"But you and your students were trapped here, just like everybody else."

"Perhaps."

"What does that mean?" I ask.

"It means I'm older than Nanuq," he says, "and there are things I know and can do that he has yet to grow into. Perhaps I was trapped, perhaps I wasn't. I don't know because I never tried to leave."

I sigh. Cousins sure do like to lay it on thick and mysterious.

"Well, I can sympathize with Nanuq's situation as much as the next guy," I say, "but I'm still taking him down."

"The more immediate concern," Cory says, "is the upcoming assassination attempt on Congressman Householder. Auntie Min has been organizing cousins and people to protect him. With the dog cousins no longer under Nanuq's control, he might be all right, but I wouldn't bet on it. Nanuq obviously has other allies, and his strategy is to pin the congressman's death on a Wildling and get them all locked up for it."

Canejo turns to Marina. "Is this Auntie Min the woman you were telling me about?" he asks.

Marina nods.

"Her full name," Cory tells him, "is Señora Catalina Mariposa, of the Black Witch Moth Clan."

Canejo's eyebrows raise. "She's still alive?"

"Why wouldn't she be?" Marina asks.

Canejo turns to her. "She's almost as old as I am, and I remember the first days."

"Well, *you're* still alive."

"This is true," Canejo tells her. "But I keep a much lower profile. Powerful cousins such as Señora Mariposa tend to attract too many enemies. But that is always the way with warriors."

I find it hard to think of Auntie Min as any kind of a warrior.

"I'm going after Nanuq and the condors," I say.

"The choice is yours," Canejo tells me. "But if Señora Mariposa advises against it, I would hear her out before you set off. And perhaps you need no reminding, but Nanuq is a formidable opponent."

"Tell that to Vincenzo."

Canejo studies me for a long moment, then nods.

"Yes, you are brave," he says. "But are you also wise?"

He stands up before I can respond and claps his hands. "Students!" he calls. "It's past time we returned to our studies. Those who wish to return to their old lives may do so, now that our friend Marina has reopened the passages between the worlds. But for the rest of us, we have work to do."

He steps up to Marina and clasps her hands. He gazes at her for a long moment, then turns to the rest of us. "I wish you all luck," he says.

He lets go of Marina and strides back into the building. Most of his students go with him, but a few remain with us. The kids I recognized from Sunny Hill. Thorn.

A Chinese girl with a lizard under her skin approaches us. She looks like she's about to cry. "Can you take us home?" she asks.

"Of course," Marina says, putting her arm protectively around her shoulders. Then she looks at Cory and me. "That's okay, right?"

"No one who wants to leave will be left behind," Cory says.

Thorn approaches Marina. She lets the girl go, then hugs Thorn hard. After a moment he gently pushes her back and places a meaty hand on each of her shoulders. "I enjoyed meeting you, Mistress Otter," he says. "Look me up if you're ever in Tal Avelle."

"I will ... and thank you for helping me," she says as he lets her go. Her eyes are glassy.

Then Thorn does the step-away thing and disappears.

Cory starts organizing those who remain, getting them ready to travel back through the worlds.

"You know," Marina says in a quiet voice, "I'm a bit surprised that Theo didn't come, as well."

I shoot Des a pained glance. He looks back at me, sympathy in his eyes. I know what he's thinking. Marina doesn't know yet that Chaingang died. She was probably grabbed and brought to this place before he actually stopped breathing.

I look at her. She's going to take this hard, I think.

But it turns out I'm the one who has it all wrong.

"He really wanted to come," Des tells her, "except Auntie Min said no. She convinced him that we could handle finding you. She's got him doing some stuff about the rally for her."

"What? He's still alive?" I ask. I can't help feeling a weird mix of happy and deflated all at once.

"Dude, why wouldn't he be? Oh, that's right. You disappeared before Cory went into his brain and brought him back."

"Say what?"

"Long story," Des says, looking over at Cory, the same sympathy in his eyes.

Marina studies him, head cocked to the side.

"What aren't you telling me?" she asks.

"Dude, there's nothing to tell."

She gives him her best don't-bullshit-me look.

Cory clears his throat. "Chaingang lured a pack of canids to the Ocean Avers' compound," Cory says. "He and his brother set up an ambush and they slaughtered them all."

Marina goes pale. She looks from Cory to Des.

"It wasn't quite like that," Des says.

"Then what was it like?" Cory asks, his posture stiff.

"They were stalking us, dude. All those dogs. They treed Donalita and me, and also went after Chaingang's grandmother and Josh's mom."

"*What?*" I yell. "If anything's happened to my mother—"

"Easy, dude," Des tells me. "Your mom's safe. The Feds got there in time to stop the attack and Chaingang's grandmother shot the one coming after her."

"I don't get it," Marina says. She looks at Cory. "If they were attacking people, why are you so mad? Wouldn't you defend yourself?"

"I would. But this wasn't defence. The canids were only *tracking* Chaingang when he set up the ambush. They hadn't attacked him."

"Yet," Donalita adds.

Cory shoots her a dirty look. "The point is, he never even tried to talk to them. He did what all the gangbangers always do—shoot first, ask questions later."

"Were they also under Nanuq's binding?" Marina asks.

Cory nods. "And they belonged to one of the same clans that you just exchanged a friendship oath with."

Marina looks at the ground and shakes her head.

"Yeah, it was harsh," Des says, "but dude, Chaingang didn't know why they were tracking him or what they were going to do."

Cory's voice is almost a growl. "Because he didn't take the time to ask."

"Sounds like they went after my mom and his grandma," I say. "Maybe we should hear Chaingang's side of the story before we start pointing fingers and calling names."

"They were my *kin*," Cory says, knocking his fist against his chest.

"Who treated you with so much respect when they captured us earlier," Donalita adds.

"Because they were under a binding."

Donalita shrugs. "If you hadn't stopped me, I would have done the same to them as Theo did."

Cory bristles. "That doesn't make either of you right."

I think of what I did to Vincenzo's corpse after he was already dead.

"We've all done things we regret," I say.

Cory nods. "Except Chaingang has no regrets."

"Neither do I," Donalita says. "That's why Theo and I get along so well." She cocks her head. "Though maybe I like his grandma better. She makes the best lemonade."

Cory gives her a tired look, which she ignores.

"I think it's because she uses fresh lemons."

Cory stands up. "We should get going."

We've got a half-dozen people who were trapped here in Nanuq's world waiting for us. All of them perk up at Cory's words.

"I can't go home," Marina says. "When I do get back, I'll be grounded forever."

"Me too," Des says.

Marina nods. "And I need to be at that rally tomorrow."

I wish I could just go home and stay there. I'd like to hug my poor mom. She must be going out of her mind.

"I don't know that I can make two trips," Cory says. "Auntie Min probably has things for me to do back in the first world."

"Go ahead," I tell him. "I can get us back. Just tell me, is this a fast world or a slow world?"

He gives me a puzzled look.

"How time flows," I add. "Is it the same as in our world, or does it move differently?"

"It's the same. Today's Friday."

"Then there's no problem. We'll get there in time for the rally."

Cory studies me for a moment, then nods. He gets his new charges to link hands, then walks them out of here. We watch them disappear, one at a time.

"What did you mean about how time flows?" Marina asks.

I turn to her. "How long has it been since we were attacked at Tiki Bay?"

"That happened last night—Thursday."

"It's been way longer for me."

"Dude," Des says. "Is that how you grew your dreads back? You must have been wandering around for freaking ages for them to get that long. Or were you in Rip Van Winkle land, sleeping?"

"No, it was something else."

The three of them look expectantly at me.

"So dish," Marina says when I don't explain.

There's no need for me to glance up to know that there's still a hawk circling above. It was obvious that Tío Goyo didn't want me to tell anybody, but he didn't specifically ask me not to, either.

These are my friends. My best friends. Or at least Marina and Des are, and we've learned the hard way that keeping secrets is a big fail in our gang of three. And considering how Donalita is snuggling up against Des's side, I guess she might end up becoming a friend as well.

"Let's move away from the doors," I say.

I get up from the steps by the front of the building and walk over to one of the campfires abandoned by the canids. I don't say it, but I don't want to talk about my experiences where Canejo or his students might overhear me.

I add some wood to the fire and sit down on a flat rock,

waiting for the others to join me. The three of them settle in, Marina to my right, Des and Donalita across the fire.

"I'll go first," I say.

I tell them everything that happened to me since I jumped off the cliff by Tiki Bay in pursuit of Vincenzo, including how I went crazy and tore his body to pieces. Then they fill me in on what's been happening with them.

It takes us a while to exchange war stories.

"So, are you *two* kinds of Wildling now?" Des asks. "Because, dude, that's freaking awesome."

I shake my head. "I'm not really a hawk—you just saw me that way."

"It sounds amazing," Marina says.

Des is nodding. "Yeah, except I'm still trying to get my head around it. It's not like astral projection, right? You just leave your body and it *what*? Dissolves into the ground? And when you want it back, you just call it up and it'll be whatever you want it to be? Like, with the longer dreads?"

"That's pretty much it."

"So dude, you should make yourself all tall and buff when you come back."

I shake my head. "That's not who I am."

"But you got your dreads back."

"Yeah, but they were stolen from me. I just put things back the way they were, except a little longer."

Des snickers.

Marina punches his shoulder at the same time as I say, "I'm talking about my dreads."

"Dude," he says with an innocent look. "Get your mind out of the gutter. I knew you were talking about your dreads."

But he laughs out loud, and Donalita joins him. I try to keep a smile from my face, but it's not working very well, especially when Marina gives in and starts chuckling. It's so stupid and not even all that funny, but I guess we've been stressing so much that we're all looking for some kind of release. We're all about to dissolve into ridiculous laughter—the kind that's too loud and you just can't stop—except the map in my head pings a warning that Tío Goyo is approaching.

Donalita senses it, too. She's on her feet in a fluid motion. There's a knife in her hand and I have no idea where it came from.

"It's okay," I say as Tío Goyo comes around the corner of a building, a couple of large backpacks hanging from either shoulder. "He's a friend."

"The hawks of Halcón Pueblo have never been friends to cousins."

"Chill," Des tells her. "That's the dude from Josh's story."

Donalita nods, but she doesn't relax and she doesn't put away her knife.

Tío Goyo pays no attention to the threat she presents. When he reaches us he gives everybody a friendly nod and dumps the backpacks on the ground.

"You left these behind," he tells me. "Food and blankets."

I was wondering before where he got this stuff when we were camping. Now I know. He calls them up the same way we call up our bodies when we're finished being in our spirit shapes. Instead of just focusing on bringing himself back, he brings himself back with a couple of backpacks and fresh supplies.

I make introductions.

"Don't worry, my young coati," he says to Donalita. "Your soul is your own, so you have nothing to fear from me."

Donalita continues to glare at him. "I'm not scared of you."

"Which is as it should be since I mean you no harm."

I grab one of the backpacks. "Can you get that?" I ask Des, nodding at the other.

We open them at the fire and Donalita brightens right up as the smell of fresh warm burritos wafts up from the foil container that I open. Her knife, I note, has disappeared again.

"Oh, I *love* burritos," she says.

She grins happily, snatching one out of the container along with a bottle of water. A few moments later, and we've all got food and drink, with blankets to sit on.

Tío Goyo doesn't eat. I don't really feel that I have to, either—when I regain my body from the earth, it's rested, healthy and nourished—but I can't resist the smell of the burritos. And I already know that they taste even better than they smell.

"You found your friend," Tío Goyo says.

I nod and swallow. "But she didn't need rescuing. Or rather, she does, but it's the kind of rescuing she has to do for herself."

"I'm sorry it didn't work out."

I feel Marina shift on the blanket and I lean slightly toward her.

"Me too," I say to Tío Goyo. "Hey, you were watching from above. Nanuq—the polar bear guy—does he have an evil spirit inside him?"

Tío Goyo shakes his head. "Just a great deal of anger."

He takes a kettle and a bottle of water from one of the packs, then fills the kettle and places it on a stone by the coals. When he pulls a clear plastic pouch of tea leaves from his pocket, Des regards it with interest.

"Is that your special tea?" he asks. "The one that lets you fly like a hawk?"

Tío Goyo gives me a look.

"You didn't specifically tell me not to talk about anything," I say. "And these are my friends. I don't hide things from them."

I find Marina's hand and give her fingers a squeeze. When I look at her, her eyes are a little shiny in the firelight. She squeezes back.

"I'm afraid this is normal tea," Tío Goyo tells Des.

"Too bad," Des says. "I'm the only one in this crew without any superpowers, so I could totally use some of that magic tea."

Tío Goyo smiles. "That's not exactly how it works. It takes years of study and practice."

"But Josh—"

"Has apparently been given more than one gift from the Thunders. He should not be able to do many of the things that he can. But nothing is ever freely given. There is always a cost. A responsibility one must assume."

I sigh. "A destiny."

Tío Goyo's smile widens. "Precisely."

Marina gives my hand another squeeze. "It's not so bad, is it?" she says. "Having the opportunity to help people and do some good? And you know we'll stand by you."

"Dude," Des says. "Was there ever a doubt?"

And even though we've only just met, Donalita adds an enthusiastic nod of support.

"You will speak to Señora Mariposa before you do anything?" Tío Goyo asks me.

"Sure. Why not. I can find Nanuq whenever I have to."

"Good. Then I will see you later. I have some thoughts on how to address the concerns of the cousins who think of you as unborn. I will look into that now."

I nod. "Thanks for …" I wave a hand at the backpacks. "You know … everything."

I'm sure he knows that I mean more than just the food and blankets he brought.

"It was my pleasure … Tíoito."

He winks and steps out of this world.

"What did he just call me?" I ask Marina.

She smiles. "Little uncle."

"Dude," Des says. "You've got your stage name!"

"Great, it sounds like a bird call."

They all laugh and we talk a little longer until Des starts yawning.

"I'm beat," he says. "I need to turn in."

He makes a bed near the fire and lies down. Donalita immediately brings her blanket over to where he is and snuggles in beside him. I can see the hesitation in his body language before he puts his arm around her. But that's Des. God forbid he should actually commit to a girl.

Turning away, I add some more wood to the fire. Marina and I watch the flames until their breathing evens out.

"Are they an item?" I ask.

She laughs. "Who knows? It's Des. Girls just like him."

I smile. "True, that," I say, remembering the business with Joanie Jones. That makes me think about pheromones.

"It must be nice to know that Ampora's worried about you," I say. "From what Des was saying, she doesn't totally hate you."

"She's just feeling guilty because she kicked me out of the house that night."

"Harsh."

She nods. "Except that's Ampora for you. Though I'm guessing you must know her softer side." She gives me a gentle prod with her elbow.

"Oh, God. That was totally *her*. I mean, it was the pheromones that got her going, but then it was her. I didn't initiate anything. And I've had them clamped right down ever since I found out about them."

"I know," she says. "I'm just teasing."

Any other time and we would move on to talking about some TV show, what the waves were like this morning. Maybe a song, or a movie.

But the life we had is gone. We're still kids, but we don't get to be kids anymore. Once upon a time we couldn't wait until we were old enough to do whatever we wanted. Get a tattoo. Have a beer in a bar. Go out to some surfer's party and stay out all night, then hit the waves when the sun's rising.

The world seemed bigger than we'd ever need, and filled with cool possibilities. Right now I'd give anything to be stuck at home on a school night with my biggest worry being about some test the next day.

"So, how are things with Chaingang?" I find myself asking, though I don't really want to know.

Marina doesn't answer right away. Instead her hand slips back into mine as she stares into the fire.

"I like Theo," she says. "I like him a lot. He's always been nice and kind of sweet to me, and because of that, I saw this whole other side of him—one I really care for. I guess I've wanted to ignore what he really is."

"A gangbanger," I say when she falls silent.

She nods. "And a bookie, and a drug dealer, and a guy who's been to jail. A guy who solves his problems with his fists and guns."

"So he needs to change," I say, "if you're going to be able to stay with him."

"That's the problem. He is who he is. Why should he have to change if he doesn't want to? But I don't see how I can be with him if he doesn't. He says he doesn't like the gang life, but I can't be the only reason he gets out of it. He has to want to do it for himself."

"And you don't think he wants to."

"I don't think he can. I think the only reason we got involved in the first place was because I was just reaching for a lifeline to hold on to when … you … we … you know …"

"When I messed everything up."

"But I'm the one who didn't tell you I was a Wildling when you were the first person I should have told."

I let go of her hand and put my arm around her shoulder.

"Can we agree to just let all of that go?" I ask. "My fault, your fault—what does it matter if it's all in the past? It's not like either of us is going to make that mistake again."

She leans against me. It's amazing how well she fits under my arm.

"Sure," she says. "That's easy."

We stare into the flames for a while. I'm dying to kiss her, but I know we should go slow. Everything we've been through is too fresh, and it sounds like she's still confused about Chaingang. No matter what happens, I don't want to mess up our friendship, so I try to ignore everything my body's screaming at me to do, and just content myself with being close to her.

It's very quiet out here in this abandoned city, and even with Wildling sight, it's hard to make out much beyond the light cast by the fire. It's so dark. The map in my head tells me what's out there on those deserted streets, but there's nothing to see. This is such a weird place. I don't know all the constellations back home, but when I look up here, I know they're different. I wish someone could tell me why. Regardless, I love being close to Marina under any starlight.

"So what are you going to do?" I finally ask.

She gives a slow shrug. The movement of her shoulders gives me the start of an unbidden erection.

"I don't know," she says. "It's hard. The story Cory told gave me serious creeps, but—and maybe this is a mean thing to say—what Chaingang did doesn't surprise me. I just don't see that I can get past the violence of his lifestyle. It's a part of who he is. It could just as easily have been a bunch of the Kings that got in his way as those dog cousins."

"Maybe it's not all his fault. Tío Goyo thinks we're having these anger and violence issues because we were made Wildlings instead of being born to the animals under our skin. He thinks it's a temporary thing—a kind of adjustment."

"I guess ..."

"You've talked about how you tore into your sister," I say, "and you fought off those canids that attacked you in the playground. And when you think of the awful things I've done ..." I don't have to mention Vincenzo or the researcher in the laboratory. We both know what I'm referring to.

"But you regret what you did," she says. "Cory's right. Theo never will."

I'm tired of defending Chaingang. Yeah, he's had my back, and I'd step up for him if he ever needed my help, but I don't want to see Marina with him, even if she's not with me. I can't see her as one of those hard girls who hang around the Ocean Avers' compound or ride around on the back of their bikes.

"Marina," I start, but I don't know what to say. A wave of emotion comes over me and I can't help myself. I pull her in and kiss her. She stiffens for the briefest moment, then she draws me closer, her lips parting, her tongue slipping slowly into my mouth.

It seems the most natural thing in the world for us to lie down on the blankets, the fire between us and where Des and Donalita are sleeping. My hand goes up under the back of her shirt and she arches toward me, pressing her hips against mine. A moment later and I've pulled her shirt over her head and she's lowering the zipper of my jeans.

I stop thinking of everything except for her.

CHAINGANG

J-Dog and I figured we'd have plenty of time to get organized if we got the boys out early, but even though we're downtown for seven a.m., the grounds are already crawling with people, most of them dorks. It's the antithesis of that old hippie Woodstock movie. There's this straight, pickle-up-the-ass vibe in the air, except for the odd Wildling or Ocean Aver.

We came in cars and we're all suited up in civvies—no gang colours, head scarves or banger gear, and definitely no weapons. Can't do much about the tats and shaved heads, though J-Dog's wearing a jaunty fedora that's pretty fly, even with that tat of a handgun on his neck. Most of us went for baseball caps. We've all got what look like Bluetooth phone earpieces, but they actually came our way courtesy of the Feds so that we can all communicate with one another.

Security looks good. I don't see any Secret Service, but then the congressman hasn't shown up yet, either. Right now there's men from the sheriff's department, state troopers, our boys and maybe ten thousand crows. Okay, that's an exaggeration, but I can't look anywhere without seeing at least one.

Whatever. There are more than enough of us to handle the

thousand or so people here so far. But the rally doesn't start until noon, so who knows how many more are going to show up? Because, oh yeah, they're still arriving, by ones and twos and in larger groups—a steady stream filling a powder keg that could blow up in our faces in a second if someone lights the wrong fuse.

I can't help but wonder if that's what the congressman wants, because why else organize this rally against Wildlings? He's got to know how bad this can go. He just didn't plan on being the target. But I'll bet he's hoping for a mini riot, which'll give him the ammunition to push through his stinking legislation.

As the crowd thickens, it seems to get more evenly divided between pro and con. Some of the pro-Wildlings are easy to spot. They're wearing animal ears and tails and crap. Others carry signs. It reminds me of when Josh's friend Dillon killed himself and so many kids showed up at school wearing the same kind of stuff.

That, I now realize, was a more innocent time.

I get pings from actual Wildlings, too—more than I expected, to be honest. I figured the kids would be lying low. But I guess they're here for the same reason I'd be here if Auntie Min hadn't already asked me to do it: morbid curiosity. I'd want a peek at all the people who hate me that much. Know your enemy.

We've been walking a circuit, checking things out. There's already some tension between the pros and cons. Raised voices here, a push there, but the cops intervene quickly.

Our own boys are all in place. They're used to spotting people carrying weapons, so that's what they're focused on. People walk differently when they're armed. We don't have to worry about hidden snipers. The crows have that covered. As in every tree and rooftop with any kind of a sightline.

"It's coming up on eight," J-Dog says.

I nod and turn on the FBI communicator in my ear like we'd arranged with Matteson. J-Dog and I move out toward the perimeter of the crowd where we can keep an eye on things, but be a little more discreet with communications.

"You with us, Washington?" Matteson's voice asks in my ear.

"We're here; all our boys are on it."

"Crowd's antsy," J-Dog adds.

"Already noted. Listen, Danny's got some information for you and the cousin bosses."

"Shoot."

Danny's voice comes on. "Two of the Secret Service detail are Wildlings."

"Well, fuck," J-Dog says. "Did you grab them?"

"And say what?" Matteson asks.

"This is messed up," I say.

A new voice comes on. "What clan?" That's Lalo, Auntie Min's crow man head of security. His tone has a bit of a crow's rasp in it.

"I can't tell," Danny says. "They're old-school cousins."

"So?" J-Dog asks.

"They might be okay, might not," Lalo says. "Some cousins are more sympathetic to Wildlings than others."

"Unless they're being controlled," I say. "Like the dogs."

"True. But we've just heard that the binding on the canids has been broken, so they're no longer a threat."

"So you're saying we can trust them now."

Beside me J-Dog is shaking his head. I know exactly what he's thinking. *Like hell.*

"Absolutely," Lalo says. "The bad news is, the canids were able to tell us who's behind all of this. It's Nanuq."

"Means nothing to me," I say.

"He's Polar Bear Clan—old and powerful, with plenty of influence among the cousins. He's also very angry."

"So put him down," J-Dog says. "End of story."

"We wouldn't do that," Lalo tells us. "He has too much sway and he's more dangerous than Vincenzo ever was. Even if he were somehow killed, it would only bring more cousins over to his way of thinking: that Wildlings are a threat to the rest of us. Better to find a way to reason with him."

"Look, if he's this big a problem, let *us* just take him down," I say. "Then it'll be on us."

"Easy, Washington," Matteson warns. "We don't want a war here."

"That's right," Lalo says. "You're not even listening. And anyway, Nanuq's not going to set foot over here; he'd send someone else."

Which makes me think of the dogs again. "So, this binding on the dogs—how did it get broken? Are you sure they're not a threat?"

"So we've been told. Apparently Marina was able to break it before—"

"Wait, homeboy," I break in. "Did you say Marina? Is she okay? Is she back?"

"Yes, she's fine. She—"

"And you were planning to tell me this—*when*?"

There's a moment's silence, then Lalo says, his voice formal, "My apologies to you, Theodore Washington. I only just received word of this myself, and my mind has been so preoccupied with security that I forgot the importance of this matter to you."

I'm just starting to wonder if Auntie Min is playing me, when a crow swoops down out of the sky and drops something at my feet. I pick it up and see it's a piece of foolscap crumpled around a small stone. I open the paper and stretch it out so that I can read what it says:

Marina's with Josh and the others and she is safe. They will be with us soon.

"You still there?" Lalo asks.

"Yeah. I just got a message from a crow about Marina."

"Does it mention the canid clans?" Lalo asks.

"No. What about them?"

"All the clans in this area have sworn fealty to Marina."

"Okay. So?"

"I hope this will not cause a problem for you, considering ..."

He lets the words trail off, but I can finish the thought. Considering how the other Avers and I mowed down a bunch of them.

"Ladies, can we get back to the business at hand?" Matteson says. "Lalo, can your boys remove these Wildlings in the congressman's detail?"

"No. But I will send someone to see who they are. In the meantime, remain vigilant. If they aren't the threat, then it's still out there."

"We're on it," I say.

The crowd's at least doubled. J-Dog checks in with the boys. No one's seen anybody who looks like an obvious threat, but the growing tension hangs in the air like a thundercloud. The sheriff's department and state police have men weaving in and out among the people, making their presence known, and that's probably the only thing that's keeping this sick party in check. For now.

"You okay?" J-Dog asks.

"Sure. I'm good. We should probably split up, cover more ground that way. This place is getting nuts."

"'Cause if you need to check in on your girl, we've got this."

"I *said* I'm good."

I'm lying. I feel like shit. What does it mean that the canids have all sworn this fealty thing to Marina—that they're her crew? And I know they're just waiting for today to be over to put the Ocean Avers in their sights, so what does that mean for Marina and me?

I realize that J-Dog's still standing beside me. I'm about to ask why, when I realize he's pissed off, and not at me. I turn to see what he's looking at, and here come Fat Boy Zaragoza and his lieutenant Chico Para sauntering through the crowd. This is not cool. They're in full gangbanger gear and I can tell by the way Para's walking that he's got a gun under that baggy T-shirt. A couple of state troopers are trailing along behind them.

I'm not surprised to see the Kings. Something this big hasn't happened in Santa Feliz for as long as I can remember. There's going to be all kinds of rubberneckers, checking it out. Why should the Riverside Kings be any different?

"Look at you boys, all cleaned up," Fat Boy says when the pair reaches us. "You on your way to some country club?"

"Now's not a good time," J-Dog manages to get out in a civil tone. I'm proud of him.

Fat Boy raises his eyebrows. "What? You haven't got the time to say hello to old friends?"

Everybody's got buttons. Between the Kings and the Avers, it doesn't have to be anything that's said, just the way it's said, the look in an eye, the way somebody's standing. It brings old drive-bys and other hurts alive like they happened yesterday.

That's why J-Dog takes a step forward, only stopping when I put a hand on his arm.

"Back off," I tell Fat Boy.

Fat Boy gives Chico a *can you believe this guy?* look.

"I wasn't talking to you, *ese*," he tells me. "And backing off's not something I do. Now you run along and let the men talk—you know, *mano a mano*, boss to boss."

I feel J-Dog stiffen at my side. I don't think Fat Boy's actually here to cause us trouble. Being an asshole is just his habit. But diplomacy's not something J-Dog knows much about—especially when it comes to dealing with the Kings—and he's taken it about as far as he can. I figure we're just an eye blink from someone throwing a punch, so I step in between the two.

"We're here at the request of the Halcón Pueblo," I tell Fat Boy, which is mostly true, since Tío Benardo was at the meeting last night.

Fat Boy's eyes narrow. "If you're bullshitting me ..."

"Where's the percentage in that?" I say. "But if you want confirmation, see all those crows?"

Fat Boy looks around and nods. Hard to miss them since there are three or four on every tree, lamppost and roofline, with more winging in lazy circles directly above the crowd.

"Go ask one of them," I say.

"Crows ain't hawks, *ese*. Those are just scavengers."

"Ask them anyway."

"You have a problem?" Matteson asks in my earpiece.

"Nothing we can't handle," I tell him.

"Who you talking to?" Fat Boy wants to know.

"Nobody."

Fat Boy gives me a thousand-yard stare, cold and hard, but hell, unless he gets Para to pull a gun, he can look at me all he wants.

"So you're telling me it's *los tíos*," he finally says.

I nod.

"And they come to *your* crew?" he goes on, though what he's really asking is, why the Avers and not the Kings? "What are you supposed to do for them?"

"Keep the congressman from getting killed."

"Shit, who cares if one more fat white dude dies?"

"*Los tíos*, apparently."

"Wrap it up," Matteson says in my ear. "The staties have just asked their captain permission to take the bunch of you in."

"Okay," I tell Fat Boy. "Here's the deal. You've got one second to walk away or I let those staties pull you in."

I know he's been as aware of them as me and J-Dog.

"They've got dick-all to hold us on," Fat Boy says.

"True. But if you fuck this up, you're going to find Josh waiting for you when you step outside state police headquarters. You remember Josh—you met him at the skatepark where *los tíos* told you to back the fuck off?"

I don't know that Josh would actually do it, but they don't know that he won't, and they know what he's capable of.

I see the state troopers start to move toward us, hands on their still-holstered guns.

"Last chance," I say.

DES

I wake up to find Donalita snuggled up tight against me. The ground's hard and I ache everywhere from the crappy bed it made, but her warmth feels nice. Sure, she makes for a psycho girlfriend, but the truth is, everything seems more interesting when I'm around her. Like, instead of watching the movie, I'm in the movie. *And* I've got the girl.

It sure beats being with most of the girls I've hooked up with. Let's just say those classic blond beach girls are cute and everything, but I could almost write out a script for what they'll say or do.

I sit up and stretch, trying to work out a few of the kinks in my back. Donalita murmurs something and wriggles until she's pretty much glued to me with her head on my lap.

I tangle a hand in her hair and look around, still blown away. I'm in a freaking otherworld, dude. I may not have superpowers, but this is still way cool. Then I realize that the blanket-covered bundle lying on the ground on the other side of last night's fire isn't one person, but two.

Josh pokes his head out, blinking in the light. He sits up, bare-chested, and I catch a glimpse of Marina's naked shoulder.

I shake my head and smile. "Du-*ude*."

He turns in my direction. "Don't say a word," he says.

And I don't want to because this is what I've wanted pretty much forever. If I couldn't be with Marina, then it had to be Josh. Oh, who am I kidding? It always had to be Josh. But the two of them hooking up *now*?

"You remember who Chaingang runs with, right?" I say. "Do you really want to get on the Avers' bad side?"

Marina sits up beside him, looking gorgeous with her mussed hair and sleepy eyes. She holds the blanket up against her chest. The pair of them look mildly guilty, but they've also got this goofy look of pure happiness in their eyes. Josh puts an arm around her shoulders.

"We know," he says. "Okay?"

"Yeah, but—"

I don't get a chance to finish. Donalita's awake now, too, and she pokes a sharp elbow in my side.

"Stop it," she says. "Don't you see that they were meant to be together?"

"Dude, I totally agree. But pissing off a gang of bikers never seems like a good idea. Especially when half of the rest of the world's already lining up to take a crack at us."

"We'll work it out," Josh says.

The door of Canejo's building opens, cutting off anything more we might say. Canejo walks out carrying a tray with a teapot and a bunch of small mugs without handles.

"Good morning!" he calls out to us.

"I need a moment," Marina says.

She wraps a blanket around herself. Picking up her clothes, she heads around the side of the building, presumably to pee.

Josh wriggles into his pants under the other blanket, then gets out from under it to put on his shirt and shoes.

"Thanks. This is generous of you," he tells Canejo.

The rabbit man sets the tray down near us, then straightens up, his nose twitching.

"You had a visitor last night," he says. His voice is calm, but there's a new edge in it.

"That's right," Josh says.

Canejo regards him, waiting.

There's a long pause. "It was Tío Goyo," Josh finally says, "from the Halcón Pueblo."

Canejo nods. "You know those men are not to be trusted."

This is new and I'd like to hear more—like, hello, why?—but Josh only shrugs.

"Who's not to be trusted?" Marina asks, rejoining us.

"The hawk uncles," Donalita says. "The ones that go around killing cousins with evil spirits in them."

She says it like she's never had a bloodthirsty thought in her own pretty head.

Marina glances at Josh and he shrugs again.

"Don't take them lightly," Canejo says. "They can be dangerous."

Josh nods. "I can be dangerous, too. Everyone has that potential. The trick is in knowing when your aggressive actions are justified, and when they're not."

He and Canejo are staring at each other and I don't know what to think. Josh has always been so easygoing. Between the two of us, if anyone was going to get into a fight, it'd be me. But he's different now. Focused. Tough. Enough of the old Josh remains that I doubt he'd try to pick a fight, but I'm damned sure he won't back down from one now. And I'd bet money that he'll be the one standing when the dust settles.

"So, the dude brought us some tea," I say. "That's nice, right? Hospitable."

Everyone turns to look at me, and my inane comment does just what I hoped for. It defuses the tension.

Josh grins. "Very hospitable." He gives Canejo a little bow. "For which we are grateful."

The rabbit man shrugs. "If I'd known you were camping out here all night, I would have offered you pallets inside."

Josh smiles. "No, we enjoyed being out here tonight." He draws Marina to him and gives her cheek a kiss, then lets her go and sinks to a cross-legged position beside the tea tray. She sits down beside him, close, all dreamy looking, like she didn't get a lot of sleep last night. Her hand is on his thigh.

This is going to be real messy when we get back home.

"Can I pour for anyone?" Josh asks.

Donalita scampers over. She picks up a mug and holds it out for him to fill.

"Sure," I say. "Why not? Kind of like a last meal, right? Or at least a last drink."

"Okay, I know this isn't going to be easy," Josh says as he pours tea for the two of us. "But we'll get through it. All of us will."

Donalita passes me my tea and settles back down beside me.

"Are you talking about when Chaingang finds out, or the rally?" I ask.

"Both, I guess."

Marina gets a pained look on her face.

Canejo looks at me, puzzled. "What is it that worries you so?" he asks.

I roll my eyes. "Dude, where do I start?"

JOSH

Really, Des? I think. We don't know anything about this guy except that he helped Marina—admittedly a big plus, but it doesn't automatically make him our new best friend.

Des shoots me a glance and I see that he's realizing that for himself. He opens his mouth, then closes it as though thinking better of saying anything more.

Canejo sits on his haunches so that we're all pretty much at eye level. I take a sip of tea and study the rabbit man over the brim of my mug. He's obviously curious about what we've been discussing. I decide to switch subjects before Des can change his mind again.

"Do you know anything about our world?" I say to the rabbit man.

"The first world? Of course. It's where everything started."

"I mean, our world *now*."

"I haven't been in Dainnan for that long," Canejo says, "so I doubt things have changed much in the brief time I've been here."

"Well, there's this congressman," I say, "who's got a hate-on for Wildlings." I go on to tell Canejo about Householder's rally, and how he wants to round us all up.

He nods in sympathy. "As you witnessed, Nanuq and some others have similar ideas about your kind, and antipathy toward ordinary humans, as well, for that matter."

"That's just it," I say. "Nanuq knows about the rally today. He's been scheming to have the congressman killed and pin it on a Wildling so that humans will turn against us and lock us all up. Maybe even give the authorities justification to euthanize us, like animals, and then conveniently forget that animal people ever existed." I shake my head. "As if that makes any sense."

"You're not looking at it from the right perspective," Canejo says.

"You can make sense out of it?"

"Nanuq can't kill Wildlings himself without arousing the ire of the cousins. But if he can get humans to start killing Wildlings, it will drive the undecided cousins to his side. They will see that they are no longer safe living alongside of you—especially the smaller, gentler cousins—and they will come to him for their own safety. He's not hunting you down because he hates you. He's building an army."

"To do what? There are billions of human beings. He can't expect to take them all on."

"I don't know," Canejo says. "But he'll have a plan—his kind always do—and the will to implement it."

"Auntie Min must have figured that out," I say. "So we have to make sure he doesn't get to the congressman. If he doesn't die, the Wildlings won't get blamed, and Nanuq will be back at square one."

Canejo nods.

"And then he can be dealt with outside of the public eye," I say.

"Perhaps. But that's not necessarily your responsibility."

"Except nobody else seems ready to take it on. Don't worry," I add, as much for my friends as for him. "It's not something I'm planning to rush into. It's not even something I want to do. But at some point, someone has to fix this."

Canejo accepts that with an incline of his head.

"And this other problem?" he asks. "Who or what is Chaingang?"

"A personal problem," I tell him.

"Ah."

"He's a friend of ours," Marina says. "He's in a biker gang and he was sort of my boyfriend." She hesitates, then adds, "I guess he still thinks he is."

Canejo glances at her hand on my thigh. *"Ah."*

"It's not like you think," she says. "Josh and I have known each other since we were little kids. Just ... not like this."

"And Chaingang—"

"Theo," she says. "His real name's Theo."

"Theo," Canejo repeats. "He will be angry?"

"I honestly don't know. He's always been hard to read. But he'll be hurt and I don't want to hurt him."

"Perhaps if he cares for you," Canejo says, "it will be enough for him that you're happy."

"It wouldn't be enough for me," I say.

Canejo leans closer, his gaze locked on Marina's.

"You're afraid that they'll fight over you," he says.

Marina nods.

"Oh, come on," I say. "It's not like we're living in the days of slavery. People aren't possessions. Marina makes the choice about who she wants to be with. Nobody can force her."

"Dude, he'll so want to fight you," Des says.

Canejo turns to me. "If the only way you could be with her was to fight for her, would you?"

"Not to own her."

"That's not what I asked," he says.

I sigh. Everybody's looking at me, waiting for my answer. But it's Marina that I'm speaking to when I finally say, "It's not something I'd want to do, but yeah, I would, if it meant protecting her right to choose. I just realized in the past few days that I've been letting her slip away for as long as we've known each other. I won't make that mistake again. The only reason I'd ever walk away now is if she said go."

I've changed in a lot of ways since I first got the mountain lion under my skin, but one thing that hasn't changed is that when I make a commitment, I stick with it. Marina knows this. Her eyes are bright with a moist sheen. She takes my hand and squeezes my fingers.

"I don't make a habit of giving advice," Canejo says, "but in this case I will make an exception because it would be a pity for things to go wrong simply because you don't see what I see. Stand together to face your challenges and always be honest with one another. This is as true for when you speak with your friend Theo as it is when you face the challenges the other cousins set before you."

"All for one and one for all," Des murmurs under his breath.

Canejo smiles and adds, "Yes. Be bold, but don't be foolish."

"I think we can do that," I say.

"Of course you can."

He stands up, and placing his palms together as though he's praying, he gives us a short bow. "I must return to my students," he says. "You can leave the tray where it is when you're done with your tea. I'll fetch it later."

We all scramble to our feet. He turns and doesn't look back as he goes into the building, the glass door whispering shut behind him.

"He's a pretty cool dude," Des says. "You know, for a horny old guy who doesn't seem to get out much."

Marina and I both spew our tea at the same time and reach out to slap Des. He dances out of our reach, laughing. Donalita grabs him and gives him a fierce grin and a hug.

I shake my head, take a last gulp of tea, and return the mug to the tray.

"I'd better go see what Auntie Min wants from me," I say. "You guys want to go to the rally first, or come with me?"

"Come with," Marina says.

Des looks down at Donalita. When she nods, he says, "Yeah, totally."

I don't know what I ever did to deserve their loyalty all those years ago when we first started hanging, but I'm so glad to have them.

"This means a lot," I say.

We collect everything that Tío Goyo brought and stuff it into the backpacks.

"We just have to make one stop along the way," I tell them. "Everybody grab hands and don't let go."

I take Marina's hand. Once Des and Donalita are linked up, I call up the maps and highlight the route I took to get here from that red rock cliff with the big pine trees. I figure out that direct connection and then take a step forward. The dead city vanishes from around us, and next we're all standing on the cliff, looking out over the canyons and forests, the sky impossibly vast and blue overhead.

Des is looking a little green, but everyone else seems fine.

"You okay?" I ask.

"Yeah, pretty much." He lets go of my hand and takes a couple of steadying breaths, looking around as he does. "What is this place, anyway?"

"It's one of those slow worlds I was talking about. We could spend the whole day here and only a few moments would pass by in our world, so we won't be late for anything."

"But we're not spending days here, right?" Des asks.

His colour's already looking better.

I shake my head. "This is where Tío Goyo brought me before. I just want to clean up our campsite."

We do the same as we did in the world of the dead city: pick up what doesn't belong here—blankets, kettle, mugs, food wrappers—and stuff it all into the other pair of backpacks. When we're done, we've got four of them in a pile.

"Give me a sec," I say.

I grab two of the packs in each hand and return my body to the earth, bringing them with me. For a moment my friends see a hawk hanging there in the air where I was standing, then I call up my body again, this time holding nothing. Donalita applauds with great enthusiasm.

"Dude," Des says. "That was friggin' awesome."

"And a handy way to get rid of trash," Marina says. "Where does it go?"

"Back into the earth."

She smiles. "When this is all over, you should open a landfill business."

"It'd be kind of hard to explain where the trash actually goes," I say. "And I'm not sure it'd be a great idea to do it on any large-scale basis."

"There's that. When are you going to teach us how to do that hawk trick?"

"I don't know if I can," I say. "And there's way more to it than what you just saw."

"Plus you need magic tea," Des says.

"Plus we need magic tea," I agree. "But I can ask Tío Goyo."

"Meh," Donalita says. "The hawk uncles never give up their secrets."

"We'll see," I tell her. "Maybe when I have some time to actually relax, I can figure out how to teach you. In the meantime, let's go find out what Auntie Min has to say."

Marina and Des both hold out their hands. I take them, make sure that Donalita is holding on to Des, then call up the maps in my mind.

"I need to focus for a moment," I say.

Auntie Min is easy to pinpoint, but she's more than one world away. If I could just change to my spirit form, I could be there as quickly as a thought, but I have no idea what will happen if I try to bring other living beings with me. And I'm sure not going to experiment with my friends, especially given how Des felt a bit ill just getting here.

So I map out the quickest route, then we cross briefly to another world, where I take a moment to express our respect and thanks for passage, and finally move us onward to our own.

It doesn't take long. Maybe half an hour after leaving the red rock cliff, we're stepping out of the otherworld onto the bluff by Tiki Bay. I feel a shock of recognition as soon as the grass and dirt are under my feet. I'm not sure if it's because this is my home world, or because it's the first world. All I know is that between the scent of the ocean air and the feel of the ground underfoot, I'm more connected than I've felt anywhere else.

There's stuff I don't like: the hum of electricity running through the wires along the highway, and a faint odour of pollution: diesel, gas, I don't know what all. But the sky's blue, the sun's shining. And maybe So-Cal is too dry, and there'll soon be fires up in the hills, and the Santa Anas will blow their smoke down to us here on the coast, but it's home.

My home.

I didn't even realize how much I missed it until right now.

Auntie Min doesn't seem surprised to see us, but we've no sooner arrived than we're surrounded by cousins—at least thirty strong, mostly crows and dogs. Des drops my hand and makes a grab for Donalita, who's already pulled her knife out.

"Dude," he says. "It's okay. The dogs are on our side now."

"So they say."

"So say we all," Auntie Min tells her.

I recognize Lupe of the East Riversea Blue Dog Clan from when she pledged her allegiance to Marina. She grins at our appearance and salutes us—or rather, Marina, I assume—by bringing a fist to her chest. The other dog cousins follow suit—all except for one male standing behind Lupe with a woman who could be his twin. He's staring daggers at Marina.

His twin nudges him. "Don't be an asshole, Jimmy," she mutters.

"Whose side are you on?" he asks. "She's Chaingang's mate."

"Look again," the woman says.

I realize that Marina and I are still holding hands.

Auntie Min sighs. "Unfortunately, there have been some problems between the Ocean Avers and the dog clans," she tells us.

Marina's hand tightens on mine. "We heard," she says.

"We also heard," I say, "that the Avers didn't start it."

Jimmy starts to move forward, but his lookalike grabs his upper arm and stops him. Lupe and a couple of other dog cousins step in front of them to block Jimmy.

"Ana," Auntie Min says without turning. "If you can't get your brother to behave, would you please take him away?"

"He won't cause any more problems, Señora," Ana says.

Auntie Min raises her eyebrows and I almost smile, but I catch myself.

"Has Lupe told you about Nanuq?" I ask.

Auntie Min and Lupe nod at the same time.

"So, are we going after Nanuq and the condors, or do you still want to save Householder's life?"

"What I want," Auntie Min says, "and what we need to do aren't the same. I don't particularly care for the congressman, but if we can stop him from being killed today, we'll be better poised to resolve other problems without bloodshed."

I nod. "We also met a jackalope named Canejo, who says you're a great warrior."

She smiles ever so slightly. "I am a warrior, yes. But a warrior knows when to go to battle and when to let diplomacy win her battles for her."

She holds my gaze until I nod to show that I understand.

"So what do you want us to do?" I ask.

"Join the others at city hall," she says. "Locate the killer and stop him. The longer we delay, the greater chance this individual has of causing a problem that we'll be dealing with for years to come."

"Okay," I say. "Can anyone give us a ride to city hall?"

Lupe steps forward. "Most of us walked or flew here, but I have access to a car down in the parking lot."

"Can you take all four of us?" I ask.

She shakes her head. "It's just a VW Bug."

"No problemo, dude," Des says.

I raise an eyebrow, but he's not looking at me. He puts out a hand, palm up.

"Come on, baby," he says. "Do your thing."

Donalita jumps up in the air where she changes into what looks like a pebble. Des snatches it with a quick move and gives it a kiss before he sticks it in his pocket.

He laughs at the look on my face. "You're not the only cousin with moves," he says.

I'm not alone in my surprise. Everybody except for Auntie Min is just staring at him, trying to figure how they did that. He cocks his head, grinning, and gives me a wink, then turns to Lupe.

"So what are we waiting for? Let's boogie," he says.

MARINA

I try to concentrate on what's going on around me, but my mind is overloaded with confusion, like some endless game of brain ping-pong—this thought, that thought bouncing back and forth—until I feel like my head might explode.

Last night …

Finally being with Josh was so right that I can still feel my body and soul humming along to the same vibration as his.

When he kissed me I just got lost in it. There was just us—a boy and a girl, perfectly in tune, making the best music ever. Everything else went away. All my worries and problems. Wildlings, otherworlds, the rally, my relationship with Theo, Mamá's inevitable freak-out when she finds out what I am and where I've been.

After all that went down in the past couple of weeks, I thought I was over Josh, that we'd never be able to repair the damage to our friendship, and any possibility of being *more* than friends was gone forever. Josh had never looked at me like that, anyway.

Theo did, and he made sure I knew it. I was vulnerable, and he made me feel special and protected in a way that I needed.

Sure, I had serious reservations because of his gang affiliations, but I was hoping we could somehow work that out. Deep down, I think I wanted to save him from that life. Move away and start all over. I think he wanted that, too.

But now everything has changed and I realize it's more like Theo was just a placeholder. Which is awful. He's going to think I was never serious—just a tease leading him on.

The horrible thing is, I can't quite convince myself that it's not true.

This morning I felt all tingly and happy until reality started creeping back in and I realized that I'm a cheater—and a lot like the skank I once accused Elzie of being. Why else would I just drop everything as soon as Josh opened himself up to me?

But then I think about what Josh said to Canejo: *I just realized in the past few days that I've been letting her slip away for as long as we've known each other. I won't make that mistake again. The only reason I'd ever walk away now is if she said go.*

He was talking to Canejo, but he was looking right at me. He wanted me to know he meant it, that this isn't some temporary thing for him.

Just as it's never been for me.

But Theo. When he finds out, the tough gangbanger he is won't let any feelings show, except for maybe anger. He'll be hurting and alone behind the new wall that he'll build to hide his disappointment. He's had so many letdowns in his life. I don't want to be one more.

So what can I do? I've known since we were kids that Josh was the boy I wanted to be with forever. Even when I dated other guys and he dated other girls. Even when Elzie came along.

"Earth to Marina," I hear Des say. "Are you with us, dude, or what?"

I start out of my reverie and focus on the here and now.

We're in Lupe's VW Bug on the Pacific Coast Highway, coming into Santa Feliz, Josh and Des squished into the back because Lupe insisted that I ride in front with her.

"Sorry," I say, then add the understatement of the year. "I was distracted for a second. What were you saying?"

"Josh thinks we should go with the buddy system once we get to city hall—you know, pair up—and we thought you might rather be with me, or Donalita, instead of Josh."

I sit up a little straighter. "Why wouldn't I want to be with Josh?"

"Hello? Because Chaingang will be there, dude."

"Well, I can't just avoid him forever."

"Yeah, but we're supposed to be focused on keeping the congressman from getting killed, so maybe now's not the time to let Chaingang know that the surf's not up for him anymore."

"Why can't you call him by his real name?"

"Because he'd probably rip off my head if I did. We're not exactly BFFs."

I turn around in my seat. "What do you think, Josh?"

"I think I'll stick to calling him Chaingang, too."

"Ha ha, not very funny. You know what I mean."

He smiles. I can tell he's been in his own reverie about last night and is still floating in the afterglow. "It's your call," he says.

"No, what do *you* think?"

"I'd rather be with you, but it could get awkward and Des is right. We need to stay focused on what we're there to do."

Lupe reaches across the console and places a reassuring hand on mine for a second. "Members of the Blue Dog Clan are in the crowd," she says. "We'll make sure he doesn't hurt you."

"Theo would never raise a hand to me," I tell her. "What I'm afraid of is him being hurt and upset when he finds out. And I don't want him finding out before I have a chance to talk to him myself."

"Then go with Des," Josh says. "Donalita can come with me."

"I'll be there," Lupe says, "as soon as I find a place to park."

Parking turns out to be the least of our problems. A dozen blocks from city hall the streets are so choked that we decide to abandon the car and continue on foot. Lupe pulls over into a back service lane, kills the engine, and everybody gets out except for Des. We all watch in fascination as Des takes the pebble out of his pocket. He taps it on the window and suddenly he's got his arms full of Donalita. She lets herself fall across the rest of the back seat and grins at us.

"Ta-da!" she says.

"Just what we need," Josh mutters. "Another clown." But he's smiling as the two of them squeeze out of the back of the car at the same time.

"I'll see you later," Lupe says. "Good hunting."

She takes off before I can thank her for the ride.

"Let's go," Josh says. "Donalita, you're with me."

"Really?" She shoots Des a pouty glance.

He gives her shoulder a light bump. "It's because of Chaingang," he says. "Marina wants to wait till this is all over before telling him." He points two fingers at us. "These two can't hide their goo-goo eyes when they're together."

She nods, but fixes me with a serious look. "You'd better keep him safe," she says.

Josh laughs and gives her a little push toward the busy street. "You need to work on your people skills, coati girl," I hear him tell her as Des and I follow.

"I have *great* people skills," she says. "Ask anyone. Well, not the javelina boys, but they're always rude first. But anyone else ..."

Josh nods. "Uh-huh."

"It's true. I once charmed a whole pod of killer whales with nothing more than a smile and my good manners."

"I can see why they'd be disarmed," Josh says. I can hear the laughter in his voice.

"Is she always like this?" I ask Des.

He grins. "This is her good behaviour."

"Sounds like you guys make a good match."

He shakes his head and looks at Donalita's back. "Dude, I don't know what we are," he says.

"But you like her."

He nods. "Probably too much for my own good. I don't expect her to stick around. I mean, she's such a free spirit, why would she?"

"I don't know. But if you want her to stay, you'd better make the effort."

They reach the street before we do. Donalita turns and wiggles her fingers at us, then dances to catch up with Josh, who's already crossing in between the bumper-to-bumper traffic that's now in gridlock.

Des and I stay on this side of the street. "How about you, dude?" he asks. "Are you making the effort?"

"What's that supposed to mean?"

He shrugs. "Don't get me wrong. I'm over the moon that you two are finally together. But I don't want to see either of you hurt."

I feel the tiniest chill crawl up my spine. "It's a bit scary," I admit. "But it's also Josh."

"A new Josh," Des says. "Not the one we grew up with. This one has a mountain lion living under his skin and some kind of weird-ass GPS in his head. He can navigate between worlds and he can turn into a hawk. Hell, he can put out pheromones and who knows what else. Maybe there's even stuff that hasn't shown up yet."

"He says he doesn't really turn into a hawk—that's just how we see it."

"Whatever. The point is, he's Josh, yeah, but he's a lot more now, too, and it seems like every time we turn around, somebody else has plans for him."

I shrug. "He's been doing a good job of handling them so far."

Des nods. "But what if it gets to be too much and he decides the only way he can deal is to go away? Are you going with him? Would you be willing to leave your family and everything you know?"

"Do you know something I don't?"

"We both know the same thing," Des says. "Josh doesn't like to be the center of attention—which, by the way, dude, has always seemed really weird to me for a guy who also wants to play lead guitar in a surf band—but the point is, push comes to shove, I can easily see him pulling a Kerouac and hitting the road."

"I don't think it will come to that," I say. "Through all of this, Josh has been trying really hard to get his old life back."

"I suppose."

But then I get it.

"You're not really worried about how *I'm* going to deal," I say.

"I am so!"

"Okay. Except you're also worried about getting left behind, yourself."

"Maybe I am. Is that so weird? I'm the only one in our little band of superheroes without a superpower. Of course I'm going to get left behind because otherwise, I'll be Jimmy Olsen, the kid that always needs to get rescued."

"Batman doesn't have superpowers and he seems to keep up just fine."

"Yeah, but—"

"Just as you have so far. For one thing, Cory would never have found me if it wasn't for you. I was the Jimmy Olsen in that dead city."

He's about to say more, except then we turn a corner and see city hall, the big stage with its "Humans for Humanity" banner and the flood of people all over the grounds. They're still streaming in.

"Holy crap!" Des says. "I never knew there were that many people in Santa Feliz."

My heart sinks at the numbers that Householder has managed to pull in, but then I notice that not everybody here is supporting the congressman. I see as many pro-Wildling signs as I do ones for Householder's cause. The crowd is huge and the atmosphere feels charged and ready to blow.

JOSH

I'm using the maps in my head to get a better sense of my surroundings, but there are so many people crowded around us that I have to dial my awareness way back. But even with the GPS tuned down, I'm getting a ton of information. Too much to sift through easily.

"I've never seen so many people," Donalita says.

"Me neither. Except on TV. This is crazy." I turn to look at her. "How are we supposed to find one whack-job in amongst them all?"

She looks as overwhelmed as I'm feeling, but then she shrugs and grins.

"We just start walking around," she says, "and look."

My gaze travels over the crowd. I spot Auntie Min's crow soldiers easily enough. They're on every vantage point—palm trees, light posts, rooflines. There are even a few of them on the edges of the big canvas canopy above the stage. I also spy local cops and state troopers, but there's no sign of the FBI, or Chaingang's crew. I could open my maps a little wider and find them, but that's not who we're looking for, anyway.

I offer Donalita my hand and she looks at it as though it's some alien object.

"We don't want to get separated," I say.

There's still a half hour before the rally officially starts. Up on the stage, techs are running around making last-minute adjustments. I finally pick out Matteson and Solana standing in a cluster of suits just by the wings on stage left. Then one of the suits moves and I see Danny Reed—Elzie's friend from her activist days before we hooked up. The one that turned into a rat for the FBI.

That can't be good.

I suppose the FBI has some kind of vetting process, but what if he's still in contact with Elzie? What if he's in on the plot to kill the congressman? Hell, what if *he's* the assassin?

It seems so obvious that I can't believe nobody else has twigged to it. But then I realize that I haven't talked to either Matteson or Solana since I got back. They don't know what I found out in the otherworld.

I reach in my pocket for my phone, but of course it's not there. I can't remember the last time I saw it.

"Do you have a phone I can borrow?" I ask Donalita.

"Sure."

I wait a moment, but she doesn't produce it.

"Um, can I borrow it now?"

"It'll have to be later," she says. "I don't have it with me. I think I left it under Des's bed."

"What were you doing—never mind." I grab her hand. "We have to get up to the stage," I tell her.

She follows in my wake as I wade into the crowd. I must say

"excuse me" a hundred times, but people move out of my way. When I pause for a moment to figure how to get through the next press of bodies, Donalita leans against my back.

"It's so funny," she says in my ear. "They're all scared of you. They don't know why, but they are."

I turn to tell her that's ridiculous, and bump into this huge guy standing beside me. If he's not one of the crew who does weightlifting down on the beach, then he should go meet them because they'd get along just fine. He stiffens and starts to react, but before I can apologize, I see something change in his eyes. It's not fear, so much as the look of a person who feels totally out of their depth.

"Sorry, man," he mumbles and quickly turns away.

I turn back to Donalita.

"You're a predator," she says, speaking softly, so that her voice doesn't carry. But I hear every word. "They can't explain how they know, but la-la-la—they can't ignore it, either."

Great. So now I'm putting out a dangerous vibe, making people uncomfortable without even realizing that I'm doing it. Just one more thing to worry about.

But that'll have to wait till later. First I need to warn Matteson about Danny Reed.

I push ahead through the crowd, very aware now of how people are shifting so that they don't touch me as I pass. But I take advantage of it to work my way closer to the stage.

CHAINGANG

I'm not sure which part of the equation Fat Boy likes the least: backing down from us, getting into it with the state troopers or knowing that if he stays on course, he's got a confrontation with Josh coming up. Which also means having to deal with *los tíos*, and I already know the hawk uncles have some weird hold over the Mexican gangs. When you add in the fact that the Kings are just plain loco, there's no way to tell what he'll do.

Turns out he opts for backing down. His eyes are spitting hate, but he's got a big fake smile on his face.

"We'll see you later, *ese*," he says. "You have your fun today."

He and Para move off through the crowd. I see the staties hesitate. Finally one of them trails along behind Fat Boy and his lieutenant, and the other watches us for a minute or so before moving on himself.

"What's the deal with the bangers and these hawk dudes?" J-Dog wants to know.

"Beats me. But I've seen one of them use just a few words to stop a whole roomful of Kings about to blow."

"You girls finished your pissing match?" Matteson asks through the earpiece.

"They teach you to talk like that in FBI school?" I ask him.

He laughs. "How's it looking out there?" he asks.

"We're shooting blanks," J-Dog says. "Yo, homies. Talk to me."

One by one the boys check in, but there's dick to report. Nobody sees anything suspicious or out of the ordinary.

"Unless you count way too many honkies," Dekker says, "got nothing better to do than whine about something that's never going to be a for-real hassle in their whole lives."

The crew laughs.

"Word," Shorty adds. "Strictly First World problems."

"How about you, Matteson?" I ask. "Anything?"

"One of Lalo's boys ID'd the Wildlings on Householder's detail as wolf guys from something he calls the Kickaha Blue Mountain Clan."

"Never heard of them."

"Yeah, like I have," Matteson says. "Lalo says a lot of them get into law enforcement and they're loyal to a fault when it comes to their jobs."

"Dogs, wolves," J-Dog says. "What's the diff? We've already seen how the dog clans play the game, so is this gospel?"

"The dog clans were under a binding," Lalo says, irritation plain in his voice.

J-Dog sighs. "Yeah, yeah. We heard. Broken record, bro. You willing to take the chance on Householder's life, seeing how you're all set on keeping the douchebag alive?"

"I am," Lalo tells him.

J-Dog looks at me and rolls his eyes.

"We'll keep an eye on things up here," Solana breaks in. "You keep doing the same out in the crowd. No news is good news."

"Got it," I say, then add to the boys, "You heard the man, homies. Eyes sharp, stay safe."

J-Dog laughs. "Stay safe? What are you now—our den mother?"

I turn to J-Dog, but before I can say anything, I see them over his shoulder. Des and Marina, working their way through the crowd in our direction. My heart does a little jump. They catch sight of me at the same time and the welcoming smile that starts on my lips dies fast and hard.

Something's wrong with Marina. Not physically. She looks fine. Mighty fine, if you want to know the truth. Whatever happened to her in the otherworld, she got through it in one piece. But there's a big sadness in her eyes. Our gazes meet and I already know that everything has changed. I couldn't tell you how or why, it just has. As if to confirm it, I see that Des—who always seems a little edgy around me anyway—is really putting out the anxious vibe. Like this is the last place he wants to be, and I'm the last person he wants to see. Normally he's like a nervous puppy, eager to please, but as soon as he spotted me, he looked uncomfortable as hell.

And then I get it.

Cory. He must have told Marina about what went down with the dogs back at the compound. They've got a hate-on for any Aver, and if she's part of their crew now, that puts us on opposite sides.

Fuck.

I reach up and turn off my earpiece.

"Bro?" J-Dog asks.

"I need a moment here," I tell him.

He follows my gaze. "That your girl?"

"I don't know," I say.

I step away so that I can meet her out of his earshot. We stop a couple of paces away from each other, but it feels like we're standing on opposite rims of the Grand Canyon. Des gives me an uneasy nod, then sidles to one side and pretends a great interest in the preparations on stage, leaving Marina and I facing each other.

I want to take her in my arms, but there are too many people around, and who knows which one is going to run off and rat us out to her mother. Plus there's the look in her eyes. Even if we were alone, she might not want that.

I shove my hands in my pockets.

"Hey," she says.

"I was worried about you."

She gives me a small smile. "I was worried about me, too."

"I heard you took on the big bad, all by yourself."

"Sure," she says. "If you can call turning invisible and shaking in my boots taking somebody on. I wouldn't have survived a minute if Josh and the dog clans hadn't stepped up to help me."

"How'd that happen?"

"You mean, Josh? It was kind of a fluke. He didn't even know I was missing, but he wanted to see me. He just went looking and there I was, in over my head."

She's looking at my shoulder instead of my eyes.

"No, I meant the dog clans," I say. "Why'd they help you?"

"I freed them from the binding that this guy Nanuq had them under."

"Good job," I say.

She shrugs. "Anybody would have done it. Well, except

maybe Donalita. She thought they'd turn on us, but just the opposite happened."

"Yeah, I heard about that, too." I hesitate, then add, "I guess Cory told you about what happened at the compound?"

She drops her gaze to her feet. "He did."

A large portion of the crowd suddenly cheers, and then I hear Congressman Householder being introduced. Right now, I couldn't care less about that piece-of-crap politician.

"I know he's on my case about it," I say, "but I've got nothing to apologize for. They came after me and mine. They took a run at my grandma."

The crowd's still going crazy, but we're Wildlings. We could hear each other if a jet was going by right over our heads.

"I understand," she says. "I might have done the same thing if they came after my little sisters, or Mamá."

I get a little flicker of hope. "So we're good?"

Maybe this weird vibe I'm getting is just because of everything she went through. But that dies with the next thing she says.

"I ... not really, Theo. I just can't do this gang thing."

"But you're part of the dog clan crew now, aren't you?"

She shakes her head. "That's their idea, not mine."

"I can be done with the gang," I tell her.

"This isn't really the time or place to get into it," she says. "We need to talk when things calm down a little."

"I'm serious," I tell her.

"I know you think you are, but—"

"Holy SHIT!" I hear J-Dog yell behind me.

I turn, bringing my earpiece back online, and then everything goes to hell.

JOSH

Even with the involuntary intimidation thing going for me, it's taking too long for us to get through the crowd. It's just too massive. I can't see over the people in front of us. Then I hear Householder being introduced. I push forward, Donalita on my heels. We reach a spot where we can see the stage just as Householder steps up to the microphone. I don't look at him. I'm too busy marking Danny's position.

Except he doesn't look particularly threatening. He's standing with Solana, the pair of them scanning the crowd. Matteson's on the other side of the stage. I spot four more guys in suits up there doing the same thing. I figure them for Secret Service.

But if Danny's not the threat, who is?

I start to push forward again. I need to get to the stage so I can get a clearer idea of what's going on. I know the assassin's going to have to come in close because Auntie Min's crows occupy every place a sniper would choose.

Almost there. I pull up the maps in my head, keeping the focus close—just the area around me and the stage. I mark the cousins and Wildlings, but except for Danny, none of them are close enough to be a problem.

The crowd keeps parting for me and finally I'm just a couple of rows of people away from the stage.

Everything still seems clear.

Donalita taps my back to get my attention.

"Stop growling," she murmurs. "You're freaking people out."

I didn't even realize I was doing it.

But the mountain lion feels my tension and he's aching to wear my skin. He doesn't like the crowd. He knows we're hunting, but he's frustrated because I can't get a bead on our prey.

I start to push him down, but suddenly it happens.

A cousin appears in the press of people to the right of me, stepping directly from the otherworld to here. People stumble around, pushed aside by his appearance. I can't see his face because of the hood he's wearing. He's small, but has a high-powered rifle in his hands. Someone screams. People scramble to get out of the way.

I'm aware of everything going on in the chaos. An Ocean Aver lunging for the guy. All the security on the stage reaching for guns. One of the Secret Service guys starting for the congressman. Householder looking startled, not knowing what's going on, but aware that something's wrong.

They're all going to be too late.

I won't be. I can't get to the shooter in time, not with the press of people. But I have another option.

I let the mountain lion out and leap for the stage so that I'll be right between the congressman and the shooter.

I hear the crack of the shot.

My leap takes me directly into the path of the bullet.

Just before it hits me, I think, crap, this is really going to hurt.

Then the bullet punches into me, lifting me right off my paws, and it's like my chest explodes.

CHAINGANG

I don't have to ask J-Dog what's going on—it's all over my earpiece, everybody shouting at the same time.

"—he came from," Tall Boy's saying. "I'm not going to get to him in—"

"Take him down!" That's Matteson.

J-Dog and I move fast, shoving our way through the crowd. I see the back of a dreadlocked kid and realize it's Josh, just as he shifts.

"—The fuck?"

"Is that a mountain lion?"

Josh leaps on stage.

The sharp crack of a rifle cuts the air.

People start screaming and trying to run away from the stage, pushing against me in a wave.

J-Dog gets swept back, unable to fight the swarm, but they can't stop me. They just bounce off me as they try to get away.

I see the mountain lion go down. By the time it hits the stage, it's shifted back into Josh.

A Secret Service man flattens the congressman behind the podium, kneels above him, gun out and pointed at Josh.

Tall Boy's on the shooter, wrestling with him. The gun goes off again, but the barrel's pointed up at the sky. Then Matteson and another Secret Service man leap off the stage to help Tall Boy.

My gaze locks on Josh. He's just lying there with an ugly hole in his chest, a pool of blood spreading out from under him.

Come on, bro, I think. I've seen you do this before in the barrio. You take the shot and you go down, but you get back up.

He doesn't move.

What are you waiting for? I want to yell at him. Enough with dragging out the drama. Get up.

Get the fuck up!

But he doesn't so much as twitch. He just sprawls there on the wooden floor of the stage, bleeding out.

Finally I reach the edge of the stage, but before I can climb up to get to Josh, the Secret Service man kneeling over Householder points his gun in my direction.

I stop moving and raise my hands.

DES

"Josh!" Marina screams when the mountain lion leaps onto the stage and gets shot.

She lunges forward, but the press of the crowd is too much. I grab hold of her as we get swept away by all the screaming people. Everybody's in a panic and only thinking of themselves. I see more than one person go down and be trampled. The same thing might have happened to us, but Marina gets her balance and uses her Wildling strength to become as immovable as a post.

People bounce off her, but they can't shift her. I stand behind her and we let the worst of the wave of people go by before we start inching our way toward the stage once more. It takes us a while to reach the place where Chaingang is standing, arms in the air with one of the Secret Service men pointing a gun at him.

And there on the stage is Josh. Not moving and there's way too much blood.

"Oh, Josh," Marina says, her voice so soft I can only just hear her.

Tears well in my eyes.

I can't believe this is it. That he's gone. I keep waiting for him to jump up the way he's supposed to have done in that taquería after he got shot point-blank. But I realize that's not going to happen.

Marina is starting to shake. I hesitate a moment, then put my arms around her. She buries her face against my shoulder. A moment later Donalita shows up. Her arm goes around my waist and she leans against my side.

I can't take my eyes off of Josh.

I can't believe this is real.

I'm vaguely aware of Agent Solana stepping across the stage.

"It's okay, Sean," he says to the Secret Service guy. "He's with us."

Sean gives a quick nod, then lowers his gun and turns to where one of the other members of the security detail is helping the congressman to his feet.

Chaingang lowers his arms, but otherwise, he doesn't move. He just stands there like me, staring at Josh. Then he gives his head a shake and starts toward the stairs by the corner of the stage where the handcuffed shooter is being held face down at ground level.

Matteson stops him before he can go more than a few steps.

"I'm sorry," Matteson says. "I really am. But you can't touch her."

Her?

Marina and I turn in the direction of the prisoner, whose back is to us. The hood is down and we can see spikes of short blond hair.

"I only need a moment," Chaingang says.

Matteson shakes his head. "She just took a shot at a US congressman. Where she's going, no one's going to see her for a long, long time."

"If you want to keep her in custody, you'll let me talk to her."

"What's that supposed to mean?"

"Think about it. She stepped right out of nowhere. She came from the otherworld. First chance she gets, she'll step right back and you guys'll be standing around with your dicks in your hands and no prisoner."

"And you can stop that from happening?"

"You bet your ass I can. I just need a few words with her. You won't like what you're going to hear, but you're welcome to listen in."

Matteson studies Chaingang for a long moment.

"I know you're hurting," he says. "I get it. She killed your friend. But you can't lay a hand on her—you understand that, right?"

Chaingang nods. "But you might want to get your Secret Service buddies out of earshot."

I hear someone growl as Matteson and Chaingang move away toward the stage. At first I think it's Donalita, but then I realize that Lupe has joined us. She's staring at Josh's body, her lips pulled back, a dark look in her eyes. I get the sense she's about to shift into her dog form and rip into something. But she gets a grip on herself.

"Say the word," she tells Marina, "and we'll take down the one who did this."

Marina shakes her head. "That ... that won't bring Josh back."

CHAINGANG

Matteson leads me to where the two Secret Service agents have their prisoner by the corner of the stage. I get a big-cousin *ping* from one of them and I can tell by the way his eyes narrow that he's reading me. I forgot about the cousins on the congressman's detail. Lot of good they did.

A half-dozen crows are perched on the scaffolding that holds up the tent covering above the stage. From the corner of my eye I see Cory. He's helping someone to their feet, but his attention's on me. I see other cousins all around.

"This is Theo Washington," Matteson says as we approach. "He's been consulting with us on this, and it was one of his men who first took down the shooter. He needs a word with the prisoner."

"Not going to happen," the human of the pair says.

But the cousin reads something in my eyes.

"Check with Sean," he says. "See how the congressman is doing. I've got this."

They lock gazes for a moment, then the human shrugs and goes back up on the stage.

"You've got two minutes," the cousin tells me.

"Only need one," I tell him.

I can't tell what kind of cousin the prisoner is, but I'm getting a familiar *ping* as though I know her. Even though she's cuffed behind her back, the Secret Service man is holding her by a bicep.

If the prisoner tries to step away into the otherworld, she's still going to be in handcuffs and she'll be dragging a cop with her. But she isn't always going to be under such close watch. Soon as she's alone in a cell, she'll be gone.

"Listen, bitch," I tell her. "I know what you are. Now here's the deal. You're going to stay in custody and you're going to take whatever's coming to you. You try to shift away, and I'll hunt you down."

She turns her head sideways, looks me in the eye and says, "I thought you were supposed to be dead."

I can't believe what I'm seeing. It's Elzie. There was Josh, going through who knows what kind of hell to save her, and she's the one who offs him. All I want to do is put my hands around her neck and squeeze the life out of her until her eyes pop out of her head.

"You killed my bro, but I'm going to play this by the book and let the authorities deal with you. But you make a break for it and I'll go after your family. Josh said you have a little brother. I'll hunt him down and you can forget the idea of him ever growing up. Your parents, grandparents, will all be history, too."

I can tell Matteson's not happy with what I'm saying, but the Secret Service cousin gets a grim smile.

Elzie gets an anguished look and tears start to roll down her face. "Josh wasn't supposed to be there. I warned him that innocent people might get hurt if they got in the way. Why did he do that?"

The tears mean nothing to me. I still want to strangle the bitch.

"Because," I say, "he had more courage and integrity than any of you and your asshole crew ever thought of having.

"So you understand what I'm saying?" I add. "About your kid brother and your folks? Am I getting through to you?"

She looks at me, chest hitching, weeping in earnest now. The Secret Service cousin applies some pressure to her bicep.

"Answer the man," he says.

She nods. "I understand. I'm sorry."

I turn to Matteson. "I'm done here," I say.

Then I walk away.

People have gotten over their panic and are starting to come back to gawk at what's going on. I see Fat Boy and Para near the front of the crowd. Guess he knows I wasn't bullshitting him now. I take a step toward him and the pair of them back away into the press of people.

I start back to where Marina and the others are, but I don't know where to start with the mess this has become. Josh dead. Elzie the shooter. Marina breaking up with me. The whole business of her affiliation with the local dog clans and what happened back at the compound.

I end up just standing there watching Des comfort her. One of the dog clan is on the other side of Marina. When she feels my gaze, she looks in my direction and bares her teeth. So much for letting bygones be bygones.

J-Dog and Tall Boy join me.

"You okay, bro?" J-Dog asks.

I'm anything but.

"I'm fine," I tell him. "Let's get the hell out of here."

MARINA

I can't stop the tears. Every time I think I've got them under control, I look at the rough grey blanket that someone put over Josh and they start up again. Finally Des puts his arm around my shoulders and turns me away from the stage.

There are cops and ambulances everywhere, sirens wailing. After the panicked rush died down, crowds of gawkers came back, all of them talking at the same time, aiming their phones at the stage, at Elzie, at themselves to prove they were here.

Elzie. I couldn't believe my eyes, it's all so wrong.

I'm having a hard time trying to tone down the cacophony of sound.

Des tries to walk me away from the stage. "We have to go," he says.

I swallow hard, then manage, "We can't just leave Josh."

"We don't have a choice—not unless you want to jump onto the stage and whisk him into the otherworld, and then what'll you do? Dude, we have to go." Des tries to lead me away.

Before we push through the crowd, I take one look back. Theo was over by Elzie. Now he's gone, and so is she and her guards. The agents must have put her in a car and driven away.

Police tape is going up everywhere and cops wearing plastic gloves are going around looking for evidence or whatever. There's a photographer on stage taking pictures of Josh before they put him in the body bag that's right beside him.

I rub the heels of my hands into my eyes and try to get my breathing to even out. All the people jostling around are driving me crazy. All I want to do is climb up on the stage and hold Josh's hand.

"Marina?" Des says.

I finally turn to him. "Where will we go?" I ask. "I can't go home. As soon as I go home, it'll be like I'm in prison."

"I can get you out of anywhere anyone puts you," Lupe says. "And I'll make them sorry for hurting you."

I shake my head. "No, this is my family. You can't do anything to them. But Mamá's going to go ballistic."

"Yours and mine," Des says. He looks pale. I know it's because of what just happened to Josh.

He puts a hand on my shoulder and again turns me away from the stage. This time I let him lead me away. Lupe and Donalita walk in front of us, parting the crowd. When I start to sob again, Des pulls my head against his shoulder, but he keeps us walking.

I don't know how long we walk or where we go. I just know that the crowds thin out, which makes it a bit easier to not feel so crazy. But each step also takes us farther from Josh, about to be zipped into a body bag with no one who really knows or cares about him at his side. A fresh wave of grief washes over me.

"Here," Des says. "Sit."

I blink and look around. We're at the end of a parking lot,

standing by a picnic table under palms, with only the boardwalk and sand between us and the ocean. I stare at the swells as they come in, automatically judging their height. I stare at the dark waters. The sea otter wants me to shed my human skin and disappear into them. To swim as far and deep as I can and never resurface.

I sit on the bench. Lupe sits beside me, Des is across the table. Donalita paces restlessly around us. Finally she stops at the end of the table.

"I don't believe it," she says. "The Thunders made all these different Wildlings until they got one big enough—Josh—but only to stop that fat old white dude from being killed? It doesn't make any sense. All the hurt and heartache Wildlings have gone through for *this*?"

Lupe nods.

"They should have just let the congressman take the bullet," Donalita says.

I shake my head. "Don't say that. When you say that, it makes Josh's … death … meaningless."

"What he did wasn't," Lupe says. "What he did was brave and selfless. It's *why* he had to do it that makes no sense."

Des nods. "I kind of see where you're coming from. Householder's life would never have been in danger if Wildlings hadn't existed in the first place. And when you think how many lives have been screwed up by this … Kids being pushed out of their families, getting diced up and killed, or killing themselves …"

"Nanuq needs to pay for this," Lupe says. "But he's a formidable foe. Old, old school. He could break us all like twigs."

"So what do we do?" Des asks.

I sigh and stand up.

"We go home," I say, "and face the music."

CHAINGANG

I thought I wanted to be at the compound until we actually get there. But while everybody goes into the house to crack themselves a beer and crank up some tunes, I go back to my crib and change out of these stupid civvies into something that lets me feel more like myself. I'm walking over to my bike when I see J-Dog leaning against a post of the back porch, looking at me.

"You going to see Grandma?" he asks.

Crap, I hadn't even thought of her. All the other bullshit that's been going on just pushed her right out of my head.

"You talk to her?" I ask.

"Yeah, she's cool. She wants to see us."

"Now?"

He shrugs. "Soon." He waits a beat, then asks, "What happened back there?"

"You mean with Josh?"

"No, I can pretty much figure that out. He turned into a tiger and stopped the shooter from taking down Householder, then died for his trouble. It's not a complicated story."

It *was* complicated, I think, but I don't want to get into it.

"Mountain lion," I say. "He was a mountain lion."

"Whatever. I meant, what happened with your girl."

"Fucked if I know."

"Lots of nice girls right here in the Orchards," J-Dog says. "Why you only want the barrio girls?"

"It's not like that."

"Then what is it like, bro? I can't count the fine ladies who'd like to park their booty in your crib, and they don't come thinking you'll take care of them forever."

"I'm sure there are."

But I'm barely paying attention to this conversation. I'm thinking more of what Marina said to me, how I can't change, and me saying I can, and then I go lay down the heavy on that Elzie, telling her if she doesn't take the fall, I'm going to hunt down and kill her family. And I meant it.

Maybe she's right. Maybe I can't change.

But the thing is, there's always going to be a situation where somebody has to take the hard road, and I've always been the guy who'll shoulder that weight. I'm only just now beginning to realize that it also means I walk that road by myself.

J-Dog punches me lightly on the shoulder. "You even listening to me?"

I shake my head.

"You're my little brother, fercrissakes," he says. "I'm only looking out for you."

"I know. And I appreciate it."

"But?" he asks. "Because I'm hearing a big fat 'but' coming up on me now."

"I need to take a ride. Clear my head."

"And then you'll come back."

I nod. "We'll go see Grandma."

"Yeah, she'll like that. Both her boys dropping by."

I can feel his eyes on me as I walk over to my bike. I check to make sure my tire iron's holstered like it's supposed to be. Then I kick the Harley into life and peel out of the compound. I take a left at the end of the driveway and open the throttle.

The familiar rumble of the motor and the solid reality of the machine between my legs doesn't give me the buzz it usually does. Neither do the clear blue skies or the light traffic. I've been dumped before. And I've had friends die, too—people I knew a lot better than I ever got to know Josh.

But it feels different.

I check the rear-view. There's only a white SUV and a jeep on the highway behind me. I half thought J-Dog might try to follow me, but I guess he's taking me at my word.

Part of what I told him is true. I do need to take a ride. But my head's as clear as it's ever going to be.

I've got unfinished business.

Somebody killed Josh and it wasn't Elzie. She only pulled the trigger. The guy responsible is still out there.

What seems like a long time ago, I told Josh I'd have his back. But I didn't. Now he's dead and I can't fix it. I can't make it right. The only thing I can do now is even the score.

I need answers, which is why a little later on, I pull into the parking lot at Tiki Bay. I kill the engine and put the Harley on its stand. Taking the tire iron from its holster, I start up the hill to the bluff where Auntie Min's holding court. I know from the crows—in both bird and human shape—that she's still here. They're turning in lazy circles above the bluff, or standing silhouetted against the sky from my vantage point as I come up the steep incline.

My Wildling radar's pinging like crazy by the time I get to the top. One of the crows notes the tire iron in my hand, but all he says is, "She's been expecting you."

Of course she has. Auntie Min knows I'm not going to let this go.

Just like the last time I came here with the Feds, she's not alone. I pause at the summit for a moment. Down there on the beach is where Lenny died. Up here is where Vincenzo broke my back and Cory brought me back from the otherworld. That was when Marina and I were still—

I shut down that line of thought and walk through the stiff grass to where Auntie Min's waiting with most of the usual gang of suspects. Rico isn't here. Neither is the hawk uncle Tío Benardo. But Cory and Lalo are, as I might have expected. Jimmy and Ana, the dog cousins, glare at me. Standing with them is a dark-haired woman I don't know. Cory introduces her as Lupe, and she seems to be the alpha in this little three-dog pack.

"We've been waiting for you to start," Auntie Min says.

Yeah, I think. Sure, you have. Like you knew I was coming. I didn't decide to come here until after I got back to the compound. But I don't bother to correct her.

"You did the best you could," Auntie Min tells me.

"Yeah, whoop-de-doo," I say. "Householder's safe and the person who tried to kill him is in jail. But Josh is dead. Doesn't seem like much of a fair trade to me."

Auntie Min nods. "The boy had so much potential. And I'm very disappointed in the young jaguarundi."

"Was it the same deal as with the dog clans?" I ask. "Was she bound?"

That gets me a snarl from the dog cousin Jimmy. I give him a cold look.

"I've got things to do," I tell him, "but I've got time to beat the crap out of you, you want to have a go at it."

Before he can respond, the woman Lupe steps in front of him.

"I apologize for Jimmy," she says. "He seems to forget that there is no longer a blood feud between your people and the East Riversea Blue Dog Clan."

I look from the pissed-off faces of Jimmy and his sister, back to the woman.

"Yeah?" I say. "And why's that?"

"All bindings were broken, but we have sworn fealty to Marina Lopez and she would not wish us to engage in hostilities with you."

Knowing that Elzie did the shooting of her own free will makes me even more pissed off, but I also know the crazy plan originated with this guy Nanuq. I just can't believe she bought into it.

Jimmy makes a grunt in the back of his throat and Lupe turns, fast, assuming a fighter's position. "You want to run the pack?" she snarls. "Then come on. Give it your best shot."

If Jimmy had a tail, it'd be between his legs. He stares at the ground and shakes his head. Ana also looks cowed.

"I get why you did what you did," Lupe says, turning back to me. "I'd probably do the same if strangers came after my pack. But the only thing that makes it okay between my people and yours is Marina. You understand?"

"I think she's breaking up with me," I say.

That gets me a wolfish grin from Jimmy.

Sure, yuk it up.

"So maybe you'll still get a chance to take a run at me," I say to him. I'd love to take the scumbag down.

Lupe shakes her head. "Breaking up with you doesn't change how she feels about you. It just means she likes someone else more."

Someone else? I hadn't even thought of that. I just assumed it was the gang life that was making her back off. But as soon as Lupe says it, I know. I mean, really, it was always there, wasn't it? They were probably the only people who didn't know—or at least one of them didn't.

"Josh," I say.

"Bingo."

Damn, that's messed up. I might have fought to stay together if it was only about the gang life, but how do I compete with a dead guy—a dead guy I liked?

And she's been mooning over him forever. I remember trying to console her when we were in the otherworld. Thinking about what came after that gives me a flicker of hope. But it dies just as quickly. Who am I kidding? I knew it was over the moment I saw her in the crowd at city hall. She'll never feel anything like that toward me.

There's a strange, tight feeling in my chest. I grip the tire iron a little harder and know I need to focus on something else. I'd like it to be this Jimmy asshole, but I have bigger fish to fry.

I turn to Auntie Min. "So, do you have a line on where we can find Nanuq or the remaining condor brothers?"

"I think so. But Theo, this is something that needs to be

handled with diplomacy. Nanuq's voice is listened to in many councils."

"You wouldn't last a minute with him," Cory adds.

I shrug. "I owe it to Josh."

"But he's—" Lupe starts, but she's smart. She doesn't finish.

Losing Marina to Josh—even to the memory of him—doesn't change anything between Josh and me.

"Don't go after Nanuq," Auntie Min says. "That's not the way we do it."

"I don't care. It's the way I do it. Will you just tell me where he is?"

"Not if you plan to harm him. Killing him now will only drive more cousins to his cause. Even just trying will make all of you young cousins look bad."

Lalo nods. "As I explained to you earlier, nothing makes a better recruiting tool than a martyr."

"Yeah," I say. "But if he's not around, will anyone even take up the cause? Is there someone just as dedicated and ruthless waiting in the wings? He's the one that sent Vincenzo, who killed Tomás—one of your own elders."

I look at Cory, who's been uncharacteristically quiet. "And he would have killed you, if you were easier to kill," I add. "He's responsible for Lenny being dead, and now Josh. Are you really telling me you can just let it slide? Because I can't."

Cory's always hard to read, but I can tell he's uncomfortable.

"It's politics," he says.

"No, it's bullshit."

He glances at Auntie Min. "Yeah," he says. "It pretty much is. But it's how the elders handle things."

Auntie Min sighs. "Why must you be so difficult, Theo? We're trying to avoid further violence."

"You should have thought about that before you got Josh killed."

The pain in her eyes is real. I know she didn't want things to turn out this way. "You seem to forget. We were trying to prevent bloodshed," she says.

"What happened to using your poster boy as an ambassador between cousins and the rest of the world? Oh, that's right. You got him killed."

There's a disturbance in the air behind her and I get a glimpse of those big moth wings of hers before she gets a rein on her temper.

"You will leave this to us," she says.

I shake my head. "That's not the way I roll. You want to avoid bloodshed, I'd advise you to stay the hell out of my way. Because I'm going to find this guy and when I do, he pays."

"With a tire iron?" Auntie Min says. "Do you remember how well that worked with Vincenzo? Nanuq is far more powerful."

I lift the tire iron. "This was only insurance in case a bunch of you decided to jump me."

"We would never—"

"And I'm not so stupid. I know it's not enough to deal with him. For that I'm going to see some brothers in L.A. and get me some real firepower. Crips up there know gunrunners. I figure they can set me up with something with real stopping power."

Auntie Min closes her eyes. "Can somebody talk some sense into him?" she says.

No one speaks and I walk away. No one tries to stop me, either.

I'm tempted to blow into the barrio on my bike and break some heads because I really need to hit something right about now. But I know I have to play this smart.

First up, talk to J-Dog. See if he can hook me up with somebody in L.A. to get what I need.

Then I need to find a cousin to help me track down Nanuq.

I smile as I get to the parking lot and swing my leg over the bike's saddle.

And I know just the bloodthirsty little coati girl for the job.

DES

I don't think I can do this. I'm already hanging on by a thread, but standing here at the front door of Josh's house ... I know I'm going to lose it.

I saw him die, yeah. But this feels even more real. This is the house where we spent so much time together, except he's never going to be here again. No more hanging out in the backyard. No more grabbing our boards and heading for the park, or the boardwalk. No more jamming late at night, earphones on, our instruments plugged into the computer.

But his mom needs to know, and I'd way rather she hear it from me than the Feds.

Knocking on this door is probably one of the hardest things I've ever had to do. Until my knuckles hit the wood, I could still walk away. But as soon as the sharp rap is echoing through the house, I'm committed. I can't back out now.

Donalita stands beside me, her palm resting on my back between my shoulder blades. It's such a simple connection, but so soothing. I don't know why she's still here with me when she could be off doing whatever it is that cousins do, but I'm grateful and I tell her so.

"Dude," she says.

Just that, and nothing more, but it says everything. I don't get a chance to figure out what that means for us, how I feel. The word's still echoing in my head when the door opens and Naomi is there, her eyes puffy and red.

She knows.

"Oh, Des," she says as she steps out on the porch and opens her arms.

I don't know which one of us gets more comfort out of the embrace. I could stay like that forever, but we finally step back from each other.

"Detective Matteson just left," she says. "Were ... were you there?"

"Yeah ... we were trying ... it was a Wildling thing ..."

She gives a sad nod. Her mouth is trembling. "Are you one, too?"

"No, I ..."

I almost say that I didn't draw the lucky card in the Wildlings sweepstakes, but then I think of what our lives have become since this all started—what happened to Josh—and I can't finish the thought because I don't believe it anymore. Instead, I just look helplessly at Josh's mom.

"I'm so sorry for your loss," Donalita says, and Naomi seems to notice her for the first time.

"Thank you. I—this is hard. Are you one of Josh's friends?"

She nods. "Through Des. I didn't know him well, but I really liked him."

Naomi's eyes fill again with tears. She wipes them on her sleeve. Clears her throat. Motions toward the door.

"Did ... did you want to come in?" she asks.

"No, I—" *can't,* I want to say. I don't know if I'll ever be able to walk through that door again. But I just say, "My parents will be worrying. We came right here from, you know, the rally."

Naomi nods. "Of course." She hugs me again. "Your coming here means so much to me," she says, her mouth close to my ear. "Go home and hug your parents. Please come back when you can."

I swallow hard. Her eyes are filling yet again and I will lose it for sure if I stay any longer.

"I—I'll come by. Soon. When I can."

She nods.

"If you need anything—" I begin.

"You're a good boy," she tells me. "Josh was lucky to have a friend like you."

She wipes her eyes again and slips back into the house, closing the door behind her.

I stand in front of the closed door for a long moment before I turn to Donalita. She puts her arm around my waist and steers me back to the street.

"We'll get through this," she says.

We, not you.

But I'm not sure that's true. The "getting through this" part. They make it look so easy in the movies. The characters feel bad, maybe there's a montage of past good times, then they carry on.

How do they carry on?

What do you do about that big black hole in the middle of your chest?

I'm not sure if I need to cry or puke.

MARINA

I always knew it would be bad when Mamá found out about the otter living under my skin. Given her fanatical religious beliefs, how could it not? But I never dreamed it would be as bad as this.

It's my own fault. I'm just barely holding it together when Lupe sees me to the top of my street and I continue home on my own. Mamá and my stepfather are waiting for me in the living room, and when they ask me where I've been, all I can think of is Josh lying dead on the stage at city hall, under that awful "Humans for Humanity" banner.

The rally was to support Householder's bill, the one that would imprison people like Josh and me in camps because we're unpredictable and dangerous. But it's Josh who died to save that fat pig of a congressman. Householder gets to live and keep spreading his hate, while Josh—the sweetest, most empathetic guy I know—is gone.

So when they ask me where I've been, I tell them. I tell them everything, and Mamá has a complete meltdown.

A couple of hours later I'm still sitting in my room, but now I'm listening to two sets of parents arguing over what to do with me. Mamá's first solution was to take me to a priest to have the demon exorcised, but when my stepfather, Jim, finally convinced her that wasn't possible, she insisted that they turn me over to the FBI, where she says I'll be safe. What she means is, everybody else will be safe from me.

They were still arguing about this when Papá and Elena arrived.

The four of them have been at it for at least another hour. Papá blames Mamá for this happening, Elena is crying. Weirdly, my stepfather is the voice of reason. Quiet Jim, who never raises his voice and certainly never gets in between my parents when they go at it. No church or Fed camps for me, which is good. But he does want to send me to live with his brother's family in Wisconsin until this all blows over and we have a better sense of what's really going on and how it affects me.

Of course, nobody asks what I think. What I might want. I'm just this freak that they have to deal with.

The worst thing is how they're scared of me. I can hear it in their voices. They talk about having to keep me away from my little sisters, as though I'd ever hurt them. Mamá thanks the saints that I didn't attack Ampora. All of them agree that I can't mix with regular kids because it's too dangerous. For the other kids.

Maybe they have no idea that I can hear every word they say. Maybe they don't care.

But more awful than any of that is the one thing I keep circling back to over and over again, like a crappy drum loop that just won't quit.

Josh is dead.

I don't want to think about it, but I can't get it out of my head. It breaks my heart. I'm sick to my stomach. I'm cold and clammy. I feel like I'm burning up.

Tears don't help. If they did, I'd have been cured hours ago. But around and around it goes, everything circling back to the body of the boy I love lying dead on that stage.

I don't know how to make it stop.

I can't just sit on my bed and stare at the wall, listening to parents and stepparents discuss my fate. I tried going online, but it doesn't help. The blogs are full of what happened at the rally.

I read several, out of some morbid curiosity. An argument's raging about whether Josh was part of the attack on Householder, or if he saved him. Householder is quoted as saying that this is exactly why stronger measures are needed to deal with the Wildling problem.

But as I keep clicking from blog, to news report, to blog, something interesting emerges. The news footage proves that Josh did deliberately save the congressman's life. Apparently, there are so many video recordings of the event that even the most pigheaded, stupid person could see that when Josh leapt onto the stage, he wasn't going for Householder. He was jumping in the path of the bullet. I don't click on any of the videos. I couldn't bear to see Josh murdered a second time.

And now Congressman Householder does a complete about-face. I hate to admit it, but I have to give him props because instead of denying and lying, and basically being an asshole like every other politician and celebrity who gets exposed in some scandal or other, Householder immediately retracts his previous position on Wildlings. He says he's withdrawing his bill, and offers his condolences to Josh, his family and friends. He also says that in light of what happened this afternoon, he wants to convene a committee to re-evaluate the whole Wildling issue.

I didn't see that coming.

It's not worth Josh's life, but it's something.

If only my parents would do a little of this re-evaluating. But from the conversation going down in the living room, it's clear that's not going to happen. There's no *Maybe Wildlings aren't dangerous.* It's just a matter of *Where do we send her?*

I'm *this* close to asking Lupe to get me out of here. She gave me her number before she left me at the top of my street. All it will take is one phone call.

And then what?

I need to ask somebody for some advice. Just a day ago, Theo would have been the obvious choice, but how do I face him, having slept with Josh last night?

I could try to contact another of the cousins. Auntie Min. Cory. But I don't feel like I know or trust them enough to ask for their opinions about what I should do. It's not just about tonight. It's about my whole life.

In which Josh is dead.

Eventually I start a text to Des: *Grounded forever. How about you?*

But before I can send it, I get one from Ampora, of all people. Asking me if I'm okay. Telling me how sorry she is about what happened to Josh.

I don't know how to respond.

She has no clue that the interest she had in him was only because of pheromones, which Josh wasn't in control of at the time. She probably has some huge romantic notion of how their relationship might have gone, and wants to talk to me about it.

I imagine how much more she'd hate me if she found out that before he died, Josh chose me.

I sit there staring at the phone for a long time before I finally punch in Lupe's number. I don't know her well, either, but at least I know that she thinks she owes me. If I go with her, no one's going to be able to make me do anything I don't want to.

I have no idea what I want. But I need the decision to be my own.

My call connects.

"Marina?" Lupe asks.

"Can you get me out of here?" I ask.

There's a moment's pause before she asks, "Do we need to come in soft or hard?"

I imagine a pack of dog cousins rampaging through the house, roughing up my parents.

"I don't want anyone hurt," I tell her. "I don't even want them to know I'm gone until somebody bothers to come into my bedroom looking for me."

"I'll be right there," Lupe says.

CHAINGANG

The party's going strong when I pull into the clubhouse. Music blasting. Laughter and shouting. A typical bash at Casa Ocean Avers. Some guys are hanging around the back porch, along with a girl who sits on the steps with her head between her knees. An early casualty of the night's festivities, I'm guessing.

Tall Boy hoists a beer bottle as I put the bike on its stand.

"Yo!" he calls over to me. "You hanging with us tonight?"

"You bet," I tell him. "I just need to get something from my crib."

He grins, then turns to say something to Shorty, standing beside him. I go into my crib, knowing that in two minutes they'll have forgotten all about me. The last thing I want to do is party. I just watched Josh die when I was supposed to have his back. My girl turns out to not be my girl anymore. I'm planning a drive-by on some über-cousin and there's a good chance I won't survive.

What the hell do I have to party about?

Then I realize I'm not alone. I've been so in my head coming inside that at first I don't notice Cory sitting on my couch. But the cousin *ping* hits me, and when I turn on the light, there he is, hands behind his head, feet up on my coffee table.

I flex my fingers. Finally, something to hit. I know he sees it in my eyes.

"Before you come at me swinging," he says, "I want to tell you that I agree with you. We need to take Nanuq down and I'll help in any way I can."

I stand there by the door processing what he said, looking for the angle he's playing. I come up shooting blanks.

"What happened to doing things the way the elders want?" I ask.

He shrugs. "It's what they wanted to hear."

"Yeah, and you're so rebel now?"

He sits up, puts his feet on the floor.

"We can be pissy all night," he says. "You can even take a shot at me. But in the end, we're both after the same thing and all you're doing is wasting time."

"What about your beef with me about the dog clans?" I ask.

"Truth is, I'm still pissed at you for that. But you heard Lupe. Nobody's going after you for payback."

"Yeah? What about *your* beef? You're coyote, not dog. You don't have to answer to her. And who says I can trust her? Maybe she just wants me to put my guard down and sic that dickwad Jimmy at me."

"She made him and his sister pledge to back off. The difference between cousins and five-fingered beings is that our word is everything. Once upon a time we didn't have possessions or territory, or any of the other crap that the five-fingered beings brought to the table. But we had our word. It's like sacred coin and no one abuses it."

"Nobody?"

He shrugs. "We're not perfect," he says. "Cousins mess up

just like people do, or they get sucked in by things that they shouldn't. But when they do, there are repercussions."

"What, you guys have your own police?"

"There have to be some rules—even if they're unwritten— or you end up with complete anarchy. When that happens it means the stronger you are, the more you can run roughshod over others."

"Like, what kind of rules?"

"Like, cousins don't eat cousins."

I just look at him for a long moment. "You're telling me that some cousins are cannibals?"

"Look, if they're in animal shape, a cousin mouse doesn't look that much different from an animal mouse."

"Huh. So who enforces these rules?"

"It's not like that," he says. "Cousins talk, and nothing stays hidden forever. If you've messed up, it gets out, and you cease to exist to us."

"Meaning?"

"You can't interact with any cousin. And you're fair game for anybody who wants to take you out. No clan feuds. No reparation to be paid."

"Paid in what? You just told me that none of you care about possessions or territory."

"We didn't. Things change. But our word is still sacred. In the long ago, payment was in favours, or alliances."

"So where does Nanuq fit into all this honour and crap?"

"We don't know that he lied to anybody," Cory says.

"No, but you're saying he enslaved all these cousins."

"He bound them, yes, but initially, at least some of them went to him. And let me tell you, the elders are looking into this right now. But they need to be careful. The Polar Bear Clan isn't big, but they're extremely powerful. The elders are going to make damn sure they have things right before they start tossing around accusations. That's why Auntie Min wants us to be patient."

"But you're not."

"Are you?" he asks.

I don't bother to answer. He already knows where I stand.

"I'm not from your world," I finally say. "Where I come from, people have to earn your trust. You don't put your life in the hands of anybody just on their say-so."

He nods, then looks right at me. "You *owe* me your life."

"I can't argue with that."

"So you could say you owe me the favour of us working together."

"I can't argue with that, either."

He rises, both palms held open, facing me.

"Theodore Washington," he says, "all debts between us are paid in full and I have neither the will, nor the right, to harm you or any of your clan."

His tone is formal, like this is supposed to mean something. He holds my gaze without blinking. And waits.

I sigh. Well, I was looking for a cousin to help me, wasn't I? And whatever he thinks of me, I know he was tight with Josh. And even if he says I don't owe him anything now, he *did* save my life.

"That stands whether I work with you or not?" I ask.

He nods.

"Well, fuck," I tell him. "Why didn't you say so in the first place? Where do we start?"

He gives me a feral grin.

"I've already got friends looking into where Nanuq's holed up," he says. "It shouldn't take long, but it might be a day or two."

"That's not a problem," I tell him. "I need time to get my hands on some decent firepower. Though J-Dog might have something stashed away."

"Why don't you ask him?" Cory says.

"You mean, right now?"

"The sooner you get what you need, the sooner we can go. Wouldn't you rather be out looking for Nanuq yourself than sitting on your ass waiting for the information to come to you?"

I nod. "Wait here," I tell him.

I find J-Dog in the kitchen after running a gauntlet of high-fives and beers pushed at me. By the time I get there, I have a beer in each hand. I sit down at the kitchen table and push one of them over to my brother, sitting across from me.

There's nobody else in here. No surprise, really. J-Dog looks to be in full brooding mode and nobody's stupid enough to interrupt that. Except me.

"You're not celebrating?" I ask.

He twists the cap from the bottle and tips the top of it in my direction. "Whoop-de-doo."

He guzzles half the bottle, gaze locked on mine, then bangs it down on the table.

"None of this bothers you?" he finally says.

"Hell, everything bothers me, depending on my mood. What exactly are you talking about?"

"Take your pick. Otherworlds. My brother's a Wildling. There's all these heavy-duty animal people living alongside of us.

How do you deal with it? I mean, I thought I knew the freaking world and where I fit in it. Now I have no clue, except I figure I'm way down the food chain."

"I know it seems messed up at first," I tell him. "But you get used to it. Pretty soon you'll see it's no different than growing up in the Orchards, or dealing with Kings. It looks different, but it all boils down to the same damn thing."

"Huh."

"And maybe you don't have their strength or speed," I say, "but so far as they're concerned, you're still a player."

"How you figure that?"

I tap my head. "You're a tactician and you're smart. They know that." Then I bang my fist against my chest. "And you've got heart. You don't back down. You don't quit."

"That's how you see me? The guy you're describing sounds like some kid's wet dream about his big brother."

"You're telling me I'm wrong?" I ask, my voice a notch louder.

"—The fuck would I know? I only see myself from the inside, looking out. How the hell would I know what people see?"

"I'm just telling you, don't sweat it. Maybe the world's a lot bigger than we thought, but the cousins are the same as anybody else."

He lifts an eyebrow.

"They bleed, bro," I tell him. "They can die."

He nods and tips the top of his bottle in my direction again before he finishes the other half.

"Well, when you put it like that …" His gaze drifts for a moment before it locks back on me. "You know I don't give a rat's ass about what any of those Wildlings tools think, right? No offence."

"Yeah, I know."

"So are we done with them now?"

"I've got one more little thing I need to do," I tell him, "and then I'm done."

"For them?"

I shake my head. "For me. One of those pricks sent the shooter that killed Josh, and that's the guy I want. But I'm going to need some serious firepower."

He gives me a considering look. "How serious?"

I remember joking with Des a million years ago.

"Like a rocket launcher."

He laughs. "Aw, bro. I was saving that for a rainy day."

I don't know why I'm surprised.

"You've *got* one?"

"Got two," he says. "But there's a catch. If you're going into that kind of a firefight, we're riding with you."

"You," I say. "Nobody else. And where we're going, they don't necessarily have roads."

"What, you want to hump those things around on your back?"

"Are you in or out?"

"You really need to ask? Who are we hunting?"

"A polar bear."

"Are you shitting me?"

"Word."

He grins. "Dibs on the pelt. When do we leave?"

"How soon can we get the artillery?"

"It's in the shed—under the floorboards."

"Then let's haul ass."

DES

I come in the front door and before I can say anything, Mom rushes down the hall from the kitchen and throws her arms around me.

"Oh, God," she says. "I saw it on the news and I was so worried. Were you there with him? Are you okay?"

I'm confused. Why isn't she yelling at me for being gone all night?

I look over her shoulder and see my little sister Molly standing in the kitchen doorway, her eyes big. Then my dad steps into view. He's wearing an unfamiliar worried look, which slowly changes into the more familiar one of being a little exasperated and a lot pissed off with me.

"So, you decided to come home," he says.

Mom steps back, but keeps an arm around me. "Ted. His best friend just died."

Dad's face softens. "I'm sorry," he tells me. "That was a brave thing Josh did."

Mom steers me toward the kitchen and sends Molly to her room, so that it's just three of us sitting around the table. And then the barrage of questions starts. Where was I last night?

How long did I know Josh was a Wildling? Didn't I understand how dangerous that was? How could I bring him here and put Molly in danger?

Mom keeps touching my arm, like she has to assure herself that I'm really there. Dad sits, back straight, arms folded across his chest.

I tell them the truth—or at least as much of it as makes sense. They know Wildlings are real, so I start there. I tell them about Josh, how Marina went missing and we were out looking for her, that we all went to the rally and Josh stopped the congressman from getting killed. I don't tell them about cousins, the otherworld, crazy-ass snipers, old Mexican hawk uncles, or Donalita, who's in my pocket in the shape of a pebble.

"You should have called," Mom says.

I'm so tired of the third degree. I understand that they're mad—I was totally expecting it—but I can't really deal with it right now. How am I supposed to? Even with my eyes open, I keep getting flashes of Josh lying there so still on the stage, a big hole in his chest and blood seeping out from under him, his vacant face turned toward us. And his eyes. Those lifeless eyes …

"We have rules in this house," Dad says. "Like your mother said, you should have called."

I snap my gaze to him. "And you would have said what? You would have told me to get my ass back home."

"Language," Dad says.

I stop myself from rolling my eyes.

"Look, it doesn't matter," I say. "You can do what you want— ground me, whatever—but I'd do it again. Marina got caught up with a rough crowd and she needed our help."

Mom's eyes are a little wide. "What kind of rough crowd?"

"I don't know. She got on the bad side of some kind of a gang or something—and no, she wasn't involved with them. She just got pulled in because she happened to be in the wrong place at the wrong time."

"You should have called the police," Dad says. "They're trained and paid to handle this sort of thing."

Yeah, dude, I think. Like that would ever happen. I'm sure they'd be all ready to head off into the otherworld and rescue her from some big-ass polar bear.

"They wouldn't have cared," I say.

"You don't know that."

I want to bang my head on the table. I know they're more worried than mad. I know that in a sane world, I should have called them, or let it all go and called the police. But there's no way I could have done that, and there's no way either they or the police could have helped.

They couldn't even keep the congressman protected. No, Josh had to die for that.

"We've pulled you out of a lot of scrapes," Dad says, "and put up with your antics at school, but—"

"Josh is dead," I break in. "Don't you get that? My best friend's *dead*. I can't think about anything else. I can't get that picture out of my head. What does any of the rest of this crap matter?"

My head is pounding. I know that I'm starting to lose it, but I can't seem to stop. It's either get mad—even though neither of them deserves it—or fall down sobbing on the floor.

"What did I say about lang—" Dad starts.

"I don't *care!*"

I push my chair away from the table.

"You sit down, young man," Dad says.

"I'm going to my room."

"I told you to sit *down!*"

"Or you'll what? If I sit down, will you bring Josh back to life? Because if you can't do that, I don't care about anything else you've got to say."

Dad stands up, his face getting redder, that little vein pulsing in his temple the way it does when he's really mad. As we stand there facing each other, I realize for the first time that I'm actually bigger than him.

"Last chance," he says.

"You want me to sit down?" I say. "Make me."

Dad's chair clatters down on the linoleum and he starts for me, but Mom grabs his arm.

"Ted, don't," she says. She looks at me. "Go to your room, Des."

I walk down the hall to my bedroom, go inside and slam the door.

Well, I handled that real well, I think, as I fall down on my bed. Digging into my pocket, I pull out the pebble and tap it lightly on the bedpost. Donalita appears and falls across the bottom of the bed with her arms open wide. I reach over and clamp a hand over her mouth as she's about to—I don't know what. Sing? Laugh? Start talking in tongues?

"You have to be super quiet, dude," I tell her as she scoots up alongside me.

From down the hall I can hear the soft murmur of my parents' voices—arguing about what to do with me, I guess. A couple of times Dad's threatened to put me in some military academy run by one of his pals from back when Dad was in the service. Mom hates the idea because she comes from old hippie stock and she's a total pacifist. God knows how they ever ended up together.

"I can be quiet," Donalita whispers back. "I can be quieter than the quietest mouse you ever didn't hear because it was so quiet."

She snuggles closer to me.

"This probably isn't a good idea," I say.

When she first insisted she had to come with me, I gave in because I needed the moral support, even if the friend I brought along was only a pebble in my pocket. But if they catch her in here now, I *will* end up in that military academy.

"Were they mean to you?" she asks.

"Depends on your perspective. Looking at it one way, I was mean to them first, by not coming home. They don't get why I didn't, and I can't tell them everything—which bites—but if they knew all the details, they'd have a total meltdown." I sigh. "This is, like, the worst day ever. I mean, Josh ..."

She gives my arm a squeeze. "I know. We should go away— just get away from everything."

"Except it'll still be waiting for me when I get back, only amped up to eleven."

She frowns.

"It'll be worse," I explain.

We lie there awhile, listening to my parents' voices.

"I keep thinking about Josh's mom," I say. "She's taking it so hard and she has to carry all that weight by herself, alone in a big empty house."

"I liked her," Donalita says. "Maybe we should go stay with her. We could all comfort each other."

I turn away from her and push my face into the pillow and try to muffle my sobs. I can't help it.

Josh is gone and everything is a shambles.

MARINA

I walk aimlessly around my bedroom while I wait for Lupe, trying to decide what to take with me. In the end, I just shove some underwear and a spare hoodie into a backpack.

I expect her to come tap on my window like Josh and Des used to when they wanted me to sneak out. Instead she just steps out of the otherworld, right into the middle of my room, which just about gives me a heart attack. She puts a steadying hand on my arm.

"Sorry," she whispers.

"It's okay."

"Where do you want to go?" she asks.

"I don't know. I don't know what to do. Maybe I'm making a huge mistake. Maybe I should let them turn me over to the authorities. Maybe I *am* dangerous."

She shakes her head and puts a hand on my shoulder. "That's them talking, not you. You know what's true. Your truth is all that matters, and you can't let them put you in a cage. Trust me. I know all about being made to do things I didn't want to do—things that someone would *never* choose to do on their own."

I think of Nanuq's binding medallion that I broke, how it controlled her and the other dog cousins.

"I guess you do."

"Come back to my place," she says. "You can lay low there while you figure out what to do next."

"Thanks. The one sure thing is, I can't stay here."

"Do you have everything you want to take with you?"

I lift my backpack from the end of the bed.

"I wish I could take my board and drum kit," I say, "but I doubt I'll have any use for them anymore."

"We can come back for them," she says. "There's not any place they can put them that I can't get into."

I don't suppose there is.

"Can we make a short stop on the way?" I ask.

"Sure. Where to?"

"The backyard of where I used to live when I was a kid. Do you know where that is?"

She nods. "But I thought you and your sister didn't get along."

How could she know that? I lift an eyebrow and she shrugs.

"Gossip. Cousins tend to know everything that goes on around them," she says. "After the two of you got involved with the Riverside Kings, you were on everyone's radar."

"I want to say goodbye to my little sisters," I say.

"Now? You're not moving out of state or even out of the county tonight. It's late. Maybe you should try to see them when things calm down a little."

"But what if my parents fix it so that I can't ever get near them again? Then they'll believe whatever they're told about me. They'll think I didn't care about them."

"There's no place they can hide them from me."

"I know."

I think of what happened to Josh today, and what happened to so many of the Wildlings. Nanuq is still out there, wanting us all dead.

"But," I add, "Wildlings don't seem to have much of a life expectancy these days."

I know she's going to say something about how the dog clans will keep me safe. I can see it in her eyes. And then I see her change her mind.

"Sure," she says. "No problem. Here, take my hand."

I do, and she steps us away into the otherworld. We walk for a while through desert scrub untouched by humans. When we come out again, we're in the backyard of Papá's house. I send Ampora a text while Lupe slips into the shadows beyond the back porch's light. A few moments later I see the kitchen curtain stir and then Ampora comes outside. She stands a couple of feet away, arms crossed across her chest.

"Did you get the text I sent?" she asks. "I meant it."

"I know you did. Thanks."

"Why are you here?"

"I'm going away and I want to say goodbye to the girls."

"Going away?" she says. Her gaze flicks around the backyard, trying to pierce the shadows. "With your *boyfriend?*"

"I'm not seeing Theo anymore."

And Josh is dead, but I'm not ready to tell her what that really means for me. Not when she thinks he'd been planning to come back to see her.

"I don't know how smart running away is," she says, "but at least you've still got *some* sense in you."

"Theo's not what you think."

"No, he's probably worse."

"I don't want to argue with you."

What I really don't want is for her to get into another hissy fit and not let me see the girls.

She just looks at me for a long moment, then she finally nods.

"It's funny," she says. "For a long time I've been kind of hoping you'd get out of my life, but now that you're going, it actually feels a little weird."

I don't say anything. I want to, but I can never tell what will set her off.

"I'll get the girls," she says and turns back to the house.

CHAINGANG

"No way," Cory says when J-Dog and I return to my crib. "We're not taking a civilian on what's probably a suicide mission."

"Excuse me?" J-Dog says. "Aren't you the piece of shit who held a gun to my head out back here?" I see the crazy start up in his eyes.

"Bygones," I say to J-Dog. "Let it go, or don't come."

J-Dog scowls. I see him weighing it out, deciding to bury his pride. That's huge for him and my heart swells a bit, knowing how much he's got my back. Of course, could be he's just itching to play with the rocket launcher.

"We aren't going to rough up some gangbangers," Cory says. "We're going after a monster who can move so fast you'll barely see him before he's ripping out your throat."

"Let him try," J-Dog says.

"I'm telling you, it'll be over before you even—"

"Shut up," I say. "The both of you."

I point a finger at Cory. "You're coming because you can get me to him." My finger moves to J-Dog. "And you're coming because you're too much of a dumbshit to do the smart thing and stay out of it. But this is my show—everybody got that? When we find Nanuq, it'll be my finger on the trigger. Sucker owes me and I'm taking him down."

"Or you'll die trying," Cory says, stepping heavy on the cliché.

"Or I'll die trying," I agree in all seriousness. "Then you can do whatever the hell you want. Everybody understand?"

Cory shrugs. J-Dog glares at both of us, but finally he nods.

"Okay, then," I say. "Cory, you heard from those friends of yours?"

"It's still early."

I nod. "Then we start walking, right? See what we can find on our own?"

"That's the plan, such as it is. We can go anytime."

I sling a sawed-off so that it hangs against my chest—easy to reach. I've got a Glock in my waistband. I pick up the rocket launcher. J-Dog's prepped me on how it works, and it's ready to rock 'n' roll. He picks up his own.

"So let's go," I say.

Cory puts a hand on my shoulder, the other on J-Dog's and he walks us out of my crib and into the middle of some desert scrub—what this part of Santa Feliz must have looked like back in the day.

"Fuck me," J-Dog says, getting his second look at the otherworld, but his first understanding of just how out of his league he is at this moment.

"No thanks," Cory says and he starts walking across the scrub.

We follow.

JOSH

I wake to find Tío Goyo sitting cross-legged on the dirt beside me. He's got an unfamiliar look in his eyes and it takes me a moment to realize that it's respect.

I sit up and look around. There's no city hall, no stage, no Santa Feliz. Just dry dirt and dead grass, with the odd island of scrubby trees. I can smell the ocean to the west, see the mountains far to the east. Other than that, the landscape doesn't change for as far as I can see.

"Where are we?" I ask.

"One world over."

"And when?"

"You've been unconscious for almost five hours."

Five hours? I've been out that long? Though, all things considered, I'm lucky to be around at all.

"That was a good trick you pulled on everyone, back at city hall," Tío Goyo says.

"I guess. To be honest," I add, "I wasn't sure it would work."

I didn't plan it. It just came to me as I leapt to intercept the bullet.

The moment of my second death is seared into my memory:

how I let everybody see me in my human shape, shifting into the mountain lion and getting shot, then finally returning to human form. How, in between that last shift from Wildling to human, I used what I'd learned from Tío Goyo—though I had to do it faster than I ever had before. Faster than should have been possible. I shifted to spirit form, but instead of returning my body to the ground, I left it there to die on the stage while I went on into the otherworld. I didn't know if I'd remain a spirit hawk forever or not, but even that seemed like a better option than dying.

So I remember shifting, and I remember crossing over, but when I tried to draw my body from the ground on the other side, everything snapped to black. Until I woke just now, I had no idea if I'd been able to pull it off or not.

"How did you learn to do that?" Tío Goyo asks.

"I didn't. But I had to try something. I couldn't let things go on the way they were."

"You mean, you weren't ready to die," he says.

"No. Well yes, but what I really meant was everybody wanting a piece of me. I needed to just disappear—at least so far as the world was concerned."

"You were successful in that," he tells me. "Everybody thinks you're dead."

"Even the authorities—the FBI?"

"Especially them. They took your body away with them."

"Good."

"But your secret won't last forever," Tío Goyo warns me. "Not among the cousins. It doesn't matter how careful you are, at some point one of them will catch your scent, and with the way they gossip, it won't be long before everybody knows."

"That's okay. I just need a bit of peace and quiet to figure out what I'm going to do with my life."

"I can help you with that," Tío Goyo says. "I had some success when I spoke to Diego Madera."

"Who's that?"

"The cousins call him Old Man Puma. He's the patriarch of the Hierro Madera Mountain Lion Clan and he says he will claim you as part of his clan. He wants you to stay with him for a while in the mountains. He's been around forever, so he'll be able to tell you everything you need to know about the cousin part of your nature."

"That's perfect," I say. "When can I go?"

"Right now."

"I can't go right now," I tell him. "I have a few loose ends to tie up."

"His acceptance of you is a great honour."

"I understand that. And I really am honoured. But I have some unfinished business to take care of. And I need to tell my mom and best friends that I'm alive. I don't care what the rest of the world thinks, but I can't leave them thinking I'm dead."

I hesitate a moment, then add, "Actually, I'm hoping it'll be okay to teach my friends what you taught me."

"You are gifted," he says. "It will not come so easily to them. They will have to work much harder."

"I get that. But you don't mind?"

"No. I will even help if I can."

"That means a lot—thanks."

Tío Goyo gives me a hard look. "And is there more unfinished business—with the girl you hoped to rescue, for example?"

"No, I've made enough mistakes when it comes to Elzie. If

she chooses to remain with Nanuq, there's nothing that I can do about it."

He regards me with a shocked expression. "You mean ... you don't know?"

"Know what?"

"Your assassin. It was her."

I shouldn't be surprised, but it still hits me like a punch to the gut. I feel sick that Elzie would actually follow through on this crazy plan—that she would be the one to pull the trigger.

"What happened to her?" I ask.

"She's been charged with murder and incarcerated, and evidently she's remorseful. She hasn't attempted to leave her cell."

I sigh. I wish she hadn't had to learn her lesson the hard way, but I can't invest any more time in Elzie than I already have. It's over in terms of her, but I still have other business to take care of.

"I'm finished with Elzie," I say, "but I have to deal with Nanuq. If I don't, he's just going to start up again."

"You think you can kill him?"

"I've already got two deaths on my conscience. I don't want any more. I'm hoping I can talk some reason into him."

Tío Goyo shakes his head. "Good luck with that."

"Will you explain the situation to Señor Madera?" I ask. "The last thing I want to do is offend him."

Tío Goyo looks over my shoulder. "Why don't you tell him yourself?"

I hadn't brought up the maps in my head yet, and I never heard anyone approach, but when I turn around, he's standing right there and my heart feels like it stops dead.

He reminds me of Tío Goyo, except where Tío Goyo gives off no cousin power reading whatsoever, Diego Madera registers right off the charts. I can't believe I didn't feel it until now. It must've had something to do with my just having regained consciousness, or he somehow dialed his presence down, but if the pings I'm getting now are any indication, I'm back to normal.

Old Man Puma is obviously old and powerful—more so than either Auntie Min or Vincenzo. He's dressed casually, like the hawk uncle—cowboy boots, jeans, a checked flannel shirt over a white T-shirt—but his hair isn't dark. It's a tawny gold, like my fur is in my mountain lion shape. His skin tone is a lighter brown than most of the cousins I've met and his eyes are a penetrating green-yellow. His shoulders are broad, his hips lean. His hands, with their thumbs hooked in his belt, are big—like a mountain lion's paws.

"It's good to meet you, little nephew," he says.

"And you, sir," I manage to get out. "I hope you don't find me ungrateful—"

He waves one of those big hands as though brushing away something of no consequence. "I expect the members of my clan to be loyal," he says. "To take responsibility for their actions and to fulfill their obligations. You've just proven your worth on all counts. Do what you must, with my blessing and the support of your clan."

"Wow, just like that?" The words pop out of my mouth before I think about what I'm saying, but Diego only smiles.

"I was here when Coyote played his first trick," he says. "When Raven stirred his pot and the world was born. I've watched the mountains rise and fall; seen oceans drain and the deserts take their place. After all that time, I have no difficulty judging the character of a being. You might be young to your cousin blood, little nephew, and the how and why of your existence is as much of a puzzle to me as it is to you and our friend Goyo, but I can read your worth as easily as I can read sign, and yours has a surety that cannot be mistaken for anything but what it is: noble and just."

Yeah, I think. He's one of the old cousins, all right, because they all sure do like to talk like they're reciting poetry. But I'm learning to dial back the wise-ass comments.

"Thanks," is all I say.

"Do you know where to find Nanuq?" he asks.

I tap a finger against my temple. "I've got something like a GPS in here and it'll take me right to him." Then I realize he might not know what I'm talking about. "Um," I add, "do you know what a GPS—"

"I'm old, not stupid."

"I didn't mean—"

The big hand waves that off as well.

"There will be things I can teach you," he says, "but I've no doubt there is much I can learn from you, as well. I appreciate your respectful attitude, but you need to know that I am not one to stand on ceremony."

"Got it," I say when I realize he's waiting for me to respond.

"Now go," he says. "Fulfill your obligations as befits a member of the Hierro Madera Mountain Lion Clan." He reaches over and taps my temple with a large finger. "You'll know where to find me when you're done."

Then he just kind of fades away.

I turn to Tío Goyo with a grin. "Okay, that was so cool. How did he do that?"

"You'll have to ask him the next time you see him," Tío Goyo says.

"Maybe I will." I wait a beat, then ask, "What about you and me? Are you still hoping I'll go hunt giant parasites with you?"

"You would be a great asset, no question," he says, "but I see now that you have a different role to play in the story of the world."

I sigh. "I'm done with destiny."

"I'm sure you are. But is destiny done with you?"

"Oh, please. Do you know how hokey that sounds?"

He smiles. "I see you'll go your own way," he says, "but being who you are, you won't be able to turn your back on injustice when you see it. You will stop and make things right with diplomacy and compassion."

I sigh. "Yeah, and then they'll make me a saint."

"We will see. Though, if you insist on going after Nanuq, we might not get the opportunity."

"Don't be so cynical."

Tío Goyo shakes his head. "Did you ever hear the story of the young javelina who thought he was a panther?"

I call up the maps in my head and focus on the pulsing dot that's Nanuq.

"No," I tell Tío Goyo. "You'll have to tell it to me when I get back."

I drop my body back into the ground and then I'm gone, heading deep into the otherworld. I appear in the sky above the campsite where I left Elzie yesterday. Most of the dog cousins are gone, but there are others here. All kinds. I note where each is, especially the two condor brothers.

Nobody takes notice of my sudden appearance except for Nanuq. His gaze immediately lifts, fixing on where I float high above them—though I'm guessing what he sees is a red-tailed hawk.

I drift down to where he's holding court by a big campfire. He stands up, white braids swinging slowly as his gaze tracks my descent. He's huge, at least seven feet tall, bulkier than Diego, all of it muscle. He must be even more formidable in animal form. But then, so am I.

When I call up my human body from the ground, I make it bigger to match his size. Cousins scramble out of the way at my sudden appearance, but Nanuq never moves. He doesn't even blink.

"You've been causing me a lot of trouble, unborn," he says.

"My mother would take issue with you calling me that," I tell him.

I've got my maps up and focused on the campsite, marking where everyone is. I count maybe thirty cousins. Most of them are now standing in a loose circle around Nanuq and me, but I note a few others moving slowly, a discreet distance away. I don't think they're nervous. I assume they've got weapons—rifles or even just bows—and are getting into position to take me down.

"I should also mention to anyone planning to take another shot at me," I say, "that if you do, you'll have to answer to the Hierro Madera Mountain Lion Clan."

"Liar. You're unborn, without any clan affiliation."

I shrug. "Tell Diego Madera that."

His eyes narrow. I can see he doesn't want to believe me, but he makes a subtle motion with his hand. I don't notice any difference in the position of the hidden cousins, but their movement stops. I assume he just told them to stand down.

"You know that makes no difference to me," he says. "I'll happily pay Madera a blood price for the pleasure of killing you."

"I wouldn't make assumptions," I tell him.

"What's that supposed to mean?"

"You're assuming that you *can* kill me."

Nanuq laughs. "Does Madera know that his latest clan member is mentally unhinged?"

I hear chuckles from the cousins gathered around us.

"Aren't you curious as to why I'm here?" I ask.

He shakes his head. "All I know is that you somehow survived, but have just saved me the trouble of weeding out another unborn."

He makes a grab for me and I disappear back into the earth, rising up again behind him.

"Don't be rude," I say over the gasps of the watching cousins.

He turns faster than I would have thought possible. This time his big hand grabs my shoulder and locks on. Then his free hand is on my throat and he's lifting me from the ground, his fingers clamped tight and cutting off my air.

Our gazes lock and I see an uneasy look come over him when he realizes that I'm not afraid. I hang there, arms limp at my side, and give him a chance to let go on his own. When he doesn't, I disappear back into the earth again. I concentrate hard as I shed my body and take his hands with me.

When I rise up again he's staggering back looking at his stumps in horror. There's no blood or torn muscles and arteries. His arms just end in smooth skin at his wrists.

He roars something unintelligible and charges me. But I've thrown him off now. He's fast, but he's not thinking, and it's easy to step out of the way. I put out a foot as he passes me and he goes tumbling to the dirt. I step closer as he tries to get to his feet. I give him a push with one foot and he goes down again.

"Next time it won't just be your hands," I tell him. "Do you understand?"

I don't think I've ever seen such pure hate in someone's eyes. But he has himself under control again and nods.

"I just came to talk to you," I say.

I move back as he struggles to his feet. I don't help him up. Around us, the cousins have gone completely silent.

"I'd say we should take this somewhere private," I say, "but I need all your people to hear what I've got to say."

He's not beaten—not by a long shot. He shakes his head. "Nobody cares what you've got to say."

"If they want to keep on living, they should."

He lifts his stumps. "Being like this isn't living."

"Don't be such a baby," I tell him. "You know as well as I do that you'll have them back the first time you shift into the polar bear. But I'm telling you right now"—I give the crowd a quick once over—"I'm telling all of you. I *can* make this permanent. You'll be gone and there'll be no coming back."

I let that sink in.

"So talk," Nanuq says finally.

"This stops," I say. "All of this. The killing. The coercion. The intimidation. The idea that you're all something special and that gives you the right to walk around like you're King Shit on Turd Island. It stops—right now."

"You have no idea what—"

"I know what you *say* you're fighting for," I break in, "but you're acting like fascists. I get it. You're losing your homelands.

Things look bleak. But killing innocent kids and starting wars against humanity is not the answer."

"What kids?" somebody calls from the crowd. "We're not killing kids."

"Maybe you don't know what I'm talking about," I say, "but Nanuq does. Ask him what he's got in mind for those he calls unborn. What do you think he meant just now, when he talked about *weeding out another unborn?*"

"You're not special," Nanuq says. "The Thunders didn't make you."

"I never said they did. None of the Wildlings asked to have this happen to us. But that doesn't give you the right to dispose of us."

I've been using the maps in my head to keep track of where everybody is around me, and the two condor brothers have resumed working their way around the crowd so that they're right behind me. I'm not surprised when they suddenly surge forward and grab me from either side.

I take them down with me into the ground, but when I call up my body again, I'm standing by myself in front of Nanuq.

"Now, *that's* permanent," I say. "Unlike Nanuq's hands, they're not coming back."

"Who's the fascist now?" Nanuq demands.

"Like their brother, they gave me no choice," I tell him. "I'm not telling you what to do. But I *am* telling you what you can't do. I think you should continue to stand up for what you believe in. You want to know the truth? I believe in the same thing. I want the first world to be healed, too. But I'm also telling you that if anyone else gets hurt—if you start killing innocents again to further your plans—you'll answer to me."

I turn away from Nanuq to address the crowd. "I can find you, no matter where you hide. Don't think I can't. And if you're hurting anyone, you'll be joining the condors. Am I making myself clear?"

Not one of them will meet my gaze.

"What about you?" I ask Nanuq. "Do you have any more arguments? Because we can finish this right here, right now. And if there's a blood price to be paid to your clan, I'll be just as happy to pay it. Except I don't think that's going to happen. I mean, who's going to blame me for defending myself?"

Nanuq doesn't respond, but I can see he's on the edge of giving in.

But then I sense the sudden appearance of three new figures approaching the camp—a cousin and two humans. I know who they are and realize that this could all go to hell.

CHAINGANG

Cory stops us when we see the campfire burning ahead. He motions with his hands, indicating we should get off the trail and work our way closer through the bush. I've never seen a landscape like this except in movies and TV shows. It's all tall pines and hardwoods and cedar, so dense that it's hard to manoeuvre through it carrying the rocket launchers. I've got to hand it to J-Dog. Even though he's smaller than me and doesn't have a Wildling's strength, he hasn't complained once about hauling that big-ass weapon.

We finally get a good vantage point and everything stops inside me.

"Fuck me," J-Dog says. "The white-haired dude's got no hands."

But I've only got eyes for one thing. Somebody's wearing Josh's shape. He's done a good job of copying, except he's got the size all wrong. The other guy has to top seven feet and the dude pretending to be Josh matches him in height.

I clench my jaw. Remembering Josh bleeding out, this just pisses me off even more. I told him I'd have his back, and in the end, I didn't. Seeing this imposter feels like a further indignity to his body.

"Do you know who that is?" I ask Cory. "The guy disguised as Josh?"

Cory shakes his head. "No. But the other one's Nanuq."

"What the hell happened to his hands?" J-Dog asks. "How do you lead a crew without hands?"

"I don't know," Cory says, a puzzled look on his face. "He had hands yesterday."

I don't give a crap about the hands. I came here planning to blow away Nanuq, but now all I want to do is to fire on the asshole pretending to be Josh and wipe him right off the earth.

It's like white noise in my brain. I don't know if I'm so pissed off because I failed to protect Josh, or because this dickhead is pretending to be Josh, or because he looks like Josh and I'm pissed that Marina chose him over me. I know that the ambush I set up for the dog cousins played a part in her dumping me, but hell, she's always known what I am. We could've talked about what happened and she'd listen to my side. It might have gone either way. But if she had someone better to go to, as in, Josh? That wouldn't have been a surprise to anybody, considering how she's been carrying a torch for him all these years. Well, except maybe Josh. Who's dead.

I can't fight a dead guy, so this imposter hanging with Nanuq is the perfect target for my anger.

I shut down my mind.

We're here to do a job.

I decide to give my brother a present. "You take the white-haired guy without hands," I tell J-Dog. "I'll get the other one."

"I thought you just needed to take down this Nanuq guy."

"So, I changed my mind."

J-Dog shrugs. "No skin off my ass."

"Wait," Cory says. "Something's not right here."

No kidding, I think, as I concentrate on the big guy pretending to be Josh and line him up in my sights.

DES

When I finally finish crying, Donalita's still there pressed against my back, holding on to me. She never said anything, didn't make any promises, she was just there. When I turn over and sit up, she lets go and puts a tissue in my hand. I blow my nose. I wipe my face on my sleeve.

I can't believe she stayed with me while I basically turned into some blubbering baby.

"This is hard," I finally say.

She nods. "It's hard for a long time," she tells me. "After a while … it doesn't go away, but you—I don't know. Get stronger or something and you bear it better. But it stays with you."

Great. So I have that to look forward to.

"I'd like to kill Elzie—the girl that shot him," I say. "I've never felt like that before—not seriously, for real. But she used to be Josh's girlfriend for God's sake. What's with that? I want to kill her and whoever talked her into it."

She gives me a long serious look.

"Did I ever tell you how I met Theo?" she asks.

I shake my head.

"I was looking for someone to help me kill Vincenzo, and when I heard about Theo, this big tough gang guy who also had a beef against Vincenzo, I thought he'd be the perfect guy to partner up with. So I went looking for him.

"You see, Vincenzo killed my sister Luisa and I wanted payback bad bad bad, and I knew there was nothing I could do by myself. But in the end I picked the wrong white knight. Theo turned out to be no stronger than me. It was your friend Josh—not much bigger than me—who got the job done."

She pauses. "Josh killed Vincenzo, but because he got caught up in all of this, he ends up dying himself."

I wait for a moment. "Maybe I'm dumb, dude, but I'm missing the point."

"The point is, revenge doesn't work out the way you think it will," she says. "It's like there's a cosmic wheel of balance, and when you get rid of your bad guy, you lose a good guy, too. The only way you can stop the cycle of violence is by stepping away from it yourself."

"So, we're supposed to let guys like Vincenzo go around doing whatever they want?"

She shakes her head. "But you have to understand the consequences. And that if you focus everything you are on getting revenge, you lose yourself. Eventually, you can't even remember how to get back to the person you once were."

"Okay. I get it. Scrap the revenge fantasies." I wait a moment, then add, "But dude, it seems like you've been pretty ready to indulge a few little revenge fantasies yourself."

She tilts her head and looks at me. "Just because I've been around a long time doesn't mean I can't still learn things."

"Okay, and what about now? What happens to us?"

"I don't know about you, *dude*," she says, smiling as she leans on the word, "but I want to be with you."

"I don't get it. I'm not complaining, but why me?"

"It started when Theo asked me to look out for you—back when I thought he and I could be a team. Except then it turned out I just liked you." She bats her eyelashes at me. "A lot."

"But I'm not a Wildling, or a cousin, or whatever. I'm nothing special at all."

She rolls her eyes. "But you're the perfect you—and that's what I like. You brought me back from the person I became to the one I once was, and I like her way better. She wants fun, not revenge."

She takes my hand and gives it a squeeze, then pulls me toward her, her lips searching for mine. It takes us a while to come up for air. I lean my head against the headboard and stare up at the ceiling.

"I'm so confused," I tell her. "You make me feel happy, but at the same time I feel guilty for even thinking of being happy. Josh is dead and that won't go away. It fogs up my head like a big black cloud."

She nods. "I know. I remember how that feels, except I didn't even have the chance to feel anything else. What you need to do is come away with me. Your parents don't understand what you're going through—they can't because there's so much you can't tell them. You need distance and space from them—from everything."

"Where would we go?"

"I don't know. There are whole worlds to explore."

"I can't up and take off again. My dad would be so royally pissed off at me, and Mom and Molly would be really hurt and worried."

She nods. "Let's go tell them, then they won't worry."

I take a deep breath and cup her hands in mine. She has a beautiful heart, but she just doesn't get what it's like to have parents.

"Right. And when they stop us from leaving?"

She smiles. "We walk out of the world where they can't follow."

Could I do that? Because she's right. Mom and Dad are going to be on my case without really understanding what that added pressure is going to do to me. Hell, Dad's probably got the brochures for military school laid out on the kitchen table right now. There's *no way* I can do that.

CHAINGANG

I'm about to squeeze the trigger when the guy I have in my sights disappears. Almost before that registers, he appears right in front of me. He grabs the end of the rocket launcher I'm holding as well as J-Dog's and vanishes once more, taking the weapons with him. Then he's back again, giving me a look that's equal parts tired and sad.

"This is why you're never going to be with the kind of girl you want," he says. "Every time your first response to a problem is violence, a little piece of the *you* that you say you want to be dies. They can see it in your eyes."

It's weird. Up close, he's the real Josh's size. He looks like Josh, smells like Josh—hell, he's even copied Josh's Wildling vibe. It's impressive. He's got Josh's voice; he's even saying the kind of thing that Josh would say.

But I was there. I saw Josh die back at city hall and it wasn't the same as when the Kings took him out in Casa Raphael. When he lay there bleeding out on the stage, he didn't get up again.

So I take a swing at him.

He catches my fist and just holds it. I try to pull free, but it's like trying to move a building.

Crap. Whoever this guy is, he's as strong as Vincenzo was.

I see J-Dog out of the corner of my eye, pulling a Glock from his waistband. But the guy holding my fist sees it, too. He turns to J-Dog, not easing up on his grip.

"Don't even think of it," he says.

But J-Dog doesn't waste time with words. He brings the Glock up fast. The Josh guy is faster and grabs the gun with his free hand, giving it a sharp twist. I hear J-Dog's trigger finger snap. The Glock goes flying away into the trees. J-Dog nurses his hand, but the crazy jumps into his eyes and I know he's about to go berserk and charge the guy holding me. I also know J-Dog's not going to survive a fight with this guy. It won't even be a fight. It'll be worse than when Vincenzo dealt with me because J-Dog doesn't have my strength or recuperative abilities. He's so outclassed here that when he goes down, he won't ever be getting up again.

"Jason, don't!" I yell.

But J-Dog's way past hearing anything.

The guy holding me turns and finally lets go, pushing me toward J-Dog.

"Stop him," he says, "or I won't be responsible for what happens next."

The difference between J-Dog and me is that I know when to retreat. You just step back and live to fight another day. But J-Dog's all-in with every damn thing he does, especially when it comes to a fight.

I grab him in a bear hug so that he can't move, then turn to glare at the guy wearing Josh's face.

"You'd better finish this now," I tell him, "because if you don't, I'll keep coming after you until one of us is dead."

The guy just looks at me. "Why?" he finally asks.

"You're wearing my friend's face, for starters."

"That *is* Josh," Cory says.

He's been standing beside us all this time, being a real big help by doing nothing. And now he comes up with this?

"Bullshit," I say.

"It's true," the Josh guy says.

I shake my head. "I saw Josh die. He didn't switch out to his mountain lion and come back in one piece. I saw the body. It wasn't like the last time. He was done."

Then it dawns on me. Are we all dead, and this is some afterlife? I don't remember dying, but that doesn't mean it didn't happen.

"Did we all die?" I ask, horrified that a version of heaven or hell might just be more of the same crap that I left behind.

The Josh guy smiles and shakes his head. "No. We're alive. I had to play it like I died," he says. "I needed to disappear, and what better way to do it than to make everybody think I'm dead?"

This is so messed up. I want it to be true and I don't at the same time. But I sure don't want to be stuck in some endless purgatory of this bullshit.

"Everybody?" I say.

He nods. "I was going to tell you and a couple of others, but I had some business to finish first."

"How's that possible? I *saw* your body. You bled out."

"It's complicated," Josh says. "But right now I need you to either leave, or stay out of my way."

"Because you're going to kill Nanuq? I want a piece of him, too."

"No," he says. "I'm just talking to him. I'm hoping to avoid anyone else having to die."

J-Dog's stopped struggling in my arms so I let him go. I half expect him to take a run at Josh, but I guess he's finally beginning to realize that he's in way over his head. He does the smart thing and follows my lead.

But I'm not feeling smart.

"Don't be stupid," I tell Josh. "Guys like that—you let them go—they just come back meaner and harder."

"Not if he gives me his word, he won't." And with that he turns his back on us and walks back to the fire.

I turn to Cory. "What kind of crap was that?"

"When are you going to get it through your head?" Cory says. "We don't break our word. It's like currency."

"Yeah?" J-Dog says. "And how do you spend it?"

Cory doesn't bother to answer. He just heads after Josh. After a moment, J-Dog and I follow along behind.

JOSH

I was keeping tabs on what was going on in the camp behind me while dealing with Chaingang and his brother, so I'm not surprised to see that most of the other cousins have grabbed the opportunity to take off. I *am* surprised that Nanuq is still standing there by the fire waiting for me. I half expected he would have beat a retreat while he could—to save face, if nothing else, so that he could come back at me another day, just like Chaingang said.

But there he is. Maybe he knows I'd find him wherever he went.

His features are schooled into a bland mask, though he can't quite hide the dark anger in his eyes. The only thing new is that he's taken the time to repair the damage I did to him because he's got both hands back.

"I'm not frightened of you, unborn," he says when I reach him.

"I don't really care. But this ends here. It's your choice how it goes."

He frowns. "You're very sure of yourself."

When I don't bother responding, he nods at the trio behind me.

"Why did you stop them from killing me?" he asks. "They would have solved all your problems."

"I don't have a problem," I tell him. "*You* do. You've had time to think about it. I'm sure you heard what I was saying to my friends."

He nods. "So you want me to stop protecting my homeland."

"Don't play stupid because I know you're not. I already told you. I want you to continue doing that. I think it's important, too. Just no more killing or intimidating innocent people."

"Or you'll kill me—like you did the condor brothers."

"I returned them to the earth," I tell him, "which I'll admit is pretty much the same thing. Don't make me do it to you."

He studies me for a long moment.

"After everything that's happened," he says, "you're prepared to simply forgive and forget?"

"That's never going to happen," I tell him. "But follow the one simple rule I've given you, and I'm prepared to let you live and go on your way."

He looks steadily at me for a long moment and I can't tell whether it's curiosity or respect in his eyes.

"It seems I've underestimated you," he says.

"Just tell me. Do I have your word that you'll stop targeting and hurting Wildlings—those that you mistakenly call unborn— and give them a fair chance to prove themselves among the cousins?"

We stand there for a long time. He holds my gaze, but I'm not interested in playing a staring game.

418 ᨀ CHARLES DE LINT

"Last chance," I tell him.

He gives me a slow nod. "You have my word," he says.

Then he steps away into another world. I track him with the maps in my head, dropping my focus on him as he keeps moving farther and farther away. A mountain of tension that I didn't realize I was holding melts away.

I turn to face Cory, Chaingang and his brother. The latter two still look sort of pissed off with me, but Cory's got that same respect in his eyes that Tío Goyo had.

"You've become what you said you didn't want to be," he says.

I shake my head. "No, I'm not anybody's puppet, or leader, or poster boy—now or ever. They'll have to find someone else because I'm going away."

"Where to?"

"Diego Madera has accepted me as part of his clan. I'm going to stay with him for a while."

Cory's brows go up in surprise. "Are you serious?"

"Pretty much."

"And that's a big deal because?" Chaingang asks.

"Old Man Puma's been around forever," Cory tells him. "Longer than anybody I know. He's been here since before."

"Before what?"

Cory waves his hand. "Before there was anything. They say he was one of the spirits that lived in the darkness and watched as Raven brought the world into being—like the crow girls, or my own ancestor, Coyote."

He turns back to me and a slow smile spreads across his face. "Being with him is exactly what you need."

"So you're just going to walk away and leave everything behind?" Chaingang says.

"Not everything."

I see something flash in his eyes and I know he's thinking about Marina, just as I am. But all he says is, "I thought you wanted to be a normal kid—to put all this behind you."

"And how's that going to happen if I go back?" I ask. "The Feds will be all over me, and even if they do leave me alone, I'll still have to deal with everybody at school looking at me like I'm some kind of freak."

"Man," J-Dog says. "If I could do what you do, I wouldn't even think about any lame-ass school or the Feds. I'd be living high on the hog—I mean, who's going to stop a guy like you from taking whatever he wants?"

Chaingang sighs. "Not now, bro."

"What? I'm just saying."

Chaingang turns back to me. "So what are you supposed to learn from hanging with this new dude you found? How do you know he hasn't got some angle?"

"I'm sure he does. But I've got one, too, so it doesn't matter. I need to understand what I am and figure out my place in the world. I figure someone like Madera—who's been alive since the world started and managed to make it work for him—can teach me something about what I need to know."

"Oh, come on," Chaingang says. "You don't buy this crap about immortal animal people do you? Or that some old bird made the world?"

J-Dog snickers, but I ignore him.

"Why not? How's that any more impossible than what's already happened to us?"

"Come on, bro. There are levels of believability. Just because one impossible thing is true, doesn't mean everything is."

J-Dog nods in agreement. "Word."

"Neither of you met Madera," I say. "I'm telling you, he's the real deal."

We fall silent then. J-Dog kicks at a stick in the fire, sending up a shower of sparks. Cory seems to have fallen into a meditative trance. And then there's Chaingang and me, neither of us looking at each other, but both all too aware of the betrayal that lies between us.

"Look," I finally start. "About Marina—"

Chaingang cuts me off, raising a hand between us.

"Don't," he says. "Don't even start."

His eyes go darker than the night around us.

J-Dog looks up from the fire and Cory's suddenly back from wherever he went in his head, both of them focused on what might happen next. Like suddenly Chaingang and I are planning to have a go at each other, never mind what a one-sided fight that would be.

I feel like crap. He's always been straight with me—always "had my back," as he likes to say. But what can I do? Yeah, I made the first move, but it was Marina's choice in the end. I guess that's what makes it hardest for him. It wasn't just me, it was her, too.

"Okay," I say. "Can you guys make your own way back home?"

"Are you serious, man?" J-Dog says.

"I meant with Cory," I say.

Cory shakes his head. "I'd rather you took them back. With everything that's been going on, I'm a little sick of being around people right now—no offence."

People always say "no offence" when they mean the opposite.

"I get it," I tell him.

"Not talking about you," he says.

Then he steps away into some otherworld, leaving me alone with the Washington brothers. I glance at Chaingang, but his face is a mask and I can't read him.

"Fuckin' dude was dissing us again," J-Dog says.

"Uh-huh," Chaingang says. He looks exhausted. "Let's go, bro. I know how he feels. I'm sick of this place. I just want to go home."

I nod. I reach out to put a hand on their shoulders. J-Dog shies back.

"Relax," Chaingang tells him. "Josh is our friend. He won't hurt us." There's a flash in his eyes that says, "Not any more than he already has."

I reach out again. With a hand on either of their shoulders, I step us all back to So-Cal.

DES

We go see my sister in her bedroom before facing the parents. Molly's eyes widen in surprise.

"You're the girl I saw in Des's bed," she says. "I *knew* I saw a girl." Then she frowns. "But then you turned into a cat, except that's not possible, right?"

"I'm sorry," I tell her. "We were just trying to avoid getting me into trouble with Mom. But it wasn't right to make you feel like you were crazy."

"You're in trouble now. Big trouble."

"I know. That's why I'm here, Molly-o. I'm going away for a while and I wanted to say goodbye."

She looks at me, waiting for the joke that always comes when I tease her.

"For real?" she finally asks when she realizes that I'm serious.

I nod.

"With her?"

"Yeah. Her name's Donalita."

Donalita lifts a hand. "Hey, dudette," she says.

Molly's eyes start to fill.

"You love her more than you love me," she says, half question, half saying it just the way she thinks it is.

"It's two different things," I tell her.

Especially since it's still too early to say where this thing with Donalita is going.

"Why can't you love me like you do her?" Molly asks.

"Because that would be creepy. You're my sister, short-stuff."

The tears are rolling down her cheeks now. "Why does it have to be different? Why do you even have to go?"

I reach down and wipe them aside with my thumb. "Mom and Dad are going to send me away anyway. This way, I leave on my own terms."

She pulls away and shakes her head. "Dad'll never let you out of the house."

"We'll see." I go down on one knee. "Come here. Give me a hug. I'll be back to see you whenever I can."

She wraps her arms around me, holding me hard and fierce, like if she puts enough into it, she can make me stay. I hug her back, my heart breaking, and feel a sudden anger at my dad for putting me in this position.

Finally I let go and stand up. I take Donalita's hand and we walk into the kitchen, Molly tagging along behind us like a mournful little puppy. Mom's eyes widen when she sees Donalita. Dad's face reddens.

"I thought we told you to go to your room," he says. "And who's this … this *girl*?"

"I just came to say goodbye," I tell them.

Mom looks like she's about to burst into tears.

"You're not going anywhere except where I decide, and when," Dad says.

I shake my head. "Yeah, not going to happen."

He stands up and blocks the doorway to the front hall.

"You are not leaving this house."

"Except for when you send me off to military school? So I can be a good little soldier boy, just like you? That's never going to happen."

He glares at me. "What have I told you about mouthing off?"

"Who knows? I stopped listening to your lectures years ago."

His face gets even redder and that big vein pops out on his forehead, larger than ever. I've never seen him this angry.

"Get back to your room right *now*. And you," he says, eyeing Donalita and pointing toward the front door. "Get out and don't come back."

He's still a big guy. Stronger than me, for sure. But this time he's not getting his way.

"Uh-uh. That's my girlfriend you're dissing," I tell him. "Bye, Mom. I'll try to keep in touch."

Then I nod to Donalita and she steps us away into the otherworld. I have time to see Mom's stricken face, Molly running toward us calling my name.

Then it all goes away.

I have to sit down on the sand after we cross over. It's so weird. You can tell this is the same landmass we just left, but there's not a trace of Santa Feliz. There's just the wild beach and the ocean. The only light is from the moon gleaming on the sand and the water.

Donalita crouches beside me and puts her arms around me.

"That was harder than I thought it would be," I say.

"He wasn't being mean," Donalita says. "I could see it behind his anger. He just wants what he thinks is best for you."

"That's the whole problem," I tell her. "I know he cares about me, but he's a control freak. In his head, he's always right. He knows best—it doesn't matter what I think. He's never had any respect for me. If it wasn't for Mom, I'd already be in that military academy. I'd never be a skateboarder or a musician or anything that *I* want to be."

"Is he still in the army?"

I shake my head. "Mom got tired of all his overseas deployments. She told him he'd done his bit and it was time for us to settle down in one place. That was years ago. I hardly remember the bases we lived on when I was a little kid. This is what I remember." I wave my hand around. "Well, the *this* that's back in the world we just left."

"I can take you back," she says.

"No, I made my choice. I just don't know what I'm going to do now."

"Me neither, dude." Then she jumps to her feet. "But I'm hungry. Let's go catch a fish."

"Sure," I say. "Why not?"

She doesn't wait for me, but goes running toward the ocean at full Wildling speed. She's probably going to catch it with her bare hands.

My heart lifts a little as I watch her run. I guess this is what attracted Josh to Elzie. She's so full of optimism and the sheer exuberance of being alive.

Elzie.

Josh.

I look up at the night sky.

"Dude," I say. "Why'd you have to go and die?"

Then I follow Donalita at my own slower pace.

JOSH

The first thing I do after dropping off the Washington brothers at the Ocean Avers compound is head for home. I arrive in my own neighbourhood in spirit form and make a slow spiral over the blocks of houses until I finally reach my house. If anybody was outside looking up, they'd see a hawk drifting in an ever-tightening circle, but the maps in my head tell me that there's nobody watching. No FBI. No snipers from ValentiCorp's goon squad. No cousins wanting to either kill me or praise me. They all think I'm dead.

I float above the house for a long moment. It's been—what—a couple of days? But everything already feels unfamiliar. This place, my old life—it's like they belong to a stranger. I can't really connect to any of it.

Except for Mom.

It breaks my heart when I slip inside and find her on the couch, pulled tightly in a fetal position, enveloped in sorrow. Her breathing is ragged, but she doesn't seem to have any more tears left in her.

Crap. How could I have put her through this?

"Mom?" I say.

She goes still, but she doesn't turn to where I'm standing in front of the couch. Her face stays pressed against cushions.

I reach out and touch her shoulder.

"Mom?" I repeat.

She turns her face. Slowly. Then she sees me. Her bloodshot eyes go wide, wide. She jumps over the back of the couch and scrambles away from me until her back touches the wall.

"It's okay." I speak in a soothing tone, like you would to a wild animal that's about to bolt.

"J-Josh? Is it really you?"

"Yeah, Mom."

I don't know what she thought she was seeing. A ghost. A hallucination. But the freak-out ends as suddenly as it began.

"Thank you, God," she says as she pushes away from the wall. She walks tentatively around the couch toward me, then reaches out and grabs me tight, holding on like she's never going to let me go. If I didn't have a Wildling's resilience, I think she might crush a few ribs.

"I've been so scared and lost," she murmurs. "First I saw it on the TV, and then Agent Matteson came by, and then Des …" She puts me at arm's length and studies my face. "How can you be alive? Agent Matteson said I shouldn't look at your body … that they identified it. He thought it would be better for me to remember you as you were before the shooting. But nothing made it better, except for seeing you now."

She lets me ease her back onto the couch where we both sit, but she keeps a tight grip on my arm.

"I know," I say. "I would have come to tell you right away, but it took me a while to recover from what I had to do."

"*What* did you do?"

"You were right, you know," I say instead of answering.

"About what?"

"That I have to go away. Everybody wants a piece of me and they're not above coming after my friends and family. If I disappear, if they keep thinking I'm dead, nobody's going to come looking for me anymore."

"But where would you go?"

"Into the otherworld. I've got a safe place to stay and I'll keep in touch with you."

Her chest does this little hitch and her eyes get all shiny. She touches my face, fingers trembling. "But I only just got you back."

"I know, Mom. I don't want to go. But I don't have another choice."

She puts her forehead on my shoulder. "How long do we have?" she asks. "When do you have to go?"

"Right now. I'm just going to let Des and Marina know that I'm still alive, and then I'll go."

"I hate this. I don't know if I'm strong enough."

"I love you, Mom, and I hate this, too. But one thing I know for sure is that you're really strong. You're amazing."

She raises her head and looks into my eyes. "I could not be more proud of you, honey. I can only let you go because I love you so much."

I pull her in for another hug, and say quietly, "Thanks, Mom. You know, for this to work, you can't tell anybody."

She leans away, takes my hands and looks at me. "Not even your grandparents?"

My heart aches, thinking about them. How they've always been there for the two of us—never judging, always solid, quiet and discreet. I know where my mom gets her character. Maybe it will be okay.

"Can you make them understand?" I say. "It's so important that they keep it to themselves. That dog that tried to attack you? If word gets out that I'm alive, something worse could come after you. And anybody around you at the time would be in danger, too. Maybe even Grandma and Grandpa."

I'm laying it on thick, but I have to. She has to understand—just as Des and Marina will—that they can't tell anybody. Not *ever*.

"I'll explain it to them," she says. "They're on their way here. I can't lie and let them keep suffering the same torture that I've just been through."

"I get that. It's okay. Tell them thanks for keeping my secret ... and I love them."

I gently pry her hands from mine and stand up.

"It's hard to let you go," she says, standing as well. "You're still my little boy."

"And I always will be," I tell her. "I love you, Mom."

She enfolds me in another hug. I squeeze her back, allowing myself to relax for just one moment more. I pretend that I'm not going away, that my whole life isn't going to be so different from now on. That my mom is going to be okay.

Then I pull back.

"You can't be touching me when I do this," I tell her.

"Do what?"

"It's going to look like I'm disappearing. Bye, Mom. I love you. I'll be in touch when I can."

She reaches for me, but lets her hands fall just short.

"And I love you, honey."

Then I step away into the otherworld.

I stand there for a long moment, feeling more alone than ever. I still have to go through this again with my two best friends and it's not going to get any easier.

I call up my maps and find Marina on them.

"Huh," I say when I realize where she is.

Now I'm going to have to wait until she's alone.

MARINA

I have second—and then third and fourth—thoughts about leaving when Ampora finally comes out the back door with the girls in tow. Ria and Suelo are heavy-eyed and a little confused to see me standing in their backyard at this time of the night. Lupe is still close, hidden in the shadows. But all eyes are on me and my sisters never notice her.

I look at those two sleepy faces. They let go of Ampora's hands and run to me, and my resolve falters even more. I go down on one knee and draw them close.

"What are you doing here so late?" Ria asks, her breath tickling my ear with the question.

Suelo nods. "Papá will be mad—but we won't tell."

I lean back so that I can look at them.

"I have to go away for a little while," I tell them. "But I couldn't go without …"

My voice falters. Of all my family, Ria and Suelo are the ones who would most accept me for being what I am. They're already fascinated by Wildlings, they devour the Animorphs books. But Ampora's here, too, and I don't want to take away the look of her disgust when I leave. I want to remember the girls, as they are right now, not upset because Ampora and I are fighting again. And we *will* fight when she finds out because I'm not going to let her get away with the things she's going to say.

"I just wanted to tell you how much I love you," I say to the girls. "No matter what you might hear about me, that's always going to be true."

"Are you never coming back?" Suelo asks.

"Of course I am. It just might not be for a while."

"I don't want you to go away," Ria says, a whine creeping into her voice.

Suelo's eyes fill and she nods in agreement.

"I don't want to go," I tell them. "But when you get older, sometimes you have to do things you don't want to do. But I promise you I'll come back to see you when I can."

Ria frowns. "But why do you have to—"

"You should go back to bed," I say. "Both of you. But first give me a kiss."

They're such good girls. They don't want to go. They want to know more. But each of them gives me a hug and a kiss, and then they go back up the stairs to the door.

"Go on back to bed," Ampora tells them. "I'll be right in."

She waits until they're gone before she turns back to me.

"He was never coming back to see me, was he?" she says.

I don't have to ask who she's talking about, not when she adds, "I mean, if he hadn't died."

"I don't know," I tell her.

She looks past me into the darkness. "I don't even know why I was flirting with him. Especially once I knew what he was." She sticks out her tongue like she's gagging, and that's enough to press my button.

"Pheromones."

"What?"

I explain. "He didn't even know he was giving them off."

"That's so sick." She shakes her head. "They are such freaks."

I hear Lupe growl in the shadows, but it's too low for Ampora to hear. I know just how Lupe feels.

"Do you know why the parents are having this big powwow about me?"

She shrugs. "I figure they found out that you've been the arm candy of one of those Ocean Aver jerks."

I feel like hitting her. It has nothing to do with my being a Wildling and how I've gotten more aggressive lately. I always feel like hitting her. But I refuse to play her hating game.

"That must be it," I say. "See ya 'round, *hermana.*"

I start to go, but turn back to look over my shoulder when she calls after me.

"Don't worry," I tell her. "I won't be back to cramp your style anymore."

"That's not what I was going to say."

I wait.

"I was just going to say be careful," she tells me.

Like she cares. But I nod.

"I will. You too."

I head off again. I hear a sharp intake of air from Ampora when Lupe drifts out of the shadows to fall in step beside me.

"That was hard," I say when we've put a few yards between ourselves and the house.

She drapes an arm across my shoulders. "Cutting ties always is."

"I don't even know if I'm doing the right thing," I say. "With Josh dead and leaving everything I know behind me ..."

"I'm taking you to a good place," she says. "We've got a squat at the end of South Shore Drive. It's safe. The cops never come to roust us and the Kings leave us alone. You'll have time to figure things out."

"What do you do there?"

She smiles. "Whatever we want. We've got a few artists, a bunch of musicians, and everybody skateboards."

I perk up a little at the idea of the music. I wonder if there's any way to get my drums from Des's garage.

"What kind of stuff do they play?" I ask.

But before Lupe can answer, she stops dead in her tracks, pulling me to a halt beside her.

"Mother of God," she says, her voice a hoarse whisper.

I stare at the figure standing there under a street light.

"I don't believe in ghosts," Lupe says.

I realize she's not talking to me. It's more that she's trying to convince herself. I don't believe in ghosts, either, but I'm seeing one right now.

And if this is all I get, I'll take it.

JOSH

I realize after a while that I'm not going to be able to talk to Marina on her own. I float in slow circles high above the house, hanging in until she finishes up with her sister and finally leaves with Lupe. Then I make contact.

I pull my body up out of the ground under a street light half a block from where they're walking and wait for them to come to me.

They both notice me at the same time and stop in unison.

They're slow to approach.

I want to sweep Marina up in my arms, but there's a look in her eyes that makes me hold back.

"Hey," I say.

She reaches with a tentative hand to stroke my cheek. "You're real?" she says. "You're not a ghost?"

"Yeah, I—"

She hauls off and shoves me hard in the chest before I can finish. I'm not expecting it and I stagger back.

"How *could* you?" she yells, closing the distance to go after me again. "How could you make us all think you were dead?"

I grab her hands before she can give me another shove.

"Yeah, not cool," Lupe says.

"It's not like you think," I say. "I mean, it is, but I didn't think it'd take so much out of me. It took me hours to recover."

"Recover from what?"

"From making it look like I'd been killed."

"Why would you even *do* something like that?"

She struggles to push me again, then aims a kick at my shins when she can't get her hands free. I dodge the kick.

"Would you listen to me?" I say before she can try again.

She glares at me for a long moment, then finally nods. I let her go, ready to grab her once more if she starts in on me, but she just folds her arms across her chest.

"So talk," she says, her words clipped. Now her eyes are brimming with tears.

"I need the world to think I'm dead so that everybody will just leave me alone," I say. "The cops, the cousins—everybody."

I look pointedly at Lupe. "I know how you cousins gossip. Can I trust you to keep my secret so that everything can finally settle down? I just need to get away from all this."

Lupe looks at Marina and then back to me. She nods and presses her palm to her chest. "As surely as the Thunders exist, your secret is safe with me, young lion."

"Yeah, sure," Marina says, her voice shaking. "I'll be happy to leave you alone. Do you know how horrible it's been for me?"

"It all happened so fast," I tell them. "There wasn't time to plan, much less let anybody in on what I was trying to do. I thought—if I was able to even pull it off—that I'd be able to come to you quicker, but it didn't work out. I was literally passed out for hours."

I go on to explain how I did it. Lupe takes it all in, wide-eyed.

Marina just stares off into the distance. It's weird. Her eyes are still brimming with tears, but she's so mad that she's shaking.

"I came as soon as I could," I tell her.

"I'm the first you've let in on your stupid little secret?"

"No, I went to see my mom first."

Her eyes soften a little then, and I see a single tear trickle down from the corner of her eye.

"How'd she take it?" she asks, absently wiping the tear away.

"Well, she was freaked, but she didn't *attack* me."

"Hey. You hurt me. Don't look for an apology."

"I'm not and I'm sorry. I'm just trying to explain."

She nods. "So we're the only ones who know? Lupe and me—and your mom?"

"And Chaingang and his brother. And Cory."

"You went and told them *first?*"

"I wasn't going to tell them at all, but I ran into them when I was dealing with Nanuq."

Her face goes very still. "You killed him?"

"I—"

Her shoulders sag. "God, you're as bad as the rest of them. Why is killing the only—"

"Will you shut up and let me talk?"

I don't quite mean it to come out with such vehemence and a little piece of me dies as I see her face close up again on me.

"I didn't go to kill him," I say, softening my tone. "And I didn't have to kill him. I just explained what would happen if he continued to use other people the way he has been. I told him to give Wildlings a chance."

"And he just agreed to that?" Lupe says.

"Eventually."

I turn back to Marina. "Don't you see? I had no choice. I had to make sure he didn't start the whole thing over again. Do you think I *wanted* to leave? All I wanted was to be with you."

She looks at me for a long moment and I can't read her expression at all. Then she sighs. "I'm being a selfish bitch, aren't I?" she finally says, and a glimmer of her old self reaches her eyes.

I smile. "Maybe a little."

She hits me again, but lightly, like old times. An affectionate little slap on the shoulder without any force behind it.

"I was so freaked," she says. "I thought you were dead. I saw your body."

Lupe nods. "Yeah, they took it away." She pauses and frowns. "Well, they took something away."

"It was the worst thing I've ever been through," Marina says.

"I know what it must have been like. I'm so sorry."

Her eyes tell me I'm forgiven, so I step up and draw her close to my chest.

"I'm sorry about Elzie being the shooter," she whispers. "That must've made it even worse."

"To be honest, I didn't even know that until after I came to. Tío Goyo told me."

I kiss her ear. "Elzie means nothing to me. It's you that I care about."

"Don't ever pull something like that again," she murmurs.

"I won't. But if mountain lions work like house cats, I do have another seven lives left."

She thumps my back with her fist. "Don't even joke about it."

When we disengage she keeps hold of my hand.

"What are you guys doing out here in the middle of the night?" I ask.

I hear the story of how her evening went with her parents, and how she just said goodbye to her little sisters.

"That is so messed up," I say when she's done. I look from one to the other. "So what are you going to do?"

"Lupe's letting me stay at her place for a while," Marina says.

Lupe nods. "You're welcome to tag along."

I squeeze Marina's hand. "Why don't you come with me, instead?" I say.

"Where are you going?"

I tell them about Old Man Puma and his invitation. Lupe gets the same look that every cousin seems to get when I mention him.

"Are you serious?" she says.

"Absolutely."

"You actually met him?"

"He was there with Tío Goyo when I woke up."

"He's a big deal?" Marina asks.

"Well, yeah," Lupe tells her. "How cool would it be to meet him?"

"But he invited *you*," Marina says to me. "What's he going to say if I come tagging along?"

"I don't know. But if he doesn't like it, we'll just set up camp near his place. We'll work something out."

"I don't know ..."

"How can you even consider not going?" Lupe asks.

"I want you to come," I tell Marina. "We've got so much lost time to catch up on."

She ducks her head and blushes.

"Not like that," I tell her. "Well, not only that."

Lupe grins and gives her a little push on the shoulder.

"Okay," Marina says. "We'll go meet this Señor Madera and see what he has to say. I take it we're leaving now?"

I nod. "I just want to drop by and see Des before we go."

I call up my maps and place him.

"That's funny," I say. "He's not at home. He's in the otherworld with Donalita."

Lupe gives me a considering look. "How do you know that?"

I tell her about the maps in my head.

Lupe looks at me with something like awe and I know it's time to get out of here.

"Okay," I say. "Let's go see him."

Marina's still holding my hand. She reaches out to Lupe with her free one, but Lupe shakes her head.

"No, you go ahead," she says. "Someone like Old Man Puma might be fine when you show up with your mate in tow, but he's not going to want some scraggly barrio dog hanging around."

"You're no scraggly—" Marina begins.

"It's cool. We're still tight. Come see me when you're in town." She nods at me. "Your lion boy here will know how to find me—wherever I am."

Marina lets go of my hand long enough to give her a hug and then I step us away to the otherworld beach where Des and Donalita are trying to start a fire.

Donalita looks up first, her eyes going wide. A moment later Des is on his feet and running toward us. Once again he grabs me in a big bear hug and wheels me around so that my feet are off the ground. When he sets me back down he holds my shoulders and stares right into my eyes.

"Dude!" he says. "How the hell did you pull that off? I mean you were dead—*dead*. Seriously. It was ugly."

"It's a long weird story. What are you doing here?"

"That's a short boring one. The old man was finally going to lay down the law and send me off to military school."

"Ouch."

"So I left before that could happen."

"Do they know where you are?"

He grins. "They so know I'm not in their world anymore." Then his good humour falters. "But I felt like crap about leaving Molly."

Marina nods. "I couldn't really tell my little sisters any more than that I was going away for a while."

"You've gone AWOL, too?" Des asks.

"It was that or Mamá was going to either put me in a convent or ship me off to the Feds."

"You want to come down the yellow brick road with us?" I ask him.

"If you're off to see the wizard, dude, I don't want brains or a heart, but I wouldn't mind a little Wildling mojo."

"I don't know about that," I say, "but I've got a few hawk uncle tricks I can try to teach you."

"Excellent."

"It won't be easy," I tell him, "but if you work as hard on it as you do your skateboard tricks, you'll get it."

"Aw, man. I'm going to miss my wheels. And playing music."

"Maybe you could take up the ukulele," Marina says with a grin. "They're easy to carry around. And I could play the bongos."

Des looks at me in mock horror. "Dude, just shoot me now."

I laugh. This feels good. This feels right. It's going to be hard, separated from our families and the world we knew, but we'll figure it out.

"One thing, *compadres*," Des says. He puts his arm around Donalita's shoulders. "I'm not flying solo now."

"Neither are we," I tell him. "Now let's go see how Old Man Puma reacts when a houseful of teenagers descends upon him."

CHAINGANG

The trip back from the otherworld goes a lot faster than going in with Cory did. We're back in the blink of an eye. Josh asks us to swear an oath of secrecy, which is cool with me. I don't want to talk about any of this crap, anyway. J-Dog says if he told anyone, he'd get laughed right out of the Avers.

Josh says he'll be in touch, then he leaves us there in the dirt yard behind the compound. I wonder if bringing us here was deliberate, or if he chose it because we can show up unnoticed. Because this is the place where the dog cousins died. No, where we ambushed them and shot them down.

I glance at J-Dog, but I doubt he's even thought about it since. I don't mention it.

We walk back to the house. As usual, we're met by bass and drums pounding on the sound system. Snoop rapping—old school. Riding on top of it all is a stew of laughter, conversation, shouts.

"Coming in?" J-Dog asks.

I shake my head. "I got no party in me."

He goes inside, but comes out a few moments later carrying a couple of beers and a joint. He offers me a toke. I shake my head, but I take the beer. We clink the tops of the bottles against each other.

"That kid Josh," J-Dog says. "What he had to say—it hit you hard."

I nod.

"So you want out of the crew?"

"It's not like you think."

"Yeah?" he says. "What do I think?"

"That I'm turning my back on you."

He shakes his head. "Only reason we got this crew is that there's no other option when you come up in the Orchards the way we did. What the hell else are we going to do? But you got a way out, that's golden, bro."

"You want out, too?"

He laughs. "Hell, no. I like my life just fine. I take what it gives me, you hear what I'm saying?"

"Yeah."

"You can't worry about what you can't have," he says.

Marina, I think.

"You make the party with what you've got, bro."

"I hear you."

He shakes his head. "But you don't feel me. I get it. The world's gone punk-ass weird on us and I don't even want to think about what you're going through. But you can't keep fishing when the river's dried up. That happens, it's time to move on."

"I will."

He slaps my back. "Course you will. But first you're going to mope around for a while because that's what you do best."

"Fuck you."

He grins. "That's better. Tonight I'm partying with the

crew—which is what you should be doing, 'cept I know you won't." He holds up his hands. "Hey. I'm just telling it like it is. Get it out of your system, bro, if that's what you need to do. But tomorrow we go see Grandma, so practice your happy face."

He goes back inside. I stay where I am and finish my beer. Then I put the bottle down on the porch and head back into my crib to slouch on the sofa. I put my feet on the coffee table and click on the remote. The big screen glows into life with some reality show.

I notice a message on my phone and scroll to the text that came in while we were gone. It's from Aina—the girl from the Harley shop.

"I'm still waiting for that story," she writes.

I know what J-Dog would do, but I put the phone down without sending an answer.

I remember telling Marina that I could change.

Maybe I can. Maybe I should.

The trouble is, when it comes right down to it, I'm not sure where to begin.

ACKNOWLEDGMENTS

My readers, young and not-so-young, have been great enthusiasts for this Wildlings series, and I'm grateful for your tremendous support. I hadn't worked in such a consecutive series format before, and given that I'm a "see what happens next" writer, there were extra challenges because I couldn't go back and change anything in the first two novels, which had already been published. Fortunately, I had several excellent helpers along the way: first and foremost, my wife, MaryAnn Harris, who always catches the small (and large) things that I've missed and adds a few of her own creative ideas into the mix; Lynne Missen and her excellent editorial team at Penguin Canada; and last but not least, my eagle-eyed copy editor, Catherine Dorton, who brilliantly caught all the things that slipped by the rest of us. Thanks to all of you for making the Wildlings series a pleasure to write.